PRAISE FOR
New York Times Bestselling Author
ELMORE LEONARD
"NO ONE IS LEONARD'S EQUAL."
—*Chicago Tribune*

"ELMORE LEONARD IS AN AWFULLY GOOD WRITER
OF THE SNEAKY SORT; he is so good, you don't notice
what he's up to."—*The Washington Post Book World*

"Whatever you call his novels, they always read like
Elmore Leonard, distinctive in style and vision, brilliantly inventive
in plot and characters."—*Los Angeles Times*

"NOBODY BUT NOBODY IN THE BUSINESS
DOES IT BETTER."—New York *Daily News*

"There are few writers who can match Leonard when it comes to
narrative moves, none who write dialogues that say so little
and mean so much." —*San Francisco Chronicle*

"LEONARD WRITES PROSE THAT IS AS GOOD
AS IT GETS: wryly funny, whiplash-plotted, peopled
with memorable characters and sly dialogue. Plus, there's a bonus:
he's prolific."
—*The Seattle Times*

BOOKS BY ELMORE LEONARD

The Bounty Hunters

The Law at Randado

Escape from Five Shadows

Last Stand at Saber River

Hombre

The Big Bounce

The Moonshine War

Valdez Is Coming

Forty Lashes Less One

Mr. Majestyk

Fifty-two Pickup

Swag

Unknown Man No. 89

The Hunted

The Switch

Gunsights

Gold Coast

City Primeval

Split Images

Cat Chaser

Stick

LaBrava

Glitz

Bandits

Touch

Freaky Deaky

Killshot

Get Shorty

Maximum Bob

Rum Punch

Pronto

Riding the Rap

Out of Sight

Cuba Libre

The Tonto Woman and
Other Western Stories

Elmore Leonard's
Western Roundup #1

Elmore Leonard's
Western Roundup #2

ELMORE LEONARD'S WESTERN ROUNDUP #2

Escape from Five Shadows
Last Stand at Saber River
The Law at Randado

ELMORE LEONARD

Delta
Trade Paperbacks

A Delta Book
Published by
Dell Publishing
a division of
Bantam Doubleday Dell Publishing Group, Inc.
1540 Broadway
New York, New York 10036

ISBN: 0-385-33323-4

Reprinted by arrangement with Dell Publishing, a division of Bantam Doubleday Dell Publishing Group, Inc.

Manufactured in the United States of America

Published simultaneously in Canada

December 1998

10   9   8   7   6   5   4   3   2   1

CONTENTS

ESCAPE
FROM
FIVE
SHADOWS

....

ONE

Karla hesitated in the doorway of the adobe, then pushed open the screen door and came out into the sunlight as she heard again the faint, faraway sound of the wagon; and now she looked off toward the stand of willows that formed a windbreak along the north side of the yard, her eyes half closed in the sun glare and not moving from the motionless line of trees.

She waited for the wagon to appear—a girl not yet twenty, with clear dark eyes, a clean-lined delicately featured face that was brown from the sun, and black hair that suggested Spanish-Indian blood, though her hair was cut short, almost boyishly short, and brushed back from her temples; a girl wearing a man's blue chambray shirt tucked into a gray skirt that fell almost to her rope-soled sandals.

Now she could hear the horses splashing over the creek that passed through the willows. The team and wagon appeared but the girl waited until the two riders who trailed the wagon came into view before she turned to the adobe.

"They're coming now."

Her father, John Demery, appeared in the doorway thumbing a suspender strap over his shoulder, up over long-sleeved woolen underwear. And now his face creased to an expression of almost pain as he looked off into the yellow-white sun glare. The willow trees added color to the scene and beyond them, towering, sloping out of the distance, the foothills of the Pinaleño Mountains were striped with the black shadow lines of barrancas and pine stands; but here on the flat land, looking straight out from the adobe east, then sweeping south, there was an unvarying sameness of mesquite and sun glare and the thin faint line of distant mountains was part of another world.

Demery's long adobe, his corral and outbuildings, were here of necessity. On the Hatch & Hodges Stage Line map his place was indicated at Station #3 on the Central Mail run. Locally, it was the Pinaleño station—thirteen miles southeast of Fuegos, the nearest town; and six miles almost due south of the convict camp at Five Shadows.

The wagon now approaching the station was from the convict camp. Karla was certain of this from the moment she'd heard the first faint creaking sound from the willows. She kept her eyes on the wagon, watching the driver gradually turning the team to come in broadside to the adobe.

Now one of the riders, a shotgun across his pommel, spurred to swing in on the near side. As he did, Karla said, "Mr. Renda himself."

Demery half turned from the door. "I'll get the voucher. The sooner they're out of here the better." But he hesitated, looking out toward the wagon again. "Is your friend along?"

"I don't know," Karla answered, not looking around, her gaze still going out across the yard. "He could be one of those two in back. But I can't see their faces yet."

"Or their numbers," Demery said. He turned back into the dimness of the adobe.

Frank Renda, with the shotgun, was coming directly toward her; but the second rider crossed the yard diagonally and remained on the far side of the wagon. He carried a Winchester straight up, the stock resting on his thigh and his hand gripping it through the lever.

The two men whom Karla could not yet see, who sat in the back of the empty wagon with their legs hanging over the end gate, and the driver, looked toward the adobe as they drew nearer. They wore curl-brimmed, preshaped straw hats. Their shirts and Levi's were faded and sweat-stained and a number was stenciled on the right thigh of each of the three men's Levi's. The same number was stenciled in back, below the beltline. The driver wore number 22; the men on the end gate, 17 and 18.

Frank Renda dismounted. He let his reins trail and came toward Karla carrying the shotgun under his arm—a man about her father's age, in his mid-forties, but heavier than her father, thicker through chest and shoulders, and wearing a mustache, a full, untrimmed tobacco-stained mustache that almost completely covered the firm line of his mouth.

He stopped in front of Karla, blocking her view of the men in the wagon. He stood close to her, the shotgun barrel touching her skirt, but she didn't move, not even her eyes, and she returned his gaze. "Where's my stuff, Karla?" He smiled saying this, but the smile was not in the sound of his voice.

"In the shed," Karla answered.

Renda motioned toward the open shed that extended out from the east wall of the adobe. Karla saw the rider who was still mounted walk his horse toward it, his Winchester across his pommel now. Then, as the wagon moved on, passing close to her, she glanced at the two convicts on the end gate.

For a moment her eyes held on the man wearing number 18. She looked away then, quickly, her gaze going to the shed: feeling an unexpected excitement in seeing him and suddenly afraid it would show on her face.

She did not try to explain the feeling, for it was not something that could be reasonably explained, even to herself. This was the ninth time she had seen him. She was sure of that. Eight times in the past month, delivering mail to the convict camp, she had taken the trail down through the canyon and passed him on the new road. Riding along the stretch of road construction, passing the convicts and the guards, then seeing him, watching him until it would be obvious that she was watching and then she would look away.

Eight times this way and always with the feeling that she knew what he was thinking, knowing that he was watching the guards, following their moves and trying to locate the ten or twelve Apache trackers who were always mounted and always somewhere above the canyon but seldom in sight.

Each time she had wanted to say to him, "Please don't try it. Please." Again for a reason she did not even attempt to understand, though she wondered if others sensed his wanting to escape as strongly as she did.

That was part of it: the knowing what he was thinking. That and the feeling that she had known him a long time; as if he were a boy she had gone to school with in Willcox and had been close to and had seen every day and was now seeing again after a lapse of six or seven years. But, she had never laid eyes on him before a month ago and even now she did not know his name. This was the first time he had been brought to Pinaleño with the supply detail.

Now she watched Renda walking off after the wagon, seeing, beyond him, the wagon pulling up in front of the open shed.

She could feel the rider with the Winchester looking at her, but she did not raise her eyes to him. Her father had said that his name was Brazil—Renda's head guard. And her father had said he was a gunman; a man paid purely and simply for his gun and probably deserved to be wearing a straw hat and numbered pants as much as any convict in the camp.

The driver was standing in the wagon bed now, his head even with the shed roof. He would stoop under it, into the straight-line shade of it to take the sacks of flour and dried beans and salt that the two men who had been on the end gate handed up to him. He would drag the sacks to the front of the wagon and stack them, taking his time, as if trying to make this last as long as possible. Now and again he would glance at Karla.

She noticed this, but most of the time her eyes remained on the convict wearing number 18.

His sleeves were cut off at the shoulders and she had never seen a man's arms burned such a deep brown. Black copper, she thought. And in the shadow of his hatbrim his face seemed even darker. It went through the girl's mind that with shoulder-length hair and features that were coarse he could pass for a San Carlos Apache. Still, even though she had never seen him without the straw hat, she knew his hair was sand colored, just as she knew his eyes would be blue.

At this moment she knew he was watching Renda and the one called Brazil. Not looking at them directly, but watching every move they made from the shadow of the curled hatbrim.

Karla half turned as the screen door opened. "He's here," she said, a trace of excitement in the tone of her voice.

Her father stepped out into the yard. He carried a Voucher for Supplies and Services Rendered, made out by Seely, Lewis & Foss, Government Contractors. As he looked toward the wagon he asked, "Which one?"

"He's wearing 18."

"I can't make out figures from here."

"The one without sleeves in his shirt."

Demery squinted in the sunlight, studying the convict. "He looks like any other jailbird to me."

"You have to see him up close," Karla said.

"Why do you think he's any different from the rest?"

"I don't know . . . haven't you ever had a feeling about a person?" She glanced at her father. "Like Ma . . . you liked her right away, didn't you? You didn't ask to see her papers before you married her."

"You're planning to marry him, are you?"

"I'm drawing a parallel."

"Sis, the difference is I didn't meet your mother in a convict camp."

"How do you know why he's there?" Karla said hotly. "For all we know he was hungry and killed somebody else's cow. You can't blame a man for something like that."

Demery nodded. "Only maybe it wasn't a cow," he said mildly, glancing at Karla. "A nice-looking boy who doesn't look like he should be in convict clothes, so you feel sorry for him."

"It's more than that," Karla said earnestly. "But I can't explain it."

"Like getting a warm feeling for a boy at school."

"You make it sound ridiculous."

"Sis, that's what I'm trying to do. You don't even know his name."

Karla looked at her father hopefully. "I was going to ask you to ask Mr. Renda."

"What good would it do you to know it?"

"I was thinking of writing to Mr. Martz," Karla said. "He's in the courthouse every day. He could look up his record—"

"You'd write all the way to Prescott to find out why he's in?"

"I can't think of any other way."

"Waste Lyall Martz's valuable time on an errand like that—"

"He'd do it for me."

"Sis, you're sure of yourself. I'll say that."

"Don't you think he would?"

"I'm not going to encourage you."

Karla hesitated. "Will you ask Mr. Renda his name?"

Demery shook his head. "You might have a pure, kindly feeling about the boy, but don't ask me to be a party to it."

"Then you won't."

"Ask him yourself."

"He'd think it was funny. A girl asking."

"No funnier than me doing it. 'Frank, what's that boy's name, number 18? Karla's got a warm feeling for him, wants to know all about him.' "

Karla grinned. "Not like that. Just say you think you recognize him from somewhere. Or he looks like someone who used to work for you. I couldn't tell Mr. Renda that, but you could."

"With Frank's shifty-eyed nature," Demery said, "right away he'd suspect something."

Karla winked at him. "Not the way you'd handle it, Pa. Smooth as silk."

Demery eyed his daughter in silence. "You know where you ought to be? Up in Prescott with Lyall. He'd use you to soften up the juries."

Karla smiled. "You'll ask him?"

Demery looked off toward Renda who stood near the wagon watching the supplies being loaded. He called out, "Frank—" and as Renda turned, "Here's your voucher!"

Renda left the wagon and as he reached them he said to Demery, "Don't strain yourself."

Demery moved to the door. He held the screen open for Renda, saying, "You generally sign the voucher on the bar, don't you? Why take extra steps?" Renda said nothing. He walked past Demery into the adobe. Demery followed him, turning to wink at Karla before the screen closed behind him.

Karla walked toward the shed now. As she reached the corner of the adobe, Brazil, still mounted, called, "Don't get too close . . . one of them's liable to grab you." He grinned at her, cradling the Winchester in the crook of his arm and took out tobacco to make a cigarette.

The man in the wagon bed, a tall, gaunt-faced dark-bearded convict, his hands on his hips, looked down at her. "That wouldn't be so bad, would it?"

Karla said nothing. She looked away indifferently, but gradually her eyes returned to the convict wearing number 18.

He lifted a bundle of pick handles over the sideboard, then leaned against a support post, removing his hat. As Karla watched, she saw it: his hair light brown though it appeared darker, wet with perspiration. His features were even, features that were almost soft, yet distinctive and would be easily remembered. Part of his forehead was a white band that the sun had not reached and it contrasted vividly with the deep tan of his jaw line.

Karla turned, hearing the screen door again. Renda was saying something as they approached. Then, as they drew nearer, she heard her father say, "They got here about suppertime yesterday."

"If I'd known," Renda said, "I could've picked them up last night."

"Do you think," Demery asked, "I should have ridden all the way up to tell you?"

"You could've sent Karla."

"Look," Demery stated. "You pay five dollars more freight costs and it's delivered right to your door."

Renda shook his head. "Willis figured this way was cheaper."

"Was he sober when he figured it?"

Renda smiled now. "That's no way to talk about our superintendent. Willis Falvey knows his figures."

Karla asked, "And how does Mrs. Falvey like living at a convict camp?"

"Lizann?" Renda said with mock surprise. "Why Lizann likes it up there fine." He would have said more, but Brazil called out to him—

"Frank! I'm sitting in the sun while you pass the time of day!"

"There's a man that's all business," Renda said. He motioned the two convicts onto the wagon, then called to Brazil, "Let's go!" He walked past Demery and Karla and mounted his chestnut mare. From the saddle he said, "Karla, we'll visit awhile the next time you bring the mail."

He reined the mare and rode straight out from the adobe to meet the wagon making a wide, slow turn to head back toward the willows.

For a moment Karla and her father watched the wagon in silence. Finally Karla said, "Did you ask him?"

Demery nodded, still watching the wagon as it drew near the willows. "I asked him."

"What did he say?"

"Enough so you won't have to write Lyall." Demery looked at his daughter then. "A year ago he was convicted of cattle rustling and tried at Prescott. He's already spent nine months in Yuma. He's been here three months and he's got six years to go of a seven-year sentence. That, Sis, is the nice-looking boy you have the warm feeling for."

For a moment Karla said nothing. Then, "And his name?"

"Corey Bowen," her father answered.

TWO

The driver, Earl Manring, drew in on the reins as the wagon reached the willow trees that lined the creek bank. He stood up, kneeling one knee on the seat, and looked back at Renda. "We better water first. Right?"

Renda neck-reined his mare closer to the wagon. "All right." He looked at Bowen and Ike Pryde sitting on the end gate. "Get a drink," he told them, then rode over to the willow shade where Brazil was dismounting.

Brazil drank first, then Renda; and now, as they watered their horses, both of them watched the three men kneeling at the creek a few feet from the wagon team.

Manring cupped the water in his hands and raised it to his mouth. He drank the water, but his hands remained at his face and he said to Bowen, "There'll be a better time than today. Today's not right for it."

Bowen said nothing. He was lying on his stomach now with his elbows propped under him, staring at the sandy creek bed.

"If I know it," Manring said, "then Renda knows it."

Not looking at him, Bowen said, "You don't know anything."

"Listen. It's written on you like a sign. You don't talk and you keep watching Renda . . . thinking he don't know it."

Ike Pryde, the convict wearing number 17, half turned. He was in his late thirties, older than Bowen and Manring by not more than ten years; though he looked old enough to be their father. He had taken off his hat and in the sunlight his skull showed white through his thin, close-cropped hair. His face was hard-lined and rarely changed its expression; but age showed in his eyes and in the stoop-shouldered way he moved. Six years at Yuma before the road gang. Six years that had added sixteen to his life. His eyes raised to Earl Manring as he turned.

"Leave him alone," he muttered.

"If he'd think for a minute," Manring said, "he'd change his mind."

Bowen leaned closer to the bank to scoop water. "I'll say it once more. You don't know anything."

"I know somewhere between here and camp you're going into the woods."

"You think what you want," Bowen said.

Manring's jaw was clenched. "This isn't the way to do it! You got no horse. You got *nothing!*"

"Earl"—Pryde's lips barely moved—"you're going to get your jaw broke."

Renda and Brazil came out of the willow shade. Bowen rose and moved to the end of the wagon, then looked forward to the team again as he saw Pryde staring in that direction. Manring stood by one of the horses adjusting the harness and Renda was leaning over his saddle horn, saying something to him.

They forded the creek. On the other side, they followed wagon tracks that formed a long, slow-sweeping curve up to the jackpines along the crest, then skirted the shoulder of the hill before sloping down again and after this the trail kept to deep, rock-rimmed draws that twisted through the hills.

Renda rode in the lead now, turning in his saddle every few minutes to look back at the wagon. Behind the supply load, he could not see the two men on the end gate. They were Brazil's concern. Brazil and his Winchester brought up the rear, keeping not more than twenty feet behind the wagon.

The two men on the end gate had not spoken since leaving the creek. Now, unexpectedly, Pryde said, "In another mile we reach the steep part."

They sat with their legs hanging, their shoulders hunched forward and their eyes on the trail falling away beneath their feet.

Bowen said nothing.

"It's steep enough," Pryde mumbled, "that we'll have to get off and lean on a wheel."

"I know that," Bowen said.

"How? This is your first trip."

"I was told."

"What else were you told?"

"That was enough."

Pryde's eyes raised momentarily to Brazil following them. "That boy's dying to use his Winchester."

"If you want to talk," Bowen said, "tell me something I don't know."

Pryde's jaw tightened, then relaxed slowly. "You're tough, huh?"

Bowen didn't answer.

"It takes more than being tough," Pryde said. He was silent for a moment. "You're thinking when we reach the grade and have to get off, that's the time to go. Then or never." Pryde paused again. "I'll tell you one time. Don't do it today."

Bowen said, "You and Manring."

"Manring has his own reason. I don't know what that was, but I'm telling you what I feel."

"You didn't say anything at the creek."

"It wasn't the same then. If you wanted to jump, that was your business. Now there's something wrong. That man with the Winchester knows what's about."

Bowen's eyes raised. "He looks the same as always."

"You don't *see* a difference," Pryde growled. "You *feel* it."

"Well, I don't *feel* it."

"You haven't been locked up long enough."

"I'd say long enough," Bowen answered.

Pryde waited. "After six years you know things. Things you didn't know before. I don't know how, but you do."

Bowen glanced up, then looked down at the wagon ruts again. "When you were at Yuma . . . did you ever try to run?"

"Twice."

"How long before they caught you?"

"A day one time. Four the next. They paid the Pimas fifty dollars to bring you back."

"When you broke out . . . did it *feel* like it was the right time?"

Pryde hesitated. "I don't remember."

"But you're telling me one time's wrong and another time isn't."

Pryde said, "Go to hell then." But he added, "Even if you get clear, Renda's got better than Pimas. You know that."

"So it's a chance all the way."

"You don't outrun the trackers he's got. They been reading sign since they were little kids."

"That's not something to worry about now."

"But that Winchester is," Pryde said.

The trail began to rise again. Bowen could feel the wagon slanting upward and his hand gripped the end gate chain close to his right leg to steady himself.

Another twenty minutes, Bowen thought. He pictured the ride in earlier that morning, coming down the steep grade and studying the country carefully as they did, then reaching this section that clung to the hill shoulder and dropped off steeply on the right side. No, he thought, may be only ten minutes to the grade. But it doesn't make any difference how long. When you reach it, they'll pull you off the wagon and you'll know.

He thought of what Pryde had told him about them being ready and expecting him to break.

That was foolishness. You don't *feel* things. Even if you do, you don't bet on a feeling. You don't stake something big on it.

They're always ready, he thought. It's just a question of moving when they're *least* ready.

A convict on the road gang named Chick Miller had described the trail between the camp and Pinaleño. Every foot of it that he could remember. He had told Bowen, "Going there isn't the time. But when you're coming back, Renda rides in front. If he was to stay behind, then the load would be between him and the driver and some places the trail is only as wide as the wagon. That means only one man's in back to watch you. Now I'd say a man's best time would be when you reach the high grade and have to get off. Now you're on the ground, getting the feel of it under your shoes . . . and your rear guard is worrying whether the wagon's going to come sliding back at him."

He remembered Chick winking and saying, "That's the time, Corey. Right then."

And when he asked Chick why he had never tried it, the answer was that he was along in years and his legs wouldn't bear up under running. "Boy . . . you'll run till they drop off."

Bowen had waited, every day thinking about it, picturing himself doing it . . . and finally this morning he was picked for the Pinaleño trip and the time had come.

Maybe Chick told Manring, Bowen thought. That's how he knows. And Pryde picked it up from Manring.

His eyes raised to Brazil again. The Winchester was across his lap. Of course they're ready, he thought again; but you catch them when they're least—

Suddenly he saw his error.

Why should they be least ready at the grade? Because Chick said so?

If Brazil thought you had even a halfway better chance there he'd be readier than he was ever ready!

Why is being on the ground an advantage? Your back's to him then!

He breathed in and out slowly and thought, more calmly: You're facing him now. You're looking right at him and you even know when he scratches himself.

He glanced over the side of the wagon. The trail dropped off abruptly, slanting steeply for twenty-five or thirty feet. Then thick brush. Brush and scrub pine and rock and beyond that a second slope that was more gradual.

But how do you make the Winchester wait five seconds?

He noticed loose stones along the edge of the trail and he thought: One of those could stop him long enough.

But how do you know there'll be one where you jump off? We could come to a bare stretch just as—

He stopped . . . his eyes on Brazil. He watched Brazil raise the rifle barrel and rest it in the crook of his left arm. His right hand came up and across his chest and two fingers hooked into the shirt pocket to bring out the tobacco sack.

You're looking at it, Bowen thought, knowing it, being sure of it, and feeling the excitement inside of him now and trying not to show it.

You don't sit and think about it. You go or you don't go.

The crook of Brazil's left arm squeezed the barrel tightly as he poured tobacco into the troughed square of cigarette paper. Both of his hands were busy; both of them away from the trigger of the Winchester.

You go!

It was in his mind and out of his mind as he pushed himself from the wagon and went over the side of the ledge, not looking at Brazil, but hearing suddenly a hoarse yell as he hit the slope falling, sliding, raising dust, the abrupt leg shock of reaching the bottom, and now rolling and hearing another yell from above and another and lunging into the brush as a shotgun blast ripped the mesquite branches above him.

He was on his feet, running, stumbling through the scrub pine, then suddenly, instinctively, swerving to the left and the shotgun roared again, spattering buckshot through the trees behind him and it went through his mind: Where's the Winchester! But he did not look back. Coming out of the trees he hesitated, but only momentarily, only long enough to be sure of his direction. His shoes dug into the loose sand and he sprinted down the open hillside, his shoulders drawn tight waiting for the gunfire.

Then it came, the whining report and sand kicking up behind him, and he knew the Winchester was at work. Three times the .45–70 slugs whined ricocheting after him; then stopped abruptly as he reached the dense trees at the bottom of the grade. Silence followed.

He stood for a moment making himself breathe in and out slowly, then started up the slope, up through heavy timber, knowing he would not be seen now. At the top of the ridge he stopped again and this time looked back.

Far across, the wagon was a small shape on the hillside. He could make out men standing behind the wagon, but he could not distinguish one from another or even count how many were standing there. His gaze dropped down the slope, following the course he had taken, but there was no movement anywhere. Minutes went by as he waited and listened, but still there was no movement, nor the sound of anyone coming up through the trees.

Now they'll put the trackers to work, Bowen thought . . . and Brazil probably already halfway there to get them.

His only chance was to make his way back to the Pinaleño station and somehow get a horse. He knew this; and he knew that he had little time before Renda's detachment of Apache police would be reading his tracks.

THREE

Willis Falvey dismounted in front of the Pinaleño adobe. There was no sound in the sunlit yard. His gaze went to the stable shed, then back to the screen door of the adobe. He hesitated uncertainly before going inside.

"Demery?"

There was no answer. His eyes moved from one end of the low-ceilinged room to the other, past Demery's open roll-top desk, past the plank table where the stage passengers ate to the small mahogany-stained bar. The dimness was a relief after the outside glare. It was quiet here, restful, and momentarily it occurred to Willis Falvey that perhaps he might stay here instead of riding all the way to Fuegos.

No, he thought then. He would want to remain all night, and that could prove embarrassing. Not like at Fuegos where he could drink all he wanted in the privacy of a hotel room—in what passed for a hotel room—then sleep it off.

Well, he could have one here . . . at least one. He called for Demery again, waited, then walked to the bar and poured himself a whisky. This would be the start. Perhaps by this evening he would have forgotten, for a time, Frank Renda and the convict camp and his wife, Lizann.

A horse whinnied—the sound coming from the backyard where the corral was located—then Karla's voice.

Falvey listened, then drank down the whisky. He left the bar, walked through the kitchen, and from the back door saw Karla outside. She was rubbing down one of the relay horses in the shade of the long, main stable that extended out from the back of the adobe almost to the corral.

Willis Falvey's eyes raised suddenly. No, there was nothing

there; but for a moment he thought he had seen someone standing on the far side of the mesquite-pole corral.

"Karla."

She looked up, seeing Falvey coming out from the adobe, his gaze shifting now and again to the corral. He was unnaturally conscious of himself, she knew, and he had to be occupied when he thought someone was looking at him—even if it was only to glance at corralled horses. The few times he had been here before, Karla noticed this—his obviously self-conscious actions, his almost complete lack of anything to say—and in a way she felt sorry for him. He was out of place at the convict camp, especially as government superintendent, and Karla was sure he realized it more than anyone else.

"Just passing by, Mr. Falvey?"

He nodded, and hesitated before saying, "I helped myself to a drink. I'll put the money on the bar when I go back in. I heard you out here and—"

"That's all right," Karla said easily. "You could pay the next time for that matter."

"I didn't see your father inside."

"He had to go to Fuegos." She said then, "Your friend Renda was here to pick up supplies. I suppose you passed him coming in."

"No, I didn't."

"They only left about an hour ago."

"I took the horse trail," Falvey said. Then asked, "Are you alone?"

She nodded, seeing his gaze move to the corral again.

"I thought I saw someone out there," Falvey said, "just as I came out of the house."

Karla looked out from the shade. "I don't know who it would be."

"No, it was probably the way the horses were standing." Falvey was silent for a moment. "You're here all alone?"

"I'm used to it," Karla said. "Pa has to go to Fuegos every once in a while, to the telegraph office."

"Oh—" Falvey nodded. "What about your mother . . . is she—"

"Dead?" Karla smiled at his uneasiness. "No, she's in Willcox with my two sisters."

"I didn't know you had sisters."

"Younger ones. They're still in school and my mother stays with them for the term. They'll be back soon for the summer."

Falvey seemed more relaxed. "It must be hard not seeing them most of the year."

"It is, but my mother says we all have to be educated. She was born in Sonora . . . You see, her mother was Mexican, but her pa was an American, a mining man, and she didn't go to school at all. That's why we have to, even if it means being away."

"She must be a fine woman."

Karla grinned. "I like her."

"Listen," Falvey said eagerly. "Why don't you come inside while I have a drink?"

"I don't serve the bar, Mr. Falvey."

"I didn't mean that. Just . . . so we can talk."

"There's a stage due just before eleven and the change team's not nearly ready."

"It'd only be ten minutes." Falvey smiled. He was trying to make the proposal sound offhand.

"I'm sorry," Karla said. "There's just not time."

"Oh, come on." He was still smiling as he reached out to take her hand, but she stepped away from him. For a moment he stood awkwardly, his arm still extended, then moved toward her again.

Karla backed away. "Maybe you've already had too much to drink."

Falvey stopped. "Karla . . . I swear, I only want someone to talk to."

"And I told you I didn't have time."

"Karla—" He hesitated, but stepped toward her again as he said more calmly, "Didn't you ever want to relax and talk to someone? Just talk about anything, as long as it wasn't important. Even the weather. I mean talk without raising your voice, without arguing, without knowing someone's going to snap at the next thing you say." He paused. "That's all I want to do, just talk."

"Don't you talk to your wife?" Karla asked hesitantly.

"Have you ever?"

"Talked to her? A few times. But I don't know your wife very well."

"You're fortunate," Falvey said.

Karla stared at him. "I think you'd better go."

"Karla, you don't understand."

"Mr. Falvey, I'm not going to stand here and discuss your wife with you."

"I'm sorry, I shouldn't have said what I did. I started wrong."

"Why don't you go in and serve yourself?" Karla said. "I'll come in when I can."

Falvey nodded. "All right." He asked then, hesitantly, "We can be friends, can't we?"

The girl smiled uneasily. "I don't have any enemies, Mr. Falvey."

"Damn it, just say yes or no!"

Karla's eyes showed irritation, and suddenly, anger. "You don't *force* friendship! It either happens or it doesn't happen!"

"I'm sorry—"

"I'm not even sure," Karla said, "I know what you're looking for."

"I'm looking for someone who acts like a human being! Is that too much to ask for?"

"It is when you ask like that!"

"I'm sorry, Karla." He seemed suddenly very tired. "I'm really sorry. I didn't mean to talk the way I did."

"That's all right."

"I'll come back some other time . . . if it's all right with you."

She nodded, then watched him turn and walk back to the adobe. A moment later she heard his horse, the sound fading into the distance.

The yard was quiet.

Then, as she turned to the horse again, an arm came around her shoulders, jerking her off balance, and a hand covered her mouth before she could cry out. She struggled, her nails digging into the arm across her chest, trying to twist away, trying to turn to see who it was, then glimpsing the bare sun-blackened upper arm close to her face she stopped struggling.

She could feel his arm relax. His hand loosened on her mouth, then came away slowly, brushing her lips.

"Don't call out." His voice was quiet, close to her face. Karla nodded her head and the hand dropped to her shoulder.

"I'm going to take this horse. You just stand still."

Karla nodded again. "All right, Mr. Bowen."

The hands on her shoulder tightened suddenly and pulled her around to face him. "How'd you know who I was?" His face showed open surprise.

"I . . . recognized your arms."

"My arms?"

"From this morning."

"But how do you know my name?"

Karla half smiled. "Mr. Renda told us." She added quickly, "You jumped off at the grade, didn't you?"

"Before that."

"And they couldn't chase you because of the other prisoners."

"That's right."

"But the trackers are probably already following."

"That's right," Bowen said again. Still he did not move. His hands were on her shoulders and he continued to study her dark face, trying to understand the calm way she looked up at him.

"Then you'd better hurry," Karla said. "The saddle's on the wall behind you."

Bowen turned, almost reluctantly. He bridled the big mare, spread the blanket, and as he swung the saddle up, Karla started to walk away.

"Where're you going?"

Karla looked back. "To get you some clothes." She waited as he stared at her and she felt that she could almost read his thoughts. "Don't you trust me?"

"I don't know why I should."

"All right, ride around with those numbers on your pants."

Bowen shook his head. "I don't understand you."

"What would you like to know?" Karla asked.

"Why're you helping me?"

"I'm not. You're taking a horse. What good would it do if I objected?"

"The clothes—"

"You would have thought of it sooner or later," Karla said. "Hurry now."

Unexpectedly, Bowen said, "Was Falvey bothering you?"

Karla smiled again. "Maybe you're not in a hurry."

"Was he?"

"Mr. Falvey was looking for a friend, that's all."

"He could use one."

"So could you."

"I was trying to figure," Bowen said hesitantly, "if there was something between you."

"You'd better think about getting something between you and Renda's trackers." She turned. This time he did not stop her and she went on to the adobe.

Bowen was leading the horse out when she returned carrying a blanket roll. "Shirt and pants are inside," Karla said. "And something to eat."

Bowen's eyes remained on her. "I'd like to know why you're doing this."

"I'm not sure why myself," Karla answered quietly. She said then, "If you're caught, they'll make it hard for you."

"Like what, working on a road?"

Karla hesitated. "Did you really steal cattle?"

"Now how would you know that?"

"That doesn't matter now. Just tell me."

"Why would you think I didn't?"

Karla's shoulders moved, her dark eyes still watching him. "I just have a feeling you didn't."

"You can sure simplify things," Bowen said.

"But did you?" Karla asked again.

"I got to go."

"Tell me!"

Bowen swung up to the saddle, then looked down at her.

"That man with the beard this morning—Earl Manring—he hired me in Prescott to help him drive a herd, even showed me a bill of sale for the stock. But the second day out we were arrested to stand trial for rustling. The man who'd sold Earl the stock said he never did such a thing and that the bill of sale Earl had was no good, and he said he could prove it because there wasn't any copy of the transaction in his books."

Karla said, "Didn't you have a lawyer?"

"The court appointed one. We didn't have any money for our own."

Karla frowned. "But the man who sold you the stock—"

"Sold Earl the stock—Earl already had the bill of sale when I met him. The man's name was McLaughlin. He took an oath that he'd never seen the bill of sale Earl had before in his life.

"Earl told me he should've known better than to deal with a man he didn't know, and no wonder the stock was offered at such a good price. He said McLaughlin took advantage of him—got his money for the stock, then didn't register it in his books, called out the law, then even got his stock back. We were arrested one day, tried the next, and there wasn't anything we could do about it. The fastest trial I ever heard of."

"And," Karla said, "you were sentenced to Yuma."

"Seven years each."

"You needed a good lawyer," Karla said thoughtfully.

"We needed more than that."

"You needed a lawyer like Mr. Martz, the Hatch & Hodges attorney. He's in Prescott. He's—" She stopped abruptly, looking up at Bowen.

Bowen shook his head. "The trial's over."

"But if he could prove you didn't know anything about it—"

"He'd be awful good." Bowen reined the mare around. "I hope I can pay you back for this."

"Don't worry about that now."

He looked down at her and seemed reluctant to leave, then said, "Goodbye, Karla." That was all.

She watched him circle the corral and disappear into the pines and only then did it occur to her that he knew her name. He could have heard Renda say it—that was it. But he remembered it—that was the important thing.

FOUR

Salvaje, sergeant of Apache police, waited. His eyes, beneath the broad hatbrim, were fixed on the dark rise of pines miles to the east—the hillcrest that overlooked the Pinaleño station. He had sent one of his Mimbres there within minutes of being told of the escape. It was something he always did; for invariably the sign led to Pinaleño. With the rest of his trackers he had followed the escaped man's trail to this point. If the signal did not come from the pines, they would continue. Sometimes it took a complete day to bring back an escaped man, but seldom longer than that.

And sometimes it was almost too easy. At least this one had not tried to cover his trail. Some of them used devices that only wasted their time: back-tracking and stream-wading tricks that even a reservation child could understand. Doing this even when their objective was almost always Pinaleño and a horse.

But one had to admit that this was better than duty at San Carlos: the endless hunting of tulapai stills and carrying back men of your own people who had jumped the reservation. Here, one had the opportunity to track white men. Salvaje's father had been a Mimbreño war chief; his mother, a Mexican woman taken in a raid on a Chihuahua pueblo. Salvaje had spent the better part of his life making war against his mother's people and against white men— the good years of riding with Victorio and Delchay, years that could not be compared with this business of recapturing escaped prisoners.

He waited patiently, one thumb hooked in the cartridge bandoleer that crossed his worn cavalry jacket. He was confident that the signal would come, that it was only a matter of time. What else could an escaped man do but go to Pinaleño?—if he had thought about it at all.

And finally the signal did come—a white-gleaming dot in the pines, then the pinpoint flashes, sunlight reflected on a metal disk and sent to him here, miles away, and what Salvaje had known all along was now confirmed.

It blinked once; then three times in quick succession. The escaped man had left the adobe and was riding to the west. His man in the pines would follow now and signal again if the escaped one changed direction.

Salvaje looked at his men. There were ten trackers here, and now he watched them remove their army-issue shirts and pants, stripping to breechclouts, then slipping on their cartridge bandoleers again. All of them wore curl-toed Apache moccasins folded and tied just below the knee; and to a man they carried single-shot Springfield carbines.

When they were ready, Salvaje nodded, and they moved off to take the escaped man.

Now the sun was directly overhead. Bowen urged the mare over a cutbank, leaning back in the saddle as the crusted sand gave way and followed them down the slope in a thin dust trail. He entered the cover of trees that grew thickly along both sides of the dry creek bed: cottonwood and sycamore and higher up, farther down the draw, black patches of pine shadowing steep shelfrock. In the dimness it seemed more quiet and he stopped to listen before crossing the creek bed to follow its course through the draw.

He moved carefully, knowing that he was leaving a trail, but more concerned with what might lie ahead than what might be following. Coming this way, he knew, would give the Mimbre trackers time to cut him off. Still, this was wild climbing country, laced with draws and heavy timber to use for cover. South and east from the Pinaleño station were desert flats, and water only if you knew the location of the wells.

Less than two hundred yards farther on, the draw widened and began to rise and here the trees ended. Bowen edged the mare close to the near wall of shelfrock, then moved out into the open and climbed the rise. He stopped then and looked back, down over the green rolling carpet of the treetops.

At first he wasn't sure. Then there was no mistaking it—a thin wisp of dust hanging motionless over the far end of the draw.

His gaze came back to the long sweep of meadow in front of him. It sloped gradually and narrowed into a trough between two pine-studded hills. He would be in the open for more than a mile. But, he thought, trying to keep himself calm, trying to ignore the uncertainty that was tightening inside of him: You go that way or you don't go at all.

Then the wind was in his face and the mare was pounding over the thick grama grass, racing for the bottom of the meadow. The trough between the hills, perhaps a hundred yards wide, opened before him as he heeled the mare again and felt her lengthen her stride reaching level ground again.

And suddenly, with the high whining report, with the solid smacking sound of the bullet, the mare went down and Bowen was over her head—rolling, stumbling, coming to his feet as the Mimbre rode out of the pines up on the right slope, then seeing the Mimbre and running hard for the opposite grade, a shot ringing behind him, then another, and he knew he would not reach the trees.

He veered sharply, running now for an outcropping of rocks at the foot of the hill, hearing suddenly the sound of horses rumbling down the far slope. Three shots sang off the rocks as he went down behind them, and abruptly he heard the horses being reined in. Then silence.

Bowen came up slowly. He brought his knees under him, but kept his head low as he separated the brush that was thick between the rocks.

The Mimbreños were off perhaps eighty yards: eleven of them, all armed and sitting their short, close-coupled horses patiently, taking their time now, as much time as they wanted, to study the rocks. Bowen watched them, wondering why they waited.

If you could think like an Apache, Bowen thought now, you'd know why. All right, then think like a white man. What would you do if you were eleven people and you had one man cornered out in the middle of nowhere? I'd march my eleven people over and drag him out. Eleven what look like Springfields are a match for a pair of bare hands any day of the week and twice on Sunday.

If you're sure they're bare hands.

They know you're not armed.

But that's one of those things you can know and still want to be clearly sure of. So you'd spread out your eleven people and edge in a step at a time and call out things about coming out with your hands up and not trying any funny business.

Only you never in your life heard of an Apache doing anything like that, so you can cross that off and throw it away.

But however they do it, they'll try to take you alive. Even if they didn't work for Renda they'd do that. Only—and there're a lot of onlys—they can take you back in all kinds of states where you'd still be alive, though you'd just as soon be dead.

Give yourself up, he thought. No . . . let them work a little bit. You never know what can happen . . . like getting one of their horses.

How do you do that?

How do you do anything! Just shut up and watch!

Not expecting it, he saw one of the Mimbres ride off from the others. His horse went into a canter heading toward the narrowing of the trough between the two hills. Suddenly then, he turned a tight circle, kicking his horse to a gallop, and he came on a dead run directly for the rocks. Bowen went down and the Mimbre passed within ten yards of him firing his Springfield as he went by.

Bowen came up cautiously. He watched the rider circle wide returning to the rest of the band and as he did another Mimbre rode out. This one also pointed off toward the narrowness, giving his horse room to run before coming around, before making his pass at the rocks. He fired as he went by, the shot glancing off rock and whining up into the trees that were high on the slope behind Bowen.

Now, watching the third Mimbre make his circle, Bowen thought: They're making a game out of it, trying to scare you. They've got all the time in the world, so they'll play with you a while—knowing they can take you any time they feel like it. And each one comes a little closer.

He went down as a Springfield roared five yards in front of him, then came up again to watch the Mimbre rejoin the others.

That's some game, he thought then. You know who the winner is before you start. But if you had a gun . . . if you had a gun you could play with them. You could make it a two-sided game. And it occurred to him then: Why didn't you get a gun from her! Clothes and a horse, but no gun.

The fourth Mimbre started to make his circle and Bowen eased down. Or, he thought, get a gun from one of them.

Just like that. Go out and grab onto a Springfield as it goes by.

You've done crazier things. Jumping off that wagon didn't make sense either . . . at first.

He thought of breaking off a mesquite branch to use as a club, but he knew he would never get close enough to use it. Not against a mounted man. No, it had to be something to throw. Something light enough to throw, but hard enough to drop a man from a running horse.

They were scattered all around him, the stones and the broken chunks of rock: but he had had to think in terms of a throwing weapon before becoming fully aware of them. The hoofbeats grew louder as his hand groped for a piece of rock, found one the size of a man's fist, jagged and uneven, and the next moment he was standing, seeing the Mimbre low on the horse, guiding it with his knees, raising the carbine, using both hands and pressing his face close to the breech—

Bowen threw the rock and went down. The carbine exploded over his head and he was up again as the Mimbre looked back, circling toward the others. He had thrown too quickly.

He saw the Mimbre who had just made the pass pointing toward him and a faint sound drifted across the openness. Now they've got something to laugh about, Bowen thought. Something to make the game better. Well, come on. If you think it's funny keep trying.

He went down, his hand searching for another rock as the fifth Mimbre circled wide to make his pass. But this time, Bowen continued to think, we'll do it different. We'll make up new rules.

He found the right-sized rock, then moved over and away from the boulders almost five yards. Here there was less protection, but enough low brush to cover him. The rider would not see him until he was directly in front of the brush, and then it would be too late to do anything about it.

Now he could hear the Mimbre coming, the quick sound of the hoofs growing steadily. Bowen crouched, judging the distance by the sound. Almost to the rocks, getting ready, bringing up the carbine. Now. He was firing as Bowen came up, rushing past as Bowen hurled the rock, and starting to look back as it caught him in the face.

The Mimbre went back out of the saddle and Bowen was through the brush running for the carbine, picking it up and swinging it suddenly as the Mimbre started to rise. The stock caught the Mimbre's head and he crumpled. Bowen was on him, pulling the bandoleer up over his shoulder; but firing broke suddenly from the other slope and he knew there wasn't time to take the belt. His fingers snatched cartridges from the belt loops and again he was running for the rocks. The firing stopped abruptly as he reached cover.

He looked out again, pushing a cartridge into the breech of the Springfield, then placed the other four cartridges he had taken on a shelf of level rock next to him.

It wasn't even worth it, Bowen thought. Five shots. That's all you've got. What do you do with five bullets against eleven. No, against ten. He looked over to the motionless form of the Mimbre. You should've dragged him back with you. Then you'd have the whole belt . . . And you'd have a sore-headed 'Pache to watch.

No, it wouldn't have made any difference. What would you do, shoot all eleven of them? You don't run away from jail because you shouldn't be there in the first place, but kill eleven men doing it. Then you might just as well stay in prison.

You're all mixed up, aren't you? You got yourself into something and now you don't know how to get out.

Maybe scatter them and make a run for it, he thought then. He rolled to his side to study the pine stands up on the hill behind him. The trees were green-brown and motionless against the sky.

Only it's a long run for not knowing what's on the other side. What do you do once you get up there?

Then you think of something else. Just take it a step at a time . . . you're not going any faster than that.

He rolled to his stomach again and now saw one of the Mimbres leave the band. This one did not move off as if to make a circle, but came directly toward the rocks.

The brave one, Bowen thought, pressing his cheek against the smooth stock of the carbine. Well, give the brave one something to think about.

He squeezed the trigger and the horse went down. The Mimbre rolled clear and ran back to the others. Then, as he reached them, Bowen fired again. Another horse stumbled, sinking to its knees, and the Mimbres were suddenly wheeling their mounts to move out of range.

And as they scattered in momentary confusion, Bowen moved. He snatched up the cartridges and turned from the rocks, running now for the nearest stand of pines that straggled down the slope behind him. Fifty yards to the trees . . . then the beating of hoofs bearing down on him. He was loading the Springfield as he ran— dropped a cartridge—knew that he was holding only two more in his hand, and jammed one of them into the breech.

He came around, dropping to one knee, and brought up the Springfield. But the Mimbre veered off to the left, aiming his carbine at Bowen with one hand and both fired at the same time, both shots going wide.

Bowen hesitated. He saw the Mimbre rein a tight circle, starting to reload, and then he was running for the Mimbre—seeing the sudden look of surprise on the Mimbre's face, now seeing the horse jump as it was spurred forward—then dodging the horse's head he swung the carbine up at its rider.

The Mimbre swayed in the saddle, dropping his carbine, but he did not go down. He came back at Bowen to run him down, but again Bowen dodged aside. This time he released the carbine as he swung it and the stock slammed against the Mimbre's head knocking him from the saddle.

The horse came about, feeling its rider go off, slowed to a trot, then a walk—then suddenly broke into a run as Bowen swung up on the saddle and pointed the horse slanting across the slope back toward the long sweep of meadow. But he covered barely a hundred yards before the Mimbres were all around him. He reined abruptly to come back on them, but they closed in before he could break through and he was forced to a stop with seven Springfields leveled at him.

The Mimbres dismounted. One of them, on Bowen's left, reached up to drag him from the saddle. Bowen's fist chopped at him viciously and he staggered back. A carbine barrel jabbed into Bowen's right side. He turned his body, swinging a fist backhanded at the Springfield, and as he did a rawhide loop dropped over his head, and before he could free himself of it the line tightened and he was dragged from the saddle.

The Mimbres swarmed over him and the one Bowen had struck a moment before swung down at him with the butt of his carbine. Bowen rolled and the stock missed him. The Mimbre brought back the carbine to swing it again, but one abrupt, clearly spoken word in the Mimbreño dialect stopped him.

Bowen came to his feet. He looked for the Mimbre who had spoken and saw Salvaje then standing in front of his horse, the reins over his shoulder and hanging down in front of him. He spoke again and the Mimbres near Bowen stepped back from him.

Salvaje continued to stare at Bowen, openly appraising him and for a moment the hint of a smile softened his mouth. He nodded his head then, slowly, as if to say: It was a good game and it is too bad it had to end—

FIVE

At one time, the convict camp at Five Shadows had been a cavalry station—founded during the raiding days of Cochise and garrisoned until Geronimo and his renegade Chiricahuas were sent off to Florida. Officers' row, the troopers' barracks, and even the log stable—forming a U around three sides of the quadrangle—were constructed of a double thickness of adobe brick, for although Five Shadows had been designated a temporary station, there was always a feeling of permanency about the Apache campaigns.

It had been deserted for almost seven years when Frank Renda began using it as a camp for his road construction operation.

In appearance, the camp was much the same as it had always been—even to the windmill and the half dozen Apache *jacales* off beyond the stable where the Mimbreño trackers and their families lived. But now a ten-foot barbed wire fence—three feet of it angled to the inside—enclosed the compound. Over the gate a sign read:

CONVICT LABOR CAMP
KEEP OUT
This camp is under the jurisdiction of the U.S. Territorial Government. Unauthorized persons found entering will be fired on without warning.
F. W. Renda Const. Co.

The five separate quarters of officers' row now housed Renda, his five guards, and the government superintendent, Willis Falvey, and his wife. Across the compound, parallel to this adobe, was the stable. The troopers' barracks, in which the convicts were now kept, formed the base of the U and six doors of this adobe faced directly south to the camp's only gate. Five of the doors entered directly into the long dirt-floor barracks. The sixth door opened into a single room that had originally been part of the barracks, but was now bricked off and did not have a window. This was the punishment cell.

At three o'clock Frank Renda rode into the compound. He had been out at the construction site since returning with the supply wagon. But less than a half hour ago, one of the Mimbres had come to him with word that Bowen had been taken. He placed Brazil in charge then and started back to camp, wanting to be there when they brought in Bowen.

Crossing the open yard, he saw Lizann Falvey come out of the stable. He dismounted in front of her and brought his horse into the shade of the wide, open doorway.

"Have a nice ride?"

Lizann shrugged, removing her gloves and not bothering to look at Renda as he spoke. She wore a green riding suit and hat, the hat straight over her eyes and resembling a small derby, and her auburn hair was pulled back severely into a chignon at the nape of her neck.

"I was out on the road," Renda said, "and saw you go by." Beneath the heavy mustache, his lips barely moved. "I thought I told you not to go near there."

She looked at him now; her expression described boredom and even raising her eyes seemed an effort. Still she did not speak.

"So we're not talking today," Renda said mildly.

Lizann shrugged. "There isn't really much point in it."

"We could talk about Willis going to Fuegos again."

"I didn't know he had."

"Maybe," Renda suggested, "Willis's got a woman there."

Lizann looked at him again. "Willis wouldn't know the first thing about getting one."

"He got you."

"Did he?"

"Then you must've got him," Renda said. He nodded thoughtfully, even though he had thought about this before, months before, when Willis Falvey and his wife had first arrived. He had reasoned it out for himself at that time. "Sure," he said now, "you got him . . . seeing him with Washington friends and thinking he was due for something big. I don't blame you, Lizzy." Renda paused. "But why did he end up here?"

"You're talking to yourself," Lizann said.

"Well," Renda shrugged. "It doesn't make much difference how it happened, when you get right down to it. Does it? You're here and there isn't a solitary thing you can do about it."

"Isn't there?" Their eyes held momentarily. Then Lizann turned from him and started across the quadrangle. Renda slapped his chestnut into the stable and caught up with her.

"So you're still after Willis to quit."

She didn't bother to look at him, but she answered, "That isn't any of your business."

"You might think it isn't," Renda said. "I'll tell you this—the only way Willis quits while I'm here is to get carried out feet first."

"I'm surprised you let him go to Fuegos."

"Willis's got to have *some* fun."

"What if he should run away?"

Renda shook his head. "He doesn't even think about it any more."

Lizann said, "You must have someone there to watch him, or you wouldn't be so sure."

"No, Lizzy . . . you know it and Willis knows it, if he runs out on me he's a ruined man. I don't need anybody bird-doggin' him."

"He's already ruined," Lizann replied.

"Let's say he realizes that," Renda said. "He still wouldn't leave you here. See how it is?"

They were almost halfway across the yard when Renda saw the riders out beyond the gate. They were perhaps a quarter of a mile out and walking their horses toward the compound. Watching them, he said, "A man tried to run away this morning."

Lizann looked up, following his gaze. "Good for him."

"That's him they're bringing back."

"And now you'll teach him a lesson."

"Even if I didn't want to," Renda said, "I would."

They went on to the ramada shade of the long adobe and stopped there to watch the Mimbres ride in.

They straggled to almost single file as the guard opened half of the gate for them, then broke into a trot as they passed into the compound, two of the horses carrying double, and now Renda and Lizann could see the man they were leading.

Bowen was on foot, fifteen feet behind the last Mimbre. His hands were tied behind him and a reata extended from his neck to the saddle horn of the rider in front of him. The reata pulled taut as the horse started to trot and Bowen was jerked forward. He stumbled but kept his feet under him and now had to run to keep up with the horse.

Renda stepped out into the sunlight and raised his arm. "Over here!" He glanced back at Lizann. "They haven't missed yet."

Lizann was watching Salvaje, seeing him coming toward them now. "Animal tracks man," she said. Her gaze moved to Bowen then.

He was hatless and from hair to shoes he was covered with a heavy film of dust. She was sure that he had fallen more than once and had been dragged by the horse. The knees were torn from his pants and his shirt was almost in shreds. Dried blood caked the left side of his jaw and his shoulder was bloodstained where he had wiped his face on it. She could picture him doing this, stumbling along in the dust from the horses with his hands tied behind his back.

"Who is he?" Lizann asked, mildly curious.

Renda was watching Salvaje dismount. "Who?"

"The prisoner?"

"Oh . . . Bowen."

"He looks as if he's already been taught a lesson," Lizann said.

"Only part of one," Renda answered. He yelled to Salvaje then, "Bring him over here!"

A Mimbre pulled loose the honda and lifted the reata loop over Bowen's head, but did not untie his hands. He took Bowen by the arm then and led him to the ramada.

Renda waited, His thumbs were hooked in his belt and he stared at Bowen, studying his face and waiting for Bowen's eyes to drop or look away. But Bowen continued to return his stare and finally Renda said, "Was it worth it?"

Bowen didn't answer. Then, he tried to turn his head and bring up his shoulder, seeing Renda suddenly shift his weight, but he was not quick enough and Renda's fist slashed backhanded across his face.

Renda's arm dropped slowly. "I asked you a question."

Bowen nodded then. "It was worth it."

"Why?"

"I learned something."

"You're going to learn more before we're through."

Bowen said nothing.

"Like your friend Pryde," Renda said. "He learned his before he got off the road."

Bowen shook his head. "He wasn't in on it."

"That's why he went for Brazil."

Now Bowen hesitated. "Ike did that?"

"He tried. He got a Winchester over the head."

"If Brazil hit Ike," Bowen said quietly, "then he rode up to the wagon to do it. Taking it out on Ike because I—"

"Listen! I'm not discussing this with you . . . I'm *telling* you!"

"And I'm telling you Ike wasn't in on it!"

Renda's fists came up together, up under Bowen's jaw, and as his head snapped back Renda's right hand fell away then swung viciously against Bowen's face. Bowen went down. He rolled to his side painfully, his head resting on the ground.

"Pick him up," Renda said.

Salvaje stooped and slid his hands beneath Bowen's shoulders. Lifting him, he said. "This one fights well . . . when he has his hands."

Renda looked at the Mimbre sergeant. "Careful now."

"I say what I know," Salvaje answered. "He fought well and deserves better than this."

Renda nodded slowly, thoughtfully, before saying, "I'll tell you something now. You went out of here with twelve horses. You came back with ten. Worry about where you're going to find two horses and I'll worry about this one."

Salvaje shook his head. "You supply horses. We bring back escaped men."

"I think you'd do better," Renda said, "if you'd never learned to talk English." His tone changed suddenly and he pointed a finger at Salvaje. "You're going to find two horses to replace what you lost, or you're going to find yourself back at San Carlos! You savvy that, Mister Indian?"

Salvaje did not answer, but his eyes remained on Renda.

"Now get out of the way," Renda told him. He waited for Salvaje to move, then stepped up to Bowen, rubbing his fist into the palm of his left hand. Suddenly then, he cocked the fist. Bowen started to roll away from it, but as he did Renda's left hand lashed against his jaw.

Lizann watched Bowen as he tried to rise, as he fell back again and rolled to his stomach. She looked at Renda then to see what he would do.

Renda's glance went to Salvaje. "Pick him up."

With the Mimbre's help, Bowen came to his feet. He stood swaying, as if ready to fall, his head hanging forward, but as Renda swung at him again he rolled with the fist, and suddenly threw himself at Renda, lowering his head to drive against him. Renda went back a half step. He pushed Bowen away from him and moved in with his fists before Bowen could lower his head again. He hit him with both hands—short body jabs that kept Bowen backing away, trying to twist with the jabs, then a hard solid left hand to Bowen's stomach and as he started to fold forward Renda's right hand hammered against his jaw and he went down.

Renda stood over him, his thick chest rising and falling as he breathed. He backed away then and said, "Pick him up."

"Don't you think" Lizann said mildly, "he's had enough?"

Renda looked at her. "Do I tell you how to take care of Willis?"

"You'd like to be able to," Lizann said.

Renda glanced at her leaning against the ramada post. She always seemed to be lounging, watching something going on, but never taking part herself. He turned to Salvaje again. "I said pick him up."

Bowen was again lifted to his feet, but this time staggered and almost went down before Renda could reach him. Renda's hand caught the front of his shirt. He held Bowen momentarily, then dropped his hand as he shifted his weight and he hit Bowen in the face as hard as he could swing his fist.

He stepped back then, his eyes raising from Bowen to Salvaje. "Throw him in with Pryde. They'll think about it over bread and water for a while." He paused. "Say twenty days. That's a good round number."

Lizann watched Renda hand Salvaje a key; then Salvaje made a sign and two of his Mimbres lifted Bowen to his feet. He stood between them, his shoulders raised awkwardly by the support of their hands under his arms. His legs moved as they led him away, following Salvaje, but his head hung heavily, chin against chest, and Lizann realized that he was barely conscious.

Her eyes followed as they took him across the compound to the convicts' barracks, then along the wind-scarred adobe front of it, past five doors to the sixth one, the punishment cell.

She was thinking of her husband, comparing him to this man Bowen, and wondering if he could have taken half the beating Bowen did.

No, Bowen was a different breed—a man who would undoubtedly again try to escape, even if failure meant another beating and a longer period in the punishment cell. A man, Lizann reflected, who would go to any extreme to escape. Any extreme.

She saw Salvaje open the heavy door, the two Mimbres move inside with Bowen, then reappear, one carrying the length of rope that had fastened Bowen's hands, then Salvaje padlock the door again, and she continued to think of Bowen, though no longer comparing him to her husband.

Pryde sat against one wall, his legs straight out in front of him. Fifteen feet away, Bowen lay on his side, his face resting on the hard-packed dirt floor. Above him was the outline of a window. It had been bricked in, all of it except a narrow space where the top row of bricks would have gone. This opening ventilated the six-by-fifteen-foot cell, and now it framed a thin line of outside light, a faint ray that penetrated the dimness of the room to show Pryde's face in a pale streak against the wall.

He waited until Bowen stirred. Then he said, "Corey—" his voice clear in the stillness though it was barely above a whisper.

Bowen raised his head. "Ike . . . is that you?" His face was numb and swollen tight and as he spoke he could not feel his lips move.

"It's me," Pryde said.

Bowen came up on his elbow. "Ike, I'm sorry." His eyes narrowed as if to see through the dimness. "Ike, did you go after Brazil?"

Pryde's head nodded.

"Why'd you do it?"

"I don't know, I saw him trying to bring up that Winchester and I went for him . . . got him off the horse and hit him once, but that's all."

"I'm obliged to you, Ike."

Pryde said nothing.

"And he gave it back to you over the head."

Pryde's eyes moved. "He gave me more than that. When we got back here, Renda said, 'Learn him a lesson,' and Brazil went and got a pick handle to do it with."

Bowen crawled over him. "You hurt bad?"

"I don't know. I can't move my back."

"Your arms are swollen."

"I think I'm swollen about all over." He said then, still calmly, "Listen . . . you got to know something."

"We have a long time to talk," Bowen said. "Go to sleep now."

"Listen to me!" Pryde's voice rose. But he relaxed again as he said, "After Renda emptied his shotgun, he ran back to where we were. Brazil fired then, but it was too late. I was on the ground and my head buzzed like hell. That's why I'm not sure of the exact words . . . though the meaning was plain enough."

Bowen shook his head. "I don't follow you."

"You will. Renda looked like he wanted to kill somebody." Pryde went on, "but there wasn't anything he could do. Then he yelled out, 'You said not till the grade!' or words just like that."

Bowen frowned. "He said that to Brazil?"

Pryde shook his head slowly. "To Manring. Somewhere along the line Earl told him you were going to run."

SIX

They counted the days by marking the wall with Pryde's belt buckle, a mark for each day scratched in a row on the adobe wall. But even with this, after little more than a week had passed, they were not sure of the count and it seemed there should be more marks on the wall than there were. Twice a day the door opened and they were given bread and water. The guard who carried the bucket and dipper and a half loaf of bread was never armed. But another guard stood in the doorway with a shotgun. They were ordered not to talk to the prisoners and would not answer with even a sign when Bowen or Pryde asked the number of days they had been there.

In the morning, they would hear Renda or Brazil in front of the barracks lining up the convicts for the wagon trip to the construction site. Then, throughout the day, there was silence, long hours of dead silence only occasionally broken by the sound of a horse crossing the compound.

In the evening, after the convicts were in the barracks again, the faint murmur of voices, bits of conversation that were never completely clear, would drift into the darkness of the punishment cell. Bowen would sit with his back against the adobe not moving, listening for Manring's voice. But thinking of Manring, wanted to be sure he would still be here at the end of twenty days, made the time pass even more slowly.

Why had Manring warned Renda that he was planning to escape?

Pryde said, because he's paid for it. He had seen the same thing at Yuma. There were special privileges for the convict who kept the guards informed on what was going on *inside* the cell blocks. And, Pryde said, there was only one way to deal with that kind.

Maybe it was that simple. But Bowen went over in his mind everything he knew about Manring, trying to find a more personal reason.

They had met in a saloon of the Commercial House Hotel in Prescott just a little more than a year ago—Bowen with a trail drive behind him and for the time being nothing to do; Manring looking for a man to help him move a small herd down to San Carlos—the two of them standing at the bar. A few minutes after they started talking, they moved to a table.

"Ordinarily," Manring had explained, "I work for a spread same as anybody else, but I heard about this cry for beef down at San Carlos and saw it was a chance to make something if you had a little capital." And taking a bill of sale out of his pocket—"The reservation's grown bigger than the government beef allowance, so now they got to buy more. But they're buying monthly, just a hundred head or so at a time and it don't pay the big owner to take a herd down there. That's why somebody like you or me can make money out of it if you got stock to sell." He pointed to the bill of sale. "Which I got."

Bowen said it sounded all right to him. He was thinking about going down to Willcox to talk to a friend about a mining venture and if he could work his way down that was all the better.

The next morning they started driving the herd—forty head they had gathered themselves. Bowen noticed none of the steers had been vent-branded and he asked Manring about it.

"Why go to the trouble of registering a brand," Manring answered, "Then waste time putting it on when you'll only have the stock about a week? A bill of sale's good enough to prove ownership."

When Bowen opened his eyes the next morning, a man he had never seen before was standing over him with a rifle. There were eight or ten others in the clearing and a moment later he saw Manring brought in. Manring was mounted and it was evident he had tried to run when the posse closed in.

They were taken back to Prescott and formally charged that afternoon, the complaint being signed by R. A. McLaughlin, the man from who Manring claimed to have bought the cattle. Luckily (the sheriff said) a district judge would be in Prescott the next day—so there wouldn't be a delay in the trial.

Bowen remembered that first night in a jail cell clearly—watching Manring lying on his bunk smoking and for a long time neither of them spoke. But there were some things Bowen wanted to say and finally—

"If you'd vented McLaughlin's brand at the time of the sale we wouldn't be in jail." He was sorry as soon as he'd said it. That if-talking was like closing the barn after everything had run out. But Manring drew on his cigarette, not bothering to answer, and Bowen could feel his anger begin to rise.

"Why didn't you vent his brand when you closed the deal?"

Manring's head turned on the mattress. "I told you."

"Earl . . . this McLaughlin said you worked for him once, about three years ago. Took you on for a Kansas drive."

"I heard him."

"You claimed that wasn't so."

Manring stubbed out the cigarette. "You going to do the hearing all over again?"

"Earl"—he remembered that his voice was calm and that he wasn't yet really angry—"did you buy those cattle or did you steal them?"

Manring was on his back, staring at the ceiling. "I don't want to hear any more about it."

"Earl, they're going to try me tomorrow for something I don't know anything about!"

"Have a good cry," Manring muttered.

Bowen rose. "I asked you a question. I want to know if you really bought that stock!"

"So does the judge," Manring said. He started to roll over, turning his back to Bowen, but suddenly Bowen was dragging him up by the arm and as he came off the bunk Bowen hit him. He hit Manring four times before the sheriff's deputy came in to separate them.

The trial began at ten o'clock the next morning. At noon they recessed for dinner and for the jury to reach a decision. Then at two o'clock that afternoon the judge passed sentence. *Seven years in the Territorial Prison at Yuma.* There had been no time wasted. It was McLaughlin's word against Manring's and as far as both the judge and the jury were concerned, this was not a two-sided question. In sentencing them, the judge admitted being lenient, since to his knowledge neither of the accused had a previous criminal record.

That night Bowen and Manring were placed in separate cells to await transportation to Yuma.

For the next nine months, on Prison Hill, Bowen saw Manring every day, but they seldom spoke. He made himself believe that Manring was also innocent. That made it easier to live with him. Still, they had little in common and there was no reason for a friendship to exist between them. Gradually, then, he ceased to even think about Manring and the trial and he began to consider him nothing more than another Yuma convict. Being in different cells—though both were in the main cell block—made it that much easier.

From the first day he entered Yuma, Bowen thought of escape. He had made up his mind that he was not going to pay with seven years for something he didn't do. But thinking of escaping from Yuma you had to consider the Gatling gun over the main gate, the hundreds of miles of desert surrounding the prison, the Pima trackers who would bring you back for a bounty and, finally, the "Snake den" cell in the dungeon block where you would live for a month or more, chained to the stone floor, if the escape failed.

During the time they were at Yuma, construction of the cell block for incorrigibles was still in progress—a project planned to carve a dungeon of twelve cells out of solid granite. Bowen was assigned to the dynamite crew; and it was the experience gained in this work that was primarily responsible for his leaving Yuma some months later.

Their transfer came unexpectedly. Bowen, Manring and four other convicts—one of them Pryde—were taken from their cells one evening soon after supper. Nineteen days later, a wagon rolled through the barbed wire gate of the convict camp at Five Shadows as Frank Renda stood by to greet them.

In their three months here, Bowen had talked to Manring more often; and only a few days before the supply trip to Pinaleño, Manring had hinted at a plan of escape. But by then, Bowen had made up his mind to try it his own way and Manring's hints had been too vague to even arouse his curiosity.

Still, he thought now, Manring had considered him in his escape plan. That was the point. That was the main reason Pryde's story of Manring informing on him left a question in his mind.

There were twenty-two marks on the wall the morning Brazil opened the door and told them to come out. As soon as they were outside, both men lifting a hand to shield the sun from their eyes, and unexpectedly noticing the convicts grouped along the front of the barracks watching them, Brazil slammed the heavy door and walked away.

"It's Sunday," Bowen said.

Pryde was looking toward the convicts. "He's not there."

"Let me worry about Manring," Bowen said.

He walked along the front of the barracks, every convict in the yard watching him, and those near him nodded as he approached then moved aside as he entered the barracks. Over the yard there was a silence.

Two convicts playing a card game looked up as he entered. They seemed to hesitate. Then one of them began dealing the cards again. The other convict looked past the dealer, down the length of the adobe, down the row of straw mats that were lined along the wall, before his gaze dropped to the cards again.

Manring was lying on his side, his eyes closed and his left arm pillowing his head. Then his eyes opened, raising from Bowen's shoes up to his face.

"Corey, you look thinner."

Bowen said nothing, but his gaze remained on Manring's bearded face. He heard a step behind and he knew it was Pryde.

"And a few shades paler," Manring said.

There was a momentary silence before Bowen said, "You might be about to get your teeth kicked out."

Manring pushed himself up. "You better go easy." His eyes shifted to Pryde, then to Bowen again. "What for?"

"You told Renda I was going to jump the wagon."

"Ike told me . . . the first day."

Manring's eyes went to Pryde again. "And what exactly did Ike tell you?"

"That Renda said something to you . . . like, 'You said not till the grade.' "

"When was that?"

"Right after I jumped."

Manring's jaw relaxed. "How would Ike know? He'd just had his head busted with a Winchester."

"But he was still awake."

"All right." Manring shrugged. "Maybe Renda said that. I don't know—there was a lot of shooting going on. But if he said it, he didn't say it to me."

"Who would he say it to, Brazil?"

"Who else is there! Listen, you're accusing me of something you don't know anything about. Get your facts straight before you come marching in here like a couple of vigilantes!"

"I got mine straight," Pryde said. "You know it and I know it." Manring shook his head. "After Brazil busted you, you started hearing things."

"Corey might not be sure," Pryde said. "But I am. I was there. I heard Renda say it right to your face—"

"What did I say to his face?"

Renda stood in the doorway behind them, then came forward a few steps as Bowen and Pryde half turned. "What did I say?"

Pryde shook his head. "Nothing."

"Ike, you want to go back in the closet?"

Pryde did not answer and for a long moment Renda stared at him. His eyes moved to Bowen then. "You two spend three weeks in the house and when I let you out you come right back in." He paused. "You like being inside?" He answered his own question saying, "All right, we'll give you some inside work. Ike, you and your friend Corey go over and clean out the stable. Rub down the horses, too." He turned to go, then looked back. "And Ike . . . don't come out till the sun goes down."

Lizann Falvey watched her husband finish the whisky in his glass, seeing his hand come down slowly to the table and release the glass almost reluctantly. The table was across the room, at least a dozen feet away, but she could see that the bottle was empty.

Now a trip to Fuegos, she thought. She was sitting in a canvas chair studying Willis and wondering how long he would last.

He'll go to Fuegos to finish what he has started and come back tomorrow with six bottles, three in each saddle bag. You can look forward to that. And in a few days you can look forward to it again. Then again . . . and again—

She sat and watched him, waiting. Waiting for him to look up from the table, but he continued to study the label of the whisky bottle and finally she said, "Willis—"

His head turned. "What?"

"In the top drawer of my dresser," Lizann said, "there's a gun. I believe you called it a .25-caliber Colt. Why don't you take it and go for a ride up into the hills."

Willis frowned. "What?"

"Or just go behind the adobe," Lizann said. "I thought at first I'd rather not hear the shot, but on second thought it really wouldn't matter."

"What are you trying to say?"

"I'm not *trying* to say anything. I'm telling you to put a gun to your head and be done with it."

The whisky had relaxed him, had made him drowsy and it cushioned somewhat the shock of her words. His expression scarcely changed.

"You sincerely hate me, don't you?"

Lizann shook her head. "That's putting it too simply. I suppose there are moments when I think I hate you, but most of the time I can feel only disgust. You hate a man like Frank Renda who is strong enough to be hated and you would hate even a memory of him. With your kind, Willis, you feel either sorrow or disgust and when that's passed you're hardly worth a memory—a feeling of indifference at best."

Willis stared. "Why don't you leave me?"

"Don't you think I would if I could?"

"What's stopping you?"

"What's stopping me?" Lizann repeated without tone in her voice. "Willis, I think I'm beginning to feel sorry for you. You don't even fully realize the kind of man you're dealing with. Do you think Frank Renda would let me leave?"

"You go for rides. You could keep going."

"I have never gone out without one of Salvaje's men following me."

"I go to Fuegos," Willis said. "No one follows me."

"Renda doesn't have to watch you. He even admitted that. You're your own watchdog, Willis."

"Renda's very sure of himself."

Lizann shrugged. "He's in a position to be." Her expression softened then. "But, Willis . . . he doesn't have any more on you than you do on him."

"So?"

"So . . . report him."

"Just like that."

"Be a *man* one time in your life!"

"Which is easy for you to say. But you're not the one that goes to prison."

"You're already in prison. We both are."

"Then," Willis said, "we might as well stay where we are."

Lizann rose from the chair and walked to the window. Her gaze went over the yard to the convicts sitting and leaning against the front of the barracks, then came back as she saw Frank Renda leave the shade of the ramada and start across toward them. Her eyes followed him until he reached the barracks and went in the first door, then she turned to her husband again.

"Are you going to Fuegos today?"

Willis looked up. "I thought I would."

"Willis . . . when you get there, what would stop you from taking the stage to Tucson?"

His breath came out wearily and he shook his head.

"Listen to me! In Tucson you could write to the Bureau. Within two weeks someone would be here to investigate."

"And two weeks later I'd be in jail."

"No! After you send the letter, go somewhere else."

"Would you meet me?"

Lizann hesitated. "Haven't you had enough of this?"

"If I thought we could start over—"

"There is only one way to do that, Willis. But not together. God knows, not together. Think about getting out of here. Let what comes later take care of itself."

He shook his head then. "Sooner or later I'd be caught. Going to prison is one thing. Perhaps I could take a year or so of it to get out of this mess. But I'd also be killing my career."

"Your career!" Lizann's voice rose. "A bookkeeper in a convict camp! That's your career—that's what your big political friends think of you. They've put you away, out of their hair. Don't you realize that?"

"You didn't think that way a year ago," Willis said.

"I'm talking about now!"

"When you married me," Willis said, "you were sure I had a future. Or else you wouldn't have considered it."

"With a clean collar on," Lizann said, "you can fool almost anyone."

Willis was silent, studying the bottle again. Lizann waited. Finally he looked up. "It wouldn't be worth the chance."

"How do you know, unless you try it?"

He shook his head. "I'd be hiding out the rest of my life."

"I wouldn't," Lizann said calmly. "I'm asking you to do it for me."

He looked at her as if to answer, but his gaze dropped and he pushed himself up from the table. Lizann watched him go into the bedroom and when he reappeared, moving past her without raising his eyes, he was carrying his hat and saddle bags. She saw him hesitate as he opened the door and he turned to her again.

"I'm sorry, Lizann. I'm sincerely sorry."

"For me, Willis . . . or for yourself?"

"I think for both of us." He stepped outside, closing the door behind him.

Lizann turned to the window again. She was watching her husband cross the yard when Bowen and Pryde came out of the barracks and followed Willis to the stable.

So he's out, Lizann thought. Why couldn't he have been Willis?

No, she thought then. You made the mistake yourself. And you'll live with it the rest of your life unless you do something. You should have been more patient. There were others. But you guessed wrong and picked Willis—who was then what he is now. So you can't really blame Willis.

They had met in Washington less than a year before. Three weeks later they were married. Lizann: a young woman whose father had been killed at Second Bull Run a year after she was born, killed in a cavalry action, leaving wife and daughter a name, but very little money to support the name. And Willis: a young man whose father, also with a name, had also died, leaving his son sole heir to a moderately large estate. But it was not until after their wedding and honeymoon that Lizann learned Willis had gambled away almost his entire inheritance. All that remained were the stories of his fortune—the same stories which had attracted Lizann to him. Still, she was not yet discouraged. Willis did have influential friends. And a political appointment was in the offing. Three months later they were in Prescott. There, Willis was told he would serve "somewhat as a liaison man" between the territorial government, the military and a privately operated road construction project. A few weeks later they were at Five Shadows. After the first day, Lizann fully realized the mistake she had made.

Now she looked out across the yard again to the stable and she thought of Bowen—remembering how she had compared her husband to him the day he was placed in the punishment cell; remembering now how she had catalogued him in her mind: *a man who would do anything to escape.*

She thought of him calmly, impersonally now, feeling that there had been something almost instinctive in choosing him from among all the convicts. As if—since Willis would no nothing—Bowen was the next logical choice to help her.

But how?

In some way that would benefit him. That, she realized already. A way that would help him escape. But, she thought now, talk to him first. He isn't on Renda's side. But neither is he necessarily on yours.

Before leaving the window to change into her riding suit, she saw her husband ride out of the gate. Less than ten minutes later, she walked across the yard and into the wide opening of the stable. She saw Pryde immediately, at the far end sweeping the aisle between the stalls—then Bowen. He was in the first stall on the right side, curry-combing Renda's big chestnut mare. She walked toward him.

"Frank didn't waste time putting you back to work, did he?"

Bowen looked up. "No, ma'am." He watched her move toward him. She came almost into the stall, stopping to lean against the end of the partition that separated this stall from the next one. This was the first time she had even spoken to him and her relaxed, almost familiar manner surprised him.

"Will you saddle my horse?"

"All right." He looked back, over the partition. "Which one?"

"The sorrel, on the other side."

Bowen turned, taking a step as he did, then stopped abruptly. Lizann, less than an arm's length from him, had not moved.

"I'm in no hurry," she said. "Finish what you're doing."

"I've got all day to do this," Bowen said.

Lizann was studying him openly. "How do you feel?"

"Not so good," Bowen said. Her eyes made him conscious of his three weeks' growth of beard, his ragged, sweat-stained appearance.

"I saw what Renda did to to you," Lizann said quietly. "I was standing behind him."

Bowen nodded. "I noticed."

"It's too bad your hands were tied."

"Maybe it was good. I might have killed him."

"Do you mean that?"

Her question surprised him. "I mean I was mad enough at the time."

Lizann nodded slowly. "I could see why you would be. You've been here, what—three months?"

"That's right."

"And Yuma before that," Lizann said. "With six years to serve of a seven-year sentence. I can't say I blame you for trying to escape."

"How do you know all that?" Bowen asked. He was reminded of Karla Demery. Now a second woman who seemed to know all about him.

"I looked up your record," Lizann said.

"For a reason?"

"Perhaps."

"What were you looking for?"

Lizann smiled. "You've a very suspicious nature. Perhaps I just felt sorry for you . . . thought you needed a friend."

Bowen shook his head. "Not in a convict camp. With a husband."

"My husband doesn't know everything I do."

"But Renda does. He has to know what everybody's doing. Even you."

"You sound very sure of yourself."

"What's going on here," Bowen said, "is black and white and you know it as well as anyone else. Renda gets seventy cents a day for each convict—thirty of us—for food, clothes and shelter. But he doesn't spend two bits a man on his best day. He buys cheap flour, full of worms. The coffee goes twice as far as it should. The Mimbres shoot most of his meat which costs him only for bullets. We sleep on straw mats you wouldn't put a dog on. Since I've been here three men have died on those mats. Not one of them had a doctor, though Renda's supposed to provide medical care. He makes money on the road contract and he's keeping it going as long as he can, for every day he can stretch it he makes that much more money off the convicts. Anybody who's been here longer than one day knows it. So it comes down to this—living here you're either his friend or his prisoner and either way he knows what you're doing."

Lizann's eyes remained on him. "You've thought it out very carefully."

"I've had the time."

"Which do you think my husband is, friend or prisoner?"

"Maybe both. But he drinks so he won't have to admit to being either."

"And I?" Lizann asked. "Which am I?"

"Until a while ago, I would've thought you and Renda got along fine."

Lizann's eyebrows raised inquiringly. "And now?"

"Now I'd say you want out."

"You just thought of that," Lizann said. "You're guessing."

Bowen moved his hand slowly over the smooth back of the chestnut. "I'll guess something else."

"I'm listening."

"You're looking for somebody angry enough to help you."

For a moment there was no sound in the stable. They were aware then of the faint sound of Pryde sweeping at the far end, but that was all. Their eyes held, neither of them moving until Lizann asked, quietly, "Are you angry enough, Corey?"

"That all depends."

"On me?"

Bowen nodded. "On what's on your mind."

"I'll be perfectly honest with you," Lizann said softly. She moved closer to him. "I don't know how it can be done. All I know is I have to get away from here. My husband has refused to help me and Renda has me watched constantly. That's why I have no choice but to—"

"Come to a convict."

"I wasn't going to say that. I have no choice but to devise my own means of getting away from here."

"You'd leave your husband?"

"He's already left me, you might say."

"Why won't he help you?"

"You said it yourself. He's Renda's prisoner."

"He could get word out somehow," Bowen said. "Mail a report from Fuegos."

"He could . . . if he wasn't accepting money from Frank."

"Renda's bribing him?"

Lizann nodded calmly. "If he reports Frank, Frank will report him. Staying here, Willis is desperately protecting what he chooses to call his career in government service."

"I didn't think Frank was making that much that he could afford to pay somebody off."

"He doesn't have a choice."

"It seems to me," Bowen said, "he could get away with just threatening your husband."

"Perhaps he could, but it wouldn't be as sure as the way he's doing it."

"How long has your husband been taking the money?"

"I suppose from almost the first day we came here. It wouldn't have taken Willis long to realize what Renda was doing. Willis keeps the books . . . That's something else, another way Renda has him. All the accounting is in Willis's handwriting—the entries of the government subsistence funds, then the recording of fictitious expenditures to cover the funds going into Renda's pocket. As far as the people in Prescott know, the convicts are getting the equivalent of seventy cents a day—in food, clothing, blankets . . . well, you know, you mentioned it a moment ago."

"How much does your husband get out of it?"

"I don't know. Perhaps just enough to cover the six bottles of Green River he buys every week."

"Maybe Renda forced him into it somehow."

"I have found," Lizann said quietly, "that worrying about my husband serves no one's purpose, not even his."

Bowen studied her thoughtfully. "All right . . . now tell me where I fit in."

"I'm not yet sure," Lizann answered. Her face was raised to his and for a moment neither of them spoke. "But," she asked then, "you'd be willing to help me, wouldn't you?"

"It still depends," Bowen said mildly. "You tell me when you think of a way to leave . . . and then I'll let you know."

SEVEN

By five thirty A.M. the roving night guard had made his last swing through the compound, checked with the gate guard and had gone to wake up the cook. Fifteen minutes later, Renda and the day men were up and dressed. They unlocked one door of the barracks, brought the convicts out single file and counted them before marching them to the outside mesquite-pole-awninged mess tables behind the barracks.

At six o'clock they were lined up in front of the barracks again. A few minutes later, three single-team wagons moved out of the compound—the first carrying equipment, the other two, the convicts. A guard rode alongside both of the convict wagons and Renda and Brazil brought up the rear. As the wagons rolled through the gate, twelve Mimbreño trackers rode out from their camp. Three of them held back to follow the wagons, but the rest went on, spreading out and running their horses now toward the looming sand-colored slope less than a mile in the distance. As the sun rose higher, five shadow lines formed by washes and rock slides would creep down the slope like a gigantic hand groping for the convict camp below.

In the third wagon, sitting next to Bowen, Pryde said, "There they go. You see them in the morning, then you see them maybe once all day."

"Unless," Bowen said, "you try to run. Then you see them again." He watched Salvaje, a good fifty yards out, ride by the wagons, and he nodded, saying to Pryde, "How'd you like to have him on our side?"

Pryde turned to watch the Mimbres. "That would do it, wouldn't it?"

That would do it all right, Bowen thought—his eyes raising to

Renda and Brazil who had separated and dropped back a dozen yards or more to be clear of the dust rising from the wagons—once you got by those two. Maybe, he continued to think, there's where Lizann comes in. To help you get by.

But how does a woman help you break out of a convict camp? No—don't underestimate her because she's a woman. Not that one. And don't think she's doing it for you. You guessed it and she admitted it. She wants out. She wants to be free of Renda . . . and the wire fence and the Mimbres and the sun and . . . even if it means running away with a convict she doesn't know from any other convict. Think about that. Think about it good and see what it tells you. A woman who's willing to leave her husband behind . . . willing to help a convict if he'll help her. Picture the way she was in the stable and the way she spoke, then add. Add it up without cluttering it with running-hiding-making-it-escaping-from-it pictures and see what you get. Put yourself in her shoes. Be sick of your husband and hating Renda and hating everything in sight. Then look at you. A weapon. Somebody Renda beat hell out of. Somebody angry enough. You said it yourself. You don't have to reason it out. You said it yourself in the stable. Somebody angry enough. She'll use you for a battering ram to bust the door down. That's all. If you can get up and run out yourself, all right. If you can't, she's not going to stop to help you up. And if she fails, then it was a convict who forced her into it.

And so you know all that just by looking at her face, guessing what wasn't said but what was almost said. Is that how you know all about her?

Yes. Some things you know.

Some things are very simple and you can take all this reasoning that really isn't reasoning and throw it out because you knew with the first word she said and the way she said it that she was after something and if she wanted it bad enough she'd get it, one way or another. With you or with somebody else. And knowing it you'll go along with her, because at least it's a chance and one chance is better than six more years of this. Even if you don't make it.

So what have you got?

He was still watching Renda and he thought: Ride over here close and look the other way and let that shotgun barrel stick out a little more.

Then get Brazil first.

Yes, that's smart thinking. Ask Pryde if he thinks that's cool, calm, smart thinking. Ask him if he *feels* anything about it. If you planned a break with one of the convicts, he wouldn't think of *you*, would he? He'd think of himself. And you'd think of *your*self. That's what it comes down to. She's as much a prisoner as anyone else. So if she wants to get out, even needing somebody else, she'll be thinking of herself. It's not surprising now, is it? Suddenly it's not surprising. Your mistake was thinking of her as a woman instead of as another convict.

So forget she's a woman and just listen to whatever she has to say. Forget she's supposed to think like a woman, however women are supposed to think. She's another convict. Put a convict's shirt on her and numbered pants if that makes it any easier.

He began to picture Lizann in a man's shirt, not doing it intentionally, but because it was already in his mind; but suddenly the woman was no longer Lizann and he was picturing Karla Demery in a faded blue chambray shirt, the one she had been wearing that day three weeks ago.

As the trail began to climb, Bowen watched Brazil come up almost to their wagon before turning his horse from the trail. He rode even with them then, but off beyond the twisted, shaggy-barked cliff rose bushes that grew close along the wagon ruts. Renda remained behind, though he seemed to be closer to the wagon now. The three Mimbres who had trailed him were no longer there.

Then, watching Renda, Bowen thought of Karla Demery again—picturing her with Renda in the station yard. Then later, when he had been close to her—

Her short black hair making her look almost like a boy yet, strangely, more feminine because of it. A slim body. Small even features. Clean-scrubbed, clean-smelling and dark from the sun, though you knew some of the warm brown was Mexican blood and you could see it in the eyes—one quarter from her mother's side. Not more than one quarter. In the eyes that were alive and didn't move from your face as you spoke, though not the way Lizann Falvey's had not moved.

Read Karla, Bowen thought. Not the giving you the clothes and the horse and the talking about the lawyer. Read what was behind her eyes the way you did Lizann's. If you can do that, you'll understand the horse and the clothes and the other thing. But it isn't as easy, is it? You don't just label her and say, There, that's why she's doing it.

Which one would you rather be with?

For what?

For anything!

You almost kissed her.

You almost kissed both of them.

No . . . Karla. You almost climbed right off the horse to kiss her. Not for what she had done but because you *wanted* to. The other was different. Lizann was trying to make you kiss her. But you didn't.

Maybe you should've gotten off the horse.

The wagons followed a dry wash down through rock-strewn, pinyon-studded talus to the wide floor of a canyon and here intersected the new road that, following the canyon, came down from the north. The wagons moved down canyon a good three hundred yards before halting at the end of construction.

Bowen waited his turn, then jumped down from the wagon. Pryde followed him. They started for the equipment wagon as Brazil rode up.

"You two unhitch the team."

Pryde looked up at him. "We're going to pull stumps?"

Brazil grinned. "Till your back breaks."

They watched Brazil ride on to the equipment wagon. "I knew we'd be pulling stumps," Pryde said.

"One job's as bad as another," Bowen said. He looked back along the new road. "We didn't miss very much. That needle rock back there. We were even with it three weeks ago."

Pryde squinted along the canyon. "Maybe two and a half miles."

"Renda's making it last," Bowen said.

Pryde nodded. "Four months to come about twelve miles and not doing much more than cutting a path."

"With another four miles to go," Bowen said. He turned to look down the canyon. "The hardest four. Up over the rocks, then down to come out somewhere behind the stage-coach station. Renda can make that last a good two months."

"He must know somebody," Pryde said.

Bowen nodded. "He'd have to. He doesn't know anything about road building."

"The government must have lots of money," Pryde said thoughtfully. "Six months to build sixteen miles of road through the mountains to save one day's travel from Willcox to San Carlos."

"To save a half day," Bowen corrected. "You *know* Renda knows somebody."

Brazil motioned to them and they brought the team up past the equipment wagon where two convicts stood waiting for them. One, a Mexican, with a twelve-foot length of chain over his shoulder; the other leaning on a long-handled shovel. Bowen nodded to them.

The convict with the shovel squinted as if he needed glasses and the lines of his face formed a nervous, half-smiling expression. He was a small man, perhaps forty. His straw hat was cocked over one eye and his shirt collar was buttoned, though it hung loosely, at least three sizes too large for him, and he gave the impression that even in convict clothes he was trying to keep up his appearance— the white collar, coat and tie appearance of a man who had been an assistant cashier at the Wickenburg bank until the day he stole five hundred and fifty dollars to cover a gambling debt. His name was Chick Miller; the man who had described the supply wagon trip to Bowen.

"Corey," he said now, "I'm sorry you didn't make it." When Bowen said nothing, he added, "I hope you don't hold it against me."

"Why should I?"

"I mean since I was the one told you to try it."

"I made up my own mind," Bowen said.

Chick grinned. "Brazil came riding like hell through here to gather the trackers and we thought for certain you'd made it."

"Chick, did you tell Earl I was going to try it?"

The question came unexpectedly and Chick Miller straightened, his hands sliding down the handle of the shovel. "Why would you think that?"

"Just tell me if you did."

"Of course not!"

"Chick, I don't care if you did."

"Maybe he saw us talking."

Bowen nodded. "Or maybe you suggested he try it."

"I might have done that."

"Then told him I was going to."

"Why would I do that?"

"Chick, I'm not holding it against you if you did. I just want to know."

"I might've mentioned you were thinking about it." Chick Miller shook his head then. "But I wouldn't have come right out and *told*!"

The Mexican, a young, clean-shaven, dark-skinned man, said, "That's why I don't even think about it. You get it in your mind to run and everyone knows about it."

Chick Miller looked at the Mexican. "You keep out of what don't concern you." He stopped then, seeing Brazil riding toward them.

Brazil pulled up, his Winchester across his lap and pointing at them. "Just passing the time of day?"

Chick Miller grinned. "We're waiting for the axe crew to give us some work."

Brazil nodded to a tree stump just beyond them. "There's one left from Saturday. Start on it."

"That one won't be in the roadway," Chick Miller said.

Brazil studied him. "You going to argue over it?"

"I just thought, why pull her out if she's going to be off the road anyway." He saw Brazil start to dismount and the half-smiling, squinting expression came over Chick's face. "I mean it's not going to be in the way."

Brazil swung down and started for him. He waved the barrel of the Winchester at the other three men and said, "Get out of the way," not taking his eyes from Chick.

"We'll take her out," Chick said. He glanced at the Mexican, seeing him move away; then to Bowen and Pryde who were watching Brazil and now he saw them back away slowly. As he turned to Brazil again the Winchester barrel was swinging toward him. He threw up his arms and fell back stumbling but keeping his feet and the barrel slashed past his head. Chick started to run.

"Stand where you are!"

He stopped, but seeing Brazil coming toward him again, began to back away.

"I said stay where you are!"

Chick held up his hand. "I don't want to get hit. Listen, we'll pull the stump. Just let me get my shovel." His extended hand pointed. "I dropped it over there." His eyes opened wide as Brazil moved toward him and at that moment he turned to run, taking one stride as the rifle barrel slammed across his back and he went down covering his head with his arms.

Brazil looked down at Chick, then turned from him. "Now pull the stump," he said.

The Mexican went to Chick and kneeled over him. Bowen watched Brazil mount and ride down canyon. There, twenty yards ahead of them, a half dozen convicts were clearing the pinyon clumps: cutting the trees close to the ground, but leaving enough stump for the chain to be wound around and fastened to securely.

As the Mexican helped Chick to his feet, Pryde and Bowen walked over to them. Pryde asked, "How are you?"

An exaggerated expression of pain was on Chick's face, "He'll be sorry he did that."

Pryde shook his head. "When the time and the day comes, you'll be second in line. I got first dibs on Mr. Brazil."

The Mexican was looking at Pryde. He smiled then. "If that day ever comes, I hope I'm there to see it. When you're through with him, maybe I'll kick him in the face."

By noon, they were not more than a hundred yards farther down the canyon. The convicts worked as slowly as Renda would let them, knowing that he wanted to stretch the job time for all it was worth. Still, two or three times a day Renda would conscientiously speed up the work pace, as if rebelling against this one small advantage they held over him.

The clearing crew would cut down the pinyon and large mesquite bushes, drag them to the side of the canyon and burn them. The stump-pulling crew followed—digging under the shallow-rooted pinyon stumps, looping the chain about the trunk stub, levering with the shovel and finally pulling it out with the wagon team. One of them would drag the stump to the nearest fire as the others went on to the next stump.

Two guards watched the clearing crew because there was usually thick brush ahead of them. From the east side of the canyon, Brazil watched the group Bowen was with and most of the time Brazil did not leave the thin strip of shade close to the slanting talus wall.

Behind them came the pick-and-shovel crew—filling the stump holes from "borrow pits" along the side of the road, breaking stones, clearing the small mesquite bushes and the yellow-blazing patches of brittlebush, raking them over to the bonfires.

The scraper came next—two timbers bolted together and pulled by a wagon team. Six men, Manring one of them, stood on the timbers to add weight. The scraper bumped along over the roadway, the convicts losing their balance, jumping off and on, and every ten or fifteen feet the team was pulled off to the side, dragging with it the loose rocks and sand that the timbers gathered.

Two men with shovels came last—filling the potholes that the scraper passed over and did not fill completely. Renda stayed even with them, walking his horse along the east-wall shade approximately one hundred feet behind Brazil.

The Mimbreños were up on the canyon patrolling along both sides. They remained in the shadows of the pinyon pines and were not seen all morning, not until Renda stopped work at noon.

As the convicts drifted over to the east wall where the equipment wagon stood, Salvaje and two of his Mimbres came down a shallow wash, a dust cloud trailing behind them. They were riding past the equipment wagon when Renda called to them and they pulled up. The two Mimbres sat their horses, motionlessly watching Salvaje rein toward Renda who was now facing the convicts grouped at the back end of the equipment wagon. He pointed to Bowen, Pryde and the Mexican. "You three step out," he called. Then turned to Salvaje again. "You're going to the creek?"

The Mimbreño nodded and held up three fingers. "That many at a time."

"Take these men with you," Renda said. "They're going to water the teams."

The Mimbres moved off one at a time as each pair of horses was brought out. Salvaje waited until Bowen came up, then fell in next to him and they moved the team down the canyon, winding through the scattered scrub brush to a stand of sycamores that showed darkly against the west slope. A trickle of water came down from the rocks and formed a shallow pool in the deep shade of the trees. From here, the creek flowed to the end of the canyon, disappeared into the rocks and came out again miles to the south, above the Pinaleño station.

They drank: the convicts first, the Mimbres one at a time, and now they rested as the horses stood over the clear, sand-bottomed pool, their muzzles touching the water, rippling the water with breath from their nostrils, raising and shaking their manes, tails fanning lazily and now and again a rump or flank quivering to dislodge an unseen something.

Salvaje touched Bowen's arm. "But for the work of getting more horses, I wish you would run away another time."

Bowen frowned. "I don't understand."

"That was a good thing with you in the meadow," Salvaje explained. "But the two horses you killed I was made to replace."

"Renda made you buy two horses?"

Salvaje shrugged. "Not buy; but it is the same thing."

"You'd think he'd supply the horses," Bowen said.

Salvaje shook his head. "He is not easy to live with. Sometimes I see him as an escaped man. If he was ever that, he would not be brought back alive."

Bowen hesitated. The Mimbre's words took him by surprise and stayed in his mind as he said, "You speak English very well."

"From San Carlos."

"I visited Cibucu many times," Bowen said. "When I was trading horses. I knew Zele and Pindah and Bu-sikisn."

Salvaje's eyes came alive. "They were of Victorio."

Bowen nodded. "I drank tulapai with Zele and he told me much about Victorio and old Mangas."

"Perhaps I was there then," Salvaje said.

"They spoke of a band still in the Sierra Madres," Bowen said. "Maybe you were there."

Salvaje nodded thoughtfully. "The good days. At San Carlos it was not easy to live among Tontos and Mojaves."

"But better than here?" Bowen asked.

"Sometimes. The men such as you make it worth staying here."

"The men who run?"

"The ones who know how to run. Some are like children about it. Others do well."

"Listen," Bowen said then, "I'm sorry I cracked a couple of heads that day. I mean that truthfully, because I don't have any fight with you or your men."

Salvaje's eyes held on Bowen and he studied him thoughtfully, as if wanting to understand all of Bowen, all of the things about him that would never be spoken. Finally he said, "Maybe you try it again some time."

Bowen nodded. "Maybe I will."

The team horses raised their heads from the pool a moment before Bowen heard the leaf-rustling, twig-snapping sound of someone coming through the trees. He looked up as Salvaje rose, expecting to see another of the Mimbres or one of the guards and his face showed open surprise as Karla Demery walked her horse into the clearing.

Bowen saw her look directly at him, then her skirt curved gracefully as she stepped from the saddle. Again, she was wearing a man's shirt and her dark hair was even shorter than he had pictured it—curving low on her forehead, but brushed back on the sides into a soft upcurl at the nape of her neck. And Bowen was thinking, watching her take her horse to the pool edge: I'll bet she can ride like hell. I'll bet she can cook and shoot and do everything like hell. But, he thought then, seeing her looking at him again and feeling the sudden quickening inside of him: Don't try to figure her out.

Karla's gaze moved from Bowen and Salvaje to Pryde and the Mexican, then raised to the two Mimbres standing behind them. To no one in particular she said, "No guards? I'm surprised at Mr. Renda."

Squatting at the edge of the pool, the Mexican pushed up his hatbrim with his thumb. "These barbarians are guards enough."

"I'm still surprised," Karla said. Her eyes returned to Bowen and Salvaje. "I'm delivering mail to the camp, but I might as well leave it with you." She looked directly at Bowen. "You'll see that Mr. Renda gets it?"

Bowen nodded. "Sure." He started to rise and Salvaje stepped in front of him.

"Your friend understands English?" Karla said.

Bowen glanced at Salvaje. "Very well."

Karla was looking at the Mimbre now. "I'll give it to this man—Bowen."

Salvaje shook his head.

"We're missing two horses," Karla said evenly. "Both of them wearing a Double-H brand. Would you like the San Carlos man to visit your ranchería?"

The Mimbre stared at her, not answering.

"Mr. Bowen," Karla said. "You'll find the mail in the left-hand saddlebag."

Bowen hesitated. He walked around the pool then, past the team horses, feeling Salvaje and the others watching him. He saw Karla leaning close to the horse patting its neck, but as he came around to its off side she straightened up and moved toward him.

"Let me help you."

"What're you up to?"

Close to him she began unbuckling the flap of the saddle bag.
"Just listen to me."

"They can hear us!"

"Then don't talk!" Her voice dropped to a half-whisper as she
said, "I heard from the lawyer in Prescott. He's agreed to look into
your trial, but he wants a few things cleared up."

Bowen frowned. "Why should he help me?"

"Because I asked him to!"

"He can't—"

"Be quiet and listen!" She spoke rapidly then, her voice a soft,
hoarse whisper. "Think back and don't waste words when I ask
you a question, Mr. Martz says there's little mention of the bill of
sale in the court records. Was it shown as evidence?"

"It was shown for a minute."

"Did Manring admit forging Mr. McLaughlin's signature?"

"That didn't come up."

"But it was a copy of McLaughlin's style of writing."

"I think so."

"Then why didn't they try to find out who filled out and signed
the bill of sale?"

"The judge assumed it was Manring."

"How would Manring know how McLaughlin wrote?"

"McLaughlin claimed Earl worked for him three years before."

"And he'd remember McLaughlin's script?"

Bowen hesitated. "Wait a minute. You're assuming Earl forged
the receipt . . . that he stole the cattle!"

"Mr. Martz is assuming it. He knows McLaughlin well, a man
with a good reputation. He's never done anything like this in his
life. He's never had to. With the land he has, taking a few hundred
dollars from Manring wouldn't be worth the bother."

"If Earl forged the receipt, I don't know how he did it."

"Neither does Mr. Martz. That's the first thing he has to find
out. Next . . . was the bill of sale made out on plain paper?"

"No, it had McLaughlin's letterhead on it."

"His regular stock-sale receipt?"

"That's what it looked like."

"Where did Manring get it?"

"All I know is what he told me. McLaughlin gave it to him."

"Which isn't true."

"Your lawyer friend's doing a lot of assuming."

"It's his business. This isn't something new to him."

"He's sure about McLaughlin?"

"Of course he's sure! He's lived in Prescott for twenty years and has known Mr. McLaughlin longer than that." Karla pulled a bundle of letters form the saddle bag and pushed it at Bowen. "Manring couldn't have known enough about McLaughlin's handwriting to copy the signature himself. He wasn't in a position to pick up a blank bill of sale form. So . . . who did?"

"Maybe I'd better ask Earl."

Karla shook her head. "Don't do anything until I hear from Mr. Martz again."

"There's not a lot I *can* do."

"Talking to Manring could lead to a fight."

"That might be all right."

"That would be fine. You'd end up out of reach in the punishment cell. What if Mr. Martz wanted information from you?"

"All right."

"Don't do *anything!*" Karla turned from him. She picked up her reins, mounted and rode into the trees without looking back.

Pryde, sitting next to the Mexican at the edge of the pool, watched Bowen come back toward them. He saw him hand the bundle of letters to Salvaje who took them but said nothing.

"Corey, you know that girl very long?"

Bowen looked down at Pryde. "I guess long enough."

The Mexican shook his head, grinning. "Too bad we couldn't hear."

When they returned with the team horses, Bowen watched Salvaje ride over to Renda and hand him the mail. They spoke for less than a minute and, watching Salvaje ride off, Bowen was sure he had not told Renda about it. They had not talked long enough.

His spirits rose. He ate his jerky and pan bread, drank the lukewarm coffee and thought about Karla Demery: picturing her, going over and over again in his mind what she had said; then projecting from there: seeing her again, this time telling him the lawyer had found something, *something,* whatever it was, that proved his innocence; then later, on an evening, Karla and the lawyer—Martz?—riding into the convict camp, the lawyer handing Renda a signed release and Renda standing, taking it, reading it with his mouth open.

Hit him then, Bowen thought.

No, you can't have everything.

And don't count on it, he thought then. What is the *something* the lawyer finds? The odds are against your getting out of here. Even with an A-1 Prescott Hatch & Hodges lawyer . . . and Karla Demery.

But even as he told himself this, his hopes were up and he went back to work almost eagerly—and with something of a feeling that he should be working harder since Karla and the lawyer were doing so much to get him out.

Pryde said nothing more to him about the girl. But after they had pulled out the first pinyon stump and the Mexican was dragging it off to the fire, Chick Miller said, "I hear you got a sweetheart." He looked at Bowen slyly, one eye almost closed beneath the cocked brim of his straw hat.

"Is that what you hear, Chick?"

"From a little bird," Chick said, grinning.

"From a little Mex bird," Pryde said.

Chick looked at him as if surprised. "What, it's supposed to be a secret? You can't stand talking close to a girl in broad daylight and expect it to be a secret."

"She was giving me the mail," Bowen said.

"To *you*, not to the Indin."

"Maybe she's the kind," Pryde said, "who figures you can't trust a 'Pache."

"Sure," Chick nodded, grinning again. "Corey, you must've known her before."

"She was giving me the mail," Bowen said again.

Chick winked at him. "I'd let her give me the mail anytime."

"Be careful now."

"I didn't mean any offense."

They moved on to the next stump and when the Mexican returned Pryde said, "You talk a hell of a lot."

"Me?"

"You know what I'm talking about."

"I told that the girl spoke to Bowen," the Mexican said. "What about it?"

"He didn't tell me what was said." Chick shook his head. "Not one word."

"Because I didn't hear," the Mexican said. "I didn't hear anything they were saying."

"Let's drop it there," Bowen said. He looked from Pryde to Chick to the Mexican. "All right?"

"Well," Chick said, "if it's something you're ashamed of.

Though she doesn't look like a girl you'd be ashamed to be seen talking to."

Over Chick's shoulder, Pryde saw Brazil coming toward them. He had left his horse close to the canyon wall, although there was no shade there now with the sun directly overhead, and was walking toward them, carrying the Winchester under his arm.

"You better shut your mouth," Pryde told Chick.

Chick turned on him unexpectedly. "Who in hell you think you are? You're no better than anybody else! You think—"

"You better shut up." Pryde saw Brazil coming up behind Chick.

"Why, because you say so?" Chick placed his hands on his hips defiantly. "I don't have to take anything from you or anybody like you! It's enough to have to stomach Renda and Brazil telling you what to do!" Chick paused. "One more year and I'm out of here and they're going to pay. Sure as there's a God upstairs they're going to pay for every last dirty thing they've done to me."

"You're sure about that?"

Chick did not move. Pryde saw the shocked surprise, then fear come over his face—his eyes wide and his mouth open as if to cry out. Then, with an effort, with a lip-biting jaw-tensed effort, his expression slowly changed and his face was almost relaxed as he turned to Brazil.

"What're you going to do to me?"

"What do you think?" Brazil asked mildly.

"I don't want to get hit."

"I'll bet you don't."

"Listen"—Chick swallowed and the fear was in his eyes again—"I was just talking. You know how you get mad and say funny things—"

"I didn't think it was funny."

"Not *funny*. You know, you say things you don't mean."

"The first thing that comes into your mind."

"That's right. No! Wild, crazy things that you don't mean, but just so you'll be saying something."

"Like making me pay."

Chick tried to smile. "That's right. How could I make you pay? See what I mean, that's just crazy talk that came in my head."

Brazil raised the Winchester, holding it across his chest. "And you don't think I ought to hit you?"

Chick swallowed again. He started to back away. "Beating me wouldn't solve anything."

"Maybe it wouldn't at that," Brazil said. He lowered the Winchester so that the stock was beneath his right arm. His right hand gripped through the lever. He moved toward Chick who half turned and began edging away.

"What are you going to do?"

"Run down and tell Renda to come here," Brazil said.

"You mean it?"

"I wouldn't say it 'less I did."

"You're not going to do anything to me?"

"Go on."

Chick edged away, still half turned looking at Brazil. He glanced up canyon to locate Renda, looked back at Brazil once more then turned, his quick short steps developing into a run. He had gone no more than thirty feet when Brazil fired. Chick stumbled as if trying to turn and Brazil fired again, the stock of the Winchester still under his arm and held just above his waist. He levered another shell into the chamber before his gaze returned from Chick Miller to the three men near him. His eyes moved slowly from Bowen to Pryde to the Mexican.

"He tried to run," Brazil said. "You saw him. He tried to run away."

EIGHT

Renda made them remove Chick Miller's clothes before burying him. Bowen and Pryde took turns digging a grave close to the canyon slope; then, after they had lowered Chick's body into it and pushed in the dirt, the Mexican covered the low mound with stones and marked the grave with a cross he had made by tying together two mesquite sticks with a length of pinyon root.

"He never learned to keep his mouth shut," Pryde said. They were walking back to the team now, the Mexican ahead of them dragging the chain to the next stump.

"There wasn't any sense to it," Bowen said. "I saw him do it, but if I hadn't, I wouldn't believe it. You don't just kill a man like that—like you don't have anything better to do."

"Now you know what kind Brazil is," Pryde said.

"It's hard to believe," Bowen said. "A man with only a year left and he had to say the wrong thing."

"I wonder," Pryde said, "if Renda will write to his wife."

"He's got a family?"

"Sure, a wife and two girls in Wickenburg."

Bowen shook his head. "If he could've held out just one more year, maybe he could've made them pay. Like he said."

"That was talk," Pryde said. "By the time you get out Renda'll be in some other business. Even if he's still working convicts, how're you going to prove anything?"

"I was thinking—maybe twist Willis Falvey's arm."

"If you can get to him."

"Renda'll have Willis write the letter," Bowen said.

"Which is about all Willis's good for."

"Ike . . . do you have a family?"

"I wouldn't be here if I did."

Bowen said, "Something like that can't happen too many times. All of a sudden every convict here will start swinging picks and shovels. There's only so much a man can take. They'll say it's better to get killed with a chance of escaping than getting cut down for saying the wrong thing . . . Ike, what if all of a sudden the thirty of us rushed them? Thirty against four."

"Thirty against three Winchesters and a scatter gun," Pryde said.

"But if it was timed right—"

"And if the Mimbres were on our side."

"Let's take one thing at a time."

"It's all at the same time," Pryde said. "Soon as one shot is fired the Mimbres are aiming down the slopes, on both sides."

But it's got to be done somehow. Bowen thought. And soon. You keep still so long then one day you say the wrong thing and Brazil says, "Go get Renda." He could say anything. "Go over and get that shovel," or he could pull the trigger right in front of you. What difference would it make? Nobody's bringing him to court for it. In the records it's still *killed while trying to escape*. Picture six years of pulling stumps and trying not to say the wrong thing. Six years of Renda . . . and Brazil. After this camp, some other one, and if not Renda and Brazil, men just like them, because you don't get the love-thy-neighbor kind to boss convicts. Or else you go back to Yuma . . . to the granite cells and the desert and the Gatling gun over the main gate.

And if not six years, he thought picturing Karla, then how long? A year? Two years? How long do you think it'll take that lawyer— assuming he'll get you freed? Longer than you could stand. She's some girl and it would be fine to know her better, but it even takes a week to get a letter from Prescott. So add up how many letters and how many weeks. Can you stand it even that long, a week? Maybe. But you have to be looking forward to something to do it.

Cross the lawyer off, Bowen thought. Cross off everything that isn't certain or anything that's more than a week away. Then concentrate on one thing. She's some girl, he thought then, but it would've been better if she gave you a gun instead of a lawyer.

Renda stopped work at six o'clock. The convicts filed past the equipment wagon to drop shovels, picks and axes, then boarded the two wagons that waited behind. Bowen hitched the team to the third wagon. He walked back to the end gate then to climb on and as he did, Earl Manring held our his hand to help him.

"That was too bad," Manring said, "about Chick."

The wagons strained over the uneven ground, were pulled in a wide slow turn and started back up canyon to the wash they had come down that morning. Bowen moved with the swaying, jolting motion of the wagon, his eyes on Renda and Brazil again bringing up the rear.

"I said that was too bad about Chick," Manring repeated.

"I heard you."

"Don't you think it was?"

"Earl, if you have something to say, say it."

Manring grinned. "I hear you got a sweetheart."

Bowen turned to him. "That's the way Chick started. He went right on talking till the end."

"That was too bad about Chick," Manring said thoughtfully. "Something that could happen to anybody. Right?"

Bowen shrugged.

"Corey, I got something to talk over with you." Manring leaned closer to him to say it.

"What about?"

"Later on tonight we'll talk about it."

"Then what'd you bring it up for?"

"To see if you were still as agreeable as ever," Manring grinned.

The last red reflection of the sun showed in the sky behind them as the wagons rolled down the slope toward the camp— toward the silent, cold-looking, deserted-looking adobes that were already enveloped in the dull shadow of this slope the wagons were descending.

Now, at the gate, a lantern flickered, then went up to full brightness. Minutes later, off to the right of the gate, another light appeared showing the black square of the stable entrance. As the wagons neared the gate, a third lantern blinked on, this one to the left. It hung from the ramada in front of Renda's quarters, and now a shadowy figure could be seen standing close to one of the support posts.

One of the night guards turned the corner of the convict's barracks as the wagons pulled up. He struck a match to light the lantern that hung head-high next to the middle door, then leaned against the wall, the match stick in the corner of his mouth, and watched the convicts unload. When they were lined up he counted them. Then counted them again before looking at Renda.

"You're one short."

"We're supposed to be," Renda answered. "Feed 'em and put 'em to bed." He turned away, walking across the yard toward the lantern that hung from the ramada. In the dimness a figure waited for him, then stepped into the light as Renda approached the adobe.

"I heard what that guard said."

Renda looked up. "Then you got good ears, Willis."

"You let somebody escape, didn't you?"

"I didn't let anybody escape."

"Damn it, the guard said you were short one!"

"Willis, we buried a man today. That's why we're short."

"What happened?"

"What do you think? He tried to run. Brazil shot him."

Falvey exhaled slowly. "What if he'd made it?"

"Nobody has yet," Renda answered.

"But what if he had?"

"What if you stop worrying about it?"

"Frank, if a man got out and told what's going on here—"

"Who'd listen to him? It'd be your word against his."

Falvey shook his head. "We can't take a chance on even the possibility of it."

"Willis, nobody's ever escaped from me and nobody's going to."

"Those men are thinking about it all the time."

"Let them. Thinking about it and doing it are about seven hundred miles apart."

"But sooner or later—"

Renda shook his head. "Not sooner or later or any time. I'll talk to them, Willis. All I got to do is talk to them."

After the evening meal, the convicts were marched to the stock tank in back of the stable—a round, waist-high tin-lined tank fed by a thin but steady flow of water that emptied from a rusted pipe connected to the well shaft of the windmill.

They were given fifteen minutes to wash as much of themselves as they cared to, and shave if they wanted to do that. Part of a mirror was fastened to a timber of the windmill structure and above it a lantern hung from a nail. One mirror, four dull razors and a few chunks of soap for thirty men. For that reason few of the men shaved more than twice a week and almost a third of them wore beards. For them, Renda produced a pair of scissors once a week.

Most of the convicts removed only their shirts, splashed water over their faces and upper bodies to remove twelve hours of grime and sweat, then dried themselves with the shirts before putting them on again.

After that, they were marched back to the barracks, counted again, then moved inside. The three lanterns that hung from wires hooked to the ceiling would burn for an hour and a half. At the end of that time, a night guard would come in for a last check and order the lanterns out.

But this night did not follow the usual routine.

Shortly before nine o'clock, one of the guards came in. Two of the convicts rose from their mats to put out the lanterns.

"Keep them on!"

They looked at the guard. Then every man in the room looked at him and a silence followed. They watched him glance over his shoulder then step aside as Renda came in, his shotgun under his arm, followed by Brazil and the two day guards who were all carrying Winchesters. Brazil stopped near Renda, but the two guards moved past him to cover the convicts nearer the end of the room.

Renda waited and his eyes moved slowly over the convicts. Most of them were on their own mats now, but a few of them here and there were still grouped together over a card game. Renda waited until he was sure they were all looking toward him, until there was not the smallest foot-scuffing sound.

Then he began: "Chick Miller got killed today," Renda stated. "He was trying to escape. Brazil warned him—called out for Chick to halt, but Chick kept going, so he didn't have any choice but to shoot him. That's what happened, so that's what the official report will say that goes to Prescott," Renda paused. "Does anybody say it happened any different?"

No one spoke. Renda's eyes moved along the line of men, then stopped at Bowen. "Stand up."

Bowen pushed himself up, turned to face Renda.

Renda's eyes held on him. "Isn't that how it happened?"

Calmly, quietly, Bowen said, "If you say so, then that's how it happened."

"Chick tried to run and Brazil had to shoot him," Renda stated.

Bowen nodded. "All right."

"Sit down." Renda's eyes moved to Pryde, then to the Mexican. He asked them the same question and both of them agreed that it had happened as Renda said it did.

"Now I'll tell you something," Renda said, including all the convicts. "Nobody here's going to ever try that again. I'm giving the orders to shoot, the least move out of line. You hesitate one second when you're told to do something, you're dead. You take one step in the wrong direction and you won't know what hit you. I want you to understand that. I want you to get it in your heads so clear you won't move without thinking about it." He turned to Bowen suddenly. "You understand that?"

Bowen nodded, looking up at Renda.

"You understand it," Renda said. "You were standing close to Chick. Listen, I'll tell you something else. That stunt you pulled a while back . . . jumping off the wagon. You wouldn't get just twenty days for it the second time."

He looked over all the convicts. "You get past the guards, the Mimbres have got orders to take your scalp. You won't be brought back here . . . just part of you. To prove you're dead.

"I'm giving you warning now," Renda continued. "One move out of line and somebody shoots. You'll even think before spitting over the side of the wagon. What you're doing to get shot don't matter to me. It goes in the report as trying to escape and the report's the only thing that means anything. So you think about that."

Again his gaze moved slowly over the convicts, then he turned and left the barracks. Brazil and the guards followed him, the last one giving the order for the lanterns to be put out. Outside, they heard the lock snap on the door, the sound of footsteps fading away, then silence.

Moments later, something touched Bowen's foot. He sat up quietly.

"Who is it?"

"Come over here."

He recognized Earl Manring's voice. As he rose, Manring moved away. A moment later he saw Manring's outline against the window that was almost directly across from him. It was early and there was little moonlight, but enough to show the narrow shape of the window. Half of the opening had been boarded up from the outside, the other half covered by a heavy-gauge wire screen.

As Bowen reached him, Manring asked, "He scare you?"

Bowen's hand touched the window sill. "He gave you something to think about."

"That's all talk."

"You didn't see Chick get shot."

"Brazil didn't like Chick. He never did. That's why he killed him."

"Brazil doesn't like anybody."

Manring shook his head. "If you don't make any noise, you don't get in any trouble. Chick was always talking. Brazil got to the point he couldn't stand it any more. He might've thought he was even doing everybody a favor shooting him."

"That's a nice thought," Bowen said.

"You're in the same spot as Chick," Manring went on. "They're watching you because you tried to run one time. I told you it wasn't the right time, but you wouldn't listen to me . . . Corey, they're no meaner than they ever were. They'll shoot anybody they don't like . . . let you alone if you don't make trouble."

"You're one of the good ones, Earl?"

"One of the smart ones if you want to get down to it. I didn't spend no twenty days in the hole."

"You were out working."

"And looking around," Manring said.

"Go on."

"You're still thinking about it . . . after what Renda said?"

"Frank makes you want to get out all the more."

"I've got to be sure of you," Manring said.

"As sure as I am of you?"

Manring's eyes narrowed. "What's that supposed to mean?"

"You think about it a while."

"Look," Manring said. "I don't have to include you. If you're going to start accusing me again we'll forget about it. I'll get somebody else."

"Earl, the only reason you're asking anybody is because getting out of here is something you can't do alone. I'm not sure yet why you're picking me. Maybe because you thought I was easy to manage before. Whatever the reason, it's something that'll do you the most good."

Manring shrugged. "Forget about it then."

"I can, Earl, but you can't. I just told you why."

"You're pretty sure of yourself."

Bowen started to turn away.

"Wait a minute—" Manring's hand came out to take his arm. "Listen, there's no sense in arguing over it. Let's get down to cases . . . you either want to go or you don't. Which is it?"

"I haven't heard any plan yet," Bowen said.

"That'll come."

"It'll come right now, or I don't."

"I'll tell you part of it," Manring paused. Then, his voice was lower as he said, "You know what happens at the end of the canyon."

"We climb," Bowen said.

"That's right. Have you figured how we're going to cut a road up through the rocks?"

"It isn't my problem."

"It wasn't mine either," Manring said, "till I was taken on Renda's survey party. That was over a month ago . . . when we planned this swing through the canyon. We got up to the end and he says, 'How in hell we going to get out of here?' Right then is when the idea came. I said to him, 'What're you worrying about those big rocks for when you got a gang of Yuma boys on your payroll?' He stopped to listen and I told him how at Yuma we cut whole cell blocks out of granite and shaped them just right. He thought about it and then says, 'You're making work for yourself, aren't you?' That's when I told him. I said, 'Well, it's not so bad if you got dynamite.' "

"So he's going to use it?" Bowen prompted.

"It's already ordered," Manring said. "Should be here by next week."

"Earl, are you going to tell me you talked him into using dynamite?"

"I put the idea in his head. You can call it whatever you want."

"You think," Bowen said, "he would've plotted down that canyon without planning on dynamite?"

"Renda don't know anything about road building!"

Bowen paused. "Let me ask you something else, Earl. Do you know how to use dynamite?"

"I saw enough of it at Yuma."

"That's right, you *saw* it . . . but there's only one man here you're sure ever worked with it. That's where I figure in. You've got the plan, but you need me to set it off."

"You're taking on a lot of credit all of a sudden," Manring muttered. "Next you'll tell me you were planning on it all the time."

"No," Bowen admitted. "I never thought of breaking out of here as being worth blowing somebody up."

"Well, think about it now," Manring said quietly. "Think about this afternoon, the way that gunhand busted Chick Miller . . . think about them watching you, looking for the littlest excuse to bust you . . . and let me know what you come to."

That same evening, Lizann Falvey learned from her husband that a convict had been killed. She thought of Bowen, and for some time was very sure that he was dead. Willis did not know the convict's name. He knew only what Renda had told him—that a convict had tried to run away and Brazil had no choice but to shoot him. By then, the convicts were locked in the barracks for the night and Lizann had no way of finding out whether or not the man had been Bowen.

She considered asking Renda directly, but almost immediately decided against it. Her interest in Bowen could arouse Renda's suspicion and she could not risk any word or action which might do that. Not now. Not with the plan that would enable her to leave here already in her mind. She had thought it out carefully and deliberately. It was the simplest way, as far as Lizann's part in it was concerned, and it offered the least chance of error. Still, the decision to carry out the plan remained with Bowen.

The next morning Lizann was up before six o'clock and standing at the window as the wagons made their slow turn coming away from the barracks. There. Bowen was in the third wagon. She watched him until the wagon passed through the gate, relieved now in knowing she would not have to go to the trouble of—as she heard it in her own mind—breaking in a new man. Now her only problem was to get Bowen alone.

The opportunity came the next Sunday. It came unexpectedly and Lizann was almost unprepared for it.

Willis had left for Fuegos by midmorning. For almost an hour after that Lizann gazed out of the window watching the convicts standing along the front of the barracks. Bowen was among them. Bowen, and next to him, the man who had been with him in the punishment cell.

He could be sent to the stable again, Lizann thought. She went into the bedroom and changed to her riding suit, but when she returned, Bowen was still there.

Be patient, she thought. But even while thinking this she decided to take her horse out.

Frank Renda closed his door behind him as Lizann stepped outside.

"Going for a ride?" Renda asked.

How do you answer a question like that? Lizann thought and decided not to answer it at all. She started across the compound and Renda fell in next to her.

"You're not very sociable today."

"Is today different from any other?"

"It's Sunday. The day of rest . . . Rest for most." Renda was looking toward the convicts. His eyes found Bowen and Pryde and he called out to them. As they came toward him Renda said, "But no rest for these two."

"The stable?" Pryde asked.

"What'd you think?" Renda said. "That's your permanent Sunday job."

Inside the stable, Lizann watched Pryde pick up a broom and walk down to the far end. She heard Renda say to Bowen, "Saddle up my chestnut."

As he moved to Renda's stall, Lizann said, "Ask him to saddle mine, too."

Renda glanced at her. "You like to be waited on, don't you?"

"No more than you do," Lizann answered.

Renda shrugged, looking at Bowen then. "Do what she says."

Now—Lizann thought.

"Frank," she said, turning to leave the stable. "Have him bring it over to me . . . I've forgotten something."

She walked out, not waiting to hear Renda's answer, then took her time crossing the yard, glancing indifferently from the convicts to the guard at the main gate. She entered her adobe, leaving the door open, then hurried into the bedroom. From the top drawer of the dresser, she took the .25-caliber Colt revolver and returned with it to the front room. As she did, looking out through the open door and across the wide expanse of yard, she saw Renda ride out of the stable toward the gate. A few minutes later Bowen came out leading her sorrel.

Lizann smiled and she was thinking: Frank, if you knew how easy you were making it.

She remained back out of the doorway, now holding the revolver at her side, hidden in the folds of her full riding skirt. Bowen approached the ramada, then halted at the edge of the shade. He could not yet see her, but he called out, "Here's your horse."

Lizann answered, "Come inside."

Bowen hesitated. He glanced toward the barracks, then let the reins fall and entered the adobe. He nodded, seeing Lizann. "You worked that good."

"Thank you." Lizann smiled momentarily. "Where is Frank going?"

"He didn't say."

"He made it very easy for us."

"I can still get caught in here. Brazil's about."

Lizann moved toward him. "I heard a man was killed the other day and I thought it was you. I was almost sure it was."

"If it was," Bowen said, "you'd have to break in a new man."

Lizann hesitated. "I'm never quite sure what you're going to say."

"It's true, isn't it?"

She moved closer to him and put her hand on his arm. "I was thinking of you, Corey. Not just a man who's willing to help me."

Bowen said nothing.

Lizann's eyebrows raised. "What happened to our beautiful friendship?"

"It's as beautiful as it ever was."

"Do you still want to help me?"

"If it means helping myself."

Lizann gazed up at him, studying his face. "You seem farther away, Corey. Do you feel I'm not acting like a lady?"

"I haven't been picturing you as one."

She dropped her eyes. "I was, once. Before I was brought here."

Come on, Bowen thought. Get to the point.

"It isn't just Renda and having to live here like a prisoner—which is more than any woman should be asked to bear. It's also my husband."

"We've been over your husband before."

"I thought you were more understanding."

"I'm trying to understand one thing—why you brought me in here."

Her eyes lowered again. "If you really knew what kind of a man my husband is . . . The way he treats me—"

"Look," Bowen said patiently. "I'm convinced. Let's get to the point."

She looked at him calmly now, without pretense. "You don't think very highly of me, do you?"

"It wouldn't matter one way or the other," Bowen said. "Do you have something, or don't you?"

Lizann's hand came out of the folds of her skirt and she pressed the barrel of the revolver against Bowen's belt buckle. "I have this," she said and caught the momentary surprise in Bowen's eyes as he saw the revolver. "Will it help?"

Bowen nodded slowly, thoughtfully. "It'll help."

"Then it's yours," Lizann said. "On one condition."

Bowen's hand went to the revolver. The short barrel remained pressed against him and he could feel her finger on the trigger. "What's the condition?"

"How you escape from here is your business," Lizann said. "You can have the gun and use it however you like. That will be no concern of mine. I'm not asking you to take me with you."

"What's the condition?" Bowen asked again.

"That you kill my husband first," Lizann said calmly.

NINE

The second letter from Lyall Martz, the Hatch & Hodges attorney, arrived on the Saturday afternoon stage. It came unexpectedly, for Karla had written to him only the day after talking to Bowen, Tuesday, and there had not been time for her letter even to reach Prescott, much less receive an answer already.

Her father watched her. "Well, go ahead and read it."

"I'm afraid to," Karla said.

"You're not going to change what's inside by staring at the envelope."

"It's bad news," Karla said tonelessly. "Either he's decided not to work on it or else he's run up against a stone wall."

"Sis, that's some gift you have—being able to read letters without opening them."

She glanced at her father. "It has to be one or the other. Mr. Martz hasn't even received my letter yet. He couldn't have been working on it—he needed the information he asked for first."

"Then," Demery said, "he couldn't have run into a stone wall . . . not yet."

Karla nodded dejectedly. "He's decided he can't spare the time. That must be it."

"Sis, if you don't hurry up and read it, I'll have to."

"I will," Karla said.

Demery watched her finger work open the envelope, take out the letter and unfold the pages bearing Lyall Martz's large, down-slanting scrawl. He watched her—a frown, a somber tight-lipped expression on her face, now biting her lower lip lightly, thoughtfully, now her lips parting and not biting them, her eyes opening, opening wide, glancing up, but only for part of a moment, concentrating on the letter again, and her mouth began to form a smile.

She looked up again and the smile was in her eyes: a moist, glistening smile that struck John Demery as the most genuinely happy smile he had ever seen in his life.

"Bad news?"

Karla's lips moved, but no sound came from them.

"Are you going to read it to me," Demery said, "or do I have to guess."

She stared at him, still smiling, and handed him the letter. "Read it out loud."

"This must be some letter," Demery said. He began to read:

Dear Karla,
    As soon as I accepted this "spare-time job" as you call it, I had to admit to a weakening of the will. I am afraid my giving in has touched off a complete breakdown of my mental faculties, for now I must admit to even a weakening in the intellect department. (Don't tell your father that, though he wouldn't understand it anyway.)

Demery looked up, but before he could speak Karla said, "Go on, read."

    After I wrote to you [Demery continued] outlining the information I needed, it occurred to me: how is Karla going to get information from a man locked up in a convict camp? That could be difficult even for Karla. Then I realized that all I need do was talk to McLaughlin myself. He was at the trial and, of course, he saw the bill of sale. Which I did.
    Mac stated that the handwriting on the bill of sale was clearly an imitation of his own, and a fairly good one, especially the signature. My reasoning then eliminated both your friend Bowen and the other one, Manring, as the forger. It is possible that they know how to write but highly improbable they write well enough to copy the ornate signature Mclaughlin has been practicing for fifty years.
    That pointed to a third man. I asked Mac if the identity of the forger was established at the trial. He recalled that it had not even been brought up. He also told me that Manring had worked for him once before, though had denied it at the trial. Could Manring have procured a blank bill of sale at that time? Yes, but that had been three years ago, Mac stated.

Only six months before the trial, he had purchased new stationery and forms. The bill of sale was of the new batch.

Now, so far we have established that there must be a third man. But, who?

Probably anyone who worked for McLaughlin could have come by a blank bill of sale. He admitted that. But again, we eliminated three-quarters of his hands on the basis of not being able to write at all. So it must be a man who wrote well enough himself to copy another so exactly. Still, a man who worked for McLaughlin.

His bookkeeper? No, Mac said. He kept his own books since firing Roy Avery. McLaughlin looked at me and I looked at him and that, Karla, was how it happened. You see, McLaughlin always tended his own paper work until deciding a man of his holdings should have a bookkeeper of his own. (It took him twenty years to decide this.) So he hired Avery, who lasted two months. He did nothing dishonest, then. But Mac didn't care for him in general and when he fired him they had an argument over the justice of it.

If the identity of the forger had been investigated at the trial, Mr. Avery's name would already appear in the record. That is how obvious it was his doing. Being obvious, Roy Avery of course left Prescott at the time the two men were apprehended. But—and it is questionable whether this is evidence of nerve or imbecility—Mr. Avery returned to Prescott upon learning there had been no mention of him made at the trial. Hence, he was arrested right here in Prescott, McLaughlin having agreed to proffer charges.

Yesterday morning Roy Avery signed a statement admitting his part in the case. He stated that his dealings were with Earl Manring only, that he had never met a Corey Bowen, had never even heard of him until the trial.

As far as he knew, Manring had planned to take the cattle alone. If Bowen helped him, Avery stated, then he was fairly certain Bowen was working at what he believed to be an honest job. Avery reasoned it this way: if Bowen knew it was rustled stock, he would have demanded a close to equal share in the profit. Knowing Manring, Avery said, Manring would never have agreed to that. Therefore, since Bowen *did* go along, Avery believes he was drawing nothing more than trail wages. We must compliment Mr. Avery on a piece of uncommonly sound reasoning.

This morning, Karla, I filed a motion for a new trial. The date has not yet been set, but I think your friend has a much better than average chance of winning an acquittal. And I generally do not make predictions.

Incidentally, the court record stated that neither of the two men had been arrested previously. However that meant only that the Prescott sheriff's office did not have a wanted dodger on either of them. Tracing Manring's past seemed almost impossible to begin with and after a wire to the Tucson authorities, and receiving a negative reply, I gave up on him. However I was able to find out something about Bowen.

His last job was with a cattle company headquartered in the San Rafael valley. But before that he seemed to have spent most of his time mining. His record showed his first job had been with the Moctezuma people in Bisbee. I wired them and found out he had lived there most of his life. His father had been a mine foreman with Moctezuma and Bowen worked for him on and off, sometimes going up into the hills alone to try his own luck, until the father was killed in a mine shaft cave-in. Shortly after that, Bowen left Bisbee. He worked for a horse trader about two years then joined the San Rafael cattle outfit. His mother had passed away some time before the father and as far as I can discover, your friend has no other kin in the territory.

Girl, if all this sounds overly quick and simple, put it out of your head. I have been working harder at my "spare time job" than at my regular practice or for Hatch and Hodges. It is fortunate, Karla, that you have a pretty face (even if your father does claim you are half boy), or you never would have talked me into this.

I expect to be in Willcox some time next month and look forward to seeing your mother and sisters. If I have time, I will stop by Pinaleño on the way back.

> With love,
> Your UNCLE LYALL

"Your Uncle Lyall," Demery repeated, looking up at Karla. "I hope he isn't claiming kinship from my side of the family."

Karla was still smiling. "And you said he'd be wasting his time."

"He hasn't *proved* anything, Karla."

"He has for me."

"And now you'll want to go up and tell your friend about it."

"I have to take the mail anyway."

"Not today, you won't. It'd be dark before you got back."

They were in the main room standing near the roll-top desk and now Karla glanced toward the open door. "I might have time."

Demery shook his head. "It'd be dark before you even *started* back."

"Well . . . I'll go in the morning then."

"Tomorrow's Sunday," her father reminded her. "They don't work on Sunday. So how're you going to get to him?"

"That's something you can't plan," Karla said. "A way just happens."

"Sis, even with your sunny outlook, how do you think it's going to just happen?"

"It happened the other day."

"You were lucky. Tomorrow they'll be standing in front of the barracks smoking, your friend one of them. Or maybe he'll be inside."

"If I don't see him tomorrow," Karla said, "then the next day. One more day isn't going to matter now that he's as good as out."

"You're taking a lot for granted. Lyall still has to prove his innocence."

"He will."

"You're sure of that."

"Pa, when something that looks almost impossible to start with all of a sudden turns possible and everything falls into place as if all you have to do is wish and it happens, then you know it's going to turn out all right."

"You figured that out all by yourself?"

"It makes sense."

"Do you know that your talking to him, even though he might be innocent—"

"Might be!"

"Listen to me. Your talking to him like that, even though he might be innocent, is against the law. You know that, don't you?"

"Sending an innocent man to jail is against the law, too, if you all of a sudden want to be ethical about it."

"Karla, if I told you not to see him, but wait for Lyall to do something . . . would you listen to me?"

"Of course I'd listen to you."

"But you'd go ahead and try to see him."

"It's only fair. If you were in prison, and were going to get out, wouldn't you want to know about it?"

"You're taking things for granted again," Demery reminded her.

"You just want to argue," Karla said.

Demery shook his head. "I'm glad I don't have your sweet faith in human nature."

"Some men," Karla said pointedly, "have to put on a big front of not believing in anything—hoping, I don't know why, that everybody will think they're very smart."

"You're some keen observer."

"If we had time, I'd tell you some other things."

"I guess you would," Demery said. "Listen, I'll tell you something now. I'll bet you four bits you don't talk to him tomorrow or the next day."

"You sound pretty sure of yourself."

"I'm just playing law of averages, Sis."

"Make it a dollar," Karla said, "and you've got a bet."

It was almost ten o'clock, the next morning, before Karla finished helping her father with the monthly report to the main office. She put aside the mail for the convict camp, then saddled her horse and brought it around to the front of the adobe. The next quarter of an hour was spent carrying in water from the pump to the big wooden tub in her bedroom. Her cold-water bath took only a few minutes and after it she brushed her hair and put on a fresh blouse and skirt.

John Demery's eyes studied her appraisingly as she came out of her bedroom. "Something special about today?"

Karla smiled. "I don't have time to be drawn into one of your traps."

"You're the only girl I know who can look dressed up in a man's shirt. Maybe if Willis had seen you, he would've stayed."

"Mr. Falvey was here?"

"He waved going by. Headed for the bar at Fuegos."

"The last time he was here," Karla said, "I think I frightened him. I told you—he was talking about wanting somebody to talk to—I felt sorry for him, but the way he was going about it I had to tell him to leave."

"Well, I don't imagine even his wife understands him," Demery said. He picked up the small bundle of convict camp mail from the desk and handed it to Karla. "There's a couple there for Willis. I didn't think about it . . . I could've given them to him."

"I'll give them to Lizann," Karla said.

"Don't get too close to her," Demery said. "Some of that gild might brush off."

"Now . . . you can't judge people just by looking at them."

"It seems to me I said the same thing not too long ago—about a man not having to look like a jailbird to be one."

Karla shook her head. "When you look at Corey Bowen, you know he's good. When you look at Lizann, you give her the benefit of the doubt." She leaned toward her father and kissed him on the cheek. "I'm going now. Before you think of something else to argue about."

She rode for the willow stand, passed through the dim silence of the trees, then entered the vast sunlight of the slope beyond and followed the sweeping curve of wagon tracks to the shoulder of the hill. There she left the tracks, riding straight on, up into the close-growing pines that covered the crest of the hill, following a horse trail now that twisted narrowly through the trees. Coming out of the trees, the horse trail dropped down a steeper grade, crossed the wagon ruts that had circled the hill, then followed the length of a narrow grama meadow before climbing again up through fields of house-sized boulders.

A mile farther on Karla emerged from a thin, steep-walled pass to stand above the canyon which the new road followed. Far below her, the dead end of the canyon was choked with pinyon and mesquite. The brush clumps thinned gradually as they spread and finally the dusty green patches of color disappeared completely, almost evenly, before reaching the end of new road construction.

Karla walked her horse along the west rim until she reached the trail that dropped down into the canyon: a rock-slide draw that fell to a shelf, the shelf hugging the wall narrowly until it reached the floor of the canyon. Karla descended and a quarter of a mile farther on, she stopped at the waterhole among the sycamores where she had talked to Bowen.

She let her horse drink. Coming out of the trees, her gaze caught the wisp of dust farther up canyon; but she reached the stretch of new road, passed the timbers that were used for grading, passed fire-blackened circles where brush had been burned, before she saw the rider who was leading the dust trail down the wash, down into the canyon and following the road now toward her.

It was Frank Renda. As she recognized him—her gaze going to him then sharply away from him—she saw the grave and the crude cross marking it off to the side of the canyon. Renda came directly toward her, making her rein in. His horse crowded Karla's and as their knees touched, Karla prodded her quirt at Renda's horse, backing away as she did.

Renda was smiling and he wiped the back of his hand over his heavy mustache. "This must be my day."

Karla was thinking of the new grave and she nodded to it, saying, "Someone was killed?" consciously making the question and the tone of her voice sound natural.

Renda followed her gaze. "Somebody tried to run away."

"Who was it?"

"What difference does it make?"

"I might have a letter for him," Karla said. She reached back, her hand touching the strap of the left-side saddlebag.

"His name was Miller," Renda said. Karla's hand hesitated on the strap. Now her fingers unfastened it and she drew out the bundle of letters. "You got something for him?"

She knew there was nothing for a Miller, but she loosened the string binding the letters and leafed through them. "None for that name."

"What about me?" Renda asked.

Karla glanced down and up again. "Nothing for you either."

"What's all the mail about then?"

"One for Mr. Brazil . . . one, two for Mr. Falvey."

"I'll take them back for you," Renda said.

Karla looked up. "It's all right. I'll take them. You go ahead wherever you're going."

Renda nodded to the letters. "That's where I was going. So I'm saving you a trip."

"I'd just as soon ride up and leave them myself," Karla said.

"There's no sense in that, if you don't have to."

She tried to smile. "I don't have anything to do anyway. Sunday's a funny day. There's nothing ever to do."

"Let me have the mail, Karla."

"Honestly, it's no trouble for me to ride to the camp. I *want* to."

"I don't care where you ride," Renda said. "Long as you give me the mail."

She was aware of his stare and the cold, threatening tone of his voice and only then did she realize that he wanted the letters for another reason, not simply to save her a trip to the camp. Still, she hesitated.

"Karla, you hand them over else I'll take them off you."

"If you're that anxious," Karla said, "all right." She leaned over to hand him the bundle then sat back in the saddle and watched him leaf through the envelopes. He pulled one of them out and looked at the return address on the envelope flap. Then, before Karla could speak, he had ripped open the envelope and was unfolding the letter.

"You can't read other people's mail!"

"Not looking at her, Renda said, "Keep quiet."

"That's against the law!" Karla screamed. Then, more calmly, "Mr. Renda, you're tampering with the United States mail. You can go to prison for what you just did."

Renda looked up then. He was smiling and his eyebrows raised as if to show surprise. "I didn't know it was a personal letter."

"It wasn't addressed to you!"

Renda nodded calmly. "It was addressed to Willis. But Willis ain't at camp. What if it was something had to be tended to right away? Honey, it was my business to open it." He held up the second letter addressed to Falvey. "This one, too," he said, and tore it open.

The quirt, thonged to Karla's wrist, dropped from her hand as she kicked her horse against Renda's and reached for the letter. "Give me that!"

Renda pushed her and his horse side-stepped away. "Now don't get excited." She came at him again and he held her away until he finished reading the letter.

"No," Renda said. "That one wasn't business either." He grinned then. "It seems Willis put in for a transfer, but this"—he glanced down at the return address on the envelope—"Everett C. Allen, of Washington, D.C., thinks Willis ought to stay right here. Says there aren't any good openings now, but he'll let him know when one comes along and in the meantime, superintending a"— he looked down at the letter again—"a territorial penal institution was valuable experience and would equip him for a more responsible position when the opportunity presented itself."

Renda was still smiling. "Karla, did you know Five Shadows was a territorial penal institution?"

"My father's going to hear about this," Karla said.

"Your father's going to hear about it. Now that's something."

"You won't think it's funny then—opening other people's mail." Renda crumpled both of the letters in his fist. "What mail?"

"Give me those!"

He held Karla away as she came at him again and threw the tight ball of paper over his shoulder. "I don't have anything, Karla. Just this pack of letters. That what you want?"

For a moment she stared at him, feeling a rage she could do nothing about. She dismounted then, looping her reins about the saddle horn, and walked around Renda's horse to pick up the crumpled letters.

"I'm giving this to my father," Karla said. "Just the way it is. You can count on a United States marshal visiting you within two weeks."

"Why? Because you found a piece of thrown-away paper?"

"You won't talk like that to a marshal."

"Whatever you're holding, I never saw before in my life," Renda said. "And you and all the United States marshals in the country aren't going to prove I did."

"We'll see," Karla said.

Renda swung down from the saddle and walked toward her. Watching him Karla began to back away. "What's the matter with you?" Renda said. "I only want to give your letters back. You're so anxious to ride them up to the camp, all right. Here."

As Karla took them, Renda's hand went to her shoulder. "Karla, there's no good reason we have to fight."

"Take your hand off me."

"Why don't we just talk awhile. Get all the misunderstanding cleared away."

"I'm happy the way it is," Karla said. She shifted the mail to her left hand and her right hand closed around the quirt that hung from her wrist.

"Karla, we could go over and sit in that sycamore shade. Let the horses water—"

"I said take your hand off me!"

Renda grinned. "Like nobody ever touched you before."

The quirt came up. Before Renda saw it, the rawhide lashed across his face; before he could bring up his hands the whip came back stinging across his eyes, and as he covered his face Karla ran.

Five strides and she was in her saddle, spurring, reining tight to the left, cracking the quirt across the rump of Renda's mount, then at Renda as he ran to her, as he caught her leg, almost pulling her from the saddle. She swung viciously again and again, the quirt hissing, slashing at his straining upturned face, until suddenly he was no longer there.

As Renda went down, Karla's horse broke into a gallop. Over her shoulder she saw Renda on the ground, now rising to his feet and pausing to look after her, now running for his horse as it disappeared into the sycamore grove.

It rushed through Karla's mind that she was heading up canyon. To return home the way she had come, she would have to come about and run past Renda. He would have caught his horse by the time she passed the sycamores and would overtake her easily before she reached the end of the canyon. So there was no choice.

She would go to the camp. There were people there, and even if they worked for Renda it would be better there than being alone. He would follow her; but he would have had time to think of what he had done. Lizann would be there. She would tell Lizann about it and Frank Renda would have something else to think about. She could worry about returning home when the time came.

To her right, the wagon-trail wash came winding down through the talus and Karla reined toward it. Reaching the rim of the canyon she stopped long enough to look back. Far below her Renda, mounted again, was moving unhurriedly up the new stretch of road.

Minutes later, Karla was riding down the slope that stretched to the convict camp. The gate guard recognized her two hundred yards out. He unlocked the chain and swung half of the gate open to let Karla ride in.

"Is Mrs. Falvey home?"

The guard looked over toward the ramada. "That's her horse. I judge she's fixing for a ride."

"I want to deliver her mail," Karla said.

"Go right ahead, honey."

Karla dismounted. She glanced at the bundle of letters as if to leaf through them. "Maybe there's something for you."

The guard shook his head. "Don't take the bother to look."

"If you're that sure—" Karla said. She looked back as the guard started to swing the gate closed. He hesitated, squinting out into the glare and she knew he had seen the dust line coming down the slope.

"You might as well leave it open," Karla said.

Now they could make out the form of horse and rider. Still squinting the guard asked, "Who is it?"

"Your boss," Karla said. She moved away then, leading her horse toward the main adobe. Reaching the end of the building, she entered the shade of the ramada and moved along the edge of it to the support post where Lizann's horse stood. She half-hitched her reins to the post and walked over to the Falveys' quarters.

As she stepped into the doorway, Bowen and Lizann turned, moving apart, Lizann's arms coming down from Bowen's shoulders. Bowen's hand pushed into his shirt front, but not quickly enough. Karla had already seen the revolver in his hand.

TEN

"Renda's coming," Karla said tonelessly.

Bowen moved to the door. He looked out, then to Karla close to him in the doorway. "You didn't see anything, did you?"

She shook her head.

"Listen," Bowen said urgently. "I want to say a lot of things, but there isn't time. Just promise me you won't—"

"You'd better hurry," Karla said. Her eyes moved from Bowen's. She felt him brush past her. Then, when she turned, she saw him out beyond the two horses, walking across the yard toward the stable, glancing toward the gate as Renda entered the compound.

Lizann said, "Is he there?" She moved closer to the door in time to see Renda ride over to stop Bowen. There was a silence in the adobe as they watched the two men: Bowen standing in front of Renda's horse looking up at him and they could see Renda was speaking. In front of the barracks, the convicts were watching and now the yard was quiet. They saw Renda step out of the saddle. Bowen's hand went to the front of his shirt and the hand scratched at his stomach idly. Renda was speaking. Bowen nodded. A minute passed, not more than a minute. Then, Bowen nodded again and turned away, going on toward the stable, as Renda caught up his reins and led his horse toward the abode quarters.

Close to her, Karla heard a soft, exhaling sigh from Lizann. Karla's gaze remained on Bowen. She did not turn, not even when Lizann spoke.

"You and Corey have met before."

Karla nodded. "Did you give him the gun?"

"What gun?"

"That's not the way to help him!" Karla turned as she spoke.

"I don't know what your talking about."

"I saw the gun—"

"You told Corey you didn't see anything."

"As far as anyone else is concerned."

"Why do you think *I* gave it to him?"

Karla glanced through the doorway, seeing Renda approaching, then back to Lizann. "Tell him not to use it. Please tell him that. Not now. Something has come up."

"You make very little sense," Lizann said.

"You don't have to understand it. Just tell him! If you wanted to help him enough to give him a gun then tell him!"

"Tell him what?"

"That the lawyer has found new evidence. Important enough to warrant a new trial. He's already filed the motion and it's only a matter of weeks—" Karla broke off hearing Renda's voice.

"Well . . . Miss Demery."

Lizann turned back into the room. She went to the canvas chair and sat down. Karla stepped back from the doorway as Renda entered.

"Why don't you come in?" Lizann said. "Make yourself at home."

Renda looked at her. "What're you edgy about . . . something this girl told you?"

"She hasn't told me anything."

He turned to Karla. "You change your mind about causing a fuss?"

"I told you what I'm going to do."

"You want me to tell Lizann?" Renda asked.

"If you don't," Karla said. "I will."

"You could be a damn sight easier to get along with." He looked at Lizann again. "I opened a couple of Willis's letters by mistake, but Karla thinks I done it on purpose."

"You know he did," Karla said.

"So Karla thinks she's going to make trouble for me," Renda went on. "Going to tell her father about it. And claims he'll call in a federal marshal. So if Karla's going to go to all that trouble, I'm not about to admit reading the letters. Am I, Lizzy?"

"You're admitting it right now," Karla said. "In front of Mrs. Falvey."

Renda's gaze moved to Lizann. "Did you hear me admit

anything?" Lizann said nothing and Renda's eyes returned to Karla. "If a federal marshal stopped by here, Lizzy wouldn't know anything about it."

Karla began, "When I tell Mr. Falvey——"

"And Willis," Renda broke in, "will tell the marshal that he read the letters and threw them away when he was finished, and if some girl out for a ride happened to find them, that's no concern of his. All Willis will know is that he threw the letters away. You see how it is, honey?"

Karla looked at Lizann who returned her gaze almost without expression, telling nothing, least of all offering assistance. Then, to Renda again, "I don't see how you have the nerve to admit what you just did."

Renda shrugged. "You're the only one hearing it. You got no witnesses. I got a man who'll admit reading the letters and throwing them away for you to find."

"You're very sure of yourself," Karla said.

"Honey, when you're minding thirty convicts you got to be sure of yourself."

"I'm still going to tell my father."

"You go right ahead . . . And tell him for me, I want to know the day my supplies come in this week. I don't want them laying around for some stage passenger to drop a cigar butt on. You hear me? Soon as they come in, I want to know about it."

"You'll notice," Lizann said mildly, "he's worried about his investment and not your station."

"I'll hear from you in a minute," Renda said. He looked at Karla again. "You run home now. And remember what I said. Soon as it comes in I want to know about it."

"I'm dismissed now?" Karla said.

"You're double dismissed. Ride directly through that gate and don't let me see your face around here till my stuff comes."

"Mr. Renda," Karla said. "you're a real gentleman."

Renda smiled pleasantly. "Thank you, Karla. Now get out before I kick you the hell out!" He saw her about to speak and he yelled, "Go on!" then kept his eyes on her until she had left the adobe, mounted her horse and ridden off toward the gate.

Lizann asked, "What did all that prove?"

"When somebody talks like that," Renda said, "I get sick to my stomach."

"Maybe it's your conscience backing up on you."

"A sermon now?"

Lizann shook her head. "Not even if I thought it would do you good."

Renda moved to the table. He half sat on the edge of it, hooking his leg over one corner, and leaned his weight heavily against the table. Watching him, still sitting in the canvas chair, Lizann said, "Don't make yourself too comfortable."

"I thought we'd have a talk," Renda said.

"About what?"

"Willis's letters."

"I'm not interested."

"You want me to think you're not," Renda said. "You're bustin' to know what was in them."

"Then keep it to yourself," Lizann said, "and see if I bust."

"They were from Washington."

"I told you, I'm not interested."

Renda came to his feet. "I'm interested! You understand that? I'm interested and we're going to damn-well talk about them whether you want to or not!"

"As usual," Lizann said calmly, "you'll be talking to yourself."

The table creaked as Renda leaned his weight on it again. "Let's find out," he said mildly, and noticed the look of momentary surprise on Lizann's face. "We don't have to yell at each other, Lizzy. Pretend you're in Washington and you're talking to one of Willis's political friends. Like Mr. Everett C. Allen."

"The letters were from him?"

"That's better," Renda grinned.

"Were they?"

"They were from him."

"What did he say?"

"He was answering Willis."

"I didn't know Willis had written him."

"You expect me to believe that?"

"I don't care what you believe!"

"You should. It makes a difference."

"I didn't know Willis had written to him," Lizann said evenly. "You can believe that or not."

"Let's say I don't. Who is he?"

"Everett? He's with the Department of the Interior."

"High up?"

"High enough."

"High enough to get Willis away from here?"

Lizann nodded. "What did he say?"

Renda's leg, hooked over the corner of the table, began to swing slowly back and forth. He stared at Lizann and for perhaps a full minute he said nothing. Then, "What're you so anxious to know for? You don't even know what Willis said to him first."

"Does it matter?" Lizann asked.

"You know damn well it matters."

"If you are going to insist that I know what Willis wrote," said Lizann, "there's no use discussing it further."

"I'll bet you even told him what to write."

Lizann sat lower in her chair. Her gaze went to the open doorway and she ignored Renda.

"I'll bet Willis didn't even want to write it. But you made him."

Lizann's gaze came back to Renda. "Willis asked for a transfer!"

"That's pretty good," Renda said. "You must've been rehearsing—opening your big brown eyes, looking surprised—"

"What did Everett say," Lizann demanded.

"What do you think he said?"

Lizann hesitated thoughtfully. "Something to the effect that Willis was gaining valuable experience . . . that there were no openings elsewhere, but when the right opportunity presented itself—"

"You know this man pretty well," Renda said.

"I have seen his letters before."

"So Willis is stuck," Renda said. "I told him that a long time ago."

Lizann said nothing.

"I told him. I said, 'Willis, relax and enjoy it. You're gaining valuable experience here and if you do good, maybe they'll make you superintendent at my next camp.'"

"God help him," Lizann murmured.

"That could happen, Lizzy."

"I wish you wouldn't call me that."

"It bothers you?"

"How do you know there's going to be a next camp?"

"Same way I got this one."

"You bribed someone for the contract?"

"That's a bad word."

"You must have."

"Mine was low bid, Lizzy."

"You know nothing about road construction. Someone must have told you what to bid—for a price. Someone on the inside."

Renda grinned. "A silent partner."

"What I don't understand," Lizann said, "is why you bother. You have to use bribes. You have to watch every move anyone makes. You hire a man like Brazil, who would come higher than the ordinary guard. You're constantly in danger of being found out. For what?"

"For fifteen dollars a day profit, free and clear," Renda said.

"Which isn't very much," Lizann said.

"Besides what I make on the road contract."

"But with your expenses, there couldn't be much left of that."

"Enough," Renda said. "Which adds on to the fifteen a day—"

"How do you come to that amount?"

"The government subsistence!" He sounded surprised that she had to ask. "I don't know why they think each man's worth seventy cents a day—when you only need about twenty cents to take care of one. But as long as they want to pay it, I'll make my fifteen a day. Figure that back over four months. Then go ahead a couple more months. See how it adds up? I figure I'll make three thousand on that alone . . . something I didn't even count on when I got the contract."

"Do you think it's worth the effort?"

"Lizzy, I'm not straining. I sit in the shade all day counting my money. When this job's over, I spend the money. Then I get another contract."

"Considering the chances you're taking," Lizann said, "I would think you'd play for higher stakes."

"Why? I'm not greedy."

"How much do you pay my husband?"

"Whatever I feel like, now."

"Just enough to keep him drunk."

"He started low." Renda grinned. He said then, "You better have a talk with Willis about his letter writing. I don't want to hear any more about trying to get transferred."

"If it bothers you," Lizann said, "talk to him yourself."

"Lizzy, I'm being nice about this. I don't have to be."

"What Willis does is no concern of mine," Lizann said evenly. "I want to make that clear to you. As far as I'm concerned, Willis doesn't exist. At one time I wanted him to leave here and I tried to persuade him with every argument I could think of. Willis was afraid to do anything—afraid for his life and afraid for what he chooses to call his career. So I stopped trying to persuade him. Willis is on his own—and I'm on my own."

"Well," Renda said pleasantly, "if it's all right with you, I'll still consider you and Willis a pair. Whatever he does, you're behind it; and whatever you do, he at least knows about it. As long as you're living together that makes it easier to keep track of both of you."

Lizann nodded. "As long as we're living together."

Renda studied her. "Is that supposed to mean something?"

"Think it over."

"I don't have to. I'm asking you."

"You'll find out soon enough."

"Lizann . . . now don't do anything you'll be sorry for."

"It's already done. And I won't be sorry."

"What're you talking about?"

"Wait and see."

"I don't wait on anybody!" Renda came off the table. "I'm telling you right now, if you're planning to leave, forget about it. You try anything, I'll fix you once and for all!"

"Frank," Lizann said patiently. "I've already told you how I feel about Willis. You can ruin him, cause him to go to prison, and it won't make the least difference to me."

"Who says I'm talking about Willis?"

"You've been holding him over me like a club."

Renda shook his head. "Let's get it right out in plain sight. Lizzy, I'll tell you one time and one time only." His hand came up and he pointed a finger at her. "You try to leave here without my knowing about it, I'll kill you." His hand dropped. "It's that cut and dried."

Slowly, Lizann shook her head and her expression was composed as she said, "I'm going to leave here, Frank. And there won't be a thing you'll be able to do about it."

"You're bluffing," Renda said.

"Am I? You'll see." Lizann smiled then. "Start thinking about it now—go over in your mind every possible way I could leave here—and you'll still be thinking about it when it happens."

ELEVEN

The new road had reached as far as the sycamore grove the morning Manring arranged to work with Bowen's stump-pulling detail.

He waited until the wagons were unloaded and the convicts had moved off before he went over to Frank Renda, who had dismounted and was standing near the equipment wagon.

Manring touched the brim of his straw work hat. "Mr. Renda—"

"What do you want?"

Manring leaned over the end gate of the equipment wagon then, reaching for the handle of a shovel. "I want to work with the stump pullers."

Renda rolled a fresh cigar between his lips and clamped it in the corner of his mouth. He moved leisurely to the end of the wagon to scratch a match against the gate board. "Before," Renda said, "it was to get off that job."

"I'm not talking about permanent," Manring murmured. "Put me on it a couple of days . . . long enough to find something out."

"What've you heard?"

"Nothing yet. Bowen and Ike got their heads together. That's all I know. Set me with them a couple of days and we'll know more."

"What's your price this time?"

"I'll let you know. After I think about it."

"Keep talking like that," Renda said, "your price'll be the punishment cell."

Manring's eyes raised briefly. "Look, I don't have time to be polite. Either put me with them or don't."

"They find out what you're doing," Renda said, "some morning we'll shovel you out of the barracks."

"That's my worry."

"I know it is," Renda said. "I'm just curious to know what you want in return. You got about the softest job now—riding that scraper."

"If I'm going to pull stumps," Manring said impatiently, "I better get at it."

"Go ahead."

"I'll have to get rid of the Mexican."

Renda nodded. "Send him over. I'll put him on the scraper." He watched Manring shoulder the long-handled shovel and walk off toward Bowen's group.

Now another one to watch, Renda thought. And he wondered if it was worth it. You didn't trust anybody in this business, least of all a man who would inform on his own kind. Still, a man like that could be valuable and sometimes having one around was worth it, even if you couldn't trust him.

Manring had been right about Bowen planning to jump the supply wagon that day. It had marked the beginning of Manring as an informer. And it was a strange beginning, because he had given the information without first asking for a reward. It was not until days later, after Bowen and Ike were in the punishment cell, that he asked to be taken off the stump-pulling detail. And then only hinted that perhaps he would learn other things that would be worth passing along.

Because he had been right the first time, there was no reason to doubt Manring now. That Bowen and Pryde might be up to something made considerable sense. Some men you could beat till your arms fell off and they still wouldn't learn. Bowen had tried it once. You could tell by looking at him that he had the itch to run, and you could bet safely that he'd try it again.

And Pryde. Serving thirty years. Only six of them behind him. Thirty years for killing a man with a broken whiskey bottle in a saloon fight. Yes, Pryde qualified. With twenty-four years to go—no time off—he'd be more likely to run than Bowen. But Ike would be more choosy about how the break would be made, because he had more time to think about it.

So let Manring snoop, Renda thought. Make him tell whatever he learns. And if his price is out of line, then throw him the hell in solitary. Let him think it over by himself. He thought then: Which is what you ought to do with Lizann.

But you wouldn't be sure of Willis's reaction. Willis was weak, and by now too whiskey-soaked to think for himself. But if something were to happen to Lizann—No, you couldn't be sure what Willis would do . . . even afraid as he was.

Since his talk with Lizann, Renda had thought it out very carefully. There were only two ways she could leave Five Shadows. Either try to run away by herself, or try to summon help from the outside. Both of these avenues were blocked. He read every piece of mail she wrote or received and a Mimbre followed her whenever she took her sorrel out. So Renda told himself she was bluffing. She was being wearisome, trying to get him excited, because there was nothing she could do about her situation.

Still, as Lizann had predicted, he continued to think about it, and merely telling himself that she was bluffing did not ease his mind.

Manring was confident now that Renda would believe almost anything he might tell him. That was a sign that his luck was still running. No, it wasn't all luck. Getting in with Renda wasn't luck. Arousing Bowen's interest in the dynamite wasn't luck either. It was work and thinking and sweating and being five jumps ahead of any luck that could turn against you.

The luck had been in the beginning. First, seeing the basis of a plan come apart with the word that Bowen was ready to run. Bowen the dynamiter, without whom the plan was nothing. So there had been no choice and informing on Bowen had been a good way to test his luck.

Manring reasoned it this way: If Bowen escaped, or, if he were killed in the attempt, the dynamite plan was finished. But if Renda knew beforehand that Bowen was going, they would be ready for him and Bowen would have only a slim chance at best. He *might* be killed; but, to Manring, the odds leaned slightly toward his being taken alive. Perhaps with gunshot wounds, but nevertheless alive.

As it happened, Bowen was taken and Manring's luck began its run. That he had tested his luck with a man's life in the balance rose to his conscience only briefly. He shrugged it off with the thought that if Bowen had been killed, he deserved it. He would be repaid for that night in the Prescott jail cell: the night Bowen slugged him four times before the deputy pulled him off.

It was not until a few days after Bowen and Pryde had been thrown into the punishment cell that Manring realized that he had not asked Renda for a reward. He could not risk Renda suspecting that he had informed on Bowen for any other reason than for a reward. So he asked to be taken off stump pulling.

Now he was doing the same thing in reverse. Nearing the end of the canyon, it was time to be working with Bowen again. When the dynamite arrived he would still be with Bowen. Renda would be asking what he had learned and he would have to stall Renda. But that could be done, he was sure. And Pryde. It was too bad Ike was still working with Bowen. But maybe something would happen to Ike.

Bowen was backing the team into position, Pryde pushing down on the long handle of his shovel, levering the stump, and the Mexican was passing the chain through the stump's shallow roots. Pryde saw him first. He said, "Here comes Earl." And now the three of them paused. They waited expectantly, watching Manring coming toward them.

As he reached them, Manring's eyes went to the Mexican and he lowered the shovel. "Renda wants to see you."

The Mexican's hand moved to his chest. "Me? What does he want with me?"

"Don't get overheated. You're going on the scraper."

"On the scraper? But why does he want *me*?"

"Ask him. I don't run the place."

The Mexican rose slowly, wiping his hands on his thighs. "Maybe he thinks I did something that I didn't do."

"You're going on the *scraper*. That isn't punishment."

The Mexican shook his head. "Something's wrong."

"You're just jumpy," Manring said.

"I'm jumpy since the time Chick Miller went to see Renda."

"Go on, get out of here."

Manring's eyes followed the Mexican as he started off toward the equipment wagon, then his gaze returned. He looked from Pryde to Bowen as he said, "I got transferred."

Bowen only nodded, but Pryde said, "We saw you talking to Renda."

"Sure. He was sending me over here."

"You're talking to him all the time, aren't you?"

Manring looked over at Bowen. "Your friend don't trust me."

"Maybe I don't either," Bowen said. He backed the team up to the stump and there was no more said until they had pulled the stump and Pryde moved off with the team, dragging the stump to the nearest bonfire.

Manring said then, "I talked Renda into sending me over here. We got to be working together, Corey, if we're going to pull it."

"You can talk in front of Ike," Bowen said. "I already told him about it."

"You told Ike!"

"He wants to get out just like you do."

"We don't need three!"

"But you need me. And if Ike doesn't go, I don't."

"Corey . . . it's different with you and me. We got no business being here in the first place. Ike *killed* a man. He *deserves* to be here."

"I'm not judging him," Bowen said. "If I go, so does Ike."

By late afternoon, the road had passed the sycamore grove and was halfway to the horse trail that slanted gradually up the western tree-covered slope of the canyon.

"By tomorrow afternoon the brush cutters will be on the slope," Manring said. His shovel jabbed at the roots of the stump they were working on. As Bowen went to his knees, Manring stooped, pushing down on the shovel and one side of the stump lifted, popping the roots that held it. Pryde passed the end of the chain to Bowen and they fastened it to the stump. As they worked, their eyes would raise to the tree-covered slant of the canyon wall looming above them.

"More or less," Manring said, "the road's got to follow that natural trail."

Pryde said, "I don't see any trail. Though it must be there. The girl passes this way and so does Willis."

"You can't see it for the trees," Manring said. "It goes up a shelf, all the way up, that looks like it was put there for the purpose. When the trees are cleared, maybe the shelf would be wide enough for a wagon. But it'd be *just* wide enough, without any room to spare."

"So," Bowen said. "You blast the wall out and use the rock to build up the shoulder of the road."

"That's the way I see it," Manring said.

"Is that the way you and Renda both see it?" Bowen sad.

"What do you mean by that?"

"You and he surveyed it together, didn't you? Is that the way Renda said it would be done?"

"Something like that," Manring said guardedly. "He wasn't sure and he just talked about it generally."

"So you weren't sure either how it would be done," Bowen said.

"As sure as anybody," Manring insisted. "There's only one way to get out."

"We want to hear your idea," Bowen said.

"You're awful damn anxious. We got about a week yet."

"Earl, I don't think you have a plan."

"You'll find out."

Bowen nodded. "We'll find out right now."

"It'd be easier to tell it once we got up on the slope."

"Earl, I think you're stalling."

"I can't give you details now! You got to be up there to see what I'm talking about, else it won't mean anything to you."

"Try us anyway," Bowen said.

"Well," Manring began, "it's based on three things. We got to do three things else it isn't going to work." He spoke slowly, as if giving himself time to think.

"First we got to take care of the guard that'll be on us. I figure Renda or Brazil. We get hold of him, but without anybody else knowing about it. Second, we set the charge so as to close the road on anybody coming up from below. Lay a rock slide over it or else blow a hole in it that a horse couldn't cross. Third, we got to take care of the Mimbres. I figure we can force Renda or Brazil, whichever one we're holding, to call them out. See, we'll have another charge planted. All this is timed to the second and just as they come out—boom—they're blown sky-high."

"Then what?" Bowen said.

"Then we run for the station. For horses."

Bowen looked at Pryde. "What do you think?"

"He don't anymore have a plan than I do."

"He must've just thought it up," Bowen said.

Manring looked from one to the other. "What're you trying to pull?"

"You got a lot of holes in your idea," Bowen said. "That's all."

"Well, sure," Manring said. 'You can't work everything out until you got the stuff."

"You can't work anything out," Bowen said.

"It'll go like I said, or it won't go at all."

"Maybe some of it will," Bowen said. "You've wanted us to believe you had a plan so we'd get it in our heads we need you. You supplying the brains and Ike and me lighting the fuse. But it comes out all you have is a sketchy idea . . . and now we're not sure if we do need you, Earl."

Manring remained calm, as if he had anticipated this and already knew how he would answer it. He shook his head saying, "You won't do it without me. If you don't like my idea, think it's got holes, then figure your own way. But whatever way you do it, I'm going to be along."

"Now he's threatening us," Pryde said.

"You can call it whatever you want," Manring said.

Pryde shrugged. "I was thinking you wouldn't want to go up there with us. A man could fall and kill himself."

"Ike," Manring said, "I can fix it for you right now."

"You're going, Earl," Bowen said easily. "We might not need your help, but we sure as hell need you in plain sight."

As Manring predicted, the "brush cutters"—the convicts who cleared the pinyon and scrub brush—were working their way up the slope by midafternoon of the next day. On the morning of the day after that, the crews that followed, including the scraper, had reached the beginning of the trail and could go no farther—not until dynamite widened the narrow, uneven horse trail. But the dynamite had not yet arrived.

By noon, two thirds of the convicts were idle—until Renda devised something for them to do. He was reluctant to put more men up on the slope. That would increase the rate of construction, shorten the job time and consequently decrease his daily profit. Still, the convicts had to be kept busy. So he put them to work clearing the canyon area beyond the point at which the road would begin ascending the west slope.

"Cleaning out the brush is for your own good," Renda told the convicts. "Then later on when we're working high up and somebody falls off, we'll be able to find the body for a decent burial."

There were three bonfires to consume the brush as it was hacked down and cleared away. Bowen was given the job of tending to one of them. Shirtless in the close, almost unbearable heat, he would throw the dry brush into the flames. Then, waiting for more to be dragged over to him, his gaze would raise to the jagged, climbing trace of the horse trail that became visible, foot by foot, as the pinyon was toppled into the canyon.

Now it was a matter of patience, of waiting and using the time to think it out clearly, to think of every possibility. No, there was not that much time—not time to think of everything—so you eliminated some of the things right away. The things you had thought of already and had seen no hope in. Like Karla . . . and the lawyer . . . and walking out with a pardon or a parole or an acquittal or whatever you wanted to call it.

It was nice to think about that. It was nice to think about her. But it didn't do you any good. And now you think about only the things that'll do you some good. And it's the bad things that do you good. Do you realize that? You get good from bad. That isn't possible, but that's what you're getting. From Lizann. And from Earl.

A gun from Lizann and an idea from Earl.

Bowen had hidden the gun in the stable. In the stall where Renda's chestnut mare was kept, he had pried loose one of the boards against the back wall and slipped the gun behind it. There, because the barracks offered no safe place to hide it. Getting it again, when the time came, would be another problem.

But there were a lot of problems and one more didn't make much difference. Shooting Willis Falvey, though, was not one of the problems.

Lizann's plan, when he realized it, was very simple. It was not a question of running away. That had no part in it. If her husband were killed, there would be an investigation. Someone would come down from Prescott—if not for a formal investigation, at least to take over Willis's duties. When he did, Lizann would leave, and Renda would be able to do nothing about it. It was that simple. A convict, trying to escape, had killed Willis. The convict either got away or was recaptured. That was the convict's problem.

But it won't be your problem, Bowen thought. And it won't be anybody else's problem, unless she had more than one gun.

He imagined that she would be confident, patiently waiting for it to happen, rehearsing what she would say to the man from Prescott—perhaps even taunting Renda with hints that she would be leaving soon.

Lizann had a surprise coming.

So you are left with Earl. Earl and the dynamite. And you have to be careful how you mix them if you expect to get out of this alive.

On the morning of the second day of tending the brush fire, Bowen saw Karla Demery ride down the canyon. The convicts on the slope stopped working to watch her go by; and those below, on the floor of the canyon, turned and followed her with their eyes as she crossed to Renda sitting in a shaded section of the east wall.

She spoke to Renda for only a moment, then reined her horse in a tight circle. As she did, her gaze found Bowen. She nudged her horse toward the fire, toward the motionless naked-to-the-waist figure who stood in front of the swirling, wind-caught rise of smoke. Renda called to her and she drew in the reins. Bowen watched. She was not more than fifty feet away, still looking toward him. She wanted to tell him something, he could see that by her expression. Then it was too late. Renda, mounted now, came up next to her and they rode off together toward the nearest team of horses.

A few minutes later they passed Bowen again, heading up the canyon. Behind them came a wagon carrying three convicts, one of them Manring. A guard followed, bringing up the rear.

She wanted to tell you something, Bowen thought. But it could've been bad news as easily as good, so don't think about it. You've got enough to figure out already. But through the rest of the day his thoughts would go to Karla Demery. She was not that easily put from his mind.

That evening the convicts were in the barracks when the wagon returned. Six men were called out to help unload it and they did not return for over a half hour. When they did, Manring was with them.

The lean, bearded man came over to Bowen's mat. He sat down at the foot of it and rolled a cigarette. "Let me have a match."

Bowen handed him a box of matches and watched silently.

Manring struck the match. As he held it to his cigarette he said, "Boy, we just unloaded it in the stable. Enough to blow everybody clean to hell."

TWELVE

"**W**ait a minute," Renda called. "This is far enough!" He brought up his shotgun as the four men on the climbing trail ahead of him stopped.

Brazil, leading the file, called back, "He says you got to start at the top."

"You believe everything he tells you?" Renda's face, flushed from the climb, showed sudden anger.

To Bowen who was second in line, carrying two coils of fuse over his shoulder and a box of detonators in his hand, Brazil said, "The old man can't take it, so he's got to yell at somebody."

Bowen turned and looked past Pryde and Manring who followed him to Renda. "You want to stand here with fifty pounds of dynamite and talk about it?"

Renda edged along the inside of the trail close to the wall, past Manring and Pryde. As he reached Bowen, Pryde lowered the case of dynamite from his shoulder, placed it against the wall and sat down on it.

Manring, carrying a shovel, a hand axe and a sapling pole, looked at him uncertainly. "You better be careful."

As Manring spoke, Renda turned quickly. "What are you doing!"

"I'm resting," Pryde said, "while you talk it out."

"You can't sit on dynamite!"

"And I can't stand with it a hunnert feet above nowhere while you get over your nervous state."

Bowen said to Renda, "I explained it once. You got to start at the top."

"He don't take to high places," Pryde said. "Or marching behind fifty pounds of charge."

Renda turned on him angrily. "Pick it up!"

Pryde remained seated, leaning back against the wall. "There's more chance of dropping it than my hind-end heat setting it off."

"I said pick it up!" The tight-muscled, open-eyed expression of Renda's face was dark with anger. He was aware of the four men watching him, and wanting to show neither anger nor fear he said to Bowen, more calmly, "All right. We'll talk about it upstairs."

Rising, lifting the case of explosives, Pryde said, "Frank, you want to carry this a while?"

But Renda, refusing to be angered further, ignored Pryde. He remained in line where he stood and followed Bowen the rest of the way up the trail, along the slanting wall, then into a depression where the rock had fallen away and the trail was less steep. The depression cut into the wall and formed a forty-foot draw from the shelf up to the rim of the canyon.

As he came up out of the draw, Bowen saw a Mimbreño tracker off in the trees. He was there for a moment, then gone. That's your big problem, Bowen thought.

Renda was still breathing heavily as he reached level ground. He stepped aside as Pryde and Manring came up and said to Bowen, "All right, why do you start at the top?"

"I figure—" Bowen began.

"You figure!"

"I never blew up a mountain before."

Renda exhaled. "Go on."

"I figure," Bowen said again, emphasizing the word, "If you start from the bottom, as you work up you'll be covering what you just uncovered every time you set a blast. You get your road widened and the shoulder built up, then touch one off higher up and"—he snapped his finger—"like that, no more road."

Manring said, "That makes sense."

Renda glanced at him. Then to Bowen he said, "What do you do first?"

"Test the fuse." Bowen placed the box of detonators on the ground carefully and took the two coils of fuse from his arm, dropping one of them and handing the end of the other fuse to Manring. Then he walked away from them, straightening the line as he did, measuring it with the length of his hand as he unwound it. With ten feet of it played out he said to Renda, "I need a knife."

"What for?"

"To cut the fuse!"

"I'll do the cutting."

Bowen shrugged. "Then over the next couple of weeks you're going to be living on an awful lot of dynamite."

Renda brought out a pocket knife. He hesitated, then handed it to Bowen. "Every day when we quit, you give this back to me. Closed."

Bowen smiled. "You don't trust anybody." He cut the fuse, then stretched it out on the ground. "Have you got a clock with a sweep hand on it?" When Renda nodded, Bowen said, "Start timing as soon as it catches." He pulled a match from his hatband, struck it on the bottom of his shoe and touched it to the fuse.

The fuse hissed and a small flame spurted from the end of it. There was little smoke, but the fuse moved and seemed alive with the flame burning through its powder-filled core. "It's slow enough," Renda said.

"Mind your clock," Bowen told him. When the fuse had burned all the way, he looked at Renda again. "How long?"

"About three minutes."

"Mr. Renda," Bowen said mildly, "we're talking about how much time to get clear of a blast. Don't give me any *about*."

Renda glared at him, but looked at his watch again and said, "Just a little over three minutes. Maybe five seconds."

After a moment Bowen said, "That means it burns just about a foot in eighteen seconds. Maybe you think that's slow. It's not when you're lighting the end of it."

"I'm impressed," Renda said. "Now what?"

"Now we'll test the charges," Bowen answered. Manring drew the hand axe from his belt and handed it to Bowen as he moved to the case of dynamite. On the top of the case was stenciled, *This Side Up*, below that, *High Explosives—Dangerous,* and at the end which Bowen opened, *50 lbs. No. 1 Dynamite—$1\frac{1}{4} \times 8$ inches*.

"You're supposed to use a wooden hammer and wedge to open this," Bowen said.

Renda edged toward him, then back again. "Why?"

"Something about a metal tool slipping and hitting the charge," Bowen said, prying the top boards loose with the hand axe. "You never know what'll happen."

Renda's hands were tight about the shotgun and he stood without moving. "We don't need any talk. Just hurry it up."

"That's another rule," Bowen said. "You don't hurry." He lifted one of the ten paraffin-coated packets from the case and opened it.

"Here you are," Bowen said. He extended one of the dynamite cartridges to Renda.

"I don't want it!"

"I thought maybe you wanted to see one close." Bowen rose and glanced around, then moved to the edge of the draw and looked down, studying the narrow defile that reached to the trail.

"Earl," Bowen said then. "Take your stick down there and poke a hole in the left-hand wall. Right down at the end of it."

"How deep?"

"Deep as you can make it. Start about a yard in from the corner." As Manring started down the defile, Brazil following him, Bowen cut a three-foot length of fuse. He opened the box of detonators, took one of the copper capsules from its felt wrapping and began to gently push the fuse into the capsule's open end. He did this very carefully until the fuse was touching the detonating compound. Then, with his teeth, he crimped the open end of the detonator tightly to the fuse.

Pryde said, "You ought'n to use your mouth for that."

"I don't see any nippers around," Bowen said, and thought: For a man in the construction business he's missing a damn awful lot of tools.

"How many sticks?" asked Pryde.

"We'll try three," Bowen said. "And find a stick—sharp pointed and about the size of a pencil." He moved down the draw then, holding the detonator gently in his closed hand. Pryde followed, but Renda came only halfway down.

Brazil stepped back as Bowen reached them. He saw Renda then and called, "What's the matter, Frank?"

"Mind what you're paid for!"

Brazil was grinning. "You're going to miss something way up there."

"I can see all right." Renda was twenty feet up the draw standing close to one of the steeply sloping banks.

"That deep enough?" Manring asked. "The stick's no damn good."

"You'll have to get a metal rod," Bowen said. He looked closely at the hole. It was formed in a slanting crevice in the rock and was not really a hole at all, only the rock fragments cleared from the crevice, but it would serve the purpose.

Pryde handed him two cartridges and Bowen inserted them into the seam. As he did he murmured, "Look around, Ike. Get the lay of things. Figure how the Mimbres would come from the other side of the canyon."

He unwrapped one end of the third cartridge and with the pinyon twig that Pryde gave him punched a small hole. The detonator went into this, and Bowen rewrapped the paraffin-coated paper so that only the tip of the detonator, with the fuse extending from it, could be seen. This went into the crevice, then loose sand on top of it so there would be no space between the charges and the walls of the crevice. Bowen tamped the sand gently and now they were ready.

He looked down into the canyon—seeing the convicts grouped around the wagons that were pulled over to the far side and the two guards mounted and standing off from them—then lit the fuse. As he turned he saw Renda go over the top of the draw. "Frank's already cleared," Brazil said, then waited to go up last to show that he wasn't afraid.

They moved back from the rim of the canyon and a moment later the blast went off. Dust billowed up out of the draw and close on the explosion they heard the faint boom of an echo up canyon, then another, then silence and the dust hung in the sunlight above them.

As it began to clear, they went down into the draw again. The corner that met the trail was sheered off in an undercut. Shattered rock and sand were scattered over the shelf and much of it had gone over the edge into the canyon.

"That wasn't so big," Renda said. He was at ease again.

"The next one'll be bigger," Bowen said. "First you find out what a few sticks will do. Then you add to it." He glanced at Pryde, then back at Renda. "We can make them as big as you want."

Bowen organized the routine and that day they blasted three times. At Bowen's direction they began thirty feet down the trail from the defile. Four convicts were brought up and put to work digging into the wall of the canyon. Their job was to hollow a niche six feet deep and wide enough for Manring to work in. Manring would then cut a hole, parallel with the canyon wall, for the dynamite charges. As he did this, the four convicts would return to the bottom of the canyon.

Renda said, why not send them around into the draw? But Bowen objected. "Once we light the fuse that's the way we run, and we're not going to have anybody standing around in the way."

There was an anxious moment, a moment of seeing the plan that was already forming go to nothing. "That's why we started down a ways," Bowen explained, "instead of right at the defile. So we'd have cover to use. But it won't do us any good crowded with men." Renda said nothing and Bowen added, "Then, after we're about halfway down the trail and working the dynamite from the bottom, we'll come back and blow the part we skipped. Right now, though, we got to have that pass clear."

Renda thought it over. "All right," he said finally, "send them down before you set your charge"—and Bowen's anxiety was past.

They exploded the first charge at midmorning—a forty-pound charge with the cartridges tied into bundles of eight—and the convicts were kept busy until almost noon clearing the shattered rock, spreading it evenly over the widened section of road.

As Bowen thought would happen, Renda went below before the first charge was set off, leaving Brazil to watch them. Brazil remained close. He would wait until the fuse was lighted, then go for the draw with them. He seemed fascinated by the dynamite, by the force and the noise of it, and he watched every phase of the work carefully.

That afternoon they moved a dozen feet farther down the trail. This would be slow going, Bowen realized, blowing only ten or twelve feet at a time; but Renda did not have drilling equipment and without it they could use only smaller charges effectively. Another niche was carved out of the crusted sand and rock and another blast set off. Then later, after the third charge was exploded, after watching Brazil and now realizing there would be only one more day of using the draw for cover, Bowen made up his mind.

And later again, in the barracks that evening, after the lamps had been put out and the three of them crouched in the darkness beneath the window, Bowen explained his escape plan. He told Pryde and Manring exactly what each of them would do. He made sure there were no objections. He emphasized that each man had to do what he was supposed to do, and nothing else. And if they did, this would be their last night at Five Shadows.

THIRTEEN

Six hundred pounds of dynamite were brought out of the stable and loaded onto the equipment wagon the next morning. Bowen specified the amount. He remained in the stable until the wagon was loaded and when he came out he was carrying four detonator boxes. One of the boxes had been emptied and in it was Lizann Falvey's .25-caliber Colt.

Bowen drove the equipment wagon. He took it over the Five Shadows slope, down into the canyon and to the foot of the trail that reached silently up into the early morning sunlight. The floor of the canyon was in shadow and there was little talk as the dynamite was unloaded.

"We'll take eight cases up," Bowen told Renda. "Leave the other four down here. Maybe we'll use them, but I don't think so."

Renda pointed to eight men in turn, and approximately fifteen minutes later the dynamite was up on the rim of the canyon. The eight men returned to the convicts working on the ledge, spreading the results of the previous day's last explosion. And now the dynamite crew was alone with Brazil.

They were ready to plant the first charge when Willis Falvey came up the trail. He passed them without a word, without even looking to see what they were doing, kicked his dun horse up through the draw and rode along the rim until he was beyond the end of the canyon.

The way you're going, Bowen thought, watching him disappear into the deep shadow of the pass which led down to the boulder field beyond the canyon.

Through a mile of rock and across the meadow, Bowen thought. Up past the road, straight over the hill and down the grade. Cross the creek, come out of the willows. You're there.

Brazil's voice brought him back to the ledge. "You going to light the fuse?"

Bowen lit it. They went back to the draw to wait for the explosion and Bowen watched Brazil. The gunman squinted, his mouth open and tensed, waiting, and he seemed to be smiling, keenly anticipating what was to come.

And when it came, more suddenly than they could be ready for it, the rock-shattering, head-numbing violence, the thunder rolling into the distance, somewhere beyond the ringing in their ears, Brazil still smiled.

"Damn!" He shook his head slowly as if the pleasure of it had exhausted him. "I'd like to see what would happen to a man sitting on one of them."

"You never know," Pryde said. "Maybe you will."

Brazil looked at him. "Did you see anybody get blowed up at Yuma?"

"Not me," Pryde said.

"Did you?" Brazil asked Bowen.

Bowen shook his head.

Brazil seemed disappointed. "Maybe somebody got it before you were there. Didn't you hear of anybody?"

"I wasn't listening," Bowen said.

Brazil grinned. "That would be some sight."

They went down to the shelf again as Renda and a guard brought up the convicts to do the grading. Bowen looked over the edge. There were still two guards down in the canyon. So he's got another man on, Bowen thought. One of the night guards.

"That one took more slope," Renda said. "They hardly got any chipping off to do."

"We tried a bigger charge," Bowen told him. "Packing more sticks to the bundle."

"You go any bigger, we'll be filling in," Renda said. His gaze moved along the edge of the shelf, then stopped. Unexpectedly, Bowen saw his face become tensed. He followed Renda's gaze up canyon and saw a rider moving along the stretch of new road. Now all of them were watching and soon they saw that it was Lizann Falvey.

Brazil said, "What's she doing up here?"

Renda continued to watch her, his eyes half closed in the sun glare. A swirl of wind blew dust at him, fanning his hatbrim, but he did not turn away from it.

"I never saw her up this far," Brazil said.

She bothers him, Bowen thought, still watching Renda. All she has to do is show herself and he's on his guard. You thought it once. Maybe she's threatening him. Confident she's leaving and she throws it in his face. Tells him everything but *how*.

Following Lizann, trailing her perhaps fifty yards, was a Mimbreño. Bowen watched him move off to the east side of the canyon. Lizann had circled and now was riding back toward him, past him, becoming smaller, and soon she was out of sight. But even after she was gone, Renda continued to stare up canyon and a moment later he moved down the shelf.

That's good, Bowen thought. Give him something else to think about.

Bowen indicated where the next charge would be placed before they moved back up onto the rim. And now they got ready the fuses and the dynamite cartridges they would use.

"I think I'll light the next one," Brazil said.

"That's all you got to do," Bowen said, "and you're a dynamite man."

Brazil was studying his Winchester. "It's a far size bigger than this."

Bowen looked toward Manring and nodded. Manring rose, picking up his shovel and started for the draw.

Brazil's head came up. "They're not ready for you yet."

"Earl's got another job," Bowen said. He rose as Brazil did and walked over to the edge of the draw. "He's going to dig that corner where we tested yesterday."

Brazil frowned. "What for?"

"After a couple of more blasts," Bowen explained, "we'll be far enough down to come back to the part we skipped. Earl thought he'd get it ready now if it's all right with you."

"Frank know about it?"

"Ask him," Bowen said. He turned and walked back to Pryde.

Brazil glanced at Manring. "Go on. I'll see him later." He squatted then at the edge of the draw where he could watch Bowen and Pryde, to his left, and Manring below and to his right.

"The first step," Pryde murmured.

Bowen sat down with his back to Brazil. The detonator boxes were in front of him. He raised one box, then another, and raising the third one he felt the weight of the Colt revolver. He lined up the boxes and placed this one on the right.

Now he studied the dark mass of pines that were forty or fifty yards in front of him and he began setting a fuse into the open end of a detonator.

"Ike, have you seen Mimbres?"

"For about a hair of a minute. When we first came up."

"We have to figure six on this side," Bowen said. "They don't like what's going on, so they stay back in the trees."

"What would we do if they didn't mind it?"

"Think of something else."

"And six more on the other side of the canyon," Pryde said.

"We'll think of them when the time comes," Bowen said. He crimped the open end of the detonator to the fuse. He unwrapped one end of the dynamite cartridge, pushed a twig into it to form an opening, then inserted a detonator.

"How many you going to do?" Pryde asked.

"We'll have five ready," Bowen said. "Maybe we won't use that many, but we'll have them."

"Brazil wants to light the fuse," Pryde said. "It'd be purely simple to leave him with it."

"Don't even think about it."

"I can't help it. It's too good not to."

"Ike, we do it the way I said."

"I know it. I was just talking."

Bowen had attached the fuse to the fourth detonator and was inserting it into the cartridge when Brazil called to him. "Earl says he's ready."

Rising, Bowen said to Pryde, "Like he works for us." He picked up a coil of fuse and a detonator and moved down the draw. Pryde followed, a half-full case of dynamite on his shoulder.

Brazil said, "What're you in such a hurry to plant this one for?"

Bowen dropped the coil, but held an end of it. "Might as well do it now as later."

"You sure Frank knows about it?"

"Go ask him," Bowen said. He saw Brazil's gaze go down into the canyon.

"Frank would've told me," Brazil said.

"He tells you everything?"

Brazil did not answer. He was studying the small figures far below. He said then, "I don't see him."

Now the four of them looked down into the canyon. Almost at once Pryde said, "That's him . . . riding off. Way up the road there."

"Like he's going back to camp," Manring said. He looked at Brazil. "Everybody works but Frank."

"You dig your hole," Brazil snapped. "And keep your mouth shut."

"It's dug."

"Then plant the charge!"

That's it, Bowen thought. Get mad. Get your mind on something else.

When they climbed out of the draw again, a ten-foot length of fuse hung curling to the ground from the hole where the charge was buried. The hole had been dug above the undercut of their test blast of the previous day. It was approximately five feet from the ground.

"When you going to light it?" Brazil asked Bowen.

"I figure sometime this afternoon."

Brazil's gaze found the four dynamite sticks with fuses already attached. "You're doing a damn awful lot of work beforehand."

"What difference does it make when we do it? Long as it gets done."

"Maybe I ought to ask you that," Brazil said.

Bowen shrugged. "Pull the detonators out if you don't want them there. We'll walk off about a half mile and watch you."

Bowen turned from him. He went over to the equipment, sat down next to Pryde and began fitting a fuse end into the fifth detonator, thinking, now watching Brazil wander to the edge of the draw: Don't push him too far.

Manring stopped next to Bowen. "Are we ready?"

"As ready as we'll ever be."

"How much did you plant just now?"

"Twenty pounds."

"Is that enough?"

"I'd have to set more if it wasn't."

"We got to be sure."

"What do you want to do," Bowen said, "light it now and find out?"

Manring's hand scratched nervously at his beard. "We got to be sure, that's all."

Pryde got to his feet. They saw him stare off toward the pass that was beyond the end of the canyon. Then Brazil noticed him, hearing the hoof sounds at the same time. "Sit down," he told Pryde, and swung the Winchester toward the pass.

As he did, Karla Demery appeared in the shadowed opening. She looked up, showing surprise at seeing them, then walked her horse toward them.

Her gaze moved from Bowen and the two men next to him to Brazil. "I didn't think you'd be here so soon."

"We're full of surprises," Brazil grinned. He saw her move to dismount. "Sit where you are. I got enough to watch without a horse standing by."

"I wanted to see if these men had any letters," Karla said. Her hand was behind her on the saddlebag, unfastening the strap.

"Give them to Frank," Brazil said.

"It'll only take a minute." Karla brought out the letters, began going through them, then glanced at Bowen again. "Isn't your name Bowen?"

Bowen nodded. His eyes moved to Brazil. Brazil was watching Karla.

"I thought I had a letter for you," Karla said. She came to the last letter, then started through them again. "It seems to me it was from an attorney. The return address, I mean. Lyall Martz? Is that name familiar to you?"

"Yes, ma'am," Bowen said.

"But now I don't see it."

Brazil moved toward them. "What would you be hearing from a lawyer about?"

"He's a friend," Bowen said.

Karla looked up. "I know there was a letter from him. Somehow I must have misplaced it. Tomorrow . . . I'll be sure to bring it tomorrow."

"He can wait," Brazil said. "Now move out of here."

"I remember it looked like such an important letter," Karla said.

Brazil's hand came down on the horse's rump and it sidestepped away from him. Karla looked back, then reined toward the draw and Brazil called after her, "When you find Frank, tell him I want to see him!"

Manring leaned toward Bowen. "What's this lawyer business?"

"You think it concerns you?"

"We were in it together, weren't we?"

"You don't fit into it, Earl," Bowen murmured. He began taking dynamite cartridges from an open case and binding them into bundles of eight sticks.

And you don't fit into it either, he told himself. You don't hang on to a thread. Not now. Maybe when there was time, but now it's a matter of minutes. You understand that? Minutes.

A convict appeared out of the draw and told Manring the charge hole was ready to be dug. He stood with hands on hips looking about idly, to the pass, up into the trees, then his eyes dropped to Bowen who was winding twine about the dynamite sticks and he moved back down the draw. Manring followed him.

Watching him go, Pryde murmured, "We could leave Earl there too."

"All four of us walk back up here," Bowen said.

"How're you going to handle Brazil?"

Bowen glanced over his shoulder—Brazil was still at the edge of the draw—then raised the top from the detonator box which held the revolver. "Like this."

"Where'd you get that?"

"I'm not saying."

"I could guess."

"And you'd be wrong." Bowen closed the box.

"You going to shoot Brazil?"

Bowen shook his head.

"Let me have it," Pryde said. "I'll use it on him."

"You got enough to do," Bowen said; then asked, "Have you got it straight?"

"I think so."

"Tell it."

Pryde's eyes raised to Brazil, then lowered again. "When we're called to set the charge, you're going first. You carry the case with the bundles in it. Then I follow. I'm carrying another case. There're a few sticks in it and the knife. You get down to the end of the draw before you notice I'm carrying it. Then you say, 'I got enough sticks. Leave what you got here and we'll pick it up on the way back.' I set the case down where you planted the charge a while ago. Right under where the fuse is hanging. Then we go around on the trail and do what we're supposed to be doing. You light the charge and we all hurry back up the trail. We're starting up the draw and I say that I've forgot the case. I lag back to get it, take the knife out of the case, cut the fuse so only five feet is hanging out of the wall, light it and come after you."

"That gives you a minute and a half," Bowen said, "to climb out of the draw."

"It doesn't take half of that," Pryde said.

"You want to be on the safe side."

"But why a five-foot fuse?"

"We want this charge to go off as close as possible with the main one," Bowen said. "If they blow too far apart, somebody down below will start to think about it and come up too soon to find out why. But we couldn't put on just five feet when we planted the charge, because Brazil would notice it being short and wonder about it."

"But with the draw caved in," Pryde said, "nobody could get up here anyway."

"This way is called not leaving anything to chance," Bowen said. "Maybe there's a quick way up out of the canyon we don't even know about."

"All right." Pryde nodded, then asked, "When do you pull the gun?"

"As soon as the draw blows," Bowen said. "Whether it goes before or after or at the same time the main charge does, Brazil won't expect it. He'll be off guard."

"Then we tie him up," Pryde said.

"That's right." Bowen glanced at the row of long-fused dynamite cartridges next to him. "While Earl cuts the fuses on those."

"Why don't we do it now?"

"For the same reason that charge down in the draw has a ten-foot fuse," Bowen said. "Brazil isn't that dumb. If he sees six-inch fuses sticking out of these he'll know damn well what they're for."

"And the rest is up to luck," Pryde said.

Bowen shrugged. "Maybe we'll make our own."

The convict who had come for Manring a few minutes before appeared again at the top of the draw.

"Here we go," Pryde said.

Brazil looked toward them and called, "Ready for the stuff."

Rising, lifting the case to his shoulder, Bowen said, "Take your time. Cut the fuse right where it touches the ground and you'll have five feet."

Pryde nodded. "Don't worry about it." As Bowen walked off, he picked up the second wooden case and followed him. Brazil fell in behind going down the draw. No one spoke and there was only the sounds of their steps in the loose gravel. Then, as they reached the shelf, Bowen looked back.

"Ike, what've you got that for?"

Pryde stopped. "Didn't you say bring it?

"I got all we need," Bowen said. "Set it down there and we'll pick it up on the way back." His eyes moved to Brazil. No reaction. No change in his tight-jawed, narrow-eyed expression.

Bowen turned the corner and moved down the shelf, along the thirty feet which they had not yet dynamited, then over the widened, graded section—roughly fifty feet of this—to the place where they would set off the next blast.

Manring was waiting there. The grading crew had moved out and were already at the bottom of the trail. "Ready?" asked Manring.

Bowen only nodded. He stepped into the closet-sized space that had been cut into the wall and began placing the charges. The horizontal chamber that Manring had prepared was waist high and ran parallel with the wall of the canyon. It was deep enough to hold all of the charges, but it was too wide; and with each charge that he placed Bowen would tamp sand into the chamber so the dynamite would fit snugly and there would be no air space. When he finished, only the fuse could be seen extending from the packed sand.

Bowen looked at Brazil. "You said you wanted to light it."

"I'll hold your rifle," Pryde said.

"I guess you would," Brazil said. He waved the barrel of the Winchester. "You all get out of the way. Start moving up." He drew a match and stooped over the fuse, then called after the three men, "This one's ten feet?"

Bowen turned and nodded. "Three minutes' worth." He watched Brazil strike the match and hold it to the fuse. "Give him room," Bowen murmured.

He turned again, now hearing Brazil coming up behind them, and started to walk faster.

Brazil called, "What's the hurry?"

Bowen glanced back. "That one's bigger than the others. We got to get all the way up to the top."

Pryde let Bowen pass him. He was next to Brazil as they turned into the draw. Then he stopped. And as Brazil went on, Bowen and Manring ahead of him, he stooped quickly, took the knife from the wooden case and cut the fuse so that less than a foot of it remained. Bowen looked back as he brought the knife down.

"What's the matter?" Bowen called.

Brazil stopped.

Pryde stepped in front of the cut-off fuse and waved up to

Bowen, the knife palmed in his other hand. "Go on. I got to get this box is all." He watched Bowen and Manring move up through the draw. Brazil turned to follow them.

"Hey!" Pryde called sharply, bringing Brazil around. He waited. Brazil frowned. Now Bowen and Manring were reaching the top of the draw. Pryde waited a moment longer, until they were over the rim. Then he said, "Come here."

Brazil started toward him, but stopped, as if only then remembering the burning fuse down on the trail. "Pick it up . . . we got to *move!*"

Pryde stared at him. "You're not going anywhere."

"What'd you say?"

"You heard me."

Brazil's gaze went beyond Pryde and abruptly his eyes opened wide. "What'd you do to that fuse!"

Something was wrong. Something was going on that shouldn't be happening. But even as he realized it, even as his nerves came alive and he reflexively brought up the Winchester, it was too late, Pryde was on him.

He tried to go back, tried to leave the Winchester, but Pryde's left hand pushed up on the barrel. Brazil's arms went up with it and he half turned to wrench the Winchester from Pryde's grasp. As he did, Pryde's right hand drove the knife into his side. Brazil gasped and the shock of it was in his eyes and in his straining, open-mouthed expression as he slumped to the ground.

Pryde was at the fuse again. He struck a match, touched it to the fuse and started to run. A ten-inch fuse—time enough to climb out of the draw, but not for Bowen to come down after Brazil. You had to think of Bowen doing things like that.

He was twenty feet from the rim when the main charge went off and the suddenness of it made him stumble. His ears rang and there was dust in the air and the echo up canyon and suddenly Pryde fell again.

His hands clutched at his stomach. He felt a wetness and looking down saw that it was his own blood. He could not believe it, but it was there. He had been shot and the bullet had gone completely through him. But there had been no report! Only the ringing and the echo and the slamming against his back that could have been a rock—

He rolled over and felt himself sliding and then he saw Brazil at the bottom of the draw. He was lying on his stomach aiming the Winchester.

"Ike!"—above him, Bowen's voice.

Pryde saw the Winchester raise and he called out to warn Bowen.

FOURTEEN

Bowen had already seen Brazil. He went down, rolling away from the slope, hearing Pryde's one-word scream lost in the high-whining, dust-kicking report of the Winchester.

There was no time to think, yet it was in his mind to help Pryde. He had returned to the defile in time to see only part of it—Pryde lighting the fuse and running, Brazil rolling to his stomach, bringing up the Winchester, then the blast going off down on the shelf and Pryde stumbling—

And now, even knowing it was too late, Bowen thought of Lizann's revolver. He pushed up to his hands and knees, then was moving, running for the row of detonator boxes when the draw erupted behind him.

The force of it slammed him to the ground and he covered his head with his arms as the sand and rock fragments showered down on him. Then he was up again, the hissing ringing of the explosion still tight about him, seeing Manring coming toward him, Manring looking past him to where the draw had been.

The left wall of the draw had been blown in, completely filling the narrow depression, so that now a steep slope of shattered rock dropped to the shelf and covered the section of it that had curved into the draw.

"Ike's under there," Bowen murmured. "He cut the fuse short, tried to leave Brazil there, but Brazil shot him—"

Manring looked back toward the trees. What had happened to Pryde meant nothing—not with Mimbres about to appear. He said urgently, "We got to move!" and started back toward the equipment.

Bowen stared down the slope. Was it worth that? You didn't do it—it was his own fault!

"Come on!" Manring's voice.

Bowen's gaze went down into the canyon. He saw the convicts, small figures far below, and a rider moving up canyon. He turned and ran toward Manring. "Cut the fuses!"

"With what?" Manring looked at him helplessly. "Ike had the knife!" He turned to the trees nervously. "With what, damn it!"

"We'll cut them," Bowen said. "Hold on to yourself."

"We got to get out of here!"

Bowen's eyes went over the equipment. No knife . . . but the hand axe.

He picked it up, gathered the five dynamite sticks he had prepared and had lined up on the ground, ran his hand down all five fuses at once, drawing them together, then chopped down with the hatchet—once, twice, again, until he had chopped through all of them and only eight inches of fuse remained with each cartridge.

"There!" Manring was still looking at the trees. "I saw one!"

Bowen looked up. Off through the trees he could see a movement. Now you have to be careful, he thought. Not too close.

He struck a match, held it to a fuse, then picked up the stick and threw it. The dynamite exploded as it struck the ground ten yards out from the trees.

He told Manring, "When I throw the next one, run. And he thought: You don't even have to light it. But it's better to be sure.

He struck a match, touched it to a fuse and threw the stick in the same direction. It was end over end in the air as Manring started to run, striking the ground and exploding as Bowen took the revolver from the detonator box and shoved it inside his shirt and into his waist. He picked up the three remaining cartridges and ran after Manring.

They ran for the pass that wound through the rocks beyond the end of the canyon, followed its narrow, shadowed course and as they came out Bowen lighted and dropped another stick. They were running down the length of the meadow when it exploded behind them.

Now the Mimbres from the other side, Bowen told himself. He turned to stand in the open, in the thick grama grass that moved in slow waves with the wind.

Manring turned, hesitating. "Come on!"

Bowen motioned to him to go on. "I'll catch up." He turned back to face the rocks, hearing Manring moving through the tall grass, the hurried swishing sound becoming fainter. This is something, he thought. Covering for him. No, you're covering for yourself too. This is the way to do it. It's a once-and-for-all thing. If it works. If they scare easy.

He saw them then—the six riders slightly off to the right coming down through the rocks. They had seen him, he was sure of that, and now they had reached the meadow and were coming directly for him.

You can spot them by the way they ride, Bowen thought. Straight on and no games this time. All business.

He struck a match with his thumbnail, held it as he judged the distance closing between him and the Mimbres, then touched it to the dynamite and threw the stick.

It struck and exploded twenty yards in front of the Mimbres, and they swerved right and left. They started circling back out of range and Bowen threw the last stick, arching it higher into the air. It exploded closer than the first one and the next moment they were galloping back up the slope, winding through the rock formations.

Bowen ran on through the meadow, came out of it and started up the slope ahead of him. Near the wagon road that skirted the shoulder of the hill, he caught up with Manring.

"Now Pinaleño," Bowen said.

Frank Renda had descended the five-shadowed grade and was approaching the camp when the main charge went off in the canyon. He heard it faintly in the distance and in his mind saw a section of wall high above the shelf buckle out, seem to rise and hang suspended, then disappear into thick dust—as the previous blasts had appeared from the floor of the canyon.

But he pictured this for only a moment. His thoughts returned to Lizann Falvey. She was the business at hand. Something to be dealt with *now*. You let a woman get a little bit sure of herself and pretty soon she makes you sick to your stomach watching her pretend she's a man. Lizann had gone far enough. Riding into the canyon had been, in fact, too far.

He had forbidden her ever to come near the road construction. "Ride anywhere you want, but stay away from the convicts when you got a horse." That meant stay out of the canyon. But this morning she had come down the new road—telling him without words what she thought of his authority.

Maybe she was bluffing. Maybe she was only trying to worry him. But she seemed too sure of herself. Maybe she did have a plan. Whichever it was, he intended to find out now.

There was no guard at the gate. He had shifted one of the night men to day work when the dynamiting began. Why, he was not sure; but it seemed to him there should be another guard on hand while they were working with high explosives.

The night man was sleeping now and the gate was open. As Renda passed into the compound, the sound of the second explosion reached him. He reined in abruptly and sat listening.

An echo?

That's all. He relaxed, nudging the big chestnut to a walk, thinking: Brazil's there. He'll shoot if anybody even looks at him sideways.

He dismounted in front of the Falveys' quarters and entered the open doorway without knocking. As he did, Lizann came out of the bedroom. She had changed from her riding suit and was fastening the top buttons of her dress. She showed no surprise at seeing Renda.

"What do you want now?"

"I saw you in the canyon a while ago."

"You rode all the way in to tell me that?"

"I told you never to go near there."

She nodded. "Three or four times."

"I'm not going to tell you again."

"That's fine."

"Next time you go in the punishment cell."

"You wouldn't dare."

"You want to find out, go ahead."

Lizann smiled faintly. "Frank, do you honestly think you're frightening me?"

"If I'm not, you're the one's going to suffer for it."

"I don't think so," Lizann said. She moved across the room to the table, poured water into a glass from an earthenware pitcher, then sat down. She crossed her legs, sitting sideways to the table and sipped at the glass. "Frank," she said, lowering the glass, "I'd ask you to stay, but I couldn't think of anything more unpleasant to have happen."

Renda moved toward her. "Lizzy, you're bluffing, aren't you."

"About you being unpleasant?"

"About leaving here."

A smile touched Lizann's mouth. "Why do you think I'm bluffing?"

"Because you know what I'd do to you if you ever tried."

"Has it kept you awake—thinking about it?"

"If you're not bluffing, Lizzy, you'll wish you were."

"Frank, stop trying to sound menacing. You don't frighten me anymore. I'm leaving here . . . there's nothing you can do about it, and the sooner you realize it the better."

He moved to the table, raised his hip to sit on the edge and folded his arms. Looking down at her he asked, "How're you going to do it?"

Lizann took a sip of water and placed the glass down carefully. She had expected him to show his temper, but he remained calm, deliberately in control of himself. After a moment she answered, "You'd never guess."

"I don't have to," Renda said. "You're going to tell me."

"I'll tell you this, Frank—which I already have—it's going to happen and you'll still be thinking about it when it does."

Renda watched her. As she raised the glass again, his arms uncoiled and he swept it from her hand. The glass shattered against the floor and Lizann went back from the table, straightening, looking suddenly at Renda with shocked surprise.

Renda's arms were folded again. "I asked you how're you going to do it."

Lizann did not answer, though she continued to stare at him and her hand brushed at the wet stain on her skirt.

"Willis didn't write to anybody," Renda said. "You haven't either, because I've seen every letter that's gone out. What other way is there?"

"You'll have to find out for yourself," Lizann said. She saw his arms separating and tried to turn away, but she was not quick enough and the back of his hand stung across her cheek.

As she looked up at him again, Renda said, "I'm going to find out, but not by myself. You see what I mean?"

She could feel her cheek burning as she made herself return his stare. "You intend to force me to tell you?"

Renda shrugged. "One way or the other."

"You're not a man . . . you're an animal."

"I'm still asking—"

"You can go to hell."

She was expecting it, but his hand struck so suddenly there was not time to turn from the blow, and as her head came up he struck her again with his open right hand.

"I'm not fooling, Lizzy!"

She brought her arms up in front of her and as he drew back his hand again she left the chair. Renda was on her as she reached the bedroom door. He pushed her inside and against the near wall, held her against the adobe until she stopped struggling, then stepped back slowly.

"The next time I use my fist!"

"I told you—"

He brought his fist back, but at the last moment he opened it and struck her again with the palm of his hand.

"Say it!"

"I have nothing to say."

Renda stepped back. He shifted his weight and saw her eyes close as he hit her in the face with his fist. Lizann's head struck the wall and she started to go down, but Renda caught her and held her against the adobe.

"I'll bust your face wide open. Honest to God I'll fix you so no man'll look at you as long as you live."

Lizann's eyes opened. She breathed in and out slowly, painfully, and said, "Let me sit down . . . I'll tell you."

"You're stalling."

"Let me sit down—"

Renda held her against the wall. "How're you going to do it?"

"Willis wrote a letter. He mailed it from Fuegos."

"You're lying!"

"I swear it's the truth!"

Renda went back a half step and drove his fist against her cheek.

"I'll kill you! You understand that!" He moved against her before she could slide to the floor. Close to her face he said, "One more will fix you. One more and even Willis won't know you." Her head hung forward resting on his shoulder. He could feel her breathing against him, but she made no sign that she had heard.

"All right," Renda said. His left hand held her against the wall as he stepped back.

Lizann raised her head. The side of her face was deep red, her cheekbone was skinned and a thin line of blood showed at the corner of her eye. Her eyes remained closed as she said, "I wrote the letter."

"You're lying!"

"I did!"

"How could you mail it?"

"I gave it to that girl from the station." That was it. It was forming in her mind now—something to make him leave, something to give her time—but the pain made it difficult to think and she knew she had to be careful. You gave it to the girl, she thought hurriedly. But she hasn't mailed it yet. He must think he can still get it. But get him out—for God's sake get him out!

"When did you give it to her?"

Lizann opened her eyes slowly. "She was here just before you came. A few minutes before."

"Nobody passed me. Not a soul."

"Then she came the other way. I don't know . . . but I gave it to her."

"Lizzy, if you're lying to me—"

"I swear it!"

Suddenly Renda turned from her. There was the sound of a horse outside. He waited. "Stay where you are," he said then and went out into the front room. The moment he reached the doorway he saw that his horse was gone. He ran out, hearing the running hoofbeats now—two horses, one of them his, both moving through the open gate, then swinging south toward the wagon road.

"Karla!" Renda cupped his hands to his mouth and shouted after her. She did not look back, but he saw her release his horse before she disappeared over a low-swelling rise.

Lizann stood in the doorway to the bedroom. "What did you say? You called something."

"Karla . . . she was still here."

"You're sure?"

"Listening to us all the time," Renda said. "Else she wouldn't be running now."

Lizann stared at him.

"Now I'll have to go after her," Renda said. He looked at Lizann again. "I would've sworn you were lying. You're lucky she was still around. You know I just might have killed you."

Lizann nodded slowly. She did not trust herself to speak.

FIFTEEN

They had come down the wagon-road slope keeping in line with the windowless north side of the stage station and now, from the willows, they looked across the open yard to the front of the adobe.

"One horse in the shed," Manring said.

Bowen was studying it. From this angle they could see only the hindquarters and saddle. "It could be Willis Favley's dun," Bowen said. Karla wouldn't be back yet, he thought. That left her father and whoever owned the dun. That you're sure of, he thought.

"It could be," Manring said. "That'd be something if he was inside."

Bowen's hand went into the front of his shirt. "We're about to find out," he said. As he pulled Lizann's revolver he saw the look of surprise come over Manring's bearded face.

"Where'd you get that?"

"I told you, Earl, we didn't need you as much as you thought." Bowen turned and as Manring continued to stare at him, moved out from the willows.

He started to hurry across the open yard, then thought: Take your time. He slowed to a walk, keeping his eyes on the door, but not going directly for it. He reached the corner of the building, hesitated, then moved along the front of the adobe, past the two windows, to the screen door. He opened it, felt it open wider as Manring took it, and brought up the revolver as he stepped into the room.

At the far end, behind the bar, John Demery looked up. As he did, as the astonishment came over his face, Willis Falvey glanced around, then turned suddenly, pressing his back to the bar.

Bowen said. "Who else is here?" moving toward them.

Demery shook his head. "Nobody else. Karla—" he stopped. "You broke out!"

Bowen motioned with the revolver. "Come around to this side." He glanced at Manring. "Look out back."

Manring was staring at Falvey. "I got to talk to little Willis." He walked toward him, ignoring Bowen.

Falvey pressed against the bar. "I never did anything to you."

"Leave him alone," Bowen said.

Falvey looked toward Bowen. "I don't even know his name. How could I have done anything to him?"

Close to him Manring said, "You were there, boy. That's enough."

Bowen stepped toward them. "Get away from him, Earl."

Falvey's face was flushed; he'd had a lot of whisky, Bowen judged, but not enough to hide his open-eyed, lip-biting expression of fear.

"I don't care if you run away," Falvey said. "More power to you. Ask John here, I was telling him . . . I don't care anymore what goes on at that place."

"He doesn't care," Demery said. "But not enough to pull out."

Falvey turned on him. "Why should I? I do my job! What Frank does is none of my business!" He caught himself then. "You don't even know what you're talking about."

"You're doing the talking," Demery said. "Maybe I don't know everything; but living within six miles of that place, and watching you, I know enough."

Abruptly, Manring pulled Falvey around by his coat lapels. "Willis, are you packing a gun?"

Falvey shook his head emphatically. "It's on my saddle. Gun and holster both hanging on the saddle."

Manning released him, stepping back. "Let's see."

Falvey's hands went to his coat. He unbuttoned it and was holding it open when Manring's fist drove into his face. Head and shoulders snapped back and as his knees buckled Manring hit him again.

"Leave him alone!" Bowen was on Manring pushing him away and Demery caught Falvey before he could fall.

Manring stepped back, looking at Bowen now. "You're a real do-gooder, aren't you?"

"Earl, get out of here. Take a look out back; then bring the dun around and saddle another horse."

"So you're bossing," Manring said mildly.

Bowen nodded. "Now you're sure of it."

"That's a lot of order giving," Manring said, "for a man who's still got numbers on his pants."

Bowen moved the revolver toward him. "You're on a poor end for arguing about it, Earl." He held the revolver on him until Manring turned and went out through the kitchen.

To Falvey, Bowen said, "You'd better sit down."

Falvey shook his head. "I'm all right." He took out a handkerchief to wipe the blood from his mouth, then turned to the bar and drank down the whisky still in his glass.

Demery watched Bowen move to one of the front windows. "You didn't see Karla," he said. "You couldn't have."

Looking out across the yard to the willows Bowen said, "I saw her. She passed us just before . . . just before we ran off."

"I mean," Demery said, "you didn't *talk* to her."

Bowen looked at him now. "She wanted to tell me something, but Brazil was there." It seemed a long time ago and he had almost forgotten it.

"Well, it doesn't matter now," Demery said.

"What doesn't?"

"Man, you got a new trial coming up. New evidence, new trial, new everything!"

"What—"

"You heard me right—a new trial! With about an eighty per cent chance of going free. But you have to break out and ruin any chance you ever had!"

Bowen stared at him. "How do you know?"

"We heard from Lyall Martz."

"Karla didn't tell me anything about a new trial! How was I to know—"

"She told you about the lawyer!"

"That was talk."

"Talk!" Demery said hotly. "Those two have been working for you for a month—Karla pleading at Lyall and Lyall pulling more strings than a four-team driver. And all the time you're thinking how to do it the hard way. You couldn't wait. Got to bust out with your bare hands as if that would prove something." Demery moved around the end of the bar. He poured whisky into a glass and pushed it at Bowen. "Have a drink."

Bowen exhaled slowly. He raised the glass and drank off the whisky. He tried to smile then. "I guess my timing's poor."

"I guess it is," Demery said. He hesitated before adding, "But maybe not so poor to be too late."

"What do you mean?"

Demery looked at Falvey. "Willis, if this man gives himself up, will you look after him, be responsible for him till a marshal comes from Prescott?"

Falvey hesitated. "I don't see how I could."

"You could stay right here. We'll lock him in a room and you could stand right there at the bar till the Prescott man comes."

"I don't have the authority—"

"Damn it, take the authority!"

Falvey shook his head. "It's out of my jurisdiction."

"Willis, the man just saved you from getting your head beat in!"

"I'm sorry—"

Demery shook his head. "He's sorry."

Bowen placed his elbows on the bar, leaning toward Demery. "What'd the lawyer find out, Mr. Demery?"

"All the things that should've come out at the trial," the station agent said. "Lyall found the man who'd forged the cattleman's name on the bill of sale."

"Then Earl didn't do it."

"No," Demery said. "He didn't do it. He paid to have it done."

"You're sure."

"Of course I'm sure. This forger's name is Roy Avery. He confessed to his part and told everything he knew."

Bowen shook his head. "I never heard of him."

"Avery says he never heard of you either," Demery said. "He signed a statement that it was his understanding Manring was in it alone. He said you must've been hired just as a hand."

"How'd the lawyer get Avery to make the statement?" asked Bowen.

"Lyall's full of tricks," Demery said. "But he might've just held a gun on him for all I know."

"I'm obliged to him."

"You sure as hell are." Demery paused before saying, "That's some partner you've got. Takes you to jail with him."

"I don't call him a partner."

"But you break out together."

"That's a long story."

"I bet it is."

"Listen," Bowen said. "till Karla started this, Earl was innocent as far as I knew. I was mad because he got me into it, but after a while I thought: If you have to live with him then you might as well make the best of it. I never cared for his ways, but I never had cause to doubt him till Karla talked to the lawyer."

"But after she talked to him," Demery said, "and told you about it, you still teamed with him to break out."

"When you're behind the fence," Bowen said, "you don't think the same as when you're outside. A chance comes to run, you take it—even if you have doubts about the man you're running with."

"But no doubts now?"

"I guess not."

Demery said. "I still don't know why he didn't clear you at the trial. He didn't gain anything by your going to prison."

Bowen shook his head. "I don't know either. But we're going to find out."

"Knowing won't do you any good," Demery said, "unless you get out of here before Renda comes."

"No, Mr. Demery, I don't think I'll leave now."

"Frank won't accept this lawyer thing. He'll think up an excuse to shoot you."

"I'll take a chance."

"What about the Mimbres?"

"Damn—everything at once."

"You got a lot to think about."

"But you take the important one first, don't you?"

"That's what they say."

"And that's Earl. Earl's not leaving either."

As Bowen said this, he heard the back screen door slam and he stepped around the end of the bar to be facing the doorway. Lizann's revolver was in front of him on the bar. Manring's steps sounded from the kitchen, then he was in the doorway, standing hip-cocked and wearing Willis Falvey's Colt.

"You coming?"

"We're not going anywhere, Earl."

"What's that supposed to mean?"

Get to it, Bowen thought, and he said, "Your friend Avery made a statement."

Manring straightened slowly, letting his hands slide from his hips. "Are you talking to me?"

"You know I am."

"I don't know any Avery. Avery what?"

"You'll meet him again at the trial."

"Somebody's been fooling you, boy." Manring's eyes went to Demery. "What's he been making up?"

Bowen raised his elbows to the bar. "Unstrap the gun, Earl, and we won't have to talk so much."

"What's he been telling you?"

"I already said it. Avery made a statement and there's going to be a new trial. You're going to be there to tell it in your own words."

Manring shook his head. "Corey, a man can talk you into just about anything, can't he?"

"I guess he can."

"A real honest-to-God do-gooder."

"You better start unbuckling the belt."

"Corey, don't you see what's he's done?" Manring shook his head again and a faint smile showed in his beard. "He's made up that story to stall us. He figured how to get to you right away and made up this story about a new trial. We already had one. They don't try a man twice. Don't you know that? A man can't be tried twice for the same crime. That's a *law*."

Demery said, "There's a pile of poor reasoning going on in this room."

Manring's hands moved to his hips again as he glanced at Demery. "If I was in your shoes I'd quit pushing it."

Watch him, Bowen thought. Every move. Briefly his eyes dropped to the revolver on the bar. Looking up again, its position was in his mind and he knew where his hand would go if it had to.

"Corey," Manring said. "There's a reward for helping bring back escaped convicts. That's what the old man is thinking about. It's worth making up a story for."

"Earl, why didn't you tell at the trial I was innocent?"

"I did! We both were."

"You know what I mean."

Manring shook his head wearily. "If you're going to keep talking like that, I'm going on by myself."

"You're not going anywhere."

Manring paused, staring at Bowen. "I'm walking out, Corey. If you want to stop me, you'll have to shoot me in the back."

Bowen said nothing.

"Corey, I don't have any fight against you. Even right now." Manring's voice was quiet and seemed edged with disappointment. "But I can't stand here and listen to any more. If you want to stay, all right. Then we'll part company right now."

His eyes dropped and he turned to walk through the doorway, but he stopped in the middle of his stride with the unmistakable sound of a hammer being cocked—a thin, metallic *click,* and after that, silence.

Facing the doorway, Manring didn't move. Then, slowly, in the silence, he seemed to relax and he said, "All right, Corey." He turned carefully, then shook his head seeing the revolver leveled at him. "Now what're you doing that for?" He started toward Bowen. "Put the gun down, Corey. We'll talk it over—get everything out in the open."

"Unfasten the gun belt," Bowen said. "Let it drop."

Manring came on. Reaching the bar, he said, "For a minute there, Corey, you scared hell out of me. I almost thought you were going to shoot." His left hand brought the whisky bottle toward him and he glanced at Bowen. "You want one?"

Bowen shook his head. *His hand on the bottle*—he was thinking it, expecting what was to happen, the next moment going to his left away from the end of the bar as Manring's hand suddenly swept the whisky bottle at him, With the sound of it smashing against the wall, Manring's hand was drawing the Colt, clearing it from the holster as he pushed himself away from the bar, seeing Bowen with a hand and a knee on the floor, and at that moment Bowen fired. It was over as suddenly as it had started.

Manring dropped the Colt as he went down and rolled to his side, his hands clutched tightly to his right thigh.

Demery moved toward him, glancing at Bowen. "You're low today."

Bowen nodded. "I don't want Earl to miss the trial on my account."

They carried Manring into Demery's bedroom and placed him on the bed. Bowen moved to the doorway in line with the front windows and stood there as Demery bound Manring's leg to stop the bleeding.

"He's lucky," Demery said, "A bigger gun would've busted it."

"What about moving him?" Bowen said. "Can he travel?"

"I don't see why not," Demery said, "I'll take you to Fuegos in the wagon. Let the doctor look at him, then board the stage. We'll give Earl a stick to bite on for the bumps."

Bowen moved closer to the bed. "You hear that, Earl? You're going to trial."

Manring stared at the ceiling and said nothing.

"Earl, why didn't you tell them I was innocent?"

Manring looked at him then. "You must be awful lucky to get by as dumb as you are."

"You didn't gain by it," Bowen said. "Once you were sentenced, why didn't you explain how it was?"

"What's the difference?" Manring said. "You'd still be here."

"Is that the only reason—because they wouldn't believe you even if you told?"

"There's a real dumb do-gooder for you," Manring said. His expression changed to anger. "You forget that night before the trial!"

Puzzled, Bowen said, "In the jail cell?"

"In the cell—when you tried to beat my head in!"

"You let me get sent to Yuma for that?"

"Listen to him," Manring said. "You got what you drawed, boy. Thinking you're so damn better than anybody else—dumb as you are—you deserved to get sent away."

"Earl, that doesn't make sense."

"Well, think about it a while. In your case it takes longer to sink in."

Demery said, "I'd have aimed higher, Corey. About two feet up and a little to the left."

Manring glared at him. "You and your mouth can go to hell."

Bowen turned as Falvey appeared in the doorway. "Somebody's coming," Falvey said, and as he did they could hear hoofbeats in the yard.

Bowen moved past him, going to a front window. He saw her then, already dismounting, and heard Demery say, "It's Karla," going out the door, the screen slamming behind him. Through the window he saw Karla running to her father. She was telling him something, but he could hear only a few of her words: Renda . . . and Lizann Falvey . . . and Mimbres. Something about Mimbres.

He could hear their steps, the screen door opening and Karla's voice clearly now, though she was out of breath and spoke hurriedly—

"They're up on the hill—at least five or six, but I'm not sure because I came on them unexpectedly. They were all dismounted and I recognized the head one. He was there. The one who wears the hat—"

She saw Bowen then.

SIXTEEN

From the pines that crested the hill, Salvaje watched Karla Demery ride into the willows, saw her come out the other side and continue on at the same running pace across the yard. As she dismounted, a man came out of the adobe and she went to him.

The woman cannot help him, Salvaje thought in English. She will tell we are here, but what more could she do than that? And it matters little. Sooner or later he would come out and find out for himself.

He thought of Bowen as he would of another Apache. He thought of him as a man who considered carefully before he acted. A man who did not underestimate his opponent. And regarding Bowen this way, Salvaje had changed his own tactics.

Instead of sending one tracker to the station to signal the escaped man's direction, Salvaje had followed the two men-running tracks himself all the way to these pines which overlooked the station. Four men remained with him. Another five were positioned in the trees which faced the corral behind the adobe.

Perhaps they could rush the adobe and take the two men by surprise. Perhaps the two men already knew they were here, even before the woman came. And perhaps they still had sticks that exploded. There were many perhapses and one had to think carefully to outwit an opponent.

Often he thought of the time Bowen, alone, had fought his men in the meadow and he held him in high regard.

This Bowen was a good opponent, but he seemed to not want to cause injury and this put him at a disadvantage. The first time he escaped, he shot at horses, but not at men. And throwing the exploding sticks it seemed he wanted to keep them from following, to warn them; but not to injure or kill.

It was unfortunate that a man should be born with that feeling; especially a man of this one's ability. But it was also unfortunate one had to fight against him. He made it a good fight, but it would be better to be with him than against him. This man who took tulapai with Zele and Pindah.

But let him make the first move now. Watch this man. Perhaps one might even learn something from him. But if one did learn something—against whom would you use it? The good days were long past.

He is taking a long time, Salvaje continued to think. That could mean he is planning something worthwhile. Or perhaps the man who lives there shot him—though the sound might not have been that of a gun. Or perhaps he is afraid. No. That one could be afraid, but he would not show it by hiding.

A quarter of an hour had passed since the woman had gone down the slope. Then, as Salvaje watched the adobe, the screen door opened and a man stepped out. Salvaje rose.

He watched the man walk out a few strides, then stop, then raise his hat and wave it in the air in a slow come-forward signal. The man wore convict clothes and after only a moment of watching him Salvaje was sure that it was Bowen.

Now it begins. He wants to talk and he holds his arms up to show he is unarmed. Or he is giving himself up? No. He watched Bowen walk toward the willows.

All right, we talk. Salvaje motioned to one of his men and the two Mimbres walked down the slope side by side. They carried their Springfields and did not take their eyes from the figure of the man now standing in the deep shade of the willows. When he was almost to the trees, Salvaje motioned his man to stop and he went on alone.

Bowen stood waiting. He watched the Mimbreño part the hanging willow branches entering the shade, then stop directly across the narrow creek from him.

"You come armed," Bowen said.

"I am under no truce," the Mimbreño said. "Perhaps you should have arms yourself."

"I came to speak as a friend."

"Let me tell you something first," Salvaje said, speaking clearly, carefully. "If you beg to go free, I will shoot you before you can turn away."

"I didn't come to beg," Bowen said. "I'm going to tell you two things. If there is anything you don't understand, I ask you to take my word that it's the truth. If you don't, there's nothing I can do about it. When I'm through, it's up to you to decide what you want to do. You understand that?"

Salvaje nodded.

Quickly then, but explaining it as simply as he could, Bowen told the Mimbreño how he had been tried once for a crime he had not committed and now he was to be tried again. Briefly he explained Karla's part. Then Manring's, and what Manring had tried to do in the adobe—final proof that he was guilty.

But, Bowen explained, his own innocence would mean nothing if Renda returned him to the camp. Renda could even kill him on the way and report that he had tried to escape. He must remain free long enough to appear in court again. That was the important thing. If Salvaje did not believe this he could ask the girl in the house. She acted fairly, for hadn't Salvaje taken two of her horses yet she had not reported him?

Salvaje stared at Bowen. "But the man who is innocent kills two men in his escape."

"That was not my doing," Bowen said. "The one called Pryde tried to trap Brazil and he was killed himself."

"Will the men of the trial believe that?"

Bowen hesitated. "I don't know. I can only tell them how it happened."

"And what is the second thing?" Salvaje asked.

"The girl in the house who rode past you," Bowen said. "She had just left the camp where she saw Renda beating Falvey's woman." Bowen paused. "This is hard to explain; you see, Renda's been doing things against the law. The woman knew about it and wanted to leave, but he wouldn't let her. The girl, Karla, believes Renda is on his way here. Renda thinks the girl has a letter that will prove the unlawful things he has done." Bowen paused again. "You see, Falvey's woman, in order to get rid of him, told him the girl had been there earlier and had taken the letter with her. This was not true. As I said, it was only to make him leave. But the girl did happen to be there as they spoke. Renda saw her ride away and he believed she did have a letter."

Bowen shook his head. "Does that make sense?"

"Finish," Salvaje said.

"All right—Willis Falvey is in the house now. If he will report Renda, Renda will go to prison or even hang. Falvey is afraid of Renda, but now maybe he will report him."

"And if Renda is taken now," Salvaje said, "you will not go back to Five Shadows."

"That's right."

"And Renda will be finished."

"If we can prove what he's been doing."

"What would you have me do?" Salvaje asked.

Momentarily Bowen smiled. He said then, "Nothing."

"Nothing?"

"We have to handle this ourselves," Bowen said. "If you went against him you'd be liable for a court-martial; because nothing's been proved against him yet. But if you'll take your men away and let us handle it . . . well, I'll be grateful. It's up to you."

"You are sure of yourself," the Mimbreño said. "Or you wouldn't have come out here."

Bowen nodded. "I don't know why—I just had a feeling you'd agree."

"Perhaps we drink tulapai sometime."

Bowen nodded again. "Perhaps."

"I would like to see him finished," Salvaje said thoughtfully. "I don't understand everything, but I would like to see that happen."

"Then you'll take your men away?"

Salvaje nodded solemnly. "But wherever you are, we will be watching." He turned abruptly and moved up the slope.

Bowen walked back to the adobe. Demery waited for him in the doorway. "He's agreed," Bowen told him.

"Just like that." Demery held the door open.

Bowen paused. "You ever talk to a man who looks at you the way he does? He doesn't understand it all, but if you tried to lie he'd know it. I don't know how, but he would." Bowen stepped inside and saw Falvey standing at the bar. "What did Willis say?"

Demery shook his head. "He won't budge."

"He heard Karla tell it. What's the matter with him?"

"He says he doesn't believe us. Says we're trying to trick him into going against Renda."

Bowen saw Karla come out of Manring's room. Her eyes met his briefly, then looked away as she went into the kitchen. Bowen said quickly, "You'd think Willis'd want to go see for himself."

"That would be admitting he believes us," Demery said. "He doesn't even want to think about it. But if he moved away from that bar he'd have to."

"I don't know," Bowen said wearily. "Maybe I ought to just give myself up."

"You do," Demery told him, "and you'll never get to Prescott. You know that. This is twice you've made a fool of him. Frank will either think up a way to kill you or else bury you under so many charges nobody could get you out . . . The way I see it, your only chance is to get Renda before the authorities."

"If we just took him," Bowen said, "what would happen?"

"Hand him over without proof? For the same reason I didn't report some letters Frank destroyed. Letters that didn't belong to him. It would be our word against his." Demery said then, "We don't even know if he's coming."

"He'll come," Bowen said.

"He's taking his sweet time."

"Word must have reached him about the break."

"Then he won't be alone."

"His guards still have thirty men to watch. He's coming on personal business."

"If he comes."

"He'll come," Bowen said again. "If he thinks there's a letter here for Prescott, he'll come, break or no break. This is more important to him than two men running away. That's Salvaje's worry."

"He doesn't know Willis is here," Demery said. "Maybe we can make something out of that. Let's think about it."

Bowen nodded. "And the letter that's supposed to be here."

Demery nodded thoughtfully. He went to the roll-top desk, came back with an envelope and handed it to Bowen. "If you could hold a gun on Renda and tell him you've got the letter—"

"Then what?"

"I don't know. It was just a thought."

Bowen stuffed the envelope into his left pants pocket. "The holding the gun on him sounds all right . . . Well, we better be ready." He walked to the bar, picked up the Colt Manring had dropped and pushed it into his waist. As he did, Falvey turned from the bar. "Where did you get that gun?"

Bowen looked up questioningly. "Earl had it."

"I mean the one you used on him."

"Oh—" Bowen hesitated. "I got it out of your wife's saddlebag this morning." He watched Falvey turn to the bar again. "Frank will be here soon. You better get hold of yourself."

Falvey raised his glass. "I have no part in this."

"You can wash your hands all you want," Bowen said. "But if there's a hearing, you'll be dragged into it."

"I'll tell the authorities the same thing I'm telling you."

"They'll check your books," Bowen said. "Any man who can count will see what you've been up to."

Falvey came around as Bowen spoke. "What do you know about my books?"

"What I just said's enough."

"You don't know what you're talking about. My books are in order. There isn't a man who can prove otherwise."

"What about your wife?"

"Leave her out of it."

"Don't you want to see how she is?"

"If you think I believe that girl's story, you're out of your mind."

"Karla wouldn't lie."

"Then call it something else."

"I think you're afraid to go to your wife. When you see what's happened you'll have to do something. But you don't know what."

"Are you concerned over her?"

"Anybody would be."

Falvey turned from the bar. "The reason I ask is because she doesn't own saddlebags."

"What?"

"That you could have taken her revolver from."

"All right," Bowen said quietly. "I saw her one day in the stable and talked her into letting me have it."

"That easily?"

"It sounds simpler when you tell it."

"How would giving you a gun help her—did she say?"

Bowen shook his head. "Maybe she thought I'd use it on Renda. I don't know."

"Or on me," Falvey said. He turned back to the bar.

"Mr. Falvey, you know better than that."

"Get away from me!"

You must be easy to read, Bowen thought, remembering Salvaje but now thinking of Falvey. He walked to one of the front windows and leaned against the side frame as he looked out. No, not this time, he thought. This time you made a mistake and were caught at it and it didn't matter what your face told. He's not dumb. He knows what's going on . . . but you have to feel sorry for him, don't you?

How would you like to have a wife who wanted you killed? And you suspected it. If you didn't suspect it, at least you wouldn't put it past her. So why should he be concerned about her? You say that doesn't happen to people, but you wake up one morning and it's happening to you. No wonder he drinks. He's got a lot to drink about.

He began to think of Karla then—the look on her face as she came in and saw him in the room, almost going to him, but remembering and realizing he shouldn't be there and holding herself back. Was that it? Her father explained about the escape, but Karla didn't look at Bowen as he did, nor after, when she told about Renda and Lizann.

At first, Bowen believed she was angry—just as her father had been, because he had escaped instead of waited. Then he realized that hers was not anger at all, but indifference. At least a posed indifference. And finally he understood—remembering the look on her face the morning she came into Lizann Falvey's quarters and found him there. She had seen the gun, and she had seen Lizann's hands on his shoulders.

He felt someone behind him and as he turned, Karla said, "Would you like coffee?"

"Fine . . . I was just thinking about you."

"I'll bring you a cup." She started to turn away.

"Karla—" His hand touched her arm, but came away as she looked up at him again. "We never have much time to talk, do we?"

"I guess not."

"We ought to have about a week with nothing else to do but talk, to get caught up with each other." He paused. "Karla . . . I'm grateful for what you've done. I've thought about it and thought about it, but I don't know how to say it."

"Is that why you escaped, to come thank us?"

Bowen frowned. "I tried to explain that to your father." He spoke earnestly, keeping his voice low. "You can feel you've done right, but when you explain it, it doesn't sound like good sense."

Karla's eyes raised to his. "I'm sorry. I shouldn't have said that. You had no reason to believe a new trial would come through."

"I was hopeful. But then this chance came along."

"If only I could have gotten to you before—"

"Well, it's done now."

"The morning you were with Lizann"—Karla's eyes moved to the window—"I wanted to tell you about it then. But you were there and then gone. I asked Lizann to tell you we'd found out something and not to use the gun." She paused. "No . . . I even told her Mr. Martz had filed a motion for a new trial!"

Bowen shook his head. "She didn't tell me anything about it. Listen . . . that's something else. She had good reason not to tell me." He glanced toward Falvey at the bar and brought Karla closer to him. "I've got something on my mind and I don't know what to do about it. Lizann didn't just give me that gun for my sake." He glanced toward the bar again, then back to Karla. "She wanted me to use it on Willis."

Karla's lips parted. But for a moment she stared, saying nothing. "You're sure?"

"She said I could do anything I wanted with it—if I used it on Willis first."

"It's hard to believe a woman—"

"Listen, I was standing right in front of her and I had trouble believing it."

"But you took the gun," Karla said.

"Of course I took it. I wanted to get *out*. I would have promised to shoot President Cleveland if she'd asked me. That kind of promise doesn't mean anything."

Karla said, "Have you told Willis?"

"No. That's what's bothering me. But he saw me come in here with the gun and he even guessed how I got it."

"Maybe he thinks there's something between you and Lizann."

"I don't know. Maybe he does."

"Is there?" Karla asked hesitatingly.

"Because we were standing so close that time?"

"That would seem to suggest—"

"Karla, she wasn't taking any chances. If I didn't feel sorry for her enough to do it, then maybe she could make me like her enough to."

"I wasn't going to ask you that," Karla said. "It just came out."

He watched her eyes and the clean line of her nose and her mouth. "It's something, isn't it? We've only talked together twice before this."

Karla nodded looking up at him and was silent for a moment. "What are you going to do?"

"Now?"

She smiled. "What would you do after. If—"

"After, I was planning to visit Willcox. I've got a friend there in the mining business. He doesn't mine there, but that's where his office is and where he ships out of. He's been after me to join him for a long time. In fact, I was on my way there when I met Earl."

"That's where my mother is," Karla said. "My sisters are in school there."

"You've got sisters?"

"Two younger ones."

"I could look them up."

"It isn't far. I go down every once in a while."

"We could sure get to know each other, couldn't we?"

"But," Karla said, "it seems a long way off."

"Now we're back," Bowen said.

Karla smiled faintly. "I'm glad we did that." She paused. "Are you going to tell Willis?"

"I don't want to. Even if he suspects her, *knowing* it is something else."

"Maybe she's sorry now."

"Maybe she is. I don't know."

"You'd think they would have parted before this."

"Renda wouldn't let them."

"What if Willis still likes her?" Karla said.

"That'd be something."

"Corey . . . don't tell him. If he already suspects her, he must be on his guard—"

"Or else he doesn't care."

"At least wait and see how this comes out. If there's a hearing, then you know she'll take the opportunity to leave him."

"But if Renda wins there won't be a hearing and everybody'll be right back where they started."

"Don't let him win," Karla said earnestly.

"Karla, I keep going over it and going over it—I can't just use a gun on him. If I killed him I'd be back in jail—or worse—and

Willis wouldn't have to say a word. If we hold Renda and force a hearing, we can't prove anything unless Willis testifies."

"But Lizann would," Karla said.

"You can't count on her. She might keep still, afraid the plan to kill Willis would come out. Or she might just run off."

Karla nodded. "So Willis is the only hope."

"And he knows he'll go to jail if he speaks up."

"Corey . . . what will you do when he comes?"

"I wish I knew."

There was silence before Karla said, "He doesn't know Willis is here. Every other time Willis has gone to Fuegos. Sometimes he stops for a drink on the way. But this time he stayed . . . and Renda couldn't know that."

"Your father mentioned it. I don't know how it can help us—" Bowen stopped. "Unless—"

"Unless," Karla said eagerly, "you can make him tell what he did to Lizann *in front of Willis*! He won't believe it from us—"

"He doesn't want to believe it," Bowen said.

"But he'd have to believe Renda. And in front of all of us we'd have to do something—that's what I mean!"

"If I was Willis I wouldn't much care."

"But you're not Willis! He said he didn't *believe* us . . . not he didn't *care*. That's why I'd be willing to bet anything he still likes her."

"You sure have a feeling about people."

"I was right about you, wasn't I?"

"You and that Mimbre would get along fine."

Karla frowned, but she ignored this and said, "Is it worth a try or isn't it?"

"I suppose it is," Bowen said slowly. Then, "Tell your father to keep Willis out of sight when Frank comes, but close enough to hear." Bowen shook his head. "I don't even know what I'm going to say. Your father gave me an envelope to pass off as the one Frank's looking for, but I don't know how I'd work that. I've got all kinds of tricks and I don't know how I'm going to spring any of them."

"You could pretend to make a deal with him," Karla said eagerly. "Renda gets the letter if he lets you go. At least you'd have a chance of getting away from here."

Bowen shrugged. "I don't know."

Karla smiled up at him. "You'll think of something." Turning away she said, "I'll bring your coffee now."

But within thirty seconds the coffee was forgotten and there was no time to think of what he would say. As Bowen looked out across the yard again, he saw Frank Renda ride out of the willows.

SEVENTEEN

Bowen drew the Colt from his belt, pressing himself against the wall next to the window. He looked across the room seeing Karla and her father in the kitchen, then waited until Demery turned from her and started into the front room.

"He's here," Bowen said. He nodded toward Falvey, saw Falvey turn from the bar as Demery started for him, then Bowen's gaze returned to the window.

Renda came at a walk, moving easily with the motion of the big chestnut. The shotgun was across his lap and his eyes remained on the adobe as he approached.

Behind him, Bowen heard Falvey's voice. A protest. Then steps going into the kitchen. Bowen moved three steps along the wall to the next window as Renda drew closer. He watched Renda come to a stop five or six yards out from the door. Now he'll call, Bowen thought.

But there was no call. Renda waited, apparently listening, then reined the chestnut to the left and started along the front of the open shed.

Bowen pressed close to the window, then came away from it suddenly. He saw Karla in the kitchen doorway, motioned to her and moved quietly to meet her. "He's going around back. Get Willis's horse out of sight—quick!"

He stepped to the window again, saw Renda nearing the end of the shed, made sure he was turning the corner, then hurried to the kitchen. Karla was already outside. Demery, standing behind Falvey who was seated at the table, raised his eyes inquiringly.

"He's coming around," Bowen said.

"What's Karla doing?"

"She's all right."

Bowen moved to the wooden sink and pressed against the drainboard to look out the window. He saw Karla holding the dun close to the bit, her left hand on its nose, leading it along the stable shed that extended out from the house and almost to the corral. She reached the end of the shed and rounded it a moment before Renda came into the yard.

As Renda looked toward the house, Bowen stepped away from the window. Then, hearing the horse's hoofs again, he moved along the wall to the door and looked out, edging past the side frame.

The chestnut was broadside to him, facing the shed, ten yards out and directly in line with the door. Renda sat motionless, half turned from Bowen and staring off toward the end of the shed. His right hand was on the shotgun and he seemed to be listening.

He'd have to come around to use it, Bowen thought. Or turn it over and shoot left-handed.

Bowen eased open the screen door and stepped outside. Instantly the sunlight struck him and he wanted to pull his hat brim closer to his eyes, but he hesitated with the thought of his hand momentarily in front of his face. Without thinking the word fear he realized it was fear that made him hesitate, and now, deliberately, he pulled the straw brim straight over his eyes, telling himself to relax and get hold of himself, before he brought up the Colt, cocking it as he did.

"Frank—"

Renda's body twisted in the saddle. Seeing Bowen, his face showed surprise, but it was momentary and only in his eyes. He stared at Bowen intently, saying nothing, and Bowen could almost read what was passing through his mind.

"Don't even think about it," Bowen warned. "You wouldn't get it halfway around."

Renda seemed to relax. "You'll never learn, will you? Put the gun down and tell Earl to come out."

"Earl's not in this."

"He's already gone?"

Bowen shook his head. "But he's out of it. This is just between you and me."

"Listen, you're in enough trouble. Put the gun down." Renda waited. The Colt remained leveled at him. "Corey, you're going to strain yourself standing like that." Renda's left heel nudged the chestnut and its forelegs side-stepped toward the porch.

"Hold it!"

Renda was almost facing Bowen now. He smiled, saying, "You got poor nerves, Corey."

"Let the shotgun drop and they'll be all right."

"What if it went off?"

"So will this if it does."

"You won't get more than a mile," Renda said. "You know that. The Mimbres'll be all over you."

"Are you sure?"

Renda shrugged. "You ought to know it better than I do."

"Let go of the shotgun, Frank."

"If I don't what'll you do, shoot me?"

"I might have to."

"Use your head. You got, what—six years to serve. You'd trade that for a rope?"

Bowen hesitated. Something was forming in his mind, but he was not yet sure if it could be developed. He said then, "What would you trade to stay alive?"

"I don't see where I have to trade anything."

Now, Bowen thought. "What about the letter you came for?"

Renda grinned. "Little Karla's been telling you things."

"Look at it this way," Bowen said. "Would you give your life to try to get the letter?"

For a moment Renda was silent and he nodded thoughtfully. "I've been figuring you all wrong, haven't I?"

"You see what it comes to?" Bowen said carefully.

Renda shrugged. "But I'm not even sure Karla's got the letter."

"You wouldn't be here if you weren't."

"The thing is," Renda said slowly. "I don't see you come out smelling any better than you went in. What do you get out of it?"

"I get what you trade for the letter."

"So we're making a deal." Renda grinned. "I must be a little slow this morning."

Bowen nodded. "But now everything's clear."

"Where's the letter now?"

Bowen's hand touched his pocket. "Right here."

"Let's see it."

Bowen's eyes remained on Renda as his hand went to his pocket and brought out the envelope Demery had given him. He glanced at it and saw it was addressed to Demery. "Frank, it says: to the District Supervisor, Bureau of"—Bowen looked up. "I can't read all of Lizann's writing." Then, glancing at the envelope again, "Department of the Interior, Prescott, Arizona Territory . . . That mean anything to you?"

"I don't know if it does," Renda answered. "I haven't read it. Have you?"

"I don't have to—I've been living with you."

Renda leaned forward. "Let's see it."

"Not till we talk about a swap."

Renda was silent. "How about this?" he said then. "You give me the letter and I give you a ten-minute start. Take a horse and keep your gun."

Bowen smiled faintly. "You believe in starting low."

"You want a half hour?"

Get somewhere, Bowen thought, but said, still not sure where this would lead. "What about the Mimbres?"

"That's your problem."

Bowen shook his head. "They're yours now."

"All right . . . I'll call them off."

"How?"

"Ride ahead—tell them to let you through."

"Even if I trusted you, I wouldn't go for that."

"You're hard to please." Renda paused, then said, "Here's another way. You come back to the camp and we'll fix it for you to slip out at night. You'd have about a six-hour start."

"You're bidding low again," Bowen said. "The more I think about it, the more it looks like I'm only safe if I stay close to you. Even if I did get away I'd be hiding out the rest of my life . . . while you're making all that money on the road." He spoke slowly, thinking ahead of what he was saying and suddenly, there it was: a way to bring Falvey into it. A natural, part-of-the-conversation way that would arouse neither Renda's suspicion nor Falvey's—if he was listening. And Bowen thought, wanting to look around at the adobe but making himself keep his eyes on Renda: Willis, be listening!

He said then, "What I need, Frank, is a deal something like Willis Falvey's. We'd each have something on the other, and we'd get along fine."

Renda studied Bowen in silence.

"Fix me a deal like that, Frank. I get so much of your profits for not mailing the letter."

"Somebody's been talking to you," Renda said quietly.

"Maybe it was Willis," Bowen said. "Maybe he's getting tired."

"Willis knows better."

"Maybe he's so tired he's going to stand up to you."

"Where would he get the nerve?"

"He's got it, Frank. He's had enough all along to think of his wife first . . . to stay out of jail for her sake."

"You think so, huh?"

"He made a mistake getting tied to you, but once he was in, it took nerve to keep going. The wrong kind of nerve, but at least you know he's got it." Bowen paused, thinking: You hear that, Willis? "Sometimes a man will put up with anything for his wife. That's where you misjudged him."

Renda said, "You don't know as much about him as I thought."

"But now," Bowen went on, "he's tired of it. He's starting to think it would be worth going to jail for a year or two just to get it off his mind. He realizes now his wife would respect him more if he did. After that he'd be a free agent and all the Frank Rendas in the world could go to hell."

"He knows he'd get more than a jail sentence," Renda said. "I'd bust his head for him."

"Would you?" Bowen paused. He said then, slowly, clearly, "Is that what you did to Lizann?"

Renda stared at him. "Karla didn't forget anything, did she?"

"She'll probably never forget it," Bowen said, "seeing a woman beat up. Did you have a hard time?"

"She got what she asked for."

"Frank, you're a real fighter, aren't you?" A sound came from the kitchen. Bowen heard it close behind him, but he was not sure what it was. "You fight women . . . and men with their hands tied behind them."

Renda's intent expression did not change. "You're getting off the subject, aren't you?"

"We've got time," Bowen said easily. He was thinking, hurriedly: Keep him on it! "Frank, what's it like to hit a woman?"

"You're asking a lot of questions," Renda said.

"Do you let her fight back?"

This time Renda did not answer.

"Or do you get her against the wall and just keep swinging at her?"

"You're leading up to something," Renda said cautiously.

"Frank, what's Willis going to do when he finds out?"

"He'll figure he's lucky it didn't happen to him."

"You know what I'd do if I were Willis?" Bowen paused. "I'd take a pick handle to you."

"You would, huh?"

Bowen nodded. "I'd crack you ten for every one time you hit her."

Then, close behind him, not expecting it, the screen door swung open. As he heard it, Bowen moved aside, almost glancing back, but at the same moment, seeing the look of shocked surprise come over Renda's face, he knew it was Willis Falvey, just as he knew, suddenly feeling more sure of himself, that Falvey had been listening all the time. Still watching Renda, he thought: If he moves hit him in the leg. He glanced quickly to the side then. Falvey was staring up at Renda. Lizann's .25-caliber Colt in his hand.

"Frank . . . you put your filthy hands on my wife?"

Renda shifted his weight in the saddle. "Willis, I didn't know you were here."

"Answer me!"

"Listen, Willis. I'm sorry that had to happen. It was Lizann's own fault. She didn't have to get hit but she wouldn't tell me—" He stopped. "Willis, she was planning to leave you. You realize that?"

"Frank," Falvey said tonelessly. "When you're through talking I'm going to kill you."

"Use your head! She's going to leave you anyway. She don't care a damn about you."

Bowen glanced at Falvey. "Killing him isn't the way. *Testify* against him in court. He didn't just beat up your wife—men died in that place because of him, men like Chick Miller. You'll see him dead—but let a jury take care of it!"

"I'll testify," Falvey said. "But Frank won't be there to hear it."

"So you shoot him and they hang you. You think it's worth it?"

"I'd as soon that happen as go to prison," Falvey answered. "You're wasting your breath."

Renda moved uneasily in the saddle, his hands gripping the shotgun. "Willis—listen to him—he's talking sense!"

Falvey stared, "Are you through?"

"Man, stop and think for a minute!"

"You're through," Falvey murmured.

He brought up the revolver, leveling it at Renda's chest, thumbing back the hammer. It was in his mind to kill Renda and there was no persuading him otherwise—but as he pulled the trigger, Bowen slammed against him. The revolver fired wide as both of them went down, and with the report Renda was reining hard to the right, kicking the chestnut; he fired from his lap as the big mare wheeled, but the shot was hurried and ripped high through the screen door.

Falvey was up as the mare broke into a gallop angling to the left of the corral. He fired once, then again. Bowen was on one knee as he saw Renda twist in the saddle and point the shotgun back with one hand.

"Go down!"

But he called too late. Renda's second barrel exploded. He saw Falvey spin sideways as the buckshot hailed against the adobe, chipping a powdery cloud, and Falvey went down, dropping the revolver and suddenly clutching his left hip.

Then Demery was outside, lifting Falvey, holding open the shot-out screen door with his foot and dragging Falvey into the kitchen. He snapped at Bowen, glancing off at Renda, "Get him—what's the matter with you!"

"Watch," Bowen said, coming to his feet. His eyes were narrowed, his gaze following Renda as he reached the far side of the corral and rode on toward the pine-covered slope beyond.

Demery came out again. "You let him get away!"

"Watch," Bowen said again. And as their eyes followed the chestnut moving across the meadow, streaking for the dark expanse of trees, they saw it veer sharply to the right. A single file of riders had suddenly appeared, coming down out of the trees.

Renda circled, waving his shotgun in the air and the riders, the Mimbres, came after him. As he continued the wide circle, gradually coming back to the yard, another file of Mimbres rode out of the trees approximately two hundred yards farther to the right, joining the first group now and spreading out behind Renda who glanced back at them, waving them on with the shotgun, then began to rein in as he neared the corral again.

"They're backing him!" Demery hissed.

"Wait and see," Bowen said, not taking his eyes from Renda. Then asked, "Where's Karla?"

"Inside," Demery murmured. "Looking after Willis. She circled around and came in the front. Stood there biting her nails through the whole thing . . . like to got hit when Frank ripped up the door."

"What about Willis?"

"His side's scraped is all."

"Was he listening . . . before?"

"Hanging on every word you said . . . like courage being poured into him." Demery watched Renda wave the Mimbres past him. "Listen, you can't just stand there!"

Bowen said nothing, watching four of the Mimbres circle the corral to come in on the left side. The others—he counted six— Salvaje one of them, rode past Renda. They entered the yard, moving past the corral and spread out in an uneven line as they came to a halt.

Now, Bowen thought; and walked out toward them. He was halfway across the yard when Renda came through the line of Mimbres and reined in a few yards in front of them. Bowen continued toward him until less than fifteen feet separated them.

"That's far enough," Renda called. "Now drop the shooter."

Bowen held the Colt at his side, pointed at the ground. "It won't do you any good."

"Drop it!"

Bowen let it fall from his fingers.

"Now kick it out of the way."

With the side of his foot, Bowen pushed the Colt away from him.

"The deal's off." Renda grinned. He was relaxed and confident now and looked at Bowen with open amusement. "Give me the letter."

"It wouldn't do you any good even if there was one," Bowen said. "Since Willis is going to speak up against you."

Renda's eyes narrowed. "He's still alive?"

"You just scraped his hip."

"Well, I'll have a talk with Willis," Renda said easily. "I've found Willis an agreeable boy if you talk to him right." His tone changed as he snapped. "Now give me the letter!"

Bowen brought the folded envelope from his pocket. He moved close to the chestnut's right shoulder, handed the envelope to Renda and stepped back again.

Renda glanced at it, saw Demery's address and looked at Bowen again. "You just pulled twenty more days in the punishment cell."

Bowen said nothing.

Renda's gaze raised to the adobe. Demery was still at the door. "John, where's that letter your girl brought?"

Demery shook his head holding his palms up.

"I'm warning you, John—"

"He doesn't have it," Bowen said. "Nobody does."

"I can burn down the house if that's what he wants."

"There never was a letter, Frank. Lizann made it up to get rid of you. But you happened to see Karla and you believed her."

"If there's no letter," Renda said, "then why'd you try to make a deal? You think I'd have let you go without even looking at it?"

"That was leading up to something else," Bowen said. "I wasn't going anywhere."

"You sure as hell weren't."

"I didn't know how I was going to use the letter at first," Bowen said. "I just had it as an extra card. Then, somewhere along the line, it steered us to Willis."

"I'm not going to ask you again."

"Check with your men in the canyon then! They saw Karla go by *after* you left for the camp. Karla didn't even drop off the mail she had, much less pick any up."

Renda looked past Bowen toward the adobe. "We'll see."

Bowen shook his head. "You're not going in there."

"Who's going to stop me?"

"Frank, you've got a surprise coming."

"I'm getting awful sick of you," Renda said slowly.

"But you're not going in," Bowen said. "Not with Willis there."

For a moment Renda was silent. "Corey . . . I think I've had just about all I can take of you." His right hand went into his coat pocket and brought out a shell for the shotgun. He broke open the gun, still watching Bowen, and carefully inserted the shell into the right chamber.

"What you're going to do," Renda said, taking his time and seeming to enjoy what he was saying, "is make a run for it. But if you move before I give the word, these bucks will blow you apart."

Bowen watched Renda's hand move to the pocket. The hand raised then and pointed off to the far side of the corral.

"That's the way you go," Renda said. "With a ten-count start. If you can run like hell, maybe you'll almost reach the trees."

"What about the witnesses?" Bowen said. He watched Renda's hand drop to his thigh.

"Who's going to say you didn't try to run?" Renda answered. His hand moved to the pocket and brought out a shell. He glanced down at the open shotgun and started inserting the shell into the left chamber.

It was the moment Bowen was waiting for. He lunged at Renda, reaching up for him.

The shotgun snapped closed and exploded over Bowen's shoulder as he dragged Renda from the saddle, one hand on the barrel, the other gripping Renda's sleeve, twisting then, throwing his shoulder into Renda's stomach as they both went to the ground.

Renda rolled free. He started to rise, coming to one knee, swinging the shotgun in line, but he was a moment too late and as he pulled the trigger the barrel rose suddenly and fired into the air. Bowen's left hand twisted the barrel, Renda cried out, his finger caught in the trigger guard, and as he released the shotgun, Bowen's right hand slammed against the side of his face.

Renda went down, rolled again and shielded his face with his arms as he came to his knees. Then, seeing Bowen standing, holding the shotgun, not coming for him, his gaze swung to the Mimbres, to Salvaje.

"Bust him!"

Salvaje made no move.

"You hear me!" Renda screamed. "Bust him!"

Salvaje held his Springfield straight up, the stock resting on his thigh. His eyes were on Renda, but he did not move.

Renda hesitated, his chest rising and falling. His gaze moved along the line of the Mimbres, over the cloth headbands and the stone-silent stares, the slanting cartridge bandoleers and the Springfields leveled across the pommels of their saddles. All of them were watching him and only Salvaje's carbine pointed into the air.

"You hear me!" Renda screamed again. "Cut him down! Now!"

"They hear you," Bowen said.

Renda's eyes did not leave Salvaje. "What's the matter with you? I said *shoot* him!"

Then silence, and Bowen said. "There's your surprise, Frank." He watched Renda turn slowly to face him. "You were in such a rush to get back," Bowen went on, "you didn't find out if you were leading or being chased."

For a long moment Renda said nothing. "What did you tell them?" he asked finally.

"What difference does it make. You don't have your guns, you don't have any men and Willis is against you . . . Why don't you quit now?"

Renda's eyes stared from the shadow of his hatbrim, not moving from Bowen. His mustache masked the grim line of his mouth and his jaw was clenched tightly. He stared at Bowen, silent with his thoughts, and the hate came slowly into his eyes. Finally, then, he started toward Bowen, walking slowly, his head slightly down, but his eyes raised and not wavering as he came on.

Bowen held the shotgun in his right hand, the barrel pointed at the ground. "Frank, my hands aren't tied this time."

Renda came on.

"And I'm not Lizann," Bowen said.

Another two steps . . . three . . . on the next one, Renda hesitated, then rushed at Bowen. At the same moment Bowen swung the shotgun, letting it go at Renda's legs. Renda tried to dodge, bringing himself up, but the barrel cracked across his ankles and he stumbled forward.

Bowen had half turned as he threw the gun; now his body swung back and his left hand hammered against Renda's face. Renda tried to cover, bringing up his arms, but Bowen's right slammed through his guard; he tried to fight back, swinging blindly, viciously, but Bowen's right hand jabbed again and again and he was forced to cover his face. As he did, Bowen side-stepped and came in with a wide swinging left that opened Renda's guard and jolted him back off balance. Bowen followed, shifting his feet, hammering in with his right hand, and as Renda staggered back, Bowen kept with him, hooking in one hand then the other, slashing Renda across the mouth and eyes, putting almost his full weight behind each blow, until Renda dropped. He tried to rise, then fell heavily on his back. His arms were outstretched now and he didn't move.

Bowen's arms hung at his sides. The muscles in them ached and he opened and closed his hands painfully. He felt exhaustion and relief, looking down at Renda, thinking now of all that had happened over the past hour, seeing Karla and Falvey and Renda and the Mimbreños, briefly remembering words, pieces of conversations, but not seeing or thinking these things in proper order and he wasn't sure if all of it had actually happened.

He heard footsteps in the yard, someone coming out from the house, but he turned to the Mimbres first and walked toward them, to Salvaje who had dismounted.

"If we were to talk for a few days," Bowen said to him, "with tulapai between us, maybe I could tell you how I feel."

"Come to San Carlos," the Mimbreño said.

"They won't send you back," Bowen said. "Whoever comes out to take Renda's place will still want trackers."

The broad brim of Salvaje's hat moved slightly as he shook his head. "We go home. This is not like other times. I think Victorio would laugh." The Mimbre watched Bowen closely. "Do you understand that?"

Bowen's head nodded slowly. "Yes . . . I think I do."

Salvaje's eyes went to Renda. "He will be in the punishment cell until they come for him."

Demery approached. He was smiling, looking from Renda, who was still on the ground, to Bowen. "He didn't even put a hand on you!"

"Not this time," Bowen said.

"About Falvey," Demery said. "There wasn't time to tell you before . . . That was something to see. Soon as you and Frank started talking about him he got up and moved closer to the window, and after a minute he didn't seem drunk anymore, or even afraid. He just stood staring at the wall . . . I never felt so sorry for a man in all my life. There you were handing him a chance to prove himself a man and you could see him trying his damndest to work up enough courage to take it." Demery shook his head. "That's something I'll never forget." He looked toward Renda again. "And Frank not even knowing what was happening."

"I'm not sure I knew either." Bowen said. "Or know yet." He saw Karla and moved past Demery to meet her. "Is Willis all right?"

Karla smiled. "He's in bed with your friend. Propped up with a drink next to him and pen and paper on his lap. He asked for it. He said if he didn't do another thing, he was going to get it off his chest right now . . . Come see." She took his hand and as they walked off toward the house, she asked, "But what about Lizann?"

Lizann, Bowen thought wearily. You forgot Lizann. "I don't know. Maybe she's gone by now. If she is, Willis is better off without her. But maybe she's learned her lesson . . . And a few more maybes for good measure."

"You're tired," Karla said quietly.

All that he had been thinking and trying to remember was still in his mind; though less vividly now and as he walked toward the adobe, Karla close at his side and the awareness of her coming over him more strongly, more relaxingly, the pieces of conversation and the images began to dissolve: the Mimbres, Willis Falvey, the road, even Frank Renda—there was no reason to think about them now. Somehow it had happened and somehow it was over.

Only Karla remained.

LAST
STAND AT
SABER
RIVER

ONE

Paul Cable sat hunched forward at the edge of the pine shade, his boots crossed and his elbows supported on his knees. He put the field glasses to his eyes again and, four hundred yards down the slope, the two-story adobe was brought suddenly, silently before him.

This was The Store. It was Denaman's. It was a plain, tan-pink southern Arizona adobe with a wooden loading platform, but no *ramada* to hold off the sun. It was the only general supply store from Hidalgo north to Fort Buchanan; and until the outbreak of the war it had been a Hatch & Hodges swing station.

The store was familiar and it was good to see, because it meant Cable and his family were almost home. Martha was next to him, the children were close by; they were anxious to be home after two and a half years away from it. But the sight of a man Cable had never seen before—a man with one arm—had stopped them.

He stood on the loading platform facing the empty sunlight of the yard, staring at the willow trees that screened the river close beyond the adobe, his right hand on his hip, his left sleeve tucked smoothly, tightly into his waist. Above him, the faded, red-lettered *Denaman's Store* inscription extended the full width of the adobe's double doors.

Cable studied the man. There was something about him.

Perhaps because he had only one arm. No, Cable thought then, that made you think of the war, the two and a half years of it, but you felt something before you saw he had only one arm.

Then he realized it was the habit of surviving formed during two and a half years of war. The habit of not trusting any movement he could not immediately identify. The habit of not walking into anything blindly. He had learned to use patience and weigh alternatives and to be sure of a situation before he acted. As sure as he could be in his own mind.

Now Cable's glasses moved over the wind-scarred face of the adobe, following the one-armed man's gaze to the grove of willows and the river hidden beyond the hanging screen of branches.

A girl came out of the trees carrying a bucket and Cable said, "There's Luz again. Here—" He handed the glasses to his wife who was kneeling, sitting back on her legs, one hand raised to shield her eyes from the sun glare.

Martha Cable raised the glasses. After a moment she said, "It's Luz Acaso. But still it doesn't seem like Luz."

"All of a sudden she's a grown-up woman," Cable said. "She'd be eighteen now."

"No," Martha said. "It's something else. Her expression. The way she moves."

Through the glasses, the girl crossed the yard leisurely. Her eyes were lowered and did not rise until she reached the platform and started up the steps. When she looked up her face was solemn and warm brown in the sunlight. Martha remembered Luz's knowing eyes and her lips that were always softly parted, ready to smile or break into laughter. But now she wore an expression of weariness. Her eyes went to the man on the platform, then away from him quickly as he glanced at her and she passed into the store.

She's tired, or ill, Martha thought. Or afraid.

"She went inside?" Cable asked.

The glasses lowered briefly and Martha nodded. "But he's still there. Cable, for some reason I think she's afraid of him."

"Maybe." He watched Martha concentrating on the man on the platform. "But why, if Denaman's there?"

"If he's there," Martha said.

"Where else would he be?"

"I was going to ask the same question."

"Well, let's take it for granted he's inside."

"And Manuel?" She was referring to Luz's brother.

"Manuel could be anywhere."

Martha was still watching the man on the platform, studying him so that an impression of him would be left in her mind. He was a tall man, heavy boned, somewhat thin with dark hair and mustache. He was perhaps in his late thirties. His left arm was off between the shoulder and the elbow.

"I suppose he was in the war," Martha said.

"Probably." Cable nodded thoughtfully. "But which side?" That's something, Cable said to himself. You don't trust him. Any man seen from a distance you dislike and distrust. It's good to be careful, but you could be carrying it too far.

Briefly he thought of John Denaman, the man who had given him his start ten years before and talked him into settling in the Saber River valley. It would be good to see John again. And it would be good to see Luz, to talk to her, and Manuel. His good friend Manuel. Luz and Manuel's father had worked for Denaman until a sudden illness took his life. After that, John raised both of them as if they were his own children.

"Now he's going inside," Martha said.

Cable waited. After a moment he turned, pushing himself up, and saw his daughter standing only a few feet away. Clare was six, their oldest child: a quiet little girl with her mother's dark hair and eyes and showing signs of developing her mother's clean-lined, easily remembered features; resembling her mother just as the boys favored their father. She stood uncertainly with her hands clutched to her chest.

"Sister, you round up the boys."

"Are we going now?"

"In a minute."

He watched her run back into the trees and in a moment he heard a boy's shrill voice. That would be Davis, five years old. Sandy, not yet four, would be close behind his brother, following every move Davis made; almost every move.

Cable brought his sorrel gelding out of the trees and stepped into the saddle. "He'll come out again when he hears me," Cable said. "But wait till you see us talking before you come down. All right?"

Martha nodded. She smiled faintly, saying, "He'll probably turn out to be an old friend of John Denaman's."

"Probably."

Cable nudged the sorrel with his heels and rode off down the yellow sweep of hillside, sitting erect and tight to the saddle with his right knee touching the stock of a Spencer carbine, his right elbow feeling the Walker Colt on his hip, and keeping his eyes on the adobe now, thinking: This could be a scout. This could be the two and a half years still going on. . . .

As soon as he had made up his mind to enlist he had sold his stock, all of his cattle, all two hundred and fifty head, and all but three of his horses. He had put Martha and the children in the wagon and taken them to Sudan, Texas, to the home of Martha's parents. He did this because he believed deeply in the Confederacy, as he believed in his friends who had gone to fight for it.

Because of a principle he traveled from the Saber River, Arizona Territory, to Chattanooga, Tennessee, taking with him a shotgun, a revolving pistol and two horses; and there on June 21, 1862, he joined J. A. Wharton's 8th Texas Cavalry, part of Nathan Bedford Forrest's command.

Three weeks later Cable saw his first action and received his first wound during Forrest's raid on Murfreesboro. On September 3, Paul Cable was commissioned a captain and appointed to General Forrest's escort. From private to captain in less than three months; those things happened in Forrest's command. Wounded twice again after Murfreesboro; the third and final time on November 28, 1864, at a place called Huey's Mills—shot from his saddle as they crossed the Duck River to push Wilson's Union Cavalry back to Franklin, Tennessee. Cable, with gunshot wounds in his left hip and thigh, was taken to the hospital at Columbia. On December 8 he was told to go home "the best way you know how." There were more seriously wounded men who needed his cot; there would be a flood of them soon, with General Hood about to pounce on the Yankees at Nashville. Go home, he was told, and thank God for your gunshot wounds.

So for Cable the war was over, though it was still going on in the east and the feeling of it was still with him. He was not yet thirty, a lean-faced man above average height and appearing older after his service with Nathan Bedford Forrest: after Chickamauga, had come Fort Pillow, Bryce's Crossroads, Thompson's Station, three raids into West Tennessee and a hundred nameless skirmishes. He was a calm-appearing man and the war had not changed that. A clear-thinking kind of man who had taught himself to read and write, taught himself the basic rules and his wife had helped him from there.

Martha Sanford Cable was twenty-seven now. A West Texas girl, though convent-educated in New Orleans. Seven years before she had left Sudan to come to the Saber River as Paul Cable's wife, to help him build a home and provide him with a family. . . .

Now they were returning to the home they had built with the

family they had begun. They were before Denaman's Store, only four miles from their own land.

And Cable was entering the yard, still with his eyes on the loading platform and the double doors framed in the pale wall of the adobe, reining in his sorrel and approaching at a walk.

The right-hand door opened and the man with one arm stepped out to the platform. He walked to the edge of it and stood with his thumb in his belt looking down at Cable.

Cable came on. He kept his eyes on the man, but said nothing until he had pulled to a halt less than ten feet away. From the saddle, Cable's eyes were even with the man's knees.

"John Denaman inside?"

The man's expression did not change. "He's not here any more."

"He moved?"

"You could say that."

"Maybe I should talk to Luz," Cable said.

The man's sunken cheeks and the full mustache covering the line of his mouth gave his face a hard, bony expression, but it was not tensed. He said, "You know Luz?"

"Since she was eight years old," Cable answered. "Since the day I first set foot in this valley."

"Well, now—" The hint of a smile altered the man's gaunt expression. "You wouldn't be Cable, would you?"

Cable nodded.

"Home from the wars." The man still seemed to be smiling. "Luz's mentioned you and your family. Her brother too. He tells how you and him fought off Apaches when they raided your stock."

Cable nodded. "Where's Manuel now?"

"Off somewhere." The man paused. "You been to your place yet?"

"We're on our way."

"You've got a surprise coming."

Cable watched him, showing little curiosity. "What does that mean?"

"You'll find out."

"I think you're changing the subject," Cable said mildly. "I asked you what happened to John Denaman."

For a moment the man said nothing. He turned then and called through the open door, "Luz, come out here!"

Cable watched him. He saw the man's heavy-boned face turn to look down at him again, and almost immediately the Mexican girl appeared in the doorway. Cable's hand went to the curled brim of his hat.

"Luz, honey, you're a welcome sight." He said it warmly, and he wanted to jump up on the platform and kiss her but the presence of this man stopped him.

"Paul—"

He saw the surprise in the expression of her mouth and in her eyes, but it was momentary and she returned his gaze with a smile that was grave and without joy, a smile that vanished the instant the man with one arm spoke.

"Luz, tell him what happened to Denaman."

"You haven't told him?" She looked at Cable quickly, then seemed to hesitate. "Paul, he's dead. He died almost a year ago."

"Nine months," the man with one arm said. "I came here the end of August. He died the month before."

Cable's eyes were on the man, staring at him, feeling now that he had known Denaman was dead, had sensed it from the way the man had spoken—from the tone of his voice.

"You could have come right out and told me," Cable said.

"Well, you know now."

"Like you were making a game out of it."

The man stared down at Cable indifferently. "Why don't you just let it go?"

"Paul," Luz said, "it came unexpectedly. He wasn't sick."

"His heart?"

Luz nodded. "He collapsed shortly after noon and by that evening he was dead."

"And you happened to come a month later," Cable said, looking at the man again.

"Why don't you ask what I'm doing here?" The man looked up at the sound of the double team wagon on the grade, his eyes half closed in the sunlight, his gaze holding on the far slope now. "That your family?"

"Wife and three youngsters," Cable said.

The man's gaze came down. "You made a long trip for nothing." He seemed about to smile, though he was not smiling now.

"All right," Cable said. "Why?"

"Some men are living in your house."

"If there are, they're about to move."

The smile never came, but the man stared down at Cable intently. "Come inside and I'll tell you about it." Then he turned abruptly, though he glanced again at the approaching wagon before going into the store.

Cable could hear the jingling, creaking sound of the wagon closer now, but he kept his eyes on Luz until she looked at him.

"Luz, who is he?"

"His name is Edward Janroe."

"The man acts like he owns the place."

Her eyes rose briefly. "He does. Half of it."

"But why—"

"Are you coming?" Janroe was in the doorway. He was looking at Cable and with a nod of his head indicated Luz. "You got to drag things out of her. I've found it's more trouble than it's worth." He waited until Cable stirred in the saddle and began to dismount. "I'll be inside," he said, and stepped away from the door.

Cable dropped his reins, letting them trail. He swung down and mounted the steps to the platform. For a moment he watched Luz Acaso in silence.

"Are you married to him?"

"No."

"But he's been living here eight months and has a half interest in the store."

"You think what you like."

"I'm not thinking anything. I want to know what's going on."

"He'll tell you whatever you want to know."

"Luz, do you think I'm being nosy? I want to help you."

"I don't need help." She was looking beyond him, watching the wagon entering the yard.

All right, he thought, don't push her. It occurred to him then that Martha was the one to handle Luz. Why keep harping at her and get her nervous. Martha could soothe the details out of her in a matter of minutes.

Cable patted her shoulder and stepped past her into the abrupt dimness of the store.

He moved down the counter that lined the front wall, his hand gliding down the worn, shiny edge of it and his eyes roaming over the almost bare shelves. There were scattered rows of canned goods, bolts of material, work clothes, boxes that told nothing of their contents. Above, Rochester lamps hanging from a wooden beam, buckets and bridles and coils of rope. Most of the goods on the shelves had the appearance of age, as if they had been here a long time.

Cable's eyes lowered and he almost stopped, unexpectedly seeing Janroe beyond the end of the counter in the doorway to the next room. Janroe was watching him closely.

"You walk all right," Janroe said mildly. "Not a mark on you that shows; but they wouldn't have let you go without a wound."

"It shows if I walk far enough," Cable said. "Or if I stay mounted too long."

"That sounds like the kind of wound to have. Where'd you get it?"

"On the way to Nashville."

"With Hood?"

"In front of him. With Forrest."

"You're a lucky man. I mean to be in one piece."

"I suppose."

"Take another case. I was with Kirby Smith from the summer of sixty-one to a year later when we marched up to Kentucky River toward Lexington. Near Richmond we met a Yankee general named Bull Nelson." Janroe's eyes narrowed and he grinned faintly, remembering the time. "He just had recruits, a pick-up army, and I'll tell you we met them good. Cut clean the hell through them, and the ones we didn't kill ran like you never saw men run in your life. The cavalry people mopped up after that and we took over four thousand prisoners that one afternoon."

Janroe paused and the tone of his voice dropped. "But there was one battery of theirs on a ridge behind a stone fence. I was taking some men up there to get them . . . and the next day I woke up in a Richmond field hospital without an arm."

He was watching Cable closely. "You see what I mean? We'd licked them. The fight was over and put away. But because of this one battery not knowing enough to give up, or too scared to, I lost a good arm."

But you've got one left and you're out of the war, so why don't you forget about it, Cable thought, and almost said it; but instead he nodded, looking at the shelves.

"Maybe Luz told you I was in the army," Janroe said.

"No, only your name, and that you own part of the store."

"That's a start. What else do you want to know?"

"Why you're here."

"You just said it. Because I own part of the store."

"Then how you came to be here."

"You've got a suspicious mind."

"Look," Cable said quietly, "John Denaman was a friend of mine. He dies suddenly and you arrive to buy in."

"That's right. But you want to know what killed him?"

When Cable said nothing Janroe's eyes lifted to the almost bare shelves. "He didn't have enough goods to sell. He didn't have regular money coming in. He worried, not knowing what was going to happen to his business." Janroe's gaze lowered to Cable again. "He even worried about Luz and Vern Kidston. They were keeping company and, I'm told, the old man didn't see eye to eye with Vern. Because of different politics, you might say. So it was a combination of things that killed him. Worries along with old age. And if you think it was anything else, you're going on pure imagination."

"Let's go back to Vern Kidston," Cable said. "I never heard of him; so what you're saying doesn't mean a whole lot."

Janroe's faint smile appeared. "Vern came along about two years ago, I'm told. He makes his living supplying the Union cavalry with remounts. Delivers them up to Fort Buchanan."

"He lives near here?"

"In the old Toyopa place. How far's that from you?"

"About six miles."

"They say Vern's fixed it up."

"It'd take a lot of fixing. The house was half burned down."

"Vern's got the men."

"I'll have to meet him."

"You will. You'll meet him all right."

Cable's eyes held on Janroe. "It sounds like you can hardly wait."

"There's your suspicious mind again." Janroe straightened and stepped into the next room. "Come on. It's time I poured you a drink."

Cable followed, his gaze going from left to right around the well-remembered room: from the door that led to the kitchen to the roll-top desk to the Hatch & Hodges calendar to the corner fireplace and the leather-bottomed chairs, to the pictures of the Holy Family and the Sierra Madre landscapes on the wall, to the stairway leading to the second floor (four rooms up, Cable remembered), and finally to the round dining table between the front windows. He watched Janroe go into the kitchen and come out with a bottle of mescal and two glasses, holding the glasses in his fingers and the bottle pressed between his arm and his body.

Janroe nodded to the table. "Sit down. You're going to need this."

Cable pulled out a chair and stepped over it. He watched Janroe sit down and pour the clear, colorless liquor.

"Does my needing this have to do with Vern Kidston?"

Janroe sipped his mescal and put his glass down gently. "Vern's the one living in your house. Not Vern himself. Some of his men." Janroe leaned closer as if to absorb a reaction from Cable. "They're living in your house with part of Vern's horse herd grazing in your meadow."

"Well"—Cable raised the glass of mescal, studying it in the light of the window behind Janroe—"I don't blame him. It's good graze." He drank off some of the sweet-tasting liquor. "But now he'll move his men out. That's all."

"You think so?"

"If he doesn't vacate I'll get the law."

"What law?"

"Fort Buchanan. That's closest."

"And who do you think the Yankees would side with," Janroe asked, "the ex-Rebel or the mustanger supplying them with remounts?"

Janroe looked up and Cable turned in his chair as Luz entered from the store. Behind her came Martha holding Sandy's hand and moving Clare and Davis along in front of her.

"We'll see what happens," Cable said. He rose, holding out his hand as Davis ran to him and stood close against his leg.

"Mr. Janroe, this is my wife, Martha." He glanced at Janroe who had made no move to rise. "This boy here is Davis. The little one's Sanford and our big girl there is Clare, almost seven years old already." Cable winked at his daughter, but she was staring with open curiosity at Janroe's empty sleeve.

Martha's hand went to the little girl's shoulder and she smiled pleasantly at the man still hunched over the table.

"Mr. Janroe"—Martha spoke calmly—"you don't know how good it is to be back here again." She was worried one of the children might ask about Janroe's missing arm. Cable knew this. He could sense it watching her, though outwardly Martha was at ease.

Luz said, "I invited them for dinner."

Janroe was staring at Clare. She looked away and his eyes went to Davis, holding him, as if defying him to speak. Then, slowly, he sat back and looked up at Luz.

"Take the kids with you. They'll eat in the kitchen."

Luz hesitated, then nodded quickly and held out her hand to Sandy. The boy looked up at her and pressed closer into his mother's skirts.

"They're used to being with me," Martha said pleasantly. Gently she urged Clare forward, smiling at Luz now, though the Mexican woman did not return her smile. "While Cabe . . . while Paul was away the children didn't have the opportunity to meet many new people. I'm afraid they're just a little bit strange now."

"If they eat," Janroe said, "they still eat in the kitchen."

Martha's face colored. "Mr. Janroe, I was merely explaining—"

"The point is, Mrs. Cable, there's nothing to explain. In this house kids don't sit at the table with grownups."

Martha felt the heat on her face and she glanced at her husband, at Cable who stood relaxed with the calm, tell-nothing expression she had learned to understand and respect. It isn't your place to answer him, she thought. But now the impulse was too strong and she could no longer hold back her words, though when she spoke her voice was calm and controlled.

"Now that you've said it three times, Mr. Janroe, we will always remember that in this house children do not eat with grownups."

"Mrs. Cable"—Janroe spoke quietly, sitting straight up and with his hand flat and unmoving on the table—"if your husband has one friend around here it's going to be me. Not because I'm pro-South or anti-Union. Not because I favor the man who's at a disadvantage. But because I don't have a reason not to befriend your husband. Now that's a pretty flimsy basis for a friendship."

"If you think I was rude," Martha said patiently, "I apologize. Perhaps I did—"

"Just wait a minute." Janroe brought up his hand to stop her. "I want you to realize something. I want you to understand that I don't have to smile at your husband for his business. If you don't trade with me you go to Fort Buchanan and that's a two-day trip. Add to that, I do business with the Kidstons. They buy most of the goods as fast as I receive them. And I'll tell you right now, once they learn I'm dealing with your husband they're going to come in here and yell for me to stop."

"Mr. Janroe—"

"But you know what I'll answer them? I'll tell them to go to

Buchanan or hell with their business, either one. Because no man on earth comes into my house and tells me what I can do or what I can't do. Not Vern Kidston or his brother; not you or your husband here."

Janroe relaxed against the back of his chair. "That's how it is, Mrs. Cable. I'd suggest you think about it before you speak out the first thing that comes to your mind."

Again there was silence. Cable saw his wife tense, controlling herself with a fixed tightness about her nose and mouth. She stared at Janroe.

"Martha," Cable said mildly, "why don't you take the children to the kitchen? Maybe you could help Luz dish up." Martha looked at him, but said nothing. She held out her hand to Davis, gathered her children about her, and followed the girl to the kitchen.

"Your wife looks like a woman of strong character," Janroe said as Cable sat down again.

"She sticks up for what she believes."

"Yes," Janroe said. "A strong-minded woman. I noticed you *asked* her when you told her to go to the kitchen. You said, 'Why don't you take the children? . . .' "

Cable stared at him. "I think I said that."

"I've found," Janroe said, "it works a sight better to *tell* women what to do. Never *ask* them. Especially a wife. You were away for a while and your wife took on some independence. Well, now you're back I'd suggest you assume your place as head of the family."

Cable leaned forward, resting his arms on the edge of the table. "Mr. Janroe, I'd suggest you mind your own business."

"I'm giving you good advice, whether you know it or not."

"All I know about you so far," Cable said quietly, "is that you like to talk. I've got no reason to respect your advice. I've got no reason to respect you or anything about you."

He saw Janroe about to speak. "Now wait a minute. You gave my wife a lecture on what she was supposed to understand. I stood by and watched you insult her. But now I'll tell you this, Mr. Janroe: if you didn't have the misfortune of being one-armed you never would have said those things. You might be a strong-minded, hard-nosed individual who doesn't care what anybody thinks and who won't stand for any kind of dependence. You might even be a man to admire. But if you had had both your arms when you said those things, I'd have broken your jaw."

Janroe stared at Cable, his chest rising and falling with his breathing. He remained silent.

"I'm sorry I had to say that," Cable told him after a moment. "But now we know where we stand. You've got your ideas and I've got mine. If they cross, then I guess you and I aren't going to get along."

Janroe sipped his mescal, taking his time, and set the glass down gently. "You were with Bedford Forrest," he said then. "Were you an officer?"

"I reached captain."

"That speaks well of you, doesn't it—an officer with Forrest?"

"It depends from which side you view it."

"How long were you with him?"

"Since June, sixty-two."

"In the saddle most every day. Living outside and fighting—" Janroe's head nodded slowly. He raised the glass again. "You might be able to break my jaw at that."

"Maybe I shouldn't have said that."

"Don't back off. I'm being realistic, not apologizing. I'm saying you *might*."

Cable stared at him. "Maybe we should start all over again."

"No, I think we've come a long way in a short time."

"Except," Cable said, "you know more about me than I do about you."

"You don't have to know anything about me," Janroe said. "The Kidstons are your problem."

"I'll talk to them."

"But why should they talk to you?" Janroe watched him intently. "You're one man against, say, fifteen. You're an ex-Confederate in Union territory. The Kidstons themselves are Yankees. They sell most of their cattle and all of their horses to the Union army. Vern's brother Duane even held a command, but now he's back and he's brought the war with him. Has everybody calling him 'The Major' and he orders Vern's riders about like they were his personal cavalry." Janroe shook his head. "They don't have to listen to you."

Cable shrugged. "We'll see what happens."

"How do you eat?" Janroe asked. "That's your first problem."

"For now," Cable said, "I plan to buy provisions and maybe shoot something. Pretty soon I'll start buying stock and build my herd again."

"Buy it from where?"

"South. Luz's brother has friends in Sonora. I sold my stock to them when I enlisted on the agreement they'd sell back whatever I could buy when I came home."

"Manuel's down that way right now," Janroe said.

Cable's eyes raised. "When will he be back?"

"In a few days, I suppose. But your problem is now. I said before, some of Vern's men are living at your place."

"I'll have a talk with them," Cable said.

"One of them was here this morning. Bill Dancey." Janroe paused as Luz approached the table. She put plates in front of them and a serving dish of meat stew between them. Janroe asked her, "Where's his wife?"

"With the children." Luz served them as she spoke.

"Was Dancey here this morning?"

"I saw no one else."

"Who's up there with him?"

"I think Royce and the one named Joe Bob Dodd."

"Tell Mr. Cable about them."

Luz looked off, as if picturing them, before her eyes lowered to Cable. "Bill Dancey is head. He is a large man and wears a beard and is perhaps ten years older than the others. This Royce and the one called Joe Bob look much alike with their thin faces and bodies and their hats worn straight and low over their eyes. They stand with their hands on their hips in a lazy fashion and say things to each other and laugh, though not genuinely. I think they are Texans."

"They are," Janroe said. "I'm not sure about Dancey. But it's said this Joe Bob and Royce, along with Joe Bob's two older brothers, that's Austin and Wynn, deserted from Sherrod Hunter's Texas Brigade when he came through here and Duane Kidston hired them. They say if Duane knew they'd been Rebel soldiers he'd have a fit." Janroe paused. "Royce and Joe Bob are the ones at your place. Austin and Wynn are probably at the main house."

Cable said, "You're telling me not to go home?"

"I'm telling you how it is. You do what you want."

"We'll leave as soon as we load up."

From the platform Janroe watched the wagon, with Cable's sorrel trailing, move off toward the willows. He watched intently, his right hand on the stump of his arm and massaging it gently, telling himself not to become excited or hasty or jump to conclusions.

But, my God, it was more than he could have hoped blind luck would provide—an Ex-Rebel suddenly showing up here; coming home to find the Kidstons on his land.

He's your weapon, Janroe thought. Now it was right in front of him after months of waiting and watching and wondering how he could make it happen and never be suspected. If necessary he would even apologize to Martha for what he'd said. It had come out too quickly, that was all. He would smooth it over if he had to, because Cable's presence could be far more important than where kids ate, or if they ate at all, for that matter. He would have to watch himself and not let his mind clutch at petty things just to be tearing something apart.

But think it out carefully, he thought, now that there could be a way. Don't stumble; he's right here waiting, but you have to use him properly.

Cable—Janroe could feel the certainty of it inside of him—was going to help him kill Vern and Duane Kidston. And then, thinking of Cable's wife, he decided that before it was all over, Cable would be as dead as the two men he would help kill.

Cable forded the river at the store and followed it north out into the open sunlight of the mile-wide valley, then gradually west, for the valley curved in that direction with the river following close along its left, or west, slope. The far side of the valley was rimmed by a low, curving line of hills. The near slope also rolled green-black with pines; but beyond these hills, chimneyed walls of sandstone towered silently against the sky. Beyond the rock country lay the Kidston place.

Sandy was asleep. Davis and Clare sat on the endgate, Davis holding the reins of the sorrel. And Martha sat with Cable, listening in silence as he told her everything Janroe had said about the Kidstons.

When he had finished, Martha said, "What if they won't leave, Cabe? The ones in our house."

"Let's wait and see."

"I mean with the children to think of."

"The children and a lot of things," Cable said.

They talked about Luz then. Even in the kitchen, Martha said, Luz had acted strangely: tense and almost reluctant to talk even about everyday things. She did tell that the store had been left to them, to Manuel and herself, in John Denaman's will; and they would stay here. The grave of their mother in a Sonora village was the only tie they had with their birthplace; the store had been their home for a dozen years. Luz had been only six, Manuel twelve, when their father came here to work for John Denaman. The next year their father died of a sickness and John Denaman had cared for them from that day on.

But she related little more about Edward Janroe than what she had told Cable—the man's name, the fact that he owned a half interest in the store and had been here eight or nine months.

But if business was so poor, Cable asked, why would Janroe want to buy into the store?

Because of Luz? Martha offered.

Perhaps. Luz was a good-looking girl. Janroe could easily be attracted to her.

But Martha was sure that Luz still liked Vern Kidston. Luz mentioned that she used to see Vern frequently; but that was before Janroe came. Something else to wonder about. Though Janroe himself was the big question.

"What do you think of him?" Cable asked.

"All I'm sure of is that he has a low opinion of women," Martha said mildly, "judging from the lecture he gave me."

"He won't do that again," Cable said. "I talked to him."

Martha smiled. She moved closer to her husband and put her arm through his.

They rode in silence until they saw, through the willow and aspen along the river, horses grazing farther up the meadow. Martha handed her husband the field glasses and took the reins.

"About thirty, just mares and foals," Cable said after a moment. "And a man with them."

Martha kept the team moving. They were close to the base of the slope with the dark well of pines above them and the river close on their right. Their house was perhaps a quarter of a mile ahead, no more than that, set back a hundred feet from the river; but it was still out of sight, hidden by the pine stands that straggled down from the slope.

Through the glasses, Cable saw the rider come out of the trees on this side of the river. He noticed that the man was bearded and remembered Luz Acaso's description of the one named Bill Dancey: older by ten years than the other two; the one in charge.

"He must have seen us," Cable said. "He just crossed over."

"Waiting for us?" asked Martha.

"No, going for the house." He handed the glasses to Martha, feeling the children close behind him now.

Davis said, "Can I look?"

"Not right now." Cable half turned on the seat. "Listen, I want you children to stay right where you are. Even when we stop, stay there and don't jump off."

Clare's dark eyes were round and open wide. "Why?"

"Because we're not sure we're staying."

Cable looked at the boy again. "Davis, you hold on to Sandy. You won't let him jump out now, will you?"

The little boy shook his head solemnly. "No, sir."

Cable smiled at his children. His hand reached to the wagon bed, felt the short barrel of the Spencer carbine, then moved to the shotgun next to it and brought it out, placing it muzzle-down between them on the seat.

"Martha, this one's yours. Put your hand on it when I climb off, but don't lift it unless you see you have to."

He drew the Walker Colt from its holster, eased back the hammer, turned the cylinder carefully, feeling the oil-smoothness of the action, and lowered the hammer again on the empty chamber.

"There's the house," Martha said anxiously. "Part of it." She could see an adobe-colored shape through the pines close in front of them.

Then, coming out of the trees, the house was in full view: a one-story adobe with an addition made of pine logs, a shingled roof and a ramada that ran the length of the adobe section. Beyond, part of the barn could be seen.

Cable's eyes were on the bearded rider. He was near the house, still mounted but facing them now, watching them approach. A second man had come out of the house and stood near the mounted man.

"This is far enough," Cable said. They were less than fifty feet from the men now. As the wagon stopped a third man, thumbing a suspender strap up over his bare chest, appeared in the doorway of the adobe. All three men were armed. Even the one in the doorway, though half dressed, wore crossed belts holding two holstered revolvers.

"The one in the door," Cable said. "Keep a close eye on him." Martha made no answer, but he didn't look at her now. He breathed in and out slowly, calming himself and putting it off still another moment, before he jumped down from the wagon, holding his holster to his leg, and moved toward the mounted man.

"You were a while getting here," Bill Dancey said. He dismounted, swinging his leg over carefully, and stood with his feet apart watching Cable coming toward him.

Within two strides Cable stopped. "You knew we were coming?"

"Janroe mentioned it." Dancey's short-clipped beard hid any change of expression. He nodded toward the man who stood near him. "Royce here went in for something I forgot this morning and Janroe told him."

Cable glanced at the one called Royce: a tall, thin-framed man who stood hip-cocked with his thumbs hooked into his belt. His hat was tilted forward, low over his eyes, and he returned Cable's stare confidently.

Royce must have taken the horse trail, a shorter route that followed the crest of the slope, to and from the store; that's why they hadn't seen him, Cable decided.

He looked at Dancey again. "Did Janroe tell him it's my land you're on?"

Dancey nodded. "He mentioned it."

"Then I don't have to explain anything."

"That's right," Royce said. "All you have to do is turn around and go back."

There it was. Cable gave himself time, feeling the tension through his body and the anger, not building, but suddenly there as this lounging, lazy-eyed poser told him very calmly to turn around and go back. At least there was no decision to make. And arguing with him or with Dancey would only waste time. Even with Martha and the children here he knew how far he would go if necessary. He wanted to feel the anger inside of him because it would make it easier; but he wanted also to control it and he let his breath out slowly, shaking his head.

"I was afraid this was going to happen."

"Then why did you come?" Dancey asked.

The back of Cable's hand moved across his mouth, then dropped heavily. "Well, since I own this place—"

Dancey shook his head. "Vern Kidston owns it."

"Just took it?"

"In the name of the United States government," Dancey said.

"Mister, you must've been dreaming. You ever hear of Rebel land in Union territory?"

"I'm not a soldier any more."

"You're not anything any more." Dancey glanced at the wagon. "Your wife's waiting for you. And the kids. You've got kids, haven't you?"

"Three."

"A man doesn't do anything crazy with three kids."

"Not very often," Cable said mildly. His eyes moved to Royce, then past him to the bare-chested man who had come out to the edge of the ramada shade. This would be Joe Bob Dodd. He stood with one hand on his hip, the other raised to a support post. He wore his hair with sideburns to the angle of his jaw. This and the dark line of hair down the bony whiteness of his chest made him appear obscenely naked. He was somewhat shorter than Royce but had the same slim-hipped, slightly stoop-shouldered build.

Cable's eyes returned to Dancey. "I'll give you the rest of the afternoon to collect your gear and clear out. Fair enough?"

Royce looked over at Joe Bob, grinning. "You hear what he said?"

The man at the ramada nodded. "I heard him."

"You don't have the time to give." Dancey said. "I told you, you're going to turn around and go back."

"Bill," Joe Bob called, "tell him he can leave his woman."

Cable's eyes went to him, feeling the tingle of anger again. No, wait a little more, he thought. Take one thing at a time and don't make it harder than it already is. His gaze returned to Dancey.

"Go get Kidston and I'll talk to him," Cable said.

"He wouldn't waste his time."

"Maybe I would though," Joe Bob said easily. His hand came down from the post and both thumbs hooked into his crossed belts. "Reb, you want to argue over your land?"

"I'll talk to Kidston."

"You'll talk to me if I say so."

Watching him, seeing him beyond the lowered head of Dancey's horse and feeling Dancey still close to him, Cable said, "I think that's all you are. Just talk."

"Bill," Joe Bob said, "get your horse out of the way."

Cable hesitated.

He sensed Dancey reaching for the reins, his body turning and his hands going to the horse's mane.

And for part of a moment Dancey was half turned from him with his hands raised and the horse was moving, side-stepping, hiding both Royce and Joe Bob, and that was the time.

It was then or not at all and Cable stepped into Dancey, seeing the man's expression change to sudden surprise the moment before his fist hooked into the bearded face. Dancey stumbled against his horse, trying to catch himself against the nervously side-stepping animal, but Cable was with him, clubbing him with both fists, again and again and again, until Dancey sagged, until he went down covering his head.

Cable glanced at the wagon and away from it with the sound of Martha's voice and with the sound of running steps on the hard-packed ground. He saw Joe Bob beyond Dancey's horse. Now a glimpse of Royce jerking the bridle, and a slapping sound and the horse bolted.

Both Joe Bob and Royce stood in front of him, their hands on their revolvers; though neither of them had pulled one clear of its holster. They stood rooted, staring at Cable, stopped suddenly in the act of rushing him. For in one brief moment, in the time it had taken Royce to slap the horse out of the way, they had missed their chance.

Cable stood over Dancey with the Walker Colt in his hand. It was cocked and pointing directly at Dancey's head. Joe Bob and Royce said nothing. Dancey had raised himself on an elbow and was staring at Cable dumbly.

"Now you take off your belts," Cable said. He brought Dancey to his feet and had to prompt them again before they unbuckled their gun belts and let them fall. Then he moved toward Joe Bob.

"You said something about my wife."

"Me?"

"About leaving her here."

Joe Bob shrugged. "That wasn't anything. Just something I felt like saying—"

Abruptly Cable stepped into Joe Bob, hitting him in the face before he could bring up his hands. Joe Bob went down, rolling to his side, and when he looked up at Cable his eyes showed stunned surprise.

"You won't say anything like that again," Cable said.

Dancey had not taken his eyes off Cable. "You didn't give him a chance. Hitting him with a gun in your hand."

Cable glanced at him. "You're in a poor position to argue it."

"In fact," Dancey said, "you didn't give me much of a chance either. Now if you want to put the gun away and go about it fair—"

"That would be something, wouldn't it?"

Dancey said, "You're not proving anything with that gun in your hand."

"I don't have anything to prove."

"All right, then we leave for a while." Dancey looked over at Royce. "Get the stuff out of the house."

"Not now." Cable's voice stopped Royce. "You had a chance. You didn't take it. Now you leave without anything," Cable said. "Don't come back for it either. What doesn't burn goes in the river."

Royce said, "You think we won't be back?"

Cable's gaze shifted. "You'll ride into a double load of buckshot if you do. You can tell Kidston the same."

Royce seemed to grin. "Man, you're made to order. Duane's going to have some fun with you."

Dancey's eyes held on Cable. "So one man's going to stand us off."

"That's all it's taken so far."

"You think Vern's going to put up with you?"

"I don't see he has a choice," Cable answered.

"Then you don't know him," Dancey said flatly.

TWO

With daylight a wind came out of the valley and he could hear it in the pines above the house.

Cable lay on his back listening, staring at the ceiling rafters. There was no sound in the room. Next to him, Martha was asleep. In the crib, beyond Martha's side of the bed, Sandy slept with his thumb and the corner of the blanket in his mouth. Clare and Davis were in the next room, in the log section of the house, and it was still too early even for them.

Later they would follow him around offering to help. He would be patient and let them think they were helping and answer all of their questions. He would think about the two and a half years away from them and he would kiss them frequently and study them, holding their small faces gently in his hands.

The wind rose and with it came the distant, dry-creaking sound of the barn door.

Later on he would see about the barn. Perhaps in the afternoon, if they had not come by then. This morning he would run Kidston's horses out of the meadow. Then perhaps Martha would have something for him to do.

They had worked until long after dark, sweeping, scrubbing, moving in their belongings. There would always be something more to be done; but that was all right because it was their home, something they had built themselves.

Just make sure everything that belonged to Royce and Joe Bob and Bill Dancey was out of here. Make double sure of that. Then wait. No matter what he did, he would be waiting and listening for the sound of horses.

But there was nothing he could do about that. Don't worry about anything you can't do something about. When it's like that it just happens. It's like an act of God. Though don't blame God for sending Vern Kidston. Blame Vern himself for coming. If you can hate him it will be easier to fight him.

And there's always someone to fight, isn't there?

Ten years ago he had come here from Sudan, Texas—a nineteen-year-old boy seeking his future, working at the time for a freight company that hauled between Hidalgo and Tucson—and one night when they stopped at Denaman's Store he talked to John Denaman.

They sat on the loading platform with their legs hanging over the side, drinking coffee and now and then whiskey, drinking both from the same cups, looking north into the vast darkness of the valley. John Denaman told him about the river and the good meadow land and the timber—ponderosa pine and aspen and willows, working timber and pretty-to-look-at timber. A man starting here young and working hard would have himself something in no time at all, Denaman had said.

But a man had to have money to buy stock with, Cable said. Something to build with.

No, Denaman said, not necessarily. He told about his man Acaso who'd died the winter before, leaving his two kids, Manuel and Luz, here and leaving the few cattle Denaman owned scattered through the hills. You're welcome to gather and work the cattle, Denaman said. Not more than a hundred head; but something to build on and you won't have to put up money till you market them and take your share.

That was something to think about, and all the way to Tucson Cable had pictured himself a rancher, a man with his own land, with his own stock. He thought, too, about a girl who lived in Sudan, Texas.

The first thing he did in Tucson was quit his job. The same day he bought twenty head of yearling stock, spending every last dollar he had, and drove his cattle the hundred and twenty miles back to the Saber River.

In the summer of his second year he built his own adobe, with the help of Manuel Acaso, four miles north of the store. He sold some of his full-grown beef to the army at Fort Buchanan and he continued to buy yearlings, buying them cheap from people around Tubac who'd had enough of the Apache and were willing to make a small profit or none at all just to get shed of their stock and get out of southern Arizona.

The next year he left Manuel Acaso with his herd and traveled back to Sudan. The girl, Martha Sanford, was waiting for him. They were married within the week and he brought her home to the Saber without stopping for a honeymoon. Then he worked harder than he ever imagined a man could work and he remembered thinking during those days: nothing can budge you from this place. You are taking all there is to take and if you don't die you will make a success of it.

He was sure of it after living through the winter the Apaches came. They were Chiricahuas down out of the Dragoons and every few weeks they would raid his herd for meat. From November through April Cable lost over fifty head of cattle. But he made the Chiricahuas pay.

Lying prone high on the slope with a Sharps rifle, in the cover of the trees, he knocked two of them from their horses as they cut into his herd. The others came for him, squirming unseen through the pines, and when they rushed him he killed a third one with his revolver before they ran.

Another time that winter a war party attacked the house of Juan Toyopa, Cable's nearest neighbor to the west, killing Juan and his family and burning the house. They reached Cable's place at dawn—coming suddenly, screaming out of the grayness and battering against the door. He stood waiting with a revolver in each hand. Martha stood behind him with the shotgun. And when the door gave way he fired six rounds into them in half as many seconds. Two of the Apaches fell and Martha stepped over them to fire both shotgun loads at the Apaches running for the willows. One of them went down.

Then Cable rode to Denaman's to get Manuel Acaso. They returned to the willows, found the sign of six Chiricahuas and followed it all day, up into high desert country; and at dusk, deep in a high-walled canyon, they crept up to the dry camp of the six Apaches and shot three of them before they could reach their horses. The survivors fled, at least one of them wounded, Cable was sure of that, and they never bothered him again.

Perhaps they believed his life was charmed, that he was beyond killing, and for that reason they stopped trying to take him or his cattle. And perhaps it was charmed, Cable had thought. Or else his prayers were being answered. It was a good thing to believe; it made him feel stronger and made him work even harder. That was the time he first had the thought: nothing can budge you from this land. Nothing.

The next year their first child was born. Clare. And Manuel Acaso helped him build the log addition to the house. He remembered planning it, lying here in this bed with Martha next to him and Clare, a month-old baby, in the same crib Sandy was sleeping in now; lying awake staring at the ceiling and thinking how he would build a barn after they'd completed the log room.

And now thinking about that time and not thinking about the years in between, he felt comfortable and at peace. Until the murmur of Martha's voice, close to him, brought him fully awake.

"They'll come today, won't they?"

He turned to her. She was on her side, her eyes open and watching him. "I guess they will."

"Is that what you were thinking about?"

Cable smiled. "I was thinking about the barn."

"You're not even worried, are you?"

"It doesn't do any good to show it."

"I thought you might be trying out your principle of not worrying about anything you can't do something about."

"Well, I thought about it."

Martha smiled. "Cabe, I love you."

He rolled to his side, pulling her close to him and kissed her, brushing her cheek and her mouth. His face remained close to hers. "We'll come out of this."

"We have to," Martha whispered.

When Cable left the house the sun was barely above the line of trees at the river's edge. The willow branches moved in the breeze, swaying slowly against the pale morning sky. But soon, Cable knew, there would be sun glare and deep shadows, black against yellow, and the soft movement of the trees would be remembered from another time with another feeling.

With Davis and Clare he brought the four team horses out of the barn and put them on a picket line to graze. It wouldn't help to get them mixed with Kidston's herd. He saddled the sorrel gelding, but let the reins hang free so it could also graze. The sorrel wouldn't wander. After that he returned to the house.

Martha came out of the log room with Sandy. "What did you forget?"

"The Spencer," Cable said. He picked it up, then turned sharply, hearing Clare's voice.

The little girl ran in from the yard. "Somebody's coming!"

Cable stepped to the doorway. Behind him Martha called, "Davis—Clare, where is he?"

"He's all right." Cable lowered the Spencer looking out past Davis who was in the yard watching the rider just emerging from the trees. "It's Janroe."

The first thing Cable noticed about Janroe was that he wore two revolvers—one in a shoulder holster, the other on his hip—in addition to a shotgun in his saddle boot.

Then, as Janroe approached, he noticed the man's gaze. Taking it all in, Cable thought, seeing Janroe's eyes moving from the saddled gelding to the gear—cooking utensils, clothing, curl-toed boots, bedding and the three holstered revolvers on top—that was in a pile over by the barn.

Janroe reined in, his gaze returning to the adobe. "Well, you ran them, didn't you?" His hand touched his hat brim and he nodded to Martha, then fell away as Cable walked out to him. He made no move to dismount.

"I don't think you expected to see us," Cable said.

"I wasn't sure."

"But you were curious."

Janroe's gaze went to the pile of gear. "You took their guns," he said thoughtfully. I'd like to have seen that." His eyes returned to Cable. "Yes, I would have given something to see that. Was anybody hurt?"

Cable shook his head.

"No shooting?"

"Not a shot."

"What'll you do with their stuff?"

"Leave it. They'll come back."

"I think I'd burn it."

"I thought about that," Cable said. "But I don't guess it's a way to make friends."

"You don't owe them anything."

"No, but I have to live with them."

Janroe glanced at the saddled horse. "You're going somewhere?"

"Out to the meadow."

"I'll ride along," Janroe said.

They passed into the willows, jumping their horses down the five-foot bank, and crossed a sandy flat before entering the brown water of the river. At midstream the water swirled chest high on the horses, then receded gradually until they again came up onto a stretch of sand before mounting the bank.

"Now you're going to run his horses?" Janroe asked.

"I'll move them around the meadow," Cable said. "Toward his land."

"He'll move them right back."

"We'll see."

"You're got a fight on your hands. You know that, don't you?"

They were moving out into the meadow toward Kidston's horse herd, walking their horses side by side, but now Cable reined to a halt.

"Look, I haven't even met Vern or Duane Kidston. First I'll talk to them. Then we'll see what happens."

Janroe shook his head. "They'll try to run you. If you don't budge, they'll shoot you out."

Cable said, "Are you going back now?"

Janroe looked at him with surprise. "I have time."

"And I've got work to do."

"Well," Janroe said easily, "I was going to try to talk you into going back to the store with me. I've got a proposition you ought to be interested in."

"Go ahead and make it."

"I've got to show you something along with it, and that's at the store."

"Then it'll have to wait," Cable said.

"Well"—Janroe shrugged—"it's up to you. I'll tell you this much, it would end your problem all at once."

Cable watched him closely. "What would I have to do?"

"Kill Vern," Janroe said mildly. "Kill him and his brother."

Cable had felt himself tensed, but now he relaxed. "Just like that."

"You can do it. You proved that the way you handled those three yesterday."

"And why are you so anxious to see the Kidstons dead?"

"I'm looking at it from your side."

"Like hell."

"All right." Janroe paused. "You were pretty close to John Denaman, weren't you?"

"He gave me my start here."

"Did you know Denaman was running guns for the South?"

Cable was watching Janroe closely. "You're sure?"

"He was just part of it," Janroe continued. "They're Enfield rifles shipped into Mexico by the British. Confederate agents bring them up over the border and the store is one of the relay points. It was Denaman's job to hide the rifles until another group picked them up for shipment east."

"And where do you come in?"

"When Denaman died I was sent out to take his place."

Cable's eyes remained on Janroe. So the man was a Confederate agent. And John Denaman had been one. That was hard to picture, because you didn't think of the war reaching out this far. But it was here. Fifteen hundred miles from the fighting, almost another world, but it was here.

"I told you," Janroe said, "I was with Kirby Smith. I lost my arm fighting the Yankees. When they said I wasn't any more use as a soldier I worked my way into this kind of a job. Eight months ago they sent me out here to take Denaman's place."

"And Manuel," Cable said. "Is he in it?"

Janroe nodded. "He scouts for the party that brings up the rifles. That's where he is now."

"When's he due back?"

"What do you want to do, check my story?"

"I was thinking of Manuel. I haven't seen him in a long time."

"He'll be back in a day or so."

"Does Luz know about the guns?"

"You can't live in the same house and not know about them."

"So that's what's bothering her."

Janroe looked at him curiously. "She said something to your wife?"

Cable shrugged off the question. "It doesn't matter. You started out with me killing Vern and Duane Kidston."

Janroe nodded. "How does it look to you now?"

"You're telling me to go after them. To shoot them down like you would an animal."

"Exactly."

"That's called murder."

"It's also called war."

Cable shook his head. "As far as I'm concerned the war's over."

Janroe watched him closely. "You don't stop believing in a cause just because you've stopped fighting."

"I've got problems of my own now."

"But what if there's a relation between the two? Between your problems and the war?"

"I don't see it."

"Open your eyes," Janroe said. "Vern supplies remounts to the union army. He's doing as much to help them as any Yankee soldier in the line. Duane's organized a twelve-man militia. That doesn't sound like anything; but what if he found out about the guns? Good rifles that Confederate soldiers are waiting for, crying for. But even without that danger, once you see Duane you'll *want* to kill him. I'll testify before God to that."

Janroe leaned closer to Cable. "This is what I'm getting at. Shooting those two would be like aiming your rifle at Yankee soldiers. The only difference is you know their names."

Cable shook his head. "I'm not a soldier any more. That's the difference."

"You have to have a uniform on to kill?"

"You know what I mean."

"I know exactly what you mean," Janroe said. "You need an excuse. You need something to block off your conscience while you're pulling the trigger. Something like a license, so killing them won't be called murder."

Cable said nothing. He was listening, but staring off at the horse herd now.

Janroe watched him. "That's your problem. You want Vern and Duane off your land, but you don't have the license to hunt them. You don't have an excuse your conscience will accept." Janroe paused. He waited until Cable's gaze returned and he was looking directly into his eyes.

"I can give you that excuse, Mr. Cable. I can fix you up with the damnedest hunting license you ever saw, and your conscience will just sit back and laugh."

For a moment Cable was silent, letting Janroe's words run through his mind. All at once it was clear and he knew what the man was driving at. "If I worked for you," Cable said, "if I was an agent, I could kill them as part of my duty."

Janroe seemed to smile. "I could even order you to do it."

"Why me? If it's so important to you, why haven't you tried?"

"Because I can't afford to fool with something like that. If I'm caught, what happens to the gun running?"

"And if I fail," Cable said, "what happens to my family?"

"You don't have anything to lose," Janroe said easily. "What happens to them if Vern kills you? What happens to all of you if he runs you off your land?"

Cable shook his head. "I've never even seen these people and you want me to kill them."

"It will come to that," Janroe said confidently. "I'm giving you an opportunity to hit first."

"I appreciate that," Cable said. "But from now on, how would you like to keep out of my business? You stop worrying about me and I won't say anything about you. How will that be?" He saw the relaxed confidence drain from Janroe's face leaving an expressionless mask and a tight line beneath his mustache.

"I think you're a fool," Janroe said quietly. "But you won't realize it yourself until it's too late."

"All right," Cable said. He spoke calmly, not raising his voice, but he was impatient now, anxious for Janroe to leave. "That's about all I've got time for right now. You come out again some time, how's that?"

"If you're still around." Janroe flicked his reins and moved off.

Let him go, Cable thought, watching Janroe taking his time, just beginning to canter. He's waiting for you to call him. But he'll have a long wait, because you can do without Mr. Janroe. There was something about the man that was wrong. Cable could believe that Janroe had been a soldier and was now a Confederate agent; but his wanting the Kidstons killed—as if he would enjoy seeing it happen—that was something else. There was the feeling he wanted to kill them just for the sake of killing them, not for the reasons he brought up at all. Maybe it would be best to keep out of Janroe's way. There was enough to think about as it was.

Cable swung the sorrel in a wide circle across the meadow and came at the horse herd up wind, counting thirty-six, all mares and foals; seeing their heads rise as they heard him and caught his scent. And now they were moving, carefully at first, only to keep out of his way, then at a run as he spurred the sorrel toward them. Some tried to double back around him, but the sorrel answered his rein and swerved right and left to keep them bunched and moving.

Where the Saber crossed the valley, curving over to the east side of the meadow, he splashed the herd across with little trouble, then closed on them again and ran them as fast as the foals could move, up the narrowing, left-curving corridor of the valley. After what he judged to be four or five miles farther on, he came in sight of grazing cattle and there Cable swung away from the horse herd. This would be Kidston land.

Now he did not follow the valley back but angled for the near slope, crossed the open sweep of it to a gully which climbed up through shadowed caverns of ponderosa pine. At the crest of the hill he looked west out over tangled rock and brush country and beyond it to a towering near horizon of creviced, coldly silent stone. Close beyond this barrier was the Toyopa place, where Kidston now lived.

Cable followed the crest of the hill for almost a mile before he found a trail that descended the east slope. He moved along the narrowness of it, feeling the gradual slant beneath the sorrel, and seeing the valley again, down through open swatches in the trees. Soon he would be almost above the house. A few yards farther on he stopped.

Ahead of him, a young woman stood at the edge of the path looking down through the trees. Luz Acaso, Cable thought. No.

Luz came to his mind with the first glimpse of this girl in white. But Luz vanished as he saw blond hair—hair that was tied back with a ribbon and swirled suddenly over her shoulder as she turned and saw him.

This movement was abrupt, but now she stood watching him calmly. Her hand closed around the riding quirt suspended from her wrist and she raised it to hold it in front of her with both hands, not defensively, but as if striking a pose.

"I expected you to be older,'" the girl said. She studied him calmly, as if trying to guess his age or what he was thinking or what had brought him to this ridge.

Cable swung down from the saddle, his eyes on the girl. She was at ease—he could see that—and was still watching him attentively: a strikingly handsome girl, tall, though not as tall as Martha, and younger by at least six years, Cable judged.

He said, "You know who I am?"

"Bill Dancey told us about you." She smiled then. "With help from Royce and Joe Bob."

"Then you're a Kidston," Cable said.

"You'll go far," the girl said easily.

Cable frowned. "You're Vern's—daughter?"

"Duane's. I'm Lorraine, if that means anything to you."

"I don't know why," Cable said, "but I didn't picture your dad married."

Her eyebrows rose with sudden interest. "How did you picture him?"

"I don't know. Just average appearing."

Lorraine smiled. "You'll find him average, all right."

Cable stared at her. "You don't seem to hold much respect for him."

"I have no reason to."

"Isn't just because he's your father reason enough?"

Lorraine's all-knowing smile returned. "I knew you were going to say that."

"You did, huh? . . . How old are you?"

"Almost nineteen."

Cable nodded. That would explain some of it. "And you've been to school. You're above average pretty, which you'll probably swear to. And you've probably had your own way as long as you can remember."

"And if all that's true," Lorraine said. "Then what?"

Cable shook his head. "I don't know."

"What point are you trying to make?"

Cable smiled now. "You didn't react the way I thought you would."

"At least you're honest about it," Lorraine said. "Most men would have tried to bluster their way out. Usually they say, 'Well'—with what passes for a wise chuckle—'you'll see things differently when you're a bit older.' " Lorraine's eyebrows rose. "Unfortunately, there isn't the least shred of evidence that wisdom necessarily comes with age."

"Uh-huh," Cable nodded. This girl could probably talk circles around him if he let her. But if she pulled that on Martha—

Cable smiled. "Why don't you come down and meet my wife?"

Lorraine hesitated. "I don't think I should put myself in the way."

"You wouldn't be in Martha's way. She'd be glad of the chance to sit down and talk."

"I wasn't referring to your wife. I meant my father. He's coming, you know." She saw Cable's expression change. "Didn't you think he would?"

"Coming now?"

"As soon as he gathers his company," Lorraine answered. "Not Vern. Vern went up to Fort Buchanan yesterday on horse business." She looked away from Cable. "You know you can see your house right down there through the trees. I came here to watch."

She stepped back quickly as Cable moved past her, already urging his sorrel down the path as he mounted. She called out to him to wait, but he kept going and did not look back. Soon he was out of sight, following the long, gradual switchbacks that descended through the pines.

Martha had cleaned the stove for the second time. She came out of the house carrying a pail and at the end of the ramada she lifted it and threw the dirty water out into the sunlight. She watched it flatten and hang glistening gray before splattering against the hard-packed ground. She turned back to the house, hearing the sound of the horse then.

"Clare!" Her gaze flashed to the children playing in the aspen shade. They looked up and she called, not as loud, "Clare, bring the boys in for a while."

"Why do we have to—" Davis's voice trailed off. He made no move to rise from his hands and knees.

Martha looked back at the stable shed, then to the children. "Dave, I'm not going to call again." The children rose and came out of the trees.

She heard the horse again and with it a rustling, twig-snapping sound. She waved the children toward the house; but Clare hesitated, looking up toward the pines. "What's that noise?"

"Probably not anything," Martha said. "Inside now."

As they filed in, Cable turned the corner of the house. Martha let her breath out slowly and stood watching him as he dismounted and came toward her.

She wanted to say: Cabe, it's not worth it. One alarm after another, running the children inside every time there's a sound! But she looked at Cable's face and the words vanished.

"What is it?"

"They're on the way."

Martha glanced at the house, at the three children standing in the ramada shade watching them. "Clare, fix the boys a biscuit and jelly."

As she turned back, she again heard the rustling, muffled horse sound. She saw her husband's hand go to the Walker Colt a moment before Lorraine Kidston rounded the adobe.

"I decided," Lorraine said as she approached, "it would be more fun to watch from right here." She dropped her reins then, extending her arms to Cable. When he hesitated, she said, "Aren't you going to help me?"

Cable lifted her down from the side saddle, feeling her press against him, and he stepped back the moment her feet touched the ground. "Martha, this is Lorraine Kidston. Duane's girl."

Martha recognized his uneasiness. He wanted to appear calm, she knew, but he was thinking of other things. And she was aware of Lorraine's confidence. Lorraine was enjoying this, whatever it was, and for some reason she had Cable at a disadvantage. Martha nodded to Lorraine, listened as Cable explained their meeting on the ridge, and she couldn't help thinking: Soon we could be thrown to the lions and Lorraine has dressed in clean white linen to come watch.

"Come inside," Martha said pleasantly. "We can give you a chair at the window if you'd like."

Lorraine hesitated, but only for a moment. She nodded to Martha and said easily, "You're very kind."

At the door, the children stood staring at Lorraine. Martha named them as they entered the ramada shade, and reaching them, brushed Sandy's hair from his forehead. "The little Cables are about to have biscuits and jelly. Will you join them?"

"No, thank you," Lorraine said. She nodded politely to the children, but showed no interest in them, edging through the doorway now as if not wanting to touch them. Martha followed, moving the children to the table and sitting them down. Cable came in a moment later carrying the Spencer.

As he propped it against the wall between the two front windows, Lorraine said pleasantly, "I hope you're not going to shoot my father."

Cable closed both shutters of the right window, but only one shutter of the window nearer to the door. He turned then. "I hope not either."

"Oh, don't be so solemn," Lorraine said lightly. "If Duane does the talking you can be pretty sure he'll mess it up."

Cable saw Martha's momentary look of surprise. She placed a pan of biscuits on the table, watching Lorraine. "Miss Kidston," Cable said mildly, "doesn't have a very high regard for her father."

Martha straightened, wiping her hands on her apron. "That's nice."

Lorraine regarded her suspiciously. Then, as if feeling a compulsion to defend herself, she said, "If there is nothing about him personally to deserve respect, I don't see why it's due him just because he's a parent."

Cable was leaving it up to Martha now. He watched her, expecting her to reply, but Martha said nothing. The silence lengthened, weakening Lorraine's statement, demanding more from her.

"I don't suppose you can understand that," Lorraine said defensively.

"Hardly," Martha said, "since I've never met your father."

"You've met him," Lorraine said, glancing at Cable. "He's the kind who can say nothing but the obvious." Cable was looking out the window, paying no attention to her, and her gaze returned quickly to Martha.

"I know exactly what he's going to answer to every single thing I say," Lorraine went on. "One time it's empty wisdom, the next time wit. Now Vern, he's the other extreme. Vern sits like a grizzled stone, and at first you think it's pure patience. Then, after a few sessions of this, you realize Vern simply hasn't anything to say. I haven't yet decided which is worse, listening to Duane, or not listening to Vern."

"It sounds," Martha prompted, "as if you haven't been with them very long."

That brought it out. Lorraine recited a relaxed account of her life, using a tone bordering on indifference, though Martha knew Lorraine was enjoying it.

Her mother and father had separated when Lorraine was seven, and she had gone with her mother. That didn't mean it had taken her mother seven or eight years to learn what a monumental bore Duane was. She had simply sacrificed her best years on the small chance he might change. But finally, beyond the point of endurance, she left him, and left Gallipolis too, because that Ohio town seemed so typical of Duane. Wonderful years followed, almost ten of them. Then her mother died unexpectedly and she was forced to go to her father who was then in Washington. In the army. That was two or three years ago and she remained in Washington while Duane was off campaigning. Then he was relieved of his duty—though Duane claimed he "resigned his active commission"—and, unfortunately, she agreed to come out here with him. Now, after over a year with Duane and Vern, Lorraine was convinced that neither had ever had an original thought in his life.

Cable listened, his gaze going out across the yard and through the trees to the meadow beyond. You could believe only so much of that about Vern and Duane. Even if they were dull, boring old men to an eighteen-year-old girl, they could still run you or burn your house down or kill you or whatever the hell else they wanted. So don't misjudge them, Cable thought.

He heard Martha ask where they had lived and Lorraine answered Boston, New York City. Philadelphia for one season. They had found it more fun to move about.

Even with that tone, Martha will feel sorry for her, Cable thought, watching the stillness of the yard and the line of trees with their full branches hanging motionless over empty shade.

He tried to visualize the girl's mother and he pictured them—Lorraine and her mother—in a well-furnished drawing room filled with people. The girl moved from one group to another, nodding with her head tilted to one side, smiling now, saying something; then everyone in the group returning her smile at the same time.

Cable saw himself in the room—not intending it—but suddenly there he was; and he thought: That would be all right about now. Even though you wouldn't have anything to say and you'd just stand there—

He saw the first rider when he was midway across the river, moving steadily, V-ing the water toward the near bank. Now there were three more in the water and—Cable waited to make sure—two still on the other side. They came down off the meadow; and beyond them now, over their heads, Cable saw the grazing horse herd. They had returned the mares and foals.

As each man crossed the river, he dismounted quickly, handed off his horse and ran hunch-shouldered to the protection of the five-foot cutbank. One man was serving as horse holder, taking them farther down the bank where the trees grew more thickly.

Out of the line of fire, Cable thought. Behind him he heard Lorraine's voice. Then Martha's. But he wasn't listening to them now. This could be nine months ago, he thought, watching the trees and the river and the open meadow beyond. That could be Tishomingo Creek if you were looking down across a cornfield, and beyond it, a half mile beyond through the trees and briars, would be Bryce's Crossroads. But you're not standing in a group of eighty-five men now.

No, a hundred and thirty-five then, he thought. Forrest had Gatrel's Georgia Company serving with the escort.

How many of them would you like?

About four. That's all. Shotguns and pistols and the Kidstons wouldn't know what hit them. But now you're out-Forresting Forrest. He had two to one against him at Bryce's. And won. You've got six to one.

He could just see their heads now above the bank, spaced a few feet apart. He was still aware of Lorraine's voice, thinking now as he watched them: What are they waiting for?

A rifle barrel rose above the bank, pointed almost straight up, went off with a whining report and Lorraine stopped talking.

Cable turned from the window. "Martha, take the children into the other room." They watched him; the children, Martha, and Lorraine all watched him expectantly, but he turned back to the window.

He heard Lorraine say, "He's going to die when he finds out I'm here."

"He already knows," Cable said, not turning. "Your horse is outside."

Her voice brightened. "That's right!" She moved to Cable's side. "Now he won't know what to do."

"He's doing something," Cable said.

The rifle came up again, now with a white cloth tied to the end of the barrel, and began waving slowly back and forth.

"Surrender," Lorraine said mockingly, "or Major Kidston will storm the redoubts. This is too much."

Cable asked, "Is that him?"

Lorraine looked past his shoulder. Four men had climbed the bank and now came out of the trees, one a few paces ahead. He motioned the others to stop, then came on until he'd reached the middle of the yard. This one, the one Cable asked about, wore a beard, a Kossuth army hat adorned with a yellow, double-looped cord, and a brass eagle that pinned the right side of the brim to the crown; he wore cavalry boots and a flap-top holster on his left side, butt to the front and unfastened.

He glanced back at the three men standing just out from the trees, saw they had not advanced, then turned his attention again to the house, planting his boots wide and fisting his hands on his hips.

"Sometimes," Lorraine said, "Duane leaves me speechless."

"The first one's your father?" asked Cable, making sure.

"My God, who else?"

"That's Royce with the flag," Cable said.

"And Joe Bob and Bill Dancey in reserve," Lorraine said. "I think Bill looks uncomfortable."

Cable's eyes remained on her father. "Where's Vern?"

"I told you, he went to Fort Buchanan," Lorraine answered. Her attention returned to her father. "He loves to pose. I think right now he's being Sheridan before Missionary Ridge. Wasn't it Sheridan?"

"Cable!"

"Now he speaks," Lorraine said gravely, mockingly.

"Cable—show yourself!"

Cable moved past Lorraine into the open doorway. He looked out at Duane. "I'm right here."

Duane's fist came off his hips. For a moment before he spoke, his eyes measured Cable sternly. "Where do you have my daughter?"

"She's here," Cable said.

Again Duane stared in silence, his eyes narrowed and his jaw set firmly. The look is for your benefit, Cable thought. He's not concentrating as much as he's acting. He saw Duane then take a watch from his vest pocket, thumb it open and glance at the face.

Duane looked up. "You have three minutes by the clock to release my daughter. If you don't, I will not be responsible for what happens to you."

"I'm not holding her."

"You have three minutes, Mr. Cable."

"Listen, she came on her own. She can walk out any time she wants." Behind him he heard Lorraine laugh.

Cable looked at her. "You'd better go out to him."

"No, not yet," she said. "Call his bluff and let's see what he does."

"Listen, while you're being entertained my wife and children are likely to get shot."

"He wouldn't shoot while I'm in here."

"That's something we're not going to find out." Cable's hand closed on her arm. Lorraine pulled back, but he held her firmly and drew her into the doorway. He saw Duane return the watch to his pocket, and saw a smile of confidence form under the man's neatly trimmed beard.,

"All of a sudden, Mr. Cable, you seem a bit anxious," Duane said. His hands went to his hips again.

Close to him, as Cable urged her through the door, Lorraine gasped theatrically, "Would you believe it!"

"Go on now," Cable whispered. To Duane he said, "I told you once I wasn't holding your daughter. What do I have to do to convince you?"

Duane's expression tightened. "You keep quiet till I'm ready for you!" His gaze shifted to Lorraine who now stood under the ramada a few steps from Cable and half turned toward him. She stood patiently with her arms folded. "Lorraine, take your horse and go home."

"I'd rather stay." She glanced at Cable, winking at him.

"This is not something for you to see," Duane said gravely.

"I don't want to miss your big scene," Lorraine said. "I can feel it coming."

"Lorraine—I'm warning you!"

"Oh, stop it. You aren't warning anyone."

Duane's voice rose. "I'm not going to tell you again!"

Smiling, Lorraine shook her head. "If you could only see yourself."

"Lorraine—"

"All right." She stopped him, raising her hands. "I surrender." She laughed again, shaking her head, then moved unhurriedly to her horse, mounted and walked it slowly across the yard, smiling pleasantly at her father, her head turning to watch him until she was beyond his line of vision. She passed into the willow trees.

She's had her fun, Cable thought, watching her. But now the old man is mad and he'll take it out on you. Cable's gaze returned to Duane. You mean he'll try. At this moment he did not feel sorry for Duane; even after Duane had been made to look ridiculous by his own daughter. No, if Duane pushed him he would push him back. There was no time to laugh at this pompous little man with the General Grant beard; because beyond his theatrics this was still a matter of principle, of pride, of protecting his family, of protecting his land. A matter of staying alive too.

Cable said bluntly, "Now what?"

"Now," Duane answered, drawing his watch again, "you have until twelve o'clock noon to pack your belongings and get out." He looked down at the watch. "A little less than three hours."

There it is, Cable thought wearily. You expected it and there it is. He looked over his shoulder, glancing back at his wife, then turned back to Duane.

"Mr. Kidston, I'm going to talk to my wife first. You just hang on for a minute." He stepped back, swinging the door closed.

"Well?" he asked.

"This is yesterday," Martha said, "with the places reversed."

Cable smiled thinly. "We don't make friends very easy, do we?"

"I don't think it matters," Martha said quietly, "whether Mr. Kidston likes us or not."

"Then we're staying," Cable said.

"Did you think we wouldn't?"

"I wasn't sure."

Martha went to the bedroom. She looked in at the children before coming to Cable. "Clare's doing her letters for the boys."

"Martha, make them stay in there."

"I will."

"Then stand by the window with the shotgun, but don't shove the barrel out until I'm out there and they're looking at me."

"What will you do?"

"Talk to him. See how reasonable he is."

"Do you think Vern is there?"

"No. I guess Vern does the work while Duane plays war."

Martha's lips parted to speak, but she smiled then and said nothing.

"What were you going to say?" Cable asked.

She was still smiling, a faint smile that was for Cable, not for herself. "I was going to tell you to be careful, but it sounded too typical."

He smiled with her for a moment, then said, "Ready?" She nodded and Cable turned to the door. He opened it, closed it behind him, and stepped out to the shade of the ramada.

Duane Kidston had not moved; but Royce, holding the carbine with the white cloth, had come up on his right. Bill Dancey and Joe Bob remained fifteen to twenty feet behind them, though they had moved well apart.

"You have exactly"—Duane studied his watch—"two hours and forty-three minutes to pack and get out. Not a minute more."

Cable moved from shade to sunlight. He approached Duane, seeing him shift his feet and pocket his watch, and he heard Royce say, "Don't let him get too close."

Then Duane: "That's far enough!"

Cable ignored this. He came on until less than six feet separated him from Duane.

"I thought if we didn't have to shout," Cable said, "we could straighten this out."

"There's nothing to straighten," Duane said stiffly.

"Except you're trying to run me from my own land."

"That assumption is the cause of your trouble," Duane said. "This doesn't happen to be your land."

"It has been for ten years now."

"This property belonged to a Confederate sympathizer," Duane said. "I confiscated it in the name of the United States government, and until a court decides legal ownership, it remains ours."

"And if we don't leave?"

"I will not be responsible for what happens."

"That includes my family?"

"Man, this is a time of war! Often the innocent must suffer. But that is something I can do nothing to prevent."

"You make it pretty easy for yourself," Cable said.

"I'm making it easy for *you!*" Duane paused, as if to control the rage that had colored his face. "Listen, the easy way is for you to load your wagon and get out. I'm giving you this chance because you have a family. If you were alone, I'd take you to Fort Buchanan as a prisoner of war." Duane snapped his fingers. "Like that and without any talk."

"Even though I'm no longer a soldier?"

"You're still a Rebel. You fought for an enemy of the United States. You likely even killed some fine boys working for that bushwhacker of a Bedford Forrest and I'll tell you this, whether you're wearing a uniform or not, if it wasn't for your family, I'd do everything in my power to destroy you."

Joe Bob shifted his weight from one leg to the other. "That's tellin' him, Major." He winked, grinning at Bill Dancey.

Duane glanced over his shoulder, but now Joe Bob's face showed nothing. He stood lazily, with his hip cocked, and only nodded as Duane said, "I'll do the talking here."

Like yesterday, Cable thought. They're waiting to eat you up. His gaze shifted from Royce and Duane to Joe Bob.

Just like yesterday—

And the time comes and you can't put it off.

Cable's gaze swung back to Duane, though Joe Bob was still in his vision, and abruptly he said, "There's a shotgun dead on you." He waited for the reaction, waited for Joe Bob's mind to snap awake and realize what he meant. And the moment the man's eyes shifted to the house, Cable acted. He drew the Walker Colt, thumbed back the hammer and leveled it at Duane's chest. It happened quickly, unexpectedly; and now there was nothing Duane or any of his men could do about it.

"Now get off my land," Cable said. "Call a retreat, Major, or *I* won't be responsible for what happens."

An expression of shocked surprise showed in Duane's eyes and his mouth came open even before he spoke. "We're here under a flag of truce!"

"Take your flag with you."

"You can't pull a gun during a truce!"

"It's against the rules?"

Duane controlled his voice. "It is a question of honor. Something far beyond your understanding."

Royce stood with the truce-flag carbine cradled over one arm, holding it as if he'd forgotten it was there. "He makes it worthwhile. You got to give him that."

"Major"—Joe Bob's voice—"are you a chance-taking man? I was thinking, if you were quick on your feet—"

"I told you to keep out of this!" Duane snapped the words at him.

Looking at Duane as he spoke, at him and past him, Cable saw the horse and rider coming up out of the river, crossing the sand flat, climbing the bank now.

"I was just asking," Joe Bob said lazily. "If you thought you could flatten quick enough, we'd cut him in two pieces."

The rider approached them now, walking his horse out of the willows. A moment before they heard the hoof sounds, Cable said, "Tell your man to stay where he is."

Joe Bob saw him first and called out, "Vern, you're missing it!" Royce and Dancey turned as Joe Bob spoke, but Duane's eyes held on Cable.

"You've waited too long," Duane said.

Cable backed off a half step, still holding the Walker on Duane; but now he watched Vern Kidston as he approached from beyond Dancey, passing him now, sitting heavily and slightly stooped in the saddle, his eyes on Cable as he came unhurriedly toward him. A few yards away he stopped but made no move to dismount.

With his hat forward and low over his eyes, the upper half of his face was in shadow, and a full mustache covering the corners of his mouth gave him a serious, solemn look. He was younger than

Duane—perhaps in his late thirties—and had none of Duane's physical characteristics. Vern was considerably taller, but that was not apparent now. The contrast was in their bearing and Cable noticed it at once. Vern was Vern, without being conscious of himself. Thoughts could be in his mind, but he did not give them away. You were aware of only the man, an iron-willed man whose authority no one here questioned. In contrast, Duane could be anyone disguised as a man.

Vern Kidston sat with his hands crossed limply over the saddle horn He sat relaxed, obviously at ease, staring down at this man with the Walker Colt. Then, unexpectedly, his eyes moved to Bill Dancey.

"You were supposed to meet me this morning. Coming back I stopped up on the summer meadow and waited two hours for you."

"Duane says come with him else I was through," Dancey said calmly, though a hint of anger showed in his bearded face. "Maybe we ought to clear this up, just who I take orders from."

Vern Kidston looked at his brother then. "I go up to Buchanan for one day and you start taking over."

"I'd say running this man off your land is considerably more important than selling a few horses," Duane said coldly.

"You would, uh?" Vern's gaze shifted. His eyes went to the house, then lowered. "So you're Cable."

Cable looked up at him. "I've been waiting for you."

"I guess you have."

"Vern"—it was Duane's voice—"he pulled his gun under a sign of truce!"

Kidston looked at his brother. "I'd say the issue is he's still holding it." His eyes returned to Cable. "One man standing off four." He paused thoughtfully. "His Colt gun doesn't look that big to me."

Cable moved the Walker from Duane to Vern. "How does it look now?"

Vern seemed almost to smile. "There's seven miles of nerve between pointing a gun and pulling the trigger."

Cable stared at him, feeling his hope of reasoning with Kidston dissolve. But it was momentary. It was there with the thought: He's like the rest of them. His mind's made up and there's no arguing with him. Then the feeling was gone and the cold rage crept back into him, through him, and he told himself: But you don't budge. You know that, don't you? Not one inch of ground.

"Mr. Kidston," Cable said flatly, "I've fought for this land before. I've even had to kill for it. I'm not proud of saying that, but it's a fact. And if I have to, I'll kill for it again. Now if you don't think this land belongs to me, do something about it."

"I understand you have a family," Kidston said.

"I'll worry about my family."

"They wouldn't want to see you killed right before their eyes."

Cable cocked his wrist and the Walker was pointed directly at Vern's face. "It's your move, Mr. Kidston."

Vern sat relaxed, his hands still crossed on the saddle horn. "You know you wouldn't have one chance of coming out of this alive.

"How good are your chances?"

"Maybe you wouldn't have time to pull the trigger."

"If you think they can shoot me before I do, give the word."

Twenty feet to Cable's right, Joe Bob said, "Wait him out, Vern. He can't stand like that all day. Soon as his arm comes down I'll put one clean through him."

Dancey said, "And the second you move the shotgun cuts you in two."

Vern's eyes went to the house. "His wife?"

"Look close," Dancey said. "You see twin barrels peeking out the window. I'd say she could hold it resting on the ledge longer than we can stand here."

Vern studied the house for some moments before his gaze returned to Cable. "You'd bring your wife into it? Risk her life for a piece of land?"

"My wife killed a Chiricahua Apache ten feet from where you're standing," Cable said bluntly. "They came like you've come and she killed to defend our home. Maybe you understand that. If you don't, I'll say only this. My wife will kill again if she has to, and so will I."

Thoughtfully, slowly, Kidston said, "Maybe you would." A silence followed until his eyes moved to Duane. "Go on home. Take your cavalry and get."

"I'm going," Duane said coldly. "I'm going to Fort Buchanan. If you can't handle this man, the army can."

"Duane, you're going home."

"I have your word you'll attend to him?"

"Go on, get out of here."

Duane hesitated, as if thinking of a way to salvage his self-respect, then turned without a word and walked off.

Kidston looked at his three riders. None of them had moved. "Go with him. And take your gear."

They stood lingeringly until Vern's gaze returned to Cable. That dismissed them and they moved away, picked up the gear Cable had piled by the barn and followed Duane to the willows.

"Well," Cable said, "are we going to live together?"

"I don't think you'll last."

"Why?"

"Because," Kidston said quietly, "you're one man; because you've got a family; because your stomach's going to be tied in a knot wondering when I'm coming. You won't sleep. And every time there's a sound you'll jump out of your skin. . . . Your wife will tell you it isn't worth it; and after a while, after her nerves are worn raw, she'll stop speaking to you and acting like a wife to you, and you won't see a spark of life in her."

Cable's gaze went to the house and he called out, "Martha!" After a moment the door opened and Martha came out with the shotgun under her arm. Kidston watched her, removing his hat as she neared them and holding it in his hand. He stood with the sun shining in his face and on his hair that was dark and straight and pressed tightly to his skull with perspiration. He nodded as Cable introduced them and put on his hat again.

"Mr. Kidston says we'll leave because we won't be able to stand it," Cable said now. "He says the waiting and not knowing will wear our nerves raw and in the end we'll leave of our own accord."

"What did you say?" Martha asked.

"I didn't say anything."

"I don't suppose there's much you could." She looked off toward the willows, seeing the men there mounting and starting across the river, then looked at her husband again. "Well, Cabe," she said, "are you going to throw Mr. Kidston out or ask him in for coffee?"

"I don't know. What do you think?"

"Perhaps Mr. Kidston will come back," Martha answered, "when we're more settled."

"Perhaps I will," Kidston said. His eyes remained on Martha: a woman who could carry a shotgun gracefully and whose eyes were dark and clear, warmly clear, and who stared back at him calmly and with confidence. He recalled the way she had walked out to meet him, with the sun on her dark hair, coming tall and unhurried with the faint movement of her legs beneath the skirt.

"Maybe you'll stay at that," Vern said, still looking at Martha. "Maybe you're the kind that would."

Cable watched him walk off toward the willows, and he was trying to picture this solemn-faced man kissing Luz Acaso.

For the rest of the morning and through the afternoon, there was time to think about Kidston and wonder what he would do; but there was little time for Cable and Martha to talk about him.

Vern wanted the land and if Cable didn't move, if he couldn't be frightened off the place, he would be forced off at gun point. It was strange; Vern was straightforward and easy to talk to. You believed what he said and knew he wasn't scheming or trying to trick you. Still, he wanted the land; and if waiting wouldn't get it for him, he would take it. That was clear enough.

Cable chopped wood through the afternoon, stacking a good supply against the back wall of the adobe. Soon he'd be working cattle again and there would be little time for close to home chores.

Then, after supper, he heard the creaking barn door. If the wind rose in the night, the creaking sound would become worse and wake him up. He would lie in bed thinking and losing sleep. You could think too much about something like this; Cable knew that. You could picture too many possibilities of failure and in the end you could lose your nerve and run for it. Sometimes it was better to let things just happen, to be ready and try to do the right thing, but just not think about it so much.

So he went out into the dusk to see about the door. Carrying an unlit lantern, Cable opened the door and stepped into the dim stillness of the barn. He hung the lantern on a peg and was bringing his arms down when the gun barrel pushed into his back.

"Now we'll do it our way," Joe Bob said.

THREE

Royce lifted the Walker from Cable's holster. He stepped back and Joe Bob came in swinging, hooking his right hand hard into Cable's cheek. In the semi-darkness there was a grunt and a sharp smacking sound and Cable was against the board wall. Joe Bob turned him, swinging again, and broke through Cable's guard. He waded in then, grunting, slashing at Cable's face with both fists, holding him pinned to the boards, now driving a mauling fist low into Cable's body, then crossing high with the other hand to Cable's face. Joe Bob worked methodically, his fists driving in one after the other, again and again and again, until Cable's legs buckled. He had not been able to return a blow or even cover himself and now his back eased slowly down the boards. Joe Bob waited, standing stoop-shouldered and with his hands hanging heavily. Then his elbows rose; he went back a half step, came in again and brought his knee up solidly into Cable's jaw.

Abruptly, Royce said, "Listen!"

There was no sound except for Joe Bob's heavy, open-mouthed breathing. The silence lengthened until Royce said, between a whisper and a normal tone, "I heard somebody."

"Where?"

"Shhh!" Royce eased toward the open door.

"Cabe?" It came from outside. Martha's voice.

Royce let his breath out slowly. He stepped into the doorway and saw Martha in the gray dusk. She was perhaps forty feet from him, near the corner of the house.

"Who is it?"

"Evening, Mrs. Cable."

"Who's there?"

"It's just me. Royce." He stepped outside.

"Where's my husband?"

"Inside. Me and Joe Bob came back for some stuff we left"—he was moving toward her now—"and your husband's helping us dig it out."

She called past Royce. "Cabe?"

No answer. Five seconds passed, no more than that, then Martha had turned and was running—around the corner of the log section to the dark shadow of the ramada, hearing him behind her as she pushed the door open into bright lamplight and swung it closed. She heard him slam against it, hesitated—*Hold the door or go for the shotgun!*—saw Clare wide-eyed and said, "Go to the other room!" Martha was near the stove, raising the shotgun when Royce burst into the room. His hand was under the barrel as she pulled the trigger and the blast exploded up into the ceiling.

Royce threw the shotgun aside. He stood breathing in and out heavily. "You like to killed me."

"Where's my husband?"

"Old Joe Bob's straightening things out with him."

She was aware of the children crying then. Past Royce, she saw them just inside the bedroom. Clare's face was red and glistened with tears. And because she cried, Sandy was crying, with his lower lip pouted and his eyes tightly closed. Davis was staring at Royce. His eyes were round and large and showed natural fear, but he stood with his fists balled and did not move.

"There's nothing to cry about," Martha said. "Come kiss me good night and go to bed." They stood in their flannel nightshirts, afraid now to come into the room. Martha started for them, but she stopped.

Cable stood in the doorway. Joe Bob pushed him from behind and he lurched in, almost going to his knees, but caught himself against the back of a chair. Davis watched his father. His sister and brother were still crying, whimpering, catching their breath.

Abruptly both children stopped, their eyes on Joe Bob as he came toward them. He said nothing, and no more than glanced at them before slamming the bedroom door in their faces. Immediately their crying began again, though now the sound was muffled by the heavy door.

Martha poured water from the kettle, saturating a dish towel; she wrung the water from it and brought it to Cable who was bent over the back of the chair, leaning heavily on it with his arms supporting him stiffly.

"Cabe, are you all right?"

He took the towel from her, pressing it to his mouth, then looked at the blood on the cloth and folded it over, touching it to his mouth again. His teeth throbbed with a dullness that reached up into his head. He could not feel his lips move when he spoke.

"It's not as bad as it looks."

Joe Bob said, "Then maybe I should give you some more."

Martha turned the chair around, helping her husband sit down. Cable's eyes raised. "The children—?"

"They're all right. They're frightened, that's all."

"You better go talk to them."

"You better not," Joe Bob said. "They'll shut up after a while."

Martha looked at him now. "What do you want?"

"I'm not sure," Joe Bob said. "We're taking one step at a time." He glanced at Royce. "I wish Austin and Wynn were here." He was referring to his two brothers who also worked for Kidston. "They'd have some ideas. Man, would they!"

"Do you want us to leave?" asked Martha.

"Not right yet." Joe Bob glanced at Royce again, winking this time. "We might think of something." His gaze went beyond Royce, moving over the room and coming back to Martha. "You're such a fine housekeeper, maybe we'll keep you here." He winked at Royce again. "How'd you like to keep house for us?"

Martha did not speak, but she held Joe Bob's gaze until he grinned and moved away from her, going toward the kitchen cupboards.

"I don't know if I'd want her," Royce said. "She like to took my head off."

"I heard," Joe Bob said. He had opened a top cupboard and was reaching up into it. "Man, look at this." He took down an almost-full whisky bottle, smiling now and looking at Cable as he turned. "Would you've thought it of him?" Job Bob uncorked the bottle and took a drink. "Man—"

Royce was next to him now, taking the bottle and drinking from it. He scowled happily, wiping his hand across his mouth. "Now this puts a different light on the subject."

Joe Bob took the bottle again, extending it to Martha. "Sweetie?"

"No, thank you."

"Just a little one."

Royce said, "Don't pour it away. If she doesn't want any, all right." He watched Joe Bob lift the bottle and snatched it from him as it came down. Now he took his time, smiling, looking at the label before he drank again.

"I think we ought to sit down," Royce said. "Like a party."

"And talk to her about staying," Joe Bob said.

Royce grinned. "Wouldn't that be something."

"Man, picture it."

"Maybe we'd even pay her."

"Sure we would. With love and affection."

Cable said, "Does Vern know you're here?"

Royce looked at Cable. "Maybe I ought to take a turn on him."

"Help yourself," Joe Bob said.

"Vern and I agreed to settle this ourselves," Cable said.

Joe Bob looked at Royce. "He don't talk so loud now, does he?"

"He knows better," Royce said.

Joe Bob nodded thoughtfully. He drank from the bottle before saying, "You think we need him?"

"What for?" Royce took the bottle.

"That's the way I feel."

"Hell, throw him out."

"What about the kids—throw them out too?"

"Do you hear any kids? They're asleep already. Kids forget things a minute later." Royce lifted the bottle.

"Just throw him out, uh?"

"Sure. He'll lay out there like a hound. Else he'll crawl away. One way or the other, what difference does it make?"

Joe Bob considered this. "He can't go for help. Where'd he go, to Vern? To the one-arm man?"

Royce nodded. "Maybe to Janroe."

"So he does," Joe Bob said. "How's the one-arm man going to help him?" Joe Bob shook his head. "He's in a miserable way."

"Sure he is."

"Too miserable."

"Don't feel sorry for him."

"I mean, put him out of his misery."

Now Royce said nothing.

"Not us do it," Joe Bob said. "Him do it."

"I don't follow."

"You don't have to." Joe Bob drank from the bottle, then stood holding it, staring at Cable. "As long as he does." After a moment he handed Royce the bottle and walked over to Cable.

"You understand me, don't you?"

Cable straightened against the back of the chair. He shook his head.

"You will." Joe Bob stood close to him, looking down, and said then, "You're a miserable man, aren't you?"

Cable sat tensed. He could not fight Joe Bob now and there was nothing he could say. So he remained silent, his eyes going to Martha who stood with her hands knotted into slender fists. Still with his eyes on Martha, he felt the sudden, sharp pain in his scalp and in a moment he was looking up into Joe Bob's tight-jawed face.

Close to his belt, Joe Bob held Cable's head back, his hand fisted in Cable's hair. "I asked if you're a miserable man!"

Cable tried to swallow, but most of the blood-saliva remained in his mouth. He said. "I'd be a liar if I said I wasn't." The words came hesitantly, through swollen lips. But he stared up at Joe Bob calmly, breathing slowly, and only when he saw the man's expression change did he try to push up out of the chair. Then it was too late.

He went back with the chair as Joe Bob's fist slammed into his face. On the floor he rolled to his side, then raised himself slowly to his hands and knees. Joe Bob stood looking down at him with both fists balled and his jaw clenched in anger.

"I hate a man who thinks he's smart. God, I hate a man who does that."

Joe Bob was feeling the whisky. It showed in his face; and the cold, quiet edge was gone from the tone of his voice. On Royce, the whisky was having an opposite effect. He was grinning, watching Joe Bob with amusement; and now he said, "If he bothers you, throw him out. That's all you got to do."

"Better than that," Joe Bob said. He extended a hand to Royce though his eyes remained on Cable. "Give me his Colt."

"Sure." Royce pulled the revolver from his belt and put it in Joe Bob's hand. He stepped back, watching with interest as Joe Bob turned the cylinder to check the load.

"You're going to kill him?"

"You'll see." Joe Bob cocked the revolver. He pointed it at Cable and motioned to the door. "Walk outside."

Cable came to his feet. He looked at Martha, then away from her and walked toward the open door, seeing the dark square of it, then the deep shadow of the ramada as he neared the door, and beyond it, over the yard, a pale trace of early moonlight.

Now he was almost in the doorway, and the boot steps came quickly behind him. He was pushed violently through the opening, stumbled as he hit the ground and rolled out of the deep shadow of the ramada. He pushed himself to his knees, then fell flat again as Joe Bob began firing from the doorway. With the reports he heard Martha's scream. And as suddenly as the gunfire began, it was over. He heard Joe Bob say, "I wasn't aiming at him. If I was aiming he'd be dead. I got rid of four rounds is all."

Joe Bob leaned in the doorway looking out into the darkness, the whisky warm inside of him and feeling Royce and the woman watching him. He would make it good, all right. Something Royce would tell everybody about.

He called out to Cable, "One left, boy. Put yourself out of your misery and save Vern and me and everybody a lot of trouble. Pull the trigger and it's all over. Nobody worries any more."

He flipped the Walker in his hand, held it momentarily by the barrel, then threw it side-arm out to the yard. The revolver struck the ground, skidded past Cable, and the door slammed closed.

What would Forrest do?

That was a long time ago.

But what would he do? Cable thought.

He'd call on them to surrender. Not standing the way Duane stood, but with a confidence you could feel. The Yankees felt it and that part was real. He'd convince them he had more men and more artillery than they did—by having more buglers than companies and by having the same six field pieces come swinging down around the hill and into the woods, which was the reason the Yankee raider, Streight, surrendered—and only that part was unreal. And if they didn't surrender, he'd find their weak point and beat the living hell out of it.

But these two won't surrender. You're seven hundred miles away from that. So what's their weak point?

Almost a quarter of an hour had passed since the door slammed closed. Cable lay on his stomach, on the damp sand at the end of the river. He bathed his face, working his jaw and feeling the soreness of it, and rinsed his mouth until the inside bleeding stopped. The Walker Colt, with one load in it, was in his holster. And now what?

Now you think it out and do it and maybe it will work. Whatever it is.

What would Forrest do?

Always back to him, because you know he'd do something. God, and Nathan Bedford Forrest, I need help. God's smile and Forrest's bag of tricks.

When too many things crowded into Cable's mind, he would stop thinking. He would calm himself, then tell himself to think very slowly and carefully. A little anger was good, but not rage; that hindered thinking. He tried not to think of Martha, because thinking of her and picturing her with them and wondering made it more difficult to take this coldly, to study it from all sides.

Two and a half years ago, he thought, you wouldn't be lying here. You'd be dead. You'd have done something foolish and you'd be dead. But you have to hurry. You still have to hurry.

But even thinking this, and not being able to keep the picture of them with Martha out of his mind, he kept himself calm.

He was thankful for having served with Forrest. You learned things watching Forrest and you learned things getting out of the situations Forrest got you into. There had been times like this—not the same because there was Martha and the children now—but there had been outnumbered times and one-bullet times and lying close to the ground in the moonlight times. And he had come through them.

Their weak point, Cable thought. Or their weakness.

Whisky . . . its effect on Joe Bob. His act of bravado, throwing the one-load revolver out after him, telling him to use it on himself.

What if he did?

What if they heard a shot and thought he did? Would they come outside? The one-load revolver could be Joe Bob's mistake. His weak point.

There it was. A possibility. Would one come out, or both? Or neither?

Just get them out, he thought. Stop thinking and get them out. He crawled on his hands and knees along the water's edge until he found a rock; one with smooth edges, heavy enough and almost twice the size of his fist. He rose now, moved back to the chest-high bank, climbed it and stood in the dark willow shadows. Drawing the revolver, cocking it, he moved closer to the trunk of the willow. Then, pointing the barrel directly at the ground, he squeezed the trigger.

The report was loud and close to him, then fading, fading and leaving a ringing that stretched quickly to silence; and now even the night sounds that had been in the trees and in the meadow across the river were gone.

Through the heavy-hanging branches he watched the house, picturing Joe Bob standing still in the room. Wonder about it, Cable thought. But not too long. Look at your friend who's looking at you and both of you wonder about it. Then decide. Come on, decide right now. Somebody has to come out and make sure. You don't believe it, but you'd like to believe it, so you have to come see. Decide that one of you has to watch Martha. So only one of you can come out. Come on, get it through your head! That's the way it has to be!

And finally the door opened.

He saw a man framed in the doorway with the light behind him. The man stood half turned, talking back into the room. Then he stepped outside, drawing his revolver. Another figure appeared in the doorway, but the man outside came on alone. Cable let his breath out slowly.

He stood close to the trunk of the tree now, holding the rock against his stomach, watching the man coming carefully across the yard. He was not coming directly toward Cable, but would enter the trees about twelve or fifteen feet from him.

Now he was nearing the trees, moving cautiously and listening. He came on and a moment later was in the willows, out of sight.

"I don't see him!" The voice came from the trees, shouted toward the house. It was Royce.

From the doorway, Joe Bob called back, "Look along the bank."

Cable waited. He heard Royce. Then saw him, moving along the bank, stepping carefully and looking down at the sand flat. Cable tightened against the tree, waiting. Now Royce was near, now ducking under the branches of Cable's tree—his revolver in his right hand, on the side away from Cable. Royce stepped past him and stopped.

"I don't see him!"

From the house: "Keep looking!"

Royce started off, looking down at the sand flat again. Cable was on him in two strides, bringing the rock back as he came, holding on to it and slamming it against the side of Royce's head as the man started to turn. Cable's momentum carried both of them over the bank. He landed on Royce with his hand on the revolver barrel and came up holding it, cocking it, not bothering with

Royce now, but ducking down as he wheeled to climb out of the cutbank and into the trees again.

From the house: "Royce?"

Silence.

"Royce, what'd you do?"

Take him, Cable thought. Before he goes back inside. Before he has time to think about it.

He took the barrel of the revolver in his left hand. He wiped his right hand across the front of his shirt, stretched his fingers, opening and closing his hand, then gripped the revolver again and moved out of the trees.

Joe Bob saw him and called out, "Royce?"

Cable remembered thinking one thing: You should have taken Royce's hat. But now it was too late. He was in the open moving across the yard that was gray and shadow-streaked with moonlight.

"Royce, what's the matter with you!"

Cable was perhaps halfway across the yard when he stopped. He half turned, planting his feet and bringing up the revolver; he extended it straight out, even with his eyes, and said, "Joe Bob—" Only that.

And for a moment the man stood still. He knew it was Cable and the knowing it held him in the light-framed doorway unable to move. But he had to move. He had to fall back into the room or go out or draw. And it had to be done *now*—

Cable was ready. He saw Joe Bob's right-hand revolver come out, saw him lunging for the darkness of the ramada and he squeezed the trigger on this suddenly moving target. Without hesitating he lowered the barrel, aiming at where Joe Bob would have to be and fired again; then a third time; and when the heavy, ringing sound died away there was only silence.

He walked through the fine smoke to where Joe Bob lay, facedown with his arms outstretched in front of him. Standing over him, he looked up to see Martha in the doorway.

"It's all right now," Cable said. "It's all over."

"Is he dead?"

Cable nodded.

And Royce was dead.

Now, remembering the way he had used the rock, swinging viciously because there was one chance and only one, Cable could see how it could have killed Royce. But he hadn't *intended* killing Joe Bob. He had wanted badly to hold a gun on him and fire it and see him go down, doing it thoroughly because with Joe Bob also he would have only one momentary chance; but that was not the same as wanting to kill.

Cable found their horses in the pines above the barn. He led them down to the yard and slung the two men face-down over the saddles, tying them on securely. After that he took the horses across the river and let them go to find their way home. Let Vern see them now, if he put them up to it. Even if he didn't, let him bury them; they were his men.

When Cable returned to the house he said, "In the morning we'll go see Janroe. We'll ask him if you and the children can board at the store."

Martha watched him. "And you?"

"I'll come back here."

Bill Dancey came in while the Kidstons were eating noon dinner. He appeared in the archway from the living room and removed his hat when he saw Lorraine at the table with two men.

"It's done," Dancey said. "They're both under ground."

Vern looked up briefly. "All right."

"What about their gear?"

"Divvy it up."

"You could cast lots," Lorraine said.

Duane looked at her sternly. "That remark was in very poor taste."

Duane was looking at Vern now and not giving Lorraine time to reply.

"You mean to tell me you weren't present at their burial? Two men are murdered in your service and you don't even go out and read over their graves?"

"They were killed," Vern said. "Not in my service."

"All right." Duane couldn't hide his irritation. "No matter how it happened, it's proper for the commanding . . . for the lead man to read Scripture over their graves."

"If the head man knows how to read," Lorraine said.

"I didn't know you were burying them right away." Duane's voice became grave. "Why didn't you tell me? I'd have read over them. I'd have considered it an honor. Two boys giving their lives defending—"

Vern's eyes stopped him. "That enough of that. Duane, if I thought for a minute you sent those two over there—"

"I told you I didn't. They went on their own."

"Something else," Bill Dancey said. "Cable's moved his wife and kids into Denaman's."

Vern looked at him. "Who said so?"

"Man I sent to the store this morning. He saw the wagon and asked Luz about it. Luz says the woman and the kids are staying there, but Cable's going back to his place."

Vern rose from the table and walked around it toward Bill Dancey. He heard Duane say, "You'll run him out now; there's nothing to stop you. Vern, you hear me? You let me know when you're leaving because I want to be there." Vern did not reply or even look at Duane. Dancey turned and he followed him out through the long, beam-ceilinged, adobe-plastered living room, through the open double doors to the veranda that extended across the front of the house.

Dancey said, "What about their horses?"

"Put them in the remuda."

"Then what?"

"Then work for your money." As Dancey turned and started down the steps, Vern said, "Wait a minute." He moved against a support post and stood looking down at Dancey.

"How do you think he did it?"

"With a Colt and a rock," Dancey answered dryly.

"I asked you a question."

"And I don't know the answer you want." Dancey walked off, but he stopped within a few strides and looked back at Vern. "Why don't you ask Cable?"

"Maybe I will."

"With Joe Bob's brother along?"

"He hit you, too, Bill. The first time you met him."

"Not that hard," Dancey said. He turned away.

Vern watched him continue on. So now it was even starting to bother Dancey, this fighting a lone man.

He was almost sure Cable had not murdered them. He was sure Joe Bob and Royce had gone to him with drawn guns, but somehow Cable had outwitted them and had been forced to kill them. And that was the difficult fact to accept. That Cable was capable of killing them. That he could think calmly enough to outsmart them, to do that while having a wife and children to worry about; and then kill them, one of them with his hands, a rock, yes, but with his hands.

What kind of a man was this Cable?

What was his breaking point? If he had one. That was it, some people didn't have a breaking point. They stayed or they died, but they didn't give up.

And now, because he had handled Joe Bob and Royce, Cable's confidence would be bolstered and it would take more patience or more prying or more of whatever the hell it was going to take to get him off the Saber.

Kidston had made up his mind that the river land would be his, regardless of Cable or anyone else who cared to contest it with him. This was a simple act of will. He wanted the land because he needed it. His horses had grazed the lush river meadow for two years and he had come to feel that this land was rightfully his.

The news of Cable's return had caused him little concern. A Confederate soldier had come home with his family. Well, that was too bad for the Rebel. Somehow Cable had outmaneuvered three men and made them run. Luck, probably. But the Rebel wasn't staying, Kidston was certain of that.

He had worked too hard for too many years: starting on his own as a mustanger, breaking wild horses and selling them half-green to whoever needed a mount. Then hiring White Mountain Apache boys and gathering more mustangs each spring. He began selling to the Hatch & Hodges stage-line people. His operation expanded and he hired more men; then the war put an end to the Hatch & Hodges business. The war almost ruined him; yet it was the war that put him back in business, with a contract to supply remounts to the Union cavalry. He had followed the wild herds to the Saber River country and here he settled, rebuilding the old Toyopa place. He employed fourteen riders—twelve now—and looked forward to spending the rest of his life here.

During the second year of the war his brother Duane had written to him—first from their home in Gallipolis, Ohio, then from Washington after he had marched his own command there to join the Army of the Potomac—pleading with Vern to come offer his services to the Union army. That was like Duane, Vern had thought. Dazzled by the glory of it, by the drums and the uniforms, and probably not even remotely aware of what was really at stake.

But it was at this time that Vern received the government contract for remounts. After that, joining the army was out of the question.

The next December Duane arrived with his daughter. Duane had not wanted to return to Gallipolis after having been relieved of his command. They had made him resign his commission because of incompetence or poor judgment or whatever shelling your own troops was called.

It had happened at Chancellorsville, during Duane's first and only taste of battle. His artillery company was thrown in to support Von Gilsa's exposed flank, south of the town and in the path of Stonewall Jackson's advance. When Von Gilsa's brigade broke and came running back, Duane opened fire on them and killed more Union soldiers than Jackson had been able to in his attack.

Duane, of course, gave his version. It was an understandable mistake. There had been no communication with Von Gilsa. They were running toward his position and he ordered the firing almost as a reflex action, the way a soldier is trained to react. It happened frequently; naturally mistakes were made in the heat of battle. It was expected. But Chancellorsville had been a Union defeat. That was why they forced him to resign his commission. A number of able commanders were relieved simply because the Army of the Potomac had suffered a setback.

Vern accepted his explanation and even felt somewhat sorry for him. But when Duane went on pretending he was a soldier and hired four new riders for his "scouts," as he called them, you could take just so much of that. What was it? Kidston's Guard, Scouts for Colonel J. H. Carleton, Military Department of Arizona. It was one thing to feel sympathy for Duane. It was another to let Duane assume so much importance just to soothe his injured pride.

And Lorraine, spoiled and bored and overly sure of herself. The worst combination you could find in a woman. Both she and her comic-opera officer of a father living under one roof. Still, it seemed there were some things you just had to put up with.

Though that didn't include a home-coming Confederate squeezing him off the river. Not after the years and the sweat, and breaking his back for every dollar he earned. . . .

That had been his reaction to Cable before he saw Cable face to face, before he talked to him. Since then, a gnawing doubt had crept into his mind. Cable had worked and sweated and fought, too. What about that?

Duane's logic at least simplified the question: Cable was an enemy of the Federal government in Federal territory. As such he had no rights. Take his land and good damn riddance.

"His family is *his* worry." Duane's words. "But in these times, Vern, and I'll testify to it, men with families are dying every day. We are a thousand miles from the fighting, but right here is an extension of the war. Sweep down on him! Drive him out! Burn him out if you have to!"

Still, Vern wished with all his strength that there was a way of driving Cable out without fighting him. He was not afraid of Cable. He respected him. And he respected his wife.

Vern found himself picturing the way Martha had walked out from the house with the shotgun under her arm. Cable was a lucky man to have a woman like that, a woman who could keep up with him and who had already given him three healthy children. A woman, Kidston felt, who thoroughly enjoyed being a woman and living with the man she loved.

He had thought that Luz Acaso was that kind exactly. In fact he had been sure of it. But ever since Janroe's coming she seemed a different person. That was something else to think about. Why would a woman as warm and openly affectionate as Luz change almost overnight? It concerned Janroe's presence, that much Kidston was sure of. But was Luz in love with him or mortally afraid of him? That was another question.

He heard steps behind him and looked over his shoulder to see Lorraine crossing the porch. She smiled at him pleasantly.

"Cabe makes you stop and think, doesn't he?"

"You're on familiar terms for only one meeting," Vern said.

"That's what his wife calls him." Lorraine watched her uncle lean against the support post. He looked away from her, out over the yard. "Don't you think that's unusual, a wife calling her husband by his last name?"

"Maybe that's what everybody calls him," Vern answered.

"Like calling you 'Kid.' " Lorraine smiled, then laughed. "No, I think she made up the name. I think it's her name for him. Hers only." Lorraine waited, letting the silence lengthen before asking, "What do you think of her?"

"I haven't thought."

"I thought you might have given Martha careful consideration."

"Why?"

"As a way of getting at her husband."

Vern looked at her now.

"What do you mean?"

Lorraine smiled. "You seem reluctant to use force. I doubt if you can buy him off. So what remains?"

"I'm listening."

"Strike at Cable from within."

"And what does that mean?"

Lorraine sighed. "Vern, you're never a surprise. You're as predictable as Duane, though you don't call nearly as much attention to yourself."

"Lorraine, if you have something to say—"

"I've said it. Go after him through Martha. Turn her against him. Break up his home. Then see how long he stays in that house."

"And if such a thing was possible—"

"It's very possible."

"How?"

"The other woman, Vern. How else?"

He watched her calmly. "And that's you."

She nodded once, politely. "Lorraine Kidston as"—she paused— "I need a more provocative name for this role."

Vern continued to watch her closely. "And if he happens to love his wife?"

"Of course he loves her. Martha's an attractive woman if you like them strong, capable and somewhat on the plain side. But that has nothing to do with it. He's a man, Vern. And right now he's in that place all alone."

"You've got a wild mind," Vern said quietly. "I'd hate to live with it inside me." He turned away from her and walked down the steps and across the yard.

You shocked him, Lorraine thought amusedly, watching him go. But wait until the shock wears off. Wait until his conscience stops choking him. Vern would agree. He would have it understood that such methods went against his grain; but in the end he would agree. Lorraine was sure of it and she was smiling now.

Cable passed through the store and climbed the stairs to the bedroom where Martha was unpacking. He watched her removing linens and towels from the trunk at the foot of the bed, turning to place them in the open dresser drawer an arm's length away.

"The children will be in here?"

Martha looked up. "Clare and Dave. Sandy will sleep with me."

"With Luz here, I think you'll get along with Janroe all right."

"As long as the children eat in the kitchen."

"Martha, I'm sorry."

She saw his frown deepen the tightly drawn lines of his bruised face. "Someday I'm going to bite my tongue off. I shouldn't have said that."

"I can't blame you," Cable said.

"But it doesn't make it any easier."

"If you weren't here," Cable said, "it wouldn't even be possible." He moved close to her and put his arms around her as she straightened.

"I want to say something like 'It'll be over soon,' or 'Soon we'll be going back and there won't be any more waiting, any more holding your breath not knowing what's going to happen.' But I can't. I can't promise anything."

"Cabe, I don't need promises. Just so long as you're here with us, that's all we need."

"Do you want to leave? Right this minute get in the wagon and go back to Sudan?"

"You don't mean that."

"I do. You say it and we'll leave."

For a moment Martha was silent, standing close to him, close to his bruised cheekbone and his lips that were swollen and cut. "If we went back," Martha said, "I don't think you'd be an easy man to live with. You'd be nice and sometimes you'd smile, but I don't think you'd ever say very much, and it would be as if your mind was always on something else." A smile touched her mouth and showed warmly in her eyes. "We'll stay, Cabe."

She lifted her face to be kissed and when they looked at each other again she saw his smile and he seemed more at ease.

"Are you going back right now?"

"I have to talk to Janroe first." He kissed her again before stepping away. "I'll be up in a little while."

Janroe was sitting in the kitchen, his chair half turned from the table so that he could look directly out through the screen door. He paid no attention to Luz who was clearing the table, carrying the dishes to the wooden sink. He was thinking of the war, seeing himself during that afternoon of August 30, in the fields near Richmond, Kentucky.

If that day had never happened, or if it had happened differently; if he had not lost his arm—no, losing his arm was only an indirect reason for his being here. But it had led to this. It had been the beginning of the end.

After his wound had healed, seven months later, with his sleeve in his belt and even somewhat proud of it but not showing his pride, he had returned to his unit and served almost another full year before they removed him from active duty. His discharge was sudden. It came shortly after he had had the Yankee prisoners shot. They said he would have to resign his commission because of his arm; but he knew that was not the reason and he had pleaded with them to let him stay, pestering General Kirby Smith's staff; but it came to nothing, and in the end he was sent home a civilian.

He had not told Cable about that year or about anything that had happened after August 30, after his arm was blown from his body. But Cable didn't have to know everything. Like soldiers before an engagement with the enemy—it was better not to tell them too much.

Stir them up, yes. Make them hate and be hungry to kill; but don't tell them things they didn't have to know, because that would start them thinking and soldiers in combat shouldn't think. You could scare them though. Sometimes that was all right. Get them scared for their own skins. Pour it into their heads that the enemy was ruthless and knew what he was doing and that he would kill them if they didn't kill him. Beat them if they wouldn't fight!

God knows he had done that. He remembered again the afternoon near Richmond, coming out of the brush and starting across the open field toward the Union battery dug in on the pine ridge that was dark against the sky. He remembered screaming at his men to follow him. He remembered this, seeing himself now apart from himself, seeing Captain Edward Janroe waving a Dragoon pistol and shouting at the men who were still crouched at the edge of the brush. He saw himself running back toward them, then swinging the barrel at a man's head. The man ducked and scrambled out into the field. Others followed him; but two men still remained, down on their knees and staring up at him wide-eyed with fear. He shot one of them from close range, cleanly through the head; and the second man was out of the brush before he could swing the Dragoon on him.

Yes, you could frighten a man into action, scare him so that he was more afraid of you than the enemy. Janroe stopped.

Could that apply to Cable? Could Cable be scared into direct action?

He eased his position, looking at Luz who was standing at the sink with her back to him, then at the screen door again and the open sunlight beyond. He had given his mind the opportunity to reject these questions, to answer them negatively.

But why not? Why couldn't Cable be forced into killing the Kidstons? He had been a soldier—used to taking orders. No, he couldn't be ordered. But perhaps now, with his wife and children staying here, he would be more easily persuaded. Perhaps he could be forced into doing it. Somehow.

In Janroe's mind it was clear, without qualifying shades of meaning, that Vern and Duane Kidston were the enemy. In uniform or not in uniform they were Yankees and this was a time of war and they had to be killed. A soldier killed. An officer ordered his men to kill. That was what it was all about and that was what Janroe knew best.

They could close their eyes to this fact and believe they were acting as human beings—whatever the hell that meant in time of war—and relieve him of his command for what he did to those Yankee prisoners. They could send him out here to die of boredom; but he could still remember what a Yankee field piece did to his arm. He was still a soldier and he could still think like a soldier and act like a soldier and if his job was to kill—whether or not on the surface it was called gunrunning—then he would kill.

He felt his chest rising and falling with his breathing and he glanced at Luz, calming himself then, inhaling and letting his breath out slowly.

Still, an officer used strategy. He fought with his eyes open; not rushing blindly, unless there was no other way to do it. An officer studied a situation and used what means he had at hand. If the means was a brigade or only one man, he used that means to the best of his ability.

Janroe looked up as Cable entered the kitchen. He glanced at Luz then, catching her eye, and the girl dried her hands and stepped out through the back door.

"I've been waiting for you," Janroe said.

"I was with my wife." Cable hesitated. "We're grateful for what you're doing."

"I guess you are."

Cable sat down, removing his hat and wiping his forehead with the back of his hand. "Martha will be glad to help out with the housekeeping, and she'll keep the children out from under your feet."

"I took that for granted," Janroe said.

"We'll be out of your way as soon as I settle this business with the Kidstons."

"And how long will that take?"

"Look, we'll leave right now if you want."

"You lose your temper too easily," Janroe said. "I was asking you a simple question."

Cable looked at him, then at his own hand curling the brim of his hat. "I don't know; it's up to the Kidstons."

"It could be up to you, if you wanted it to be."

"If I kill them."

"You didn't have any trouble last night."

"Last night two men came to my home," Cable said. "My family was in danger and I didn't have any choice. Though I'll tell you this: I didn't mean to kill them. That just happened. If Vern and Duane come threatening my home, then I could kill them too because I wouldn't be trying to kill them; I'd be trying to protect my home and my family, and there's a difference. When you say kill them, just go out and do it; that's something else."

Janroe was sitting back in his chair, his hand idly rubbing the stump of his arm; but now he leaned forward. His hand went to the edge of the table and he pushed the chair back.

"We could argue that point for a long time." He stood up then. "Come on, I'll show you something."

Cable hesitated, then rose and followed Janroe through the store and out to the loading platform. The children were at one end, stopped in whatever they were playing or pretending by the sudden appearance of Janroe. They looked at their father, wanting to go to him, but they seemed to sense a threat in approaching Janroe and they remained where they were.

Janroe said, "Tell them to go around back."

"They're not bothering anything." Cable moved toward the children.

"Listen," Janroe said patiently, "just get rid of them for a while—all right?"

He waited while Cable talked to the three children. Finally they moved off, taking their time and looking back as they turned the corner of the adobe. When they were out of sight, Janroe went down the stairs and, to Cable's surprise, ducked under the loading platform.

Cable followed, lowering his head to step through the cross timbers into the confining dimness. He moved with hunched shoulders the few steps to where Janroe was removing the padlock from a door in the adobe foundation.

"This used to be a storeroom," Janroe muttered. He pushed the door open and moved aside. "Go on; there's a lantern in there."

Cable hesitated, then stepped past him, glancing back to make sure Janroe was coming.

Janroe followed, saying, "Feel along the wall, you'll find it."

Cable turned, raising his left hand. He heard the door swing closed and he was in abrupt total darkness.

He heard Janroe's steps and felt him move close behind him. Too close! Cable tried to turn, reaching for the Walker at the same time; but his hand twisted behind him and pulled painfully between his shoulder blades. He tried to lunge forward, tried to twist himself free, but as he did Janroe's foot scissored about his ankles and Cable fell forward, landing heavily on the hard-packed floor with Janroe on top of him.

FOUR

Now there was silence.

With Janroe's full weight on top of him and the cool hardness of the floor flat against his cheek, Cable did not move. He felt Janroe's chest pressing heavily against his back. His right arm, twisted and held between their bodies, sent tight, muscle-straining pain up into his shoulder. Janroe had pulled his own hand free as they struck the floor. It gripped the handle of Cable's revolver, then tightened on it as the boards creaked above them.

Faint footsteps moved through the store and faded again into silence. Cable waited, listening, and making his body relax even with the weight pressing against him. He was thinking: It could be Martha, gone out to call the children. Martha not twenty feet away.

He felt the Walker slide from its holster. Janroe's weight shifted, grinding heavily into his back. The cocking action of the Walker was loud and close to him before the barrel burrowed into the pit of his arm.

"Don't spoil it," Janroe whispered.

They waited. In the darkness, in the silence, neither spoke. Moments later the floor creaked again and the soft footsteps crossed back through the store. Cable let his breath out slowly.

Janroe murmured, "I could have pulled the trigger. A minute ago I was unarmed; but just then I could have killed you."

Cable said nothing. Janroe's elbow pressed into his back. The pressure eased and he felt Janroe push himself to his feet. Still Cable waited. He heard Janroe adjust a lantern. A match scratched down the wall. Its flare died almost to nothing, then abruptly the floor in front of Cable's face took form. His eyes raised from his own shadow and in the dull light he saw four oblong wooden cases stacked against the wall close in front of him.

"Now you can get up," Janroe said.

Cable rose. He stretched the stiffness from his body, working his shoulder to relieve the sharp muscle strain, his eyes returning to Janroe now and seeing the Walker in Janroe's belt, tight against his stomach.

"Did you prove something by that?"

"I want you to know," Janroe said, "that I'm not just passing the time of day."

"There's probably an easier way."

"No." Janroe shook his head slowly. "I want you to realize that I could have killed you. That I'd do it in a minute if I thought I had to. I want that to sink into your head."

"You wouldn't have a reason."

"The reason's behind you. Four cases of Enfield rifles. They're more important than any one man's life. More important than yours—"

Cable stopped him. "You're not making much sense."

"Or more important than the lives of Vern and Duane Kidston," Janroe finished. "Does that make sense?"

"My hunting license." Cable watched him thoughtfully. "Isn't that what you called it? If I was in the gunrunning business, I could kill them with a clear conscience."

"I'll tell it to you again," Janroe said. "If you worked for me, I'd order you to kill them."

"I remember."

"But it still hasn't made any impression."

"I told you a little while ago, now it's up to the Kidstons."

"All right, what do you think they're doing right this minute?"

"Maybe burying their dead," Cable said. "And realizing something."

"And Joe Bob's brothers—do you think they're just going to bury him and forget all about it?"

"That's something else," Cable said.

"No it isn't, because Vern will use them. He'll sic them on you like a pair of mad dogs."

"I don't think so. I've got a feeling Vern's the kind of man who has to handle something like this himself, his own way."

"And you'd bet the lives of your family on it," Janroe said dryly.

"It's Vern's move, not mine."

"Like a chess game."

"Look," Cable said patiently. "You're asking me to shoot the man down in cold blood and that's what I can't do. Not for any reason."

"Even though you left your family and rode a thousand miles to fight the Yankees." Janroe watched him closely, making sure he held Cable's attention.

"Now you're home and you got Yankees right in your front yard. But now, for some reason, it's different. They're supplying cavalry horses to use against the same boys you were in uniform with. They're using your land to graze those horses. But now it's different. Now you sit and wait because it's the Yankees' turn to move."

"A lot of things don't sound sensible," Cable said, "when you put them into words."

"Or when you cover one ear," Janroe said. "You don't hear the guns or the screams and the moans of the wounded. You even have yourself believing the war's over."

"I told you once, it's over as far as I'm concerned."

Janroe nodded. "Yes, you've told me and you've told yourself. Now go tell Vern Kidston and his brother."

End it, Cable thought. Tell him to shut up and mind his own business. But he thought of Martha and the children. They were here in the safety of this man's house, living here now because Janroe had agreed to it. He was obligated to Janroe, and the sudden awareness of it checked him, dissolving the bald, blunt words that were clear in his mind and almost on his tongue.

He said simply, "I don't think we're getting anywhere."

Janroe's expression remained coldly impassive; still his eyes clung to Cable. He watched him intently, almost as if he were trying to read Cable's thoughts.

"You might think about it though," Janroe said. His eyes dropped briefly. He pulled the Walker from his waist and handed it butt-forward to Cable.

"Within a few days, I'm told, Bill Dancey and the rest of them will start bringing all the horses in from pasture. That means Duane and maybe even Vern will be home alone. Just the two of them there." Janroe lifted the lantern from the wall. Before blowing it out, he added, "You might think about that, too."

They moved out of the cellar into the abrupt sun glare of the yard, and there Janroe waited while Cable went inside to tell Martha good-bye. Within a few minutes Cable reappeared. Janroe watched him kneel down to kiss his children; he watched him mount the sorrel and ride out. He watched him until he was out of sight, and still he lingered in the yard, staring out through the sun haze to the willows that lined the river.

He isn't mad enough, Janroe was thinking. And Vern seems to want to wait and sweat him out. If he waits, Cable waits and nothing happens. And it will go on like this until you bring them together. You know that, don't you? Somehow you have to knock their heads together.

Manuel Acaso reached Cable's house in the late evening. The sky was still light, with traces of sun reflection above the pine slope, but the glare was gone and the trees had darkened and seemed more silent.

Manuel moved through the streaked shadows of the aspen grove, through the scattered pale-white trees, hearing only the sound of his own horse in the leaves. He stopped at the edge of the trees, his eyes on the silent, empty-appearing adobe; then he moved on.

Halfway across the yard he called out, "Paul!"

Cable parted the hanging willow branches with the barrel of the Spencer and stepped into the open. Manuel was facing the house, sitting motionless in the saddle with his body in profile as Cable approached, his face turned away and his eyes on the door of the house.

He looks the same, Cable thought. Perhaps heavier, but not much; and he still looks as if he's part of the saddle and the horse, all three of them one, even when he just sits resting.

Softly he said, "Manuel—"

The dark lean face in the shadow of the straw hat turned to Cable without a trace of surprise, but with a smile that was real and warmly relaxed. His eyes raised to the willows, then dropped to Cable again.

"Still hiding in trees," Manuel said. "Like when the Apache would come. Never be where they think you are."

Cable was smiling. "We learned that, Manolo."

"Now to be used on a man named Kidston," Manuel said. "Did you think I was him coming?"

"You could have been."

"Always something, uh?"

"Why didn't you run him when he first came?"

Manuel shrugged. "Why? It's not my land."

"You skinny Mexican, you were too busy running something else."

The trace of a smile left Manuel's face. "I didn't think Janroe would have told you so soon."

"You haven't seen him this evening?"

"No, I didn't stop."

"But you knew I was here."

"A man I know visited the store yesterday. Luz told him," Manuel said. "I almost stopped to see Martha and the little kids, but I thought, no, talk to him first, about Janroe."

"He wants me to join you, but I told him I had my own troubles."

"He must see something in you." Manuel leaned forward, resting his arms one over the other on the saddle horn, watching Cable closely. "What do you think of him?"

Cable hesitated. "I'm not sure."

"He told you how he came and how he's helping with the guns?"

"That he was in the war before and wounded."

"Do you believe him?"

"I don't have a reason not to. But I don't understand him."

"That's the way I felt about him; and still do."

"Did you check on him?"

"Sure. I asked the people I work with. They said of course he's all right, or he wouldn't have been sent here."

Looking up at Manuel, Cable smiled. It was good to see him, good to talk to him again, in the open or anywhere, and for the first time in three days Cable felt more sure of himself. The feeling came over him quietly with the calm, unhurried look of this man who lounged easily in his saddle and seemed a part of it—this thin-faced, slim-bodied man who looked like a boy and always would, who had worked his cattle with him and fought the Apache with him and helped him build his home. They had learned to know each other well, and there was much between them that didn't have to be spoken.

"Do you feel someone watching you?"

"This standing in the open," Manuel nodded. "Like being naked."

"We'd better go somewhere else."

"In the trees." Manuel smiled.

He took his horse to the barn and came back, walking with a slow, stiff-legged stride, his hand lightly on the Colt that was holstered low on his right side, holding it to his leg. He followed Cable into the willows. Then, sitting down next to him at the edge of the cutback, Manuel noticed the horse herd far out in the meadow beyond the river.

"You let Vern's horses stay?"

"I ran them once," Cable said. "Duane brought them back."

"So you run them again."

"Tomorrow. You want to come?"

"Tonight I'm back to my gun business."

Denaman, Cable thought. The old man's face appeared suddenly in his mind with the mention of the gun-running. He told Manuel what Janroe had said about John Denaman's death. That he was worried about his business. "But I suppose that meant worried about the guns," Cable said. "Having to sit on them and act natural."

"I think the man was just old," Manuel said. "I think he would have died anyway. Perhaps this gun business caused him to die a little sooner, but not much sooner."

"I'm sorry—"

"Thank you," Manuel said, with understanding, as if Denaman had been his own father.

"At first," Cable said, "I couldn't picture John fooling with something like this—living out here, far away from the war."

"Why?" Manuel's eyebrows rose. "You lived here and you went to fight."

"It seems different."

"Because he was old? John could have had the same feeling you did."

"I suppose."

"Sure, and I think you going off to war, and the other people he knew who went, convinced him he had to do something to help. Since he couldn't become a soldier he did this with the guns."

"Did he talk to you about it first?"

Manuel shook his head. "There were already guns under the store when I found out. John got into it through some man he knew who lives in Hidalgo. He didn't want me to help, said I had no part in it. But I told him if he believed in what he was doing then so did I, so why waste our breath over it."

"Do you believe in it?"

"I believed in John; that's enough."

"But what about now?"

"He started it," Manuel said. "I'll finish it, with or without the help of this man who's so anxious to kill."

"Something else," Cable said. "Janroe told me that John was worried about Luz. That she was keeping company with Vern, and John didn't like it."

Manuel nodded. "She was seeing him often before Janroe came. Sometimes it bothered me, Vern being around; but John said, no, that was good, let him sit up there in the parlor with Luz. If we sneaked around and stayed to ourselves, John said, then people would suspect things. . . . So I don't think he was worried about Vern Kidston. If anything, John liked him. They talked well together; never about the war but about good things. . . . No, Janroe was wrong about that part. He figured it out himself and maybe it made sense to him, but he's wrong."

"Luz stopped seeing Vern?"

"Right after Janroe came."

"Do you know why?"

"I think because she was afraid Janroe would kill him, or try to, and if it happened at the store it would be because of her." Manuel paused. "Does that make sense?"

"I suppose. Since she knew Janroe and Vern were on opposite sides."

"Luz is afraid of him and admits it," Manuel said. "She says she has a feeling about him and sees him in dreams as a *nagual*, a man who is able to change himself into something else. A man who is two things at the same time."

"He could be two different people," Cable said, nodding. "He could be what he tells you and he could be what he is, or what he is thinking. I don't know. I don't even know how to talk to him. He wants me to work for him and kill Vern and Duane because of what they're doing."

Manuel stared. "He asked me to do that, months ago."

"What did you tell him?"

"To go to hell."

"That's what I wanted to say," Cable said. "But now Martha and the kids are living in his house and I have to go easy with him. But he keeps insisting and arguing it and after a while I run out of things to tell him."

In the dimness, Manuel leaned closer, putting his hand on Cable's arm. "Do you want to find out more about this Janroe?"

"How?"

"I'll take you to the man I work for. John's friend from Hidalgo. He can tell you things."

"I don't know—"

"You were at the war and you'd understand what he says about Janroe. You'd be able to ask questions."

"Maybe I'd better." Cable's tone was low, thoughtful.

"Listen, you're worried about your land; I know that. But after this I'll help you and we'll run these Kidstons straight to hell if you say it."

"All right," Cable nodded. "We'll talk to your man."

It was still sky-red twilight when they rode out, but full dark by the time they passed the store, keeping to the west side of the river and high up on the slope so they wouldn't be heard.

Martha stood at the sink, taking her time with the breakfast dishes, making it last because she wasn't sure what she would do after this. Perhaps ask Luz if she could help with something else. Luz, not Mr. Janroe. But even if there was something to be done, Luz would shake her head no, Martha was sure of that. So what would she do then? Perhaps go outside with the children.

Her gaze rose from the dishwater to the window and she saw her children playing in the back yard: Davis and Sandy pushing stick-trains over the hard-packed ground and making whistle sounds; Clare sitting on a stump, hunched over her slate with the tip of her tongue showing in the corner of her mouth.

They're used to not seeing him, Martha thought. But you're not used to it, not even after two and a half years. And now he seems farther away than before.

That was a strange thing. She had waited for Cable during the war knowing he would come home, knowing it and believing it, because she prayed hard and allowed herself to believe nothing else. Now he was within one hour's ride, but the distance between them seemed greater than when he had served with General Forrest. And now, too, there was an uncertainty inside of her. Because you haven't had time to think about it, she thought. Or not think about it. This time you haven't gotten used to not thinking anything will happen to him.

For a moment the thought angered her. She had things to do at home. She had a family to care for, husband and children, but she stood calmly waiting and washing dishes in another person's house, away from her husband again, and again faced with the tiring necessity of telling herself everything would be all right.

Was it worth it?

If it wasn't, was anything worth waiting or fighting for? And she thought, if you don't have the desire to fight or wait for something, there's no reason for being on earth.

That's very easy to say. Now wash the dishes and live with it. Martha smiled then. No, she told herself, it was simply a question of stubbornness or resignation. If you ran away from one trouble, you would probably run into another. So face the first one, the important one, and get used to it. She remembered Cable saying, years before, "We've taken all there is to take. Nothing will make us leave this place."

And perhaps you can believe that, just as you knew and believed he would come home from the war, Martha thought. So put on the big-smiling mask again. Even if it makes you gag.

But I'm tired, Martha thought, not smiling now. Perhaps you can keep the mask on only so long before it suffocates you.

She glanced over her shoulder as Luz entered the kitchen.

"I think Mr. Janroe is going out," Luz said. She pulled a towel from a hook above the sink and began drying dishes. "He's in the store, but dressed to go out."

"Where would he be going?" Martha asked.

"I don't know. Sometimes he just rides off."

"Would it have anything to with the guns?"

Luz looked at her. "You know?"

"Of course. Don't you think Paul would have told me?"

"I wasn't sure."

"Luz, do you have anything to do with it?"

The girl nodded. "On the day the guns are to arrive, I ride down to Hidalgo in the afternoon. That night I return an hour ahead of them seeing that the way is clear. Manuel follows, doing the same. Then the guns come."

"Are you due to go again soon—or shouldn't I ask that?"

"It doesn't matter." The girl shrugged. "Tomorrow I go again."

"Aren't you afraid?"

"Not when I'm away from here."

"But you're afraid of Mr. Janroe," Martha said. "I'm sure of that. Why, Luz?"

"You don't know him or you wouldn't ask that."

"I know he's gruff. Hardly what you'd call a gentleman."

"No." Luz shook her head solemnly. She glanced at the doorway to the main room before saying, "It isn't something you see in him."

"Has he ever . . . made advances?"

"No, it isn't like that either," the girl said. "It's something you feel. Like an awareness of evil. As if his soul was so smeared with stains of sin you were aware of a foulness about him that could almost be smelled."

"Luz, to your knowledge the man hasn't done a thing wrong."

"The feeling is a kind of knowledge itself."

"But it isn't something you can prove, is it?" Martha stood with her hands motionless in the dishwater, her full attention on Luz. "What if suddenly you realize that all you've said couldn't possibly be true, that it's all something out of a dream or—"

"Listen, I did dream about him! A number of times before, then again last night." The girl's eyes went to the main room and back again.

"I saw an animal in the dream, like a small wolf or a coyote, and it was slinking along in the moonlight. Then, in front of it, there was a chicken. The chicken was feeding on the ground and before it could raise its head, the animal was on it and tearing it apart with its teeth and eating it even while the chicken was still alive. I watched, cold with fear, but unable to move. And as I watched, the animal began to change.

"It was still on its haunches facing me, still eating and smeared with the blood of the chicken. First it's hind legs became human legs; then its body became the clothed body of a man. Then the face began to change, the jaw and the nose and the chin. The teeth were still those of an animal and he had no forehead and his eyes and head were still like an animal's. He was looking at me with blood on his mouth and on his hand . . . on the one hand that he had. And at that moment I ran from him screaming. I knew it was the face of Mr. Janroe."

"Luz, you admit it's a dream—"

"Listen, that isn't all of it." Luz glanced toward the main room again. "I awoke in a sweat and with a thirst burning the inside of my throat. So I left my bed and went down for a drink of water. The big room was dark, but at once I saw that a lamp was burning in here. I came to the door, I looked into this room, and I swear on my mother's grave that my heart stopped beating when I saw him."

"Mr. Janroe?"

Luz nodded quickly. "He was sitting at the table holding a piece of meat almost to his mouth and his eyes were on me, not as if he'd looked up as I appeared, but as if he'd been watching me for some time. I saw his eyes and the hand holding the meat, just as in the dream, and I ran. I don't know if I screamed, but I remember wanting to scream and running up the stairs and locking my door."

Martha dried her hands on her apron. She smiled at Luz gently and put her hand on the girl's arm.

"Luz, there isn't anything supernatural about a man eating with his fingers."

"You didn't see him." Luz stopped. Her eyes were on the doorway again and a moment later Janroe appeared. Martha glanced at him, then at Luz again as the girl suddenly turned and pushed through the screen door.

Janroe came into the kitchen. He was holding his hat and wearing a coat, but the coat was open and Martha noticed the butt of a Colt beneath one lapel in a shoulder holster. Another Colt was on his hip.

"Did I interrupt something?"

"Nothing important." Martha turned from the sink to face him. "You're going out?"

"I thought I would." He watched her with an expression of faint amusement. "Wondering if I'm going to see your husband?"

"Yes, I was."

"I might see him."

"If you're going that way, would you mind stopping by the house?"

"Why?"

"Why do you think, Mr. Janroe?"

"Maybe he's not so anxious to let you know what he's doing."

Now a new side of him, Martha thought wearily. She said nothing.

"I mean, considering how he dropped you here and ran off so quick." Janroe hooked his hat on the back of the nearest chair. Unhurriedly he started around the table, saying now, "A man is away from his wife for two years or more, then soon as he gets home he leaves her again. What kind of business is that?"

Martha watched him still coming toward her. "We know the reason, Mr. Janroe."

"The reason he gives. Worried about his wife and kids."

"What other reason is there?"

"It wouldn't be my business to know."

"You seem to be making it your business."

"I was just wondering if you believed him."

He was close to her now. Martha stood unmoving, feeling the wooden sink against her back. "I believe him," she said calmly. "I believe anything he tells me."

"Did he tell you he led a saintly life the years he was away?"

"I never questioned him about it."

"Want me to tell you what a man does when he's away from home?"

"And even if I said no—"

"They have a time for themselves," Janroe went on. "They carry on like young bucks with the first smell of spring. Though they expect their wives to sit home and be as good as gold."

"You know this from experience?"

"I've seen them." His voice was low and confiding. "Some of them come home with the habit of their wild ways still inside them, and they go wandering off again."

He watched her closely, his head lowered and within inches of hers. "Then there's some women who aren't fooled by it and they say, 'If he can fool around and have a time, then so can I.' Those women do it, too. They start having a time for themselves and it serves their husbands right."

Martha did not move. She was looking at him, at his heavy mustache and the hard, bony angles of his face, feeling the almost oppressive nearness of him. She said nothing.

Janroe asked, almost a whisper, "You know what I mean?"

"If I were to tell my husband what you just said," Martha answered quietly, "I honestly believe he would kill you."

Janroe's expression did not change. "I don't think so. Your husband needs me. He needs a place for you and the kids to stay."

"Are you telling me that I'm part of the agreement between you and my husband?"

"Well now, nothing so blunt as all that." Janroe smiled. "We're white men."

"We'll be out of here within an hour," Martha said coldly.

"Now wait a minute. You don't kid very well, do you?"

"Not about that."

He backed away from her, reaching for his hat. "I don't even think you know what I was talking about."

"Let's say that I didn't," Martha said. "For your sake."

Janroe shrugged. "You think whatever you want." He put his hat on and walked out. In front of the store, he mounted a saddled buckskin and rode off.

He could still see the calm expression of Martha Cable's face as he forded the shallow river, as he kicked the buckskin up the bank and started across the meadow that rolled gradually up into the pines that covered the crest of the slope. Then he was spurring, running the buckskin, crossing the sweep of meadow, in the open sunlight now with the hot breeze hissing past his face. But even then Martha was before him.

She stared at him coldly. And the harder he ran—holding the reins short to keep the buckskin climbing, feeling the brute strength of the horse's response, hearing the hoofs and the wind and trying to be aware of nothing else—the more he was aware of Martha's contempt for him.

Some time later, following the trail that ribboned through the pines, the irritating feeling that he had made a fool of himself began to subside. It was as if here in the silence, in the soft shadows of the pines, he was hidden from her eyes.

He told himself to forget about her. The incident in the kitchen had been a mistake. He had seen her and started talking and one thing had led to another; not planned, just something suddenly happening that moment. He would have to be more careful. She was an attractive woman and her husband was miles away, but there were matters at hand more important than Martha Cable. She would wait until later, when there were no Kidstons . . . and no Paul Cable.

Still, telling himself this, her calmness and the indifference grated on his pride and he was sure that she had held him off because of his missing arm, because he was something repulsive to her. Only part of a man.

He jerked his mind back to the reason he was here. First, to talk to Cable, to hammer away at him until he consented to go after the Kidstons. Then, to scout around and see what was going on.

The latter had become a habit: riding this ridge trail, then bearing off toward the Kidston place and sometimes approaching within view of the house. He did this every few days and some times at night, because if you kept your eyes open you learned things. Like Duane's habit of sitting on the veranda at night—perhaps every night—for a last cigar. Or Vern visiting his grazes once a week and sometimes not returning until the next morning. But always there had been people around the house while Duane sat and smoked on the veranda; and almost invariably Vern made his inspections with Bill Dancey along. Knowing that Kidston's riders would be off on a horse gather in a few days was the same kind of useful intelligence to keep in mind. He had already told Cable about the riders being away. Perhaps he would tell him everything—every bit of information he knew about Vern and Duane Kidston. Lay it all out on the table and make it look easy.

High on the slope, but now even with Cable's house, Janroe reined in. There was no sign of life below. No sounds, no movement, no chimney smoke. But Cable could still be home, Janroe decided.

Then, descending the path, keeping his eyes on the shingled roof and the open area of the front yard, he began to think: But what if he isn't home?

Then you talk to him another time.

No, wait. What if he isn't home and isn't even close by?

Reaching the back of the adobe, he sat for a moment, listening thoughtfully to the silence.

And what if something happened to his house while he was away? Janroe began to feel the excitement of it building inside of him.

But be careful, he thought.

He rode around to the front and called Cable's name.

No answer.

He waited; called again, but still the house stood silent and showed no signs of life.

Janroe reined the buckskin around and crossed the yard to the willows. His gaze went to the horse herd out on the meadow and he studied the herd for some moments. No, Cable wasn't there. No one was.

He was about to turn back to the house, but he hesitated. No one anywhere. What does that say?

No, it's too good. When a thing looks too good there's something wrong with it. Still, he knew that all at once he was looking at an almost foolproof way to jab Cable into action. He sat motionless, looking at the horse herd, making sure no riders were out beyond the farthest grazing horses, and thinking it all over carefully.

Would he be suspected? No. He'd tell Martha and Luz he went to Fort Buchanan on business and no one was home when he passed here. He could even head up toward Buchanan, spend the night on the trail and double back to the store in the morning.

But what if someone came while he was in the house? What if Cable came home?

You either do it or you don't do it, but you don't think about it any more!

It was decided then. He returned to the adobe, swung down as he reached the ramada, and pushed open the front door.

Inside, in the dim closeness of the room, an urgency came over him and he told himself to hurry, to get it over with and get out.

From the stove he picked up a frying pan, went to the kitchen cupboards, opened them and swung the pan repeatedly into the shelves of dishes until not a cup or a plate remained in one piece. With a chair he smashed down the stove's chimney flue. A cloud of soot puffed out and filtered through the room as he dragged the comforter and blankets from the bed. He emptied the kitchen drawers then, turning them upside down; found a carving knife and used it to slash open the mattress and pillows still on the bed.

Enough?

He was breathing heavily from the exertion, from the violence of what had taken him no more than a minute. Hesitating now, his eyes going over the room, he again felt the urgent need to be out of here.

Enough.

He went out brushing soot from his coat, mounted and rode directly across the yard and forded the river. He stopped long enough to convince himself that no riders had joined the Kidston herd since his last look at it. Then he rode on, spurring across the meadow now, pointing for the east slope and not until he was in the piñon, beginning the steep climb up through the trees, did he look back and across to Cable's house. Not until then did he take the deep breath he had wanted to take in the house to make himself relax.

You've pushed him now, Janroe told himself, hearing the words calmly, but still feeling the excitement, the tension, tight through his body.

You just busted everything wide open.

It was evening, but not yet dark, a silent time with the trees standing black and thick-looking and the sky streaked with red shades of sun reflection. A whole day had passed and Cable was returning home.

He had already skirted the store, wanting to see Martha but wanting more to avoid Janroe, and now he was high up in the shadows and the silence of the pines, following the horse trail along the ridge.

He would talk to Janroe another time, after he had thought this out and was sure he knew what to say to him.

This morning he had talked to a man, a small old man who was perhaps in his sixties with a graying beard and a mustache that was tobacco-stained yellow about his mouth. Denaman's friend from Hidalgo. In the dimness of the adobe room, and with the early morning sounds of the village outside, the man seemed too old or too small or too fragile to do whatever he was doing.

But he asked Manuel Acaso questions about Cable, then looked at Cable and asked more questions; and it was his eyes that convinced Cable that the man was not too old or too thin or too frail. Brown eyes—Cable would remember them—that were gentle and perhaps kind; but they were not smiling eyes. They were the eyes of a patient, soft-spoken man who would show little more than mild interest at anything he saw or heard.

He was willing enough to talk about Janroe once he was sure of Cable, and he made no attempt to hide facts or try to justify Janroe's actions. He spoke slowly, carefully, as if he had memorized the things he was saying. . . .

Edward Janroe, Cable learned, was a native of Florida, born in St. Augustine a few years before the outbreak of the second Seminole war, and had lived there most of his early life. Almost nothing was known of Janroe during this period; not until he joined the army in 1854. From then on his life was on record.

In 1858, a sergeant by this time, Janroe was court-martialed for knifing a fellow soldier in a tavern fight. The man died and Janroe was sentenced to six years of hard labor at the Fort Marion military prison. He was well into his third year of it when the war broke out. It saved him from completing his sentence.

With a volunteer company from St. Augustine, Janroe traveled to Winchester, Virginia—this during the summer of 1861—and was assigned to the 10th Virginia Infantry, part of General Edmund Kirby Smith's forces. Strangely enough, despite his prison record, but undoubtedly because of his experience, Janroe was commissioned a full lieutenant of infantry.

A year later, and now a captain, Janroe lost his arm at the battle of Richmond, Kentucky. He was sent to the army hospital at

Knoxville, spent seven months there, and was discharged some-time in March, 1863.

But Janroe didn't go home. He learned that Kirby Smith had been made commander of the Trans-Mississippi Department, headquartered at Shreveport, Louisiana, and that's where Janroe went. In the early part of April he was reinstated with the rank of lieutenant and served under Dick Taylor, one of Kirby Smith's field generals.

Up to this point Cable had listened in silence.

"He didn't tell me that."

"I don't care what he told you," the bearded man said. "He served under Taylor in the fighting around Alexandria and Opelousas."

But not for long. He was with Taylor less than two months when he was discharged for good. He was told that he had given enough of himself and deserved retirement. The real reason: his wild dis-regard for the safety of his men, throwing them into almost suici-dal charges whenever he made contact with the enemy. This, and the fact that he refused to take a prisoner. During his time with Taylor, Janroe was responsible for having some one hundred and twenty Union prisoners lined up and shot.

Janroe pleaded his case all the way to Kirby Smith's general staff—he was a soldier and soldiering was his life; but as far as every one of them was concerned, Janroe was unfit for active duty and immediately relieved of his command.

Janroe returned to St. Augustine, then in the hands of Federal forces. Through a man he had known there before, he made con-tact with Confederate Intelligence agents and went to work for them. And eventually—in fact after well over a year in Florida—he was sent to Mexico. There he was given his present assignment.

"I can see why he didn't tell me everything," Cable said.

The bearded man nodded. "Naturally."

Cable watched him. "What do you think of Janroe?"

"He's a hard man to know."

"But what do you think?"

"I don't care for his kind, if that's what you mean."

"Yet you have him working for you."

"Mr. Cable," the bearded man said, "Janroe seems to have one aim in life. To see the South win the war."

"Or to see more Yankees killed."

"What's the difference?"

"You know what I mean."

"I know he's moved over two thousand rifles through the store since coming here," the bearded man said.

"And now he wants to kill two men who aren't even in the war."

"Well, I wonder if you can blame him," the bearded man said, somewhat wearily now. "A man is sent to war and taught how to kill; but after, the unlearning of it is left up to him."

"Except that Janroe knew how to kill before he went to war," Cable said.

So you'll wait, Cable thought now, and wonder about Janroe and wonder when Vern will make his move, while you try to stay calm and keep yourself from running away.

He was perhaps a mile from his house, passing through a clearing in the pines, when he saw the two riders down in the meadow, saw them for one brief moment before they entered the willows at the river.

Cable waited. When the riders did not come out of the trees on this side of the river he dismounted, took his field glasses and Spencer from the saddle and made his way carefully down through the pines on foot. Between fifty and sixty yards from the base of the slope he reached an outcropping of rock that fell steeply, almost abruptly, the rest of the way down. Here Cable went on his stomach. He nosed the Spencer through a V in the warm, sand-colored rocks and put the field glasses to his eyes.

He recognized Lorraine Kidston at once. She stood by her horse, looking down at a stooped man drinking from the edge of the water. When he rose, turning to the girl, wiping his mouth with the back of his hand, Cable saw that it was Vern Kidston.

Two hundred yards away, but with them, close to them through the field glasses, Cable watched. He studied Vern standing heavily with his hands on his hips, his shoulders slightly stooped and his full mustache giving his face a solemn, almost sad expression. Vern spoke little. Lorraine seemed to be doing the talking. Lorraine smiling blandly, shrugging, standing with one hand on her hip and gesturing imperiously with the other.

She stopped. For a moment neither of them spoke: Vern thoughtful; Lorraine watching him. Then Vern nodded, slowly, resignedly, and Lorraine was smiling again. Now she moved to her horse. Vern helped her up. She rode off at once, heading north out into the meadow, and did not look back. Vern watched her, standing motionless with his hands hanging at his sides now.

He was close, his hat, his mustache, his shirt, his gun belt, his hands, all in detail. Then the glasses lowered and Vern Kidston was a small dark figure two hundred yards away.

There he is, Cable thought. Waiting for you.

He put the field glasses aside and took the solid, compact, balanced weight of the Spencer, his hands under it lightly and the stock snugly against the groove of his shoulder.

There he is.

It would be easy, Cable thought. He knew that most of the waiting and the wondering and the wanting to run would be over by just squeezing the trigger. Doing it justifiably, he told himself.

And it isn't something you haven't done before.

There had been the two Apaches he had knocked from their horses as they rode out of the river trees and raced for his cattle. He had been lying on this same slope, up farther, closer to the house and with a Sharps rifle, firing and loading and firing again and seeing the two Chiricahua Apaches pitch from their running horses, not even knowing what had killed them.

And there had been another time. More like this one, though he had not been alone then. Two years ago. Perhaps two years almost to the day. In northern Alabama. . . .

It had happened on the morning of the fifth day, after they had again located the Yankee raider Abel Streight and were closing with him, preparing to tear another bite out of his exhausted flank.

He lay in the tall grass, wet and chilled by the rain that had been falling almost all night; now in the gray mist of morning with a shivering trooper huddled next to him, not speaking, and the rest of the patrol back a few hundred yards with the horses, waiting for the word to be passed to them. For perhaps an hour he lay like this with his glasses on the Union picket, a 51st Indiana Infantryman. The Yankee had been closer than Vern Kidston was now: across a stream and somewhat below them, crouched down behind a log, his rifle straight up past his head and shoulder. He was in plain view, facing the stream, the peak of his forage cap wet-shining and low over his eyes; but his eyes were stretched wide open, Cable knew, because of the mist and the silence and because he was alone on picket duty a thousand miles from home. He's wondering if he will ever see Indiana again, Cable had thought. Wondering if he will ever see his home and his wife and his children. He's old enough to have a family. But he hasn't been in it long, or he wouldn't be showing himself.

I can tell you that you won't go home again, Cable remembered thinking. It's too bad. But I want to go home too, and the way it is now both of us won't be able to. They're going to cry and that's too bad. But everything's too bad. For one brief moment he had thought, remembering it clearly now: Get down, you fool! Stop showing yourself!

Then someone was shaking his foot. He looked back at a bearded face. The face nodded twice. Cable touched the trooper next to him and whispered, indicating the Yankee picket, "Take him."

The man next to him pressed his cheek to his Enfield, aiming, but taking too long, trying to hold the barrel steady, his whole body shivering convulsively from the long, rain-drenched hours. "Give me it," Cable whispered. He eased the long rifle out in front of him carefully and put the front sight just below the Indiana man's face. You shouldn't have looked at him through the glasses, he thought, and pulled the trigger and the picket across the stream was no more. They were up and moving after that. Not until evening did Cable have time to remember the man who had waited helpessly, unknowingly, to be killed. . . .

The way Vern Kidston is now, Cable thought.

There was no difference between the two men, he told himself. Vern was a Yankee; there was no question about that. The only difference, if you wanted to count it, was that Vern didn't have a blue coat or a flat forage cap with the bugle Infantry insignia pinned to the front of it.

What if the 51st Indiana man had had a different kind of hat on but you still knew what he was and what he was doing there?

You would have shot him.

So the uniform doesn't mean anything.

It's what the man believes in and what he's doing to you. What if Vern were here and you were down there, the places just switched?

The thumb of Cable's right hand flicked the trigger guard down and up, levering a cartridge into the breech. The thumb eased back the hammer. Cable brought his face close to the carbine and sighted down the short barrel with both eyes open, placing the front sight squarely on the small figure in the trees. Like the others, Cable thought. It would be quick and clean, and it would be over.

If you don't miss.

Cable raised his head slightly. No, he could take him from here. With the first one he would at least knock Vern down, he was sure of that. Then he could finish him. But if Vern reached cover?

Hit his horse. Then Vern wouldn't be going anywhere and he could take his time. He wondered then if he should have brought extra loading tubes with him. There were four of them in his saddle bag. Each loading tube, which you inserted through the stock of the Spencer, held seven thick .56-56 cartridges. The Spencer was loaded now, but after seven shots—if it took that many—he would have to use the Walker.

Vern Kidston moved out of line. Cable looked up, then down again and the Spencer followed Vern to his horse, hardly rising as Vern took up the reins and stepped into the saddle.

Now, Cable thought.

But he waited.

He watched Vern come out of the trees, still on the far side of the river, and head north, the same way Lorraine had gone. Going home probably. Either by way of the horse trail or by following the long curving meadow all the way around. But why weren't they together? It was strange that Vern would let her ride home alone at this time of day. In less than an hour it would be full dark. Cable doubted that she knew the country that well.

Another thing. Where had they been? Why would they stand there talking for a while, then ride off separately?

Instantly Cable thought: You're letting him go!

He shifted the Spencer, putting the front sight on Vern again. He held the carbine firmly, his finger crooked on the trigger and the tip of the barrel inching along with the slow-moving target. The distance between them lengthened.

You've got ten seconds, Cable thought. After that he wouldn't be sure of hitting Vern. His arms and shoulders tightened and for one shaded second his finger almost squeezed the trigger.

Then it was over. He let his body relax and eased the hammer down on the open breech.

No, you could have a hundred years and you wouldn't do it that way. There's a difference, isn't there? And you're sure of it now. You feel it, even if you can't define it.

Cable rose stiffly, watching Vern for another few moments, then trudged slowly back up through the pines.

Mounted again, he felt a deep weariness and he sat heavily in the saddle, closing his eyes time and again, letting the sorrel follow the path at a slow-walking pace. His body ached from the long all-day ride; but it was the experience of just a few minutes ago that had left the drained, drawn feeling in his mind. One thing he was sure of now, beyond any doubt. He couldn't kill Vern Kidston the way Janroe wanted it done. He couldn't kill Vern or Duane this way regardless of how logical or necessary the strange-acting, sly-talking man with one arm made it sound.

Knowing this, being sure of it now, was something. But it changed little else. The first move would still be Vern's. Cable would go home, not hurrying to an empty house, and he would hold on to his patience until he had either outwaited or outfought Vern once and for all.

He descended the slope behind the house, dismounted at the barn and led the sorrel inside. Within a few minutes he appeared again. Carrying the Spencer and the field glasses he walked across the yard, letting his gaze move out to the willows now dull gray and motionless against the fading sky. When he looked at the house he stopped abruptly. Lamplight showed in the open doorway.

His left hand, with the strap of the field glasses across the palm, took the Spencer. His right hand dropped to the Walker Colt and held it as he approached the house, passed through the semidarkness of the ramada and stepped into the doorway.

He stood rigid, seeing the strewn bedcovers, the slashed mattress, the soot filming the table and the caved-in stove chimney on the floor; seeing the scattered, broken ruin and Lorraine Kidston standing in the middle of it. She turned from the stove, sweeping aside fragments of china with her foot, and smiled at Cable. "I've been waiting for you."

FIVE

Cable said nothing, his eyes going to the shattered china still on the cupboard shelves, then to the stove again and to the battered chimney flue lying on the floor.

So Vern or Duane, or both of them, had become tired of waiting. Now they were doing something and this was a warning. Fix the house, Cable thought, then another time when you're away they tear it apart again. How much of that could you take? Do you run out of patience right now or later sometime?

He could release his anger and kick at the broken dishes or yell at Lorraine, threaten her, threaten her father and Vern. But what good would it do? That was undoubtedly their intention—to rile him, to make him start something. And once you did what the other man wanted you to, once you walked into his plan, you were finished.

Lorraine was watching him. "When the wife is away, the house just seems to go to ruin, doesn't it?"

He looked at her. "What do they expect me to do now?"

"I'm sure I don't know."

"Or care," Cable said.

"Well, I'm sorry; but there's nothing I can do about it, is there?"

"Did both of them have a hand in this?"

"I doubt if either of them did. They've been home all day."

"I just saw Vern."

"Alone?"

"You were with him."

"Do I have to explain what we were doing?"

"It doesn't matter."

"Vern and I went for a ride after supper. When we reached the meadow he said he wanted to look at his horses. I told him to go ahead, I was going home."

Cable said nothing.

"Well?" Lorraine looked at him inquiringly.

"All right. Then what?"

"Then I left him."

"And came to see what he did to the house."

Lorraine smiled, shaking her head. "Guess again."

"Some other time."

She caught the note of weariness in his tone. For a moment she said nothing, watching him stand the carbine next to the window and then move slowly to the table and place the field glasses there. "Did you see my horse outside?" she asked.

Cable glanced at her. "I didn't notice."

"No horse," Lorraine said lightly. "That's why I'm here." She watched Cable gather the blanket and comforter and pile them on the slashed mattress.

"I was going up the path behind your house, taking the short cut home, when something frightened my horse. It happened very suddenly; he lost his footing and started to slide back and that's when I fell off." Lorraine touched her hair lightly and frowned. "I hit my head."

Cable was looking at her again, sensing that she wasn't telling the truth. "Then what happened?"

"Then he ran off. I could hear him way up in the trees, but I couldn't very well chase after him, could I?"

"So you came to the house."

"Of course."

"You want me to look for your horse?"

"He's probably still running."

Cable paused. He was certain she was here for a reason and he was feeling his way along to find out what it was. "I've only got one horse here."

"I know," Lorraine said.

"You want me to ride you home?"

"The way my head hurts I don't know if I could stand it."

"Just for an hour? That's all it would take."

She was staring at Cable, not smiling now, holding him with the calm, knowing impudence of her gaze.

"We could wait until morning."

He almost knew she was going to say it; still, the shock, the surprise, was in hearing the words out loud. Cable's expression did not change. "What would your father say about that?"

"What could he say? I don't have a choice. I'm stranded."

Cable said nothing.

"Or I could tell him I spent the night outside." Lorraine smiled again. "Lost."

"You're serious, aren't you?"

"What do you think?"

"If you're ready, I'll saddle the horse."

"I told you, I couldn't bear the ride."

"You told me a lot of things."

The knowing, confident expression was in her eyes again. "I think you're afraid of me. Or afraid of yourself."

"Being alone with you?"

Lorraine nodded. "But I haven't decided which it is. The only thing I'm sure of is you don't know what to do. You can't take me home by force; and you can't throw me out. So?"

Momentarily, in his mind, he saw Lorraine at home sitting with Vern and her father evening after evening, looking up from her book and wanting to do something, anything, to break the monotony but having no choice but to sit there. Until she planned this, or somehow stumbled into it. Perhaps that was all there was to her being here. It was her idea of excitement, something to do; not part of a plan that involved Vern or Duane.

So, Cable thought, the hell with it. He was too tired to argue. Tired and hungry and her mind was made up, he could see that. He moved to the door of the next room, glanced in and saw that the two single beds had not been touched, then looked at Lorraine again.

"Take your pick."

She moved close to him in the doorway to look into the room. "It doesn't matter."

"Whichever one you want." He walked away from her and for the next few minutes concentrated on shaping and straightening the stove flue. He was able to put it up again, temporarily, but his hands and face were smudged with soot when he'd finished.

Lorraine waited until he started a fire in the stove, then told him to go outside and wash; she'd fix something to eat. Cable hesitated, doubting her ability at the stove; but finally he went out—washed up at the river, scrubbing his hands with sand and scooping the cool water into his face. He felt better being alone outside and he took his time at the river, then went to the barn and looked in at the sorrel again before returning to the house.

Coffee was on the fire; Cable smelled it as he came in. For a moment he watched Lorraine making pancakes in the iron frying pan and he thought: She wants you to be surprised. But he turned away from her and busied himself sweeping up the broken china. After that he turned the slashed mattress on the bed and spread the bedcovers over it. When it was time to sit down she served him the corn meal cakes in a pie plate and poured his coffee into a tin drinking cup. Lorraine sat down with him, watching him eat, waiting for him to say something; but Cable ate in silence.

"Well, what do you think?"

"Fine." He was finishing the last of his coffee.

"Surprised I know how to cook?"

"You're a woman, aren't you?" he answered, knowing she would react to it, but saying it anyway.

"Does that follow," Lorraine said peevishly. "Just because you're a woman all you're to be concerned with is cooking and keeping house?"

"I didn't say that."

"You're probably hopeless. You deserve to live out here with a wife and three kids."

"You make it sound like a sentence."

"You *are* hopeless."

"And tired," Cable said. He got up from the table, walked around to Lorraine's chair and pulled it out for her. "So are you."

She looked up at him. "Am I?" Her tone was mild now.

"Tired out from that long ride with Vern." He took Lorraine by the arm to the bedroom. "Have a good sleep and before you know it it'll be time to fix breakfast." He pushed her inside and closed the door before she could say a word.

Cable blew out the lamp, then walked to the open front door and stood looking out at the night, letting the stillness and the breeze that was coming off the meadow relax him. This was good. But it was a peace that lasted only as long as the night. Slowly Cable sat down in the doorway. Take advantage of the peace you can feel, he thought. Sleep was good, but it wasn't something you could enjoy each minute of and know you were enjoying it.

So he sat in the doorway, feeling the silence and the darkness about him, thinking of his wife and children, picturing them in bed in the rooms above the store; then picturing them here, seeing himself sitting with the children close to him and talking to them, answering their questions, being patient and answering the questions that were unrelated or imaginary along with the reasonable ones. Clare would ask the most questions and through her eyes that were wide with concentration he could almost see her picturing his answers. It was like the times she would relate a dream she had had and he would try to imagine how she saw it with her child's eyes and with her child's mind. While he was talking to Clare, Davis would become restless and jump on his back, Davis with enough energy for all of them and wanting to fight or be chased or swim in the river. Sandy, lying against him, listening to them contentedly with his thumb in his mouth, would scowl and yell at Davis to stop it. Then he would quiet them and they would talk about other things until Martha called.

And after the children were in bed they would sit here on the steps, watching the willows turn to silent black shapes against the sky, hearing the night sounds in the pines and far out on the meadow. They would talk in low murmurs, feeling the familiar nearness of one another. They talked about the children and the house and about things they had done and about things they would do someday; but not talking about the future, because if they accomplished or acquired nothing more than what they had, it would be enough and they would be satisfied; perhaps as happy as anyone, any family, could expect to be.

If you can hold on to what you have, Cable thought. Right now you would settle just for that and not hope for anything more.

He was certain that the Kidstons had damaged the house, as a warning. Maybe not Vern. It seemed more like something Duane would do. But regardless of who did it, the effect was the same.

He heard the sound behind him, the bedroom door opening and closing. He turned, starting to push himself up, but Lorraine was already over him. Her hand went to his shoulder and she sank down beside him.

"I thought you were tired."

"I'm going to bed in a minute," Cable said. He saw that Lorraine was wearing one of Martha's flannel nightgowns. He had felt it as she brushed against him to sit down.

"What were you thinking about?"

"A lot of things at once, I suppose."

"Vern and Duane . . . the happiness boys?"

He looked at her. "I'd like to know what you're doing here."

"I explained all that."

"You didn't any more get thrown than I did."

Lorraine smiled. "But I had to tell you something."

"Did Vern send you?"

"Don't be silly."

"Then what are you doing here?"

"Keeping you company."

"I guess you are."

Lorraine moved, rising to her knees and turning to him. Her hands went to his shoulders, then to his face caressingly as she kissed him.

"You're not very responsive, are you?" She pressed close to him, kissing him again. "In fact you're rather cold. I'm surprised."

"You've got the wrong one, that's all."

"Oh, come now——"

"Or else the wrong time and place."

"Would you like to go somewhere else?"

Quietly, Cable said, "Lorraine, you're probably the pleasantest temptation I've ever had—but I've got enough things living in my mind the way it is."

Close to him her head moved slowly from side to side. "The only halfway decent looking man within fifty miles and he has to have a conscience." She felt his hands circle her waist and when they lingered, holding her, she said, "I'll give you one more chance."

But now he pushed her away and rose, lifting her with him. "I don't think this would do either of us any good."

In the darkness her eyes remained on him, but it was some time before she said, "I suppose your wife is very fortunate. But I doubt if I'd want to be married to you. I can't help feeling there's such a thing as being too good."

The next morning Cable cleaned the main room and fixed the stove flue more securely. Later on, he decided, he would ride to Denaman's Store. He would buy plates and cups, probably tin ones if Janroe had any at all; and he would stay as long as he could with Martha and the children.

Cable was outside when the two Kidston riders came by. He saw them crossing the river, approaching cautiously, and he walked out from the ramada, the Walker on his leg. He waited then as the two riders came across the yard toward him. A vague memory of having seen them before made Cable study their faces closely. No, he was certain he didn't know them. Still—

The two riders looked somewhat alike, yet the features of one appeared more coarse and his coloring was freckled and lighter than the other man. It was as if both of their faces—both narrow and heavy boned—had been copied from the same model, but one had been formed less skillfully than the other. Both wore full mustaches and the darker of the two men showed a trace of heavy beard, at least a week's growth.

"If you're looking for Lorraine," Cable said, "you've found her."

The two riders were watching Cable, but now their eyes rose past him as Lorraine appeared.

She seemed a little surprised. "How did you know I was here?"

"Your daddy's got everybody looking everywhere," the dark man said. There was no trace of concern in his voice.

"Is he worried?"

"About out of his mind."

"I can just see him." Lorraine stepped down from the doorway and walked out to them. "You two will have to ride double," she said, looking up. Neither of the men made a move to dismount. Lorraine moved toward the dark rider's chestnut gelding. "This one." Still the man hesitated and Lorraine added, "If you don't mind."

"Where's yours?"

"I have no idea," Lorraine answered.

The dark rider's gaze moved to Cable. "Maybe we ought to use his then."

Lorraine's face showed sudden interest. "If he'll let you."

"He will."

"We can't do it while the girl's here," the other man said then. "Duane wouldn't have any part of that."

"I suppose we got time," the dark one grunted.

"All we want," the other rider said.

The dark one swung down. Not bothering to help Lorraine, he walked past her, raised his hand to the other rider and was pulled up behind him. He looked down at Cable again.

"Long as we got time."

They rode out, past the house to the horse trail that climbed the slope. In the saddle now, straddling it with her skirt draped low on both sides, Lorraine waited long enough to say, "That was Austin and Wynn Dodd."

Cable frowned. "I don't know them."

Lorraine smiled pleasantly. "You knew their brother. Joe Bob."

She rode off toward the slope, following the Dodd brothers. Before passing into the pines behind the house, Lorraine looked back and waved.

There were times when Janroe could feel his missing hand; times when he swore he had moved his fingers. He would be about to pick something up with his left hand, then catch himself in time. A moment before this Janroe had absently raised his missing arm to lean on the door frame. He fell against the timber with his full weight on the stump, and now he stood rubbing it, feeling a dull pain in the arm that wasn't there.

Luz Acaso appeared, coming from the back of the building. She was riding her dun-colored mare, sitting the saddle as a man would, her bare legs showing almost to her knees. Two of the Cable children, Clare and Davis, were following behind her as she crossed the yard toward the river.

Janroe stepped out to the loading platform.

"Luz!" The dun mare side-stepped as the girl reined in and looked back at him.

"Come over here."

She held the horse, standing almost forty feet from the platform. "I can hear you," she said.

"Maybe I don't want to shout."

"Then you come over here!"

Don't ruffle her, Janroe thought. Something was bothering her. He had first noticed it as she served him his breakfast. She seldom spoke unless he said something to her first, so her silence this morning wasn't unusual. Still, he had sensed a change in her. Her face was somber, without expression, yet he could feel a new tension between them. Even when she served him she avoided his eyes and seemed to reach out to place the coffee and food before him, as if afraid to come too close to him.

That was it. As if she was guarding something in her mind. As if she was so conscious of what she was thinking, she felt that if he looked in her eyes or even came too close to her, he would see it.

But while he was eating he would feel her eyes on him, watching him carefully, intently; although when he looked up from his plate she would be turning away or picking something up from the stove.

Now she was riding down to Hidalgo. Tonight there would be a gun shipment and Luz would lead it to the store, making sure the way was clear. Janroe said, "You're leaving a little early, aren't you?"

"I want to have time to see my brother."

"About what?"

"Nothing."

"You seem anxious enough over nothing."

"I want to see him, that's all." She waited a moment longer, watching Janroe, but when he said no more she flicked the reins and moved on across the yard. Janroe watched her pass into the willows and even after she was out of sight he continued to stare at the trees. What was it about her—was she more confident? More sure of herself since the Cables had come home. Afraid when she was alone with him, still somewhat more confident.

He noticed the Cable children then. Clare and Davis were still in the front yard, standing close to each other now and looking up at him on the platform.

"I told you once to play in the back," Janroe called out. "I'm not going to tell you again. I'll get a stick next time, you understand?"

Clare stood rigid. Davis nodded with a small jerk of his head and reached for Clare's arm. They turned to go.

"Wait a minute." Janroe looked down at them sternly. "Where's your father? Is he still here?"

"Upstairs," the boy said.

"All right." Janroe waved them away and they ran, glancing back at him as they rounded the corner of the building.

What do you have to do to a man like that? Janroe thought. A man that finds his house wrecked and comes moping in to buy tin plates and sit with his wife. Cable had arrived about mid-morning and had been here ever since.

Janroe stood for some time holding the stump of his arm, rubbing it gently. He was looking above the willows now, to the hillside beyond the full roundness of the tree tops. But it was moments before he realized a file of riders had come down out of the pines and was descending the slope.

Perhaps because his hand still held the stump, or because he had jarred it and imagined the pain still present; because of this and then abruptly seeing the riders on the hillside and for the moment not caring who they were—his mind went back to another time, another place. . . .

There had been riders then on a hillside; directly across the cornfield and not more than eight hundred yards away, a line of riders appearing along the crest of the hill, then stopping and dismounting. He had seen that they were unhitching the horses from artillery pieces—three of them—and rolling the guns into position.

He had waited then, studying the position through his field glasses for at least ten minutes, or perhaps a quarter of an hour; so by the time he brought his men out of the pines, screaming at them, shooting one and seeing the other soldier who had been afraid suddenly run by him, the field pieces were ready and loaded and waiting for him.

Janroe himself was no more than a hundred yards out from the woods when the first shell exploded. The blast was loud in his ears and almost knocked him down; but he kept moving, seeing two, then three, men come stumbling, crawling out of the smoke and dust that seemed to hang motionless in the air. One of the men fell facedown and didn't move. As he watched, a second and third shell exploded and he saw one of the crawling men lifted from the ground and thrown on his back. Close around him men were flattening themselves on the ground and covering their heads.

But the ones in front of him were still moving, and with the next explosion Janroe was running again. He saw the man who had been afraid a few moments before, running, breathing heavily, his head back as if he was looking up at the three artillery pieces. Janroe was close to the man, almost about to run past him and yell back at him to keep coming, and then the man was no more.

It was as if time suddenly stopped, for Janroe saw the man, or part of him, blown into the air and he could remember this clearly, the fraction of a moment caught and indelibly recorded in his mind. And it was the same sudden, ground-lifting, sound-smashing burst of smoke and iron that slammed Janroe senseless and cleanly severed his left arm. . . .

For some time the line of riders was out of sight, low on the slope now and beyond the bank of willow trees. Janroe waited, watching, judging where they would cross the river and appear out of the tree shadows. They would be Kidston riders, Janroe was certain of that. He wondered if he should call Cable. No, wait, Janroe decided. Act natural and just let things happen.

There were six of them. Janroe recognized Duane Kidston at once: Duane sitting a tall bay horse with one hand on his thigh, a riding quirt hanging from his wrist and his elbow extended rigidly. Duane wearing the stiff-crowned Kossuth hat squarely on his head, the brim pinned up on one side with the regimental insignia. Duane playing soldier, Janroe thought contemptuously. Pretending that he's a man.

Have your fun, Major, Janroe thought then, not taking his eyes from Duane. Have all the fun you can. Your time's about run out.

Briefly he noted the five men with Duane: Bill Dancey, the solemn, bearded one close to Duane's right; then the two Dodd brothers, Austin and Wynn. They had been here only once before but Janroe remembered them well, the brothers of one of the men Cable had killed. Austin and Wynn Dodd, one light, the other dark, but both with angular, expressionless faces. Janroe remembered their eyes; they watched you coldly, impersonally, as if you were a thing that couldn't look back at them.

Janroe was not sure if he had ever seen the two other riders before. He watched these two veer off midway across the yard and circle to the back of the store.

Moments later the two Cable children, Clare and Davis, came running around from the back yard. Then, seeing the four riders approaching the platform, they stopped and stood watching, their eyes wide with curiosity.

"Where is he?" Duane asked.

"Inside." Janroe moved nearer the edge of the platform.

"Get him out."

"What for?"

"That's my business."

"You want to kill him?"

"Duane's got things to say to him," Dancey said then.

Janroe's eyes moved to the bearded man. "I wouldn't want to think I fetched him to be killed."

"We're not going to kill him," Dancey said.

"That would be an awful thing to have on your conscience," Janroe said. "Calling a man to be killed in front of his children."

Dancey shook his head. "You've got my word."

"And with his wife here too," Janroe said. "I couldn't ever face her again."

"Mr. Janroe," Duane said, "if you don't get him out here, you can be assured we will."

Janroe looked past the men to the Cable children. His eyes settled on Clare.

"Honey, go tell your daddy there's some men here to see him."

Clare hesitated, but Davis pushed her and she ran up the steps to the platform, holding close to the wall as she ran by Janroe and into the store.

"Fine youngsters," Janroe said pleasantly. "He's got three of them." Duane wasn't listening. He glanced at Dancey. Then Dancey and the Dodd brothers dismounted and came up the steps to the loading platform. Duane remained in his saddle.

"Where is he?" Dancey asked.

"Upstairs a few minutes ago."

"He mention what happened last night?"

"Not a word." Janroe's tone indicated only mild interest. "What did?"

"About Lorraine—"

"No!" Janroe's face showed surprise, then an eager curiosity. "What happened?"

But Dancey's gaze moved beyond him. Janroe turned. He heard the steps on the plank floor then Cable, wearing his Walker Colt, was standing in the doorway. Janroe saw Martha and the little girl a few steps behind him.

"Take off that gun," Dancey said.

Cable looked from Dancey to the Dodd brothers—to Austin, the dark one, who was a step nearer than Wynn—then back to Dancey.

"What's this about?"

"Take it off," Dancey said again. "You're covered front and back."

Cable heard the quick steps behind him. He seemed about to turn, but he hesitated. The two riders who had circled the adobe had entered by the back door and had waited for Cable behind the counter. Now one of them pulled the Walker from its holster. Feeling it, Cable glanced over his shoulder. He saw the second man standing close to Martha.

As Cable turned back to Dancey, Austin Dodd moved. He

stepped in bringing his balled left hand up from his side. Before Cable saw it coming the fist slammed into his face. He fell against the door frame, went to his hands and knees with his head down and close to the platform boards. Austin Dodd followed through. His right hand came up with his Colt, his thumb already hooking back the hammer.

"Hold on!" Dancey stepped in front of him. "We didn't come here for that." He looked out at Duane Kidston angrily. "You'd have let him, wouldn't you?"

"Austin has his own reason," Duane said. "Stopping him wouldn't be any of my business."

"We didn't come here to satisfy Austin," Dancey grunted.

Duane stared at the bearded foreman. "I'm beginning to wonder why I brought you."

"You wouldn't've if Vern had been around. You said you wanted to talk to this man. That's all."

"I'm going to."

"But you'd have let Austin kill him."

"It wasn't your brother Cable shot down," Duane said flatly. "That's the difference."

"He took him in a fair fight."

"We're not even sure of that. All we know is Joe Bob and Royce came home face-down over their saddles," Duane said. "And it wasn't your daughter he—"

Duane stopped. His eyes went to Cable who was still on one knee, but watching Duane now.

"Get him up."

Dancey moved aside. He said, "Go ahead," and stepped back to the edge of the platform near Janroe. The Dodd brothers pulled Cable to his feet. They planted themselves close to him, each holding an arm with both hands. Cable stood quietly, making no attempt to free himself. Behind him, Dancey could see Martha and the little girl in the square of light formed by the doorway. Martha seemed calm, Dancey judged. But you couldn't tell about women. The little girl was afraid. And the little boy—Dancey's gaze moved to the steps where Davis was squatting now—he's wondering what they're doing to his pa and he wouldn't believe it if somebody told him.

Duane called, "Jimmie!" and one of the men who'd covered Cable from behind came out to the platform. Duane raised his reins, then dropped them and the man came down; but not until he'd picked up the reins did Duane dismount. He stepped down stiffly, straightened his coat, then walked around to the steps and up to the platform, past Davis without even glancing at him though he touched him with his riding quirt, in a gesture of brushing the boy aside.

His full attention was on Cable now. Duane stepped squarely in front of him, close to him, and stood for some moments in silence, his legs apart and his hands fisted on his hips. But before he spoke his hands dropped to his sides.

"I should let Austin kill you," Duane said. "But I can't do it. God knows everyone here would be better off for it, but I can't pass final judgment on a mortal man, not even after he's done what you did."

"What did I do?" Cable asked, not with surprise or indignation, but calmly, wondering what had suddenly brought Duane here.

"Offended innocence," Duane said. "You'd better keep your mouth shut. I've taken all of you I can stomach."

"I asked a civil question."

Duane's quirt came up and lashed across Cable's face. "And I said shut up!" He stepped back as Cable twisted to free himself. Wynn Dodd stumbled to one knee and Cable almost broke away, but Austin forced Cable's right arm behind his back and jerked up on it.

"I'll break it!"

Cable stopped struggling. He let his breath out slowly and his body seemed to sag. His eyes went to Davis still watching him from the steps, then away from the boy quickly, back to Duane.

"Do you have to do this in front of my children?"

Duane stepped close to him again. "How much respect did you show my daughter?"

"What did Lorraine say I did?"

"She didn't have to say anything. She was all night at your place."

Janroe, near the edge of the platform, looked at Martha, but her eyes were on her husband. He noticed Duane's gaze move to her then.

"You hear that Mrs. Cable? Your husband and my daughter."

"He told me about it," Martha said quietly.

"He told you, did he." Duane's mouth barely moved. "Did he tell you how he dragged Lorraine into that hut?" He turned on Cable and in the motion slashed the quirt across his face. "Did he tell you how he kept her there all night?" The quirt came back across Cable's face. "How he threatened her and forced his will on her?" He swung on Cable again and again, hacking at Cable's cheeks and forehead with the rawhide. Cable's eyes were squeezed closed and he would turn his head with each stinging blow. But he was off balance, leaning forward awkwardly, and he was unable to turn his body with Austin holding his arm twisted behind him. Duane struck him eight times before his arm dropped heavily to his side.

"Did he tell you all that, Mrs. Cable?"

"He told me everything that happened."

"His version."

"If you've finished, Mr. Kidston, may I take my husband inside?"

Duane stared at Martha, his face tight as he held back the temper ready to flare out at her calm, quiet manner.

He said then, "If you want him, take him. Take him anywhere you like, but not back to your house. You're finished here, and I believe you're intelligent enough to realize it. If you think this is unjust, that's too bad; your husband is lucky to be alive. I'll tell you frankly, if it wasn't for your children he would be dead now."

Bill Dancey watched Martha, waiting for her to speak again; but Martha said nothing, her hand on the little girl close to her side. Dancey walked across the platform. Going down the steps he patted Davis's shoulder, but the boy pulled away from him. Dancey mounted, then looked up at Duane.

"You've said it. What're you waiting for?"

Duane still faced Martha. He ignored Dancey, and said, "This evening my men leave for the horse pastures. They'll be gone one week. If you haven't cleared out by the time they return, we will take your husband out and hang him. That's my last warning, Mrs. Cable."

Duane turned and marched stiffly down the steps to his horse. The Dodd brothers followed, almost reluctantly, both of them looking back at Cable as they mounted and rode out after Duane.

Janroe came away from the edge of the platform and studied Cable's face closely. "Duane laid it on you, didn't he?"

Cable said nothing. He felt Martha standing next to him now, but he continued to watch the riders. When they had finally crossed the river and started up the slope, he looked at Janroe.

"That one Duane called Jimmie—what did he do with my gun? Did you see?"

Janroe stepped to the edge of the platform again and looked down. "He dropped it right there."

"Get it for me."

Janroe seemed to smile. "I'd be glad to."

Cable felt Martha's hand on his arm. He looked at her, at her soft, clear expression, at her eyes that seemed moist, though he wasn't sure if she was crying.

She said, "Cabe, come inside now."

He followed her through the store, through the main room to the kitchen, then sat down while Martha went to the sink. She dipped water from a bucket into a kettle, and put the kettle on the stove to heat.

Clare and Davis appeared in the doorway, staring at their father until Martha noticed them and told them to go outside and play.

Cable looked up. "No, let them stay," he said. He motioned to the children. They came in hesitantly, as if this man with the red welts across his face was someone neither of them had ever seen before. But when he smiled and held out his arms, both of them ran to him and pressed against his chest. He kissed Clare on the cheek, then Davis. The boy's arms went around his neck and clung to him and Cable felt the knot in his stomach slowly begin to relax.

Martha poured the warm water into a basin. She carried it to the table, then leaned close to her husband and began bathing the swollen red marks that crossed both of his cheeks, his nose and his forehead. A bruise colored his cheekbone where Austin Dodd had hit him.

Cable's eyes raised. "Where's Sandy?"

"Still taking his nap."

"I'm glad he didn't see it."

Martha said nothing. She moved the two children aside to give herself more room, then pressed the wet cloth gently to Cable's forehead.

"The second time they've seen me beaten," Cable said. "Beaten up twice in front of my children—standing there turning the other cheek while a man rawhides my face."

Martha raised his chin with her hand. "Cabe, you don't have to prove yourself to them. You're their father."

"Something they don't have anything to say about."

"They'd love you under any circumstance, you know that."

"Then it's a question of proving myself to me."

Martha shook her head. "It isn't a matter of principle, a question of whether or not you're a man. This is something that affects the whole family. We want to go home and live in peace. Clare and Davis and even Sandy, we want what is rightfully ours, but we don't want it without you."

"Then you want to leave here," Cable said.

"I didn't say that. If we run away, we lose. But if we have to bury you, we lose even more."

"Martha, I don't have a choice."

She leaned close to him with her hands on the arms of the chair. "Cabe, don't go after them just because of what Duane did."

"You know it's more than that."

"You were beaten up in front of the children. Right now that's all you can think about."

"Sooner or later this will be settled with guns," Cable said. "It might as well be now."

"It doesn't have to be that way," Martha said urgently. "If we wait, if we can put it off—Cabe, something could happen that would solve everything!"

"Like what?"

She hesitated. "I'm not sure."

"Martha, I'm awful tired of waiting."

She looked at him intently. "You could go to Fort Buchanan. Put it up to the authorities."

"You know who they'd side with."

"But we're not sure. Cabe, at least it's worth trying."

From the doorway Janroe said, "I've got the only way to solve your problem." He extended Cable's Walker Colt, holding it in the open palm of his hand. "Right here."

Martha turned, looking at him coldly. "That would solve nothing."

"All right," Janroe said. "Go up to Buchanan. Tell the Yankees you're a Rebel soldier come home to find a gang of Yankee horsebreakers using your land and threatening to hang you." Janroe moved into the kitchen. "You know what they'd do? Supply the rope."

Martha motioned the two children to the back door. She held it open for them, then, closing it behind them, looked at Janroe again.

"Mr. Janroe, I don't think this concerns you."

"Ask your husband whether it concerns me or not." He stopped in front of Cable and handed him the revolver. "Right?"

Cable said nothing. He took the Walker and looked at it idly, holding it in both hands.

Janroe watched him. "You're going back to your place?"

Cable nodded.

"That's the right direction," Janroe said mildly. His eyes remained on Cable's lowered head. "Did you hear what Duane said about his men going off this evening? They'll go over to some pastures Vern's got way north and west of here and start working the herds home. Duane said they'd be gone a week." Janroe shook his head. "They'll be gone longer than that. And just Duane and maybe Vern will be home, just the two of them."

Cable looked up. "You told me that once before."

Janroe nodded. "And Duane confirmed it." His voice lowered. "It would be easy for a man like you. Ride in there and take both of them."

Martha came away from the door. "You're asking my husband to commit murder!"

Janroe glared at her. "Like any soldier murders."

"This isn't war—he isn't a soldier now!"

"We've been all through that," Janroe said. "Whether it bothers his conscience or not, your husband doesn't have a choice. He's got to kill them before they kill him."

That evening, as soon as it was dark, Janroe slipped under the platform and let himself into the locked storeroom. He measured three strides to the crates of Enfield rifles stacked against the back wall, then stood in the darkness, wondering if there would be room for the wagon-load of rifles due to arrive later that night. The rifles that were here should have been picked up days ago.

You can worry about it, Janroe thought, or you can forget it and ask Luz when she comes. She should be here within two hours. Perhaps they told her in Hidalgo why the rifles had not been picked up. Perhaps not. Either way, there was something more immediate to think about. Something raw and galling, because it was fresh in his mind and seemed to have happened only moments before though it had been this afternoon, hours ago.

He had almost convinced Cable. No, not almost or maybe. He had convinced him. He had handed the man his gun and told him to kill the Kidstons or be killed himself, and Cable had seen the pure reality of this. If he had left at that moment, he would have gone straight to the Kidston place. Janroe was sure of it.

But Martha had interfered. She talked to her husband, soothing the welts on his face with a damp cloth while she soothed his anger with the calm, controlled tone of her voice. And finally Cable had nodded and agreed not to do anything that day. He would go home and watch the house—that much he had to do—but he would not carry the fight to the Kidstons; at least not while he felt the way he did. He agreed to this grudgingly, wearily, part by part, while Martha reasoned in that quiet, firm, insisting, never-varying tone.

Perhaps if he went out to see Cable now? No, the guns were coming and he would have to be here. In the morning then; though by that time the sting would be gone from the welts on Cable's face and that solid patience would have settled in him again.

He had *convinced* Cable—that was the absolute truth of it—until the woman had started in with her moral, monotonous reasoning—

Janroe straightened. He stood listening, hearing the faint sound of a horse approaching. The hoof beats grew louder, but not closer, and when the sound stopped, he knew the horse had reached the back of the store.

Luz? No, it was too early for her. He left the storeroom, carefully, quietly padlocking the door, came out into the open and took his time mounting to the platform and passing through the darkened store. He saw Martha first, standing in the kitchen, then Luz, and saw the girl's eyes raise to his as he moved toward them.

"You're early."

"They're not coming," Luz said.

"What do you mean they're not coming?"

"Not any more."

"All right," Janroe said. "Tell me what you know."

"The war's over."

She said it simply, in the same tone, and for a moment Janroe only stared at her.

"What are you talking about?"

"It's true," Martha said. "They told her as soon as she reached Hidalgo."

He looked at Martha then, seeing her face no longer composed but for the first time flushed and alive and with a smile that was warm and genuine and seemed to include even him, simply because he was here to share the news with them.

He turned to Luz again. "Who told you?"

"Everyone knows it. They told me to come back and tell you."

"But how do they know? How can they be sure?"

"They know, that's all."

"Listen, wars don't just end like that."

"How do they end?" Martha asked, not smiling now.

"There's some warning—days, weeks before, that it's going to end."

"You know how news travels out here," Martha said.

"No"—Janroe shook his head—"we would have heard something. It's a false alarm, or a Yankee trick. It's something else because a war just doesn't end like that."

"We're telling you that the war is over," Martha said. "Whether you believe it or not it ended five days ago, the day we came home."

"And they're just finding out now?" Janroe shook his head again. "Uh-unh, you don't sell me any of that."

"Would they have lied to Luz?"

"I don't even know what they told her! How do I know she even went there?"

Martha was staring at him. "You don't want to believe it."

"What am I supposed to believe—everything this girl comes in and tells me?"

"Luz"—Martha glanced at the girl—"can I take your horse?"

Janroe saw Luz nodding and he said anxiously, "What for?"

"To tell my husband," Martha answered, looking at him again.

"You think you should?" Janroe asked. It was moving too fast again, rushing at him again, not giving him time to think, and already it was the next step, telling her husband. They would not just stand and talk about it and see how ridiculous the news was; they would bring Cable into it, and if he argued about the sense of her going she would go all the quicker.

"I mean riding out alone at night," Janroe said. He shook his head. "I couldn't see you doing that."

"I think my husband should know," Martha began.

"I believe that," Janroe said. The words were coming easier now. "But I think I better be the one to go tell him."

Martha hesitated. Before she could say anything, Janroe had turned and was gone. She looked at Luz, but neither of them spoke, hearing Janroe just in the next room.

When he came into the kitchen again he was wearing a hat and a coat, the armless sleeve flat and ending abruptly in the pocket, but bulging somewhat with the shape of a shoulder holster beneath the coat.

"You *will* see him?" Martha said. "I mean make sure he finds out?"

"Don't worry about it."

"And you promise to tell him everything?"

"I won't be long." Janroe went out the back door and mounted Luz Acaso's dun mare.

He crossed the river and hurried the dun up the slope to the horse trail, following it north, almost blindly in the night darkness of the trees, brushing branches in his haste and kicking the dun. He moved along the ridge, though with no intention of visiting Cable.

He knew only that there was no time for Cable now. He could admit that to himself without admitting the other, that the war was over. Certainly it could be at the very edge of the end. This could be the last day. It might very well be the last day. All right, it *was* the last day and now there was no time for Cable. The war was not over yet, he told himself, but there was time to do only one thing now.

Four, raging, uninterrupted years of war did not end with two women standing in a kitchen and saying that it was over. You would expect that of women. It was typical. A woman would tell you anything. Lies became truth to them because they felt justified in using any means at hand to hold life to a sweet-smelling, creeping pace; to make this a woman's existence with no room for war or fighting or so many of the things that men did and liked to do and only really proved themselves as men when they were doing them.

If he had not entered the kitchen he wouldn't have heard anything. A man couldn't wait and plan for eight months and know what he had to do, and then see it all canceled by walking into a kitchen. That couldn't be.

So the two women had lied and it was stupid to think about it. And even if it was not a matter of their lying, then it was something else, something equally untrue; and whether the something was a lie from the women or a trick or an untruth from another source was beside the point.

He was hurrying, as if to keep up with time, so that not another moment of it would go by before he reached the Kidston place. But even after half admitting this was impossible he told himself that right now was part of a whole time, not a time before or a time after something. It was a time which started the day he came to live at the store and would end the day he saw the Kidstons dead. So this was part of the time of war. But almost as he thought this, it became more than that. Now, right now, was the whole of the war, the everything of a war that would not end until the Kidstons were dead.

It took him less than an hour altogether. By the time he left the horse trail he had cleared his mind of everything but the Kidstons. Winding, moving more slowly through the sandstone country, he was able to calm himself and think about what he would do after, what he would do about Cable, what he would tell Martha and Luz. Martha . . .

By the time he reached the edge of the timber stand bordering the Kidston place, looking across the open area to the house and outbuildings, he was composed and ready. He was Edward Janroe who happened to be riding by, say, on his way to Fort Buchanan. He was a man they had seen at least once a week for the past eight months. He was the one-armed man who owned the store now and didn't say much. He was nothing to be afraid of or even wonder about. Which was exactly the way Janroe wanted it.

SIX

Janroe came out of the trees, letting the dun mare move at its own pace toward the house. He was aware of someone on the veranda, certain that it was Duane when he saw the pinpoint glow of a cigar.

There was no hurry now. Janroe's eyes rose from the veranda to the lighted second-story window, then beyond the corner of the house, past the corral where a dull square of light showed the open door of the bunkhouse. There were no sounds from that end of the yard, none from the big adobe that was pale gray and solid looking in the darkness. The cigar glowed again and now Janroe was close.

"Good evening, Major."

Duane leaned forward, the wicker chair squeaking. "Who is it?"

"Edward Janroe." Now, almost at the veranda, Janroe brought the dun to a halt. He saw Duane rise and come close to the railing, touching it with his stomach.

"I didn't mean to startle you," Janroe said.

"You didn't startle me." There was indignation in Duane's tone.

"I meant you sitting here by yourself. . . . Is Vern about?"

"No, he's up at his pastures. You wanted to see him?"

"I'd like to have. But I guess you can't have everything."

"What?"

"Where's Vern, out on the horse drive?"

"Getting it started. He's been gone all day."

"You alone?"

"My daughter's in the house."

"And somebody's out in the bunkhouse."

Duane seemed annoyed, but he said, "A couple of the men."

"I thought everybody went out on the drives," Janroe said.

"We always keep one man here."

"You said a couple of men were there."

As if remembering something, Duane's frown of annoyance vanished. "The second man rode in a while ago to tell us the news. I've been sitting here ever since thinking about it." Duane paused solemnly. "Mr. Janroe, the war is over. Lee surrendered the Army of Northern Virginia to General Grant on April ninth."

"Is that a fact?" Janroe said.

"I have been thinking of a place called Chancellorsville," Duane said gravely. "I have been thinking of the men I knew who died there: men I campaigned with who gave their lives that this final victory might be accomplished."

"A touching moment," Janroe said.

Duane's eyes rose. "If you had served, you would know the feeling."

"I served."

"Oh? I didn't know that. In the Union army?"

"With Kirby Smith."

"Oh. . . . You lost your arm . . . were wounded in battle?"

"During the fight at Richmond, Kentucky."

"Is that right? I was in Cincinnati at the time. If I hadn't been on my way to Washington, I would have answered General Nelson's call for volunteers."

"That would have been something," Janroe said, sitting easily and looking down at Duane, "if we'd fought against each other."

Duane nodded gravely. "More terrible things than that have actually happened. Brother fighting brother, friend against friend. The wounds of our minds as well as those of our bodies will have to be healed now if we are to live together in peace." Duane added, for effect, "The war is over."

"You're not just telling me that?" Janroe said.

"What?"

"That the war's over."

"Of course it is. The word came direct from Fort Buchanan. They learned about it this afternoon. Their rider ran into Vern, and Vern sent a man here to tell us. Vern realized I would want to know immediately."

"I haven't been told," Janroe said. "Not officially, and your telling me doesn't count."

Duane was frowning, squinting up at Janroe in the darkness with his cigar poised a few inches from his face. "How could you learn more officially than this? The message came from Fort Buchanan, a military establishment."

"You learned it from your side," Janroe said. "I haven't been told officially from mine."

"Man, you've been out of the war for at least a year! Do you expect them to tell personally every veteran who served?"

"I haven't been out of it." Janroe paused, studying Duane's reaction. "I'm still fighting, just like you've been with your saddle-tramp cavalry, like your brother's been doing supplying Yankee remounts."

Duane was squinting again. "You've been at your store every day. I'm almost sure of it."

"Look under the store," Janroe said. "That's where we keep the Enfields."

"British rifles?"

"Brought in through Mexico, then shipped east."

"I don't believe it." Duane shook his head. "All this time you've been moving contraband arms through the store?"

"About two thousand rifles since I started."

"Well," Duane said, officially now, "if you have any there now, I advise you to turn them over to the people at Fort Buchanan. I presume Confederate officers will be allowed to keep their horses and sidearms, but rifles are another matter."

Janroe shook his head slowly. "I'm not turning anything over."

"You'd rather face arrest?"

"They can't take me if they don't know about the guns."

"Mr. Janroe, if you don't turn them in, don't you think I would be obligated to tell them?"

"I suppose you would."

"Then why did you tell me about them?"

"So you would know how we stand. You see, you can be obligated all you want, but you won't be able to do anything about it."

Duane clamped the cigar in the corner of his mouth. "You've got the nerve to ride in here and threaten me?"

"I guess I do." Janroe was relaxed; he sat with his shoulders hunched loosely and his hand in his lap.

"You're telling me that I won't go to Buchanan?" Duane's voice rose. "Listen, I'll take my saddle-tramp cavalry, as you call it, and drag those guns out myself, and I'll march you right up to the fort with them if I feel like it. So don't go threatening me, mister; I don't take any of it."

Janroe watched him calmly. "It's too bad you didn't volunteer that time you said. That would have made this better. No, it would have made it perfect—if you had been in command of that Yankee artillery company. They were upon a ridge and we had to cross a cornfield that was trampled down and wide open to get at them. They began firing as soon as we started across. Almost right away I was hit and my arm was torn clean from my body."

"I think we've discussed this enough for one evening," Duane said stiffly.

"What if you had given that order to fire?" Janroe said. "Do you see how much better it would make this?" He shook his head then. "But that would be too much to ask; like having Vern here too. Both of you here, and no one else around."

"I would advise you to go home," Duane said, "and seriously consider what I told you. I don't make idle threats."

"I don't either, Major." Janroe's hand rose to the open front of his coat. He drew the Colt from his shoulder holster and cocked it as he trained it on Duane. "Though I don't suppose you'd call this a threat. This is past the threatening stage, isn't it?"

"You don't frighten me," Duane said. He remembered something Vern had told Cable that day at Cable's house, rephrasing it now because he was not sure of the exact words.

"There is a big difference between holding a gun and using it. If you're bluffing, Mr. Janroe, trying to frighten me, I advise you to give it up and go home."

"I'm not bluffing."

"Then you're out of your mind."

"Major, I don't think you realize what's happening."

"I realize I'm talking to a man who hasn't complete control of his faculties."

"That's meant to be an insult, nothing else," Janroe said. "If you believed it, you'd be scared out of your wits."

Duane hesitated. He watched Janroe closely, in silence; the hand holding the cigar had dropped to his side. "You wouldn't dare use that gun," he said finally.

"It's the reason I came."

"But you have no reason to kill me!"

"Call it duty, Major. Call it anything you like." Janroe put the front sight squarely on Duane's chest. "Do you want to run or stand there? Make up your mind."

"But the war's over—don't you realize that!"

Janroe pulled the trigger. In the heavy report he watched Duane clutch the railing, holding himself up, and Janroe fired again, seeing Duane's body jerk with the impact of the bullet before sliding, falling to the porch.

"It's over now," Janroe said.

He reined and kicked the dun to a gallop as he crossed the yard. Behind him he heard a window rise and a woman's voice, but the sounds seemed to end abruptly as the darkness of the trees closed in on him.

Now back to the store. There was no reason to run. He would tell the women that Cable was not at home, that he'd looked for him, but with no luck. Tomorrow he would ride out again, telling the women he would try again to locate Cable.

But he would take his time, giving Vern time to learn about his brother's death; giving him time to convince himself that it was Cable who'd killed Duane; giving him time, then, to go after Cable. No, there was no need to run.

It had been a satisfying time. The best since the days near Opelousas when he'd killed the Yankee prisoners.

Bill Dancey had spent the night in a line shack seven miles north of the Kidston place. The day before, after the incident at Denaman's, after watching Duane demonstrate his authority with a rawhide quirt, after riding back to the Kidston place with Duane and the Dodd brothers and not speaking a word to them all the way, Dancey had decided it was time for a talk with Vern.

But Vern was still away. Since that morning he'd been visiting the grazes, instructing his riders to begin driving the horses to the home range. Vern could be gone all night, Dancey knew, and that was why he went out after him. What he had to say wouldn't wait.

By late evening, after he had roamed the west and north pastures, but always an hour or more behind Vern, Dancey decided to bed down in the line shack. It was deserted now, which suited him fine. It was good to get away from the others once in a while, to sit peacefully or lie in your blanket with quiet all around and be able to hear yourself think. It gave him a chance to review the things he wanted to tell Vern.

With the first trace of morning light he was in the saddle again; and it was at the next pasture that he learned about Duane. There were five men here, still at the breakfast fire. They told him that Vern had been here; but a rider came during the night with news about Duane—one before that with word about the war being over; it had sure as hell been an eventful night—and Vern had left at once, taking only the two Dodd brothers with him.

By six o'clock Dancey was back at the Kidston place. He crossed the yard to the corral, unsaddled and turned his horse into the enclosure before going on to the house.

Austin and Wynn Dodd were sitting on the steps: Wynn sitting low, leaning forward and looking down between his legs; Austin sitting back with his elbows resting on the top step, Austin with his head up, his stained, curled-brim hat straight over his eyes. Both men wore holstered revolvers, the butt of Wynn's jutting out sharply from his hip because of the way he was sitting. Austin, Dancey noticed then, was wearing two revolvers, two Colts that looked like the pair Joe Bob had owned.

Dancey stopped in front of them. "Vern's inside?"

Wynn looked up. Austin nodded.

"He told you to wait for him?"

"Right here." Wynn leaned back saying it, propping his elbows on the step behind him.

"If that's all right with you, Bill," Austin said dryly.

Dancey moved through them to the porch. He opened the screen then stood there, seeing Vern and Lorraine at the stove fireplace across the room. Dancey waited until Vern saw him before moving toward them.

"I've been looking for you." Vern said it bluntly, and the tone stirred the anger Dancey had held under control since yesterday afternoon.

He wanted to snap back at Vern and if it led to his quitting, that was all right. But now Duane was dead and before he argued with Vern he would have to say he was sorry about Duane. And Lorraine was here. Her presence bothered him too. She didn't appear to have been crying, but stood staring at the dead fire; probably not even thinking about her father, more likely wondering what was going to happen to her. She seemed less sure of herself now; though Dancey realized he could be imagining this.

He looked at Vern. "Your brother's dead?" And when Vern nodded Dancey said, "I'm sorry about it. Where is he now?"

"Upstairs. We'll bury him this afternoon."

"All right." Dancey's eyes moved to Lorraine. "What about his girl?"

"I think she'll be going back home," Vern said. "This brought her up pretty short. She might have even grown up in one day."

"It could do that," Dancey said. "When was it, last night?"

Vern nodded. "He rode in while Duane was on the porch. Lorraine was upstairs. She heard the two shots and looked out her window in time to see him riding off."

"Who's he?"

"Who do you think?"

"Did she see him clearly?"

"She didn't have to."

"It's best to be sure."

"All right, Bill, if it's not Cable, who would it be?"

"I know. It's probably him; but you have to be sure."

"I'm sure as I'll ever be."

Vern moved past him and Dancey followed out to the porch. The two Dodd brothers were standing now, watching Vern.

"There'll be just the four of us," Vern told them. He waited until they moved off, then seemed to relax somewhat, leaning against a support post and staring out across the yard. He said to Dancey behind him, "They'll bring you a fresh horse."

"I can get my own," Dancey said.

"I guess you can, but they'll bring it anyway."

"Now we go visit Cable—is that it?"

"You don't have to come."

"Then I sure as hell don't think I will."

Vern turned suddenly from the post, but hesitated then. "Bill, do you realize the man's killed three people now, one of them my brother?"

"Are you telling me you're going after Cable because you and Duane were so close?"

"Be careful, Bill."

"What would you have done if two men came to your house at night—two men like Royce and Joe Bob? What would you have done if somebody busted your house—"

"I had no part of that; you know it."

"Duane said yesterday he didn't either." Dancey paused. "Maybe Lorraine just made it up." The tone of his voice probed for an answer.

But Vern said only, "Who did it isn't my concern."

"All right," Dancey said. "How would you see it if somebody

had taken a rawhide quirt to your face while two others held your arms?"

"I don't have to see it! The man killed my brother, do you understand that?"

"You've got something to say for your stand." Dancey saw the anger etched deeply in Vern's eyes, hardening the solemn, narrow-boned look of his face. "But what are you going to do about it?"

"Take him up to Fort Buchanan."

"You better go in shooting."

"If that's the way it has to be."

"It's the only way you'll beat him," Dancey said. "And even then he'll fight harder than you will. He's got his family and his land at stake."

Vern shook his head. "This has gone beyond arguing over land."

"You've got three hundred horses up in the high pastures," Dancey said. "When you bring them down they're going to have water. That's the point of all the talk. Nothing else. You've got horses relying on you. He's got people. Now who do you think's going to swing the hardest?"

Vern watched the Dodd brothers coming, leading the horses, then looked at Dancey again. "I'll give him a chance to go up to Fort Buchanan peacefully. If he refuses, that's up to him."

Dancey shook his head. "You'll have to kill him."

"I said it's up to him."

"Maybe you'd hold back." Dancey watched the Dodd brothers approaching. "But they wouldn't. They'd give up a month's pay to draw on him." Dancey hesitated, and when Vern said nothing he added, "You've got yourself talked into something you don't even believe in."

"Listen," Vern said tightly, "I've said it, if he won't come peacefully, we'll shoot him out."

"But you're hoping he'll listen to you."

"I don't care now."

"He won't," Dancey said. "And not one person in his family would. I saw that yesterday. I saw it in his wife and kids, his little boy standing there watching his daddy get rawhided and the kid not even flinching or crying or looking the other way. The man's family is with him, Vern. They're part of him. That's why when you fight him you'll think you're fighting five men, not just one."

"There'll be four of us, Bill," Vern said. "So that almost evens it." He started down the steps.

"Three," Dancey said. "I'll drive your horses. I will this time. But I won't take part in what you're doing."

Vern was looking up at Dancey again, studying him, but he said only, "All right, Bill," as if he had started to say something else but changed his mind. He moved to his horse and mounted, not looking at Dancey now, and led the two Dodd brothers out of the yard.

They'll kill Cable, Dancey thought, watching them go. But they'll pay for it, and not all three of them will come back.

Cable was in the barn when Luz Acaso came.

Earlier, while he was fixing something to eat and had gone to the river for a bucket of water, he saw Kidston's mares and foals out on the meadow. He had planned to run them two days ago, but Manuel had come and he had forgotten about the horses until now. So after breakfast he mounted the sorrel and again chased the herd up the curving sweep of the valley to Kidston land.

He was back, less than an hour later, and leading the sorrel into the barn, when he heard the horse coming down through the pines from the ridge trail. He waited. Then, seeing Luz Acaso appear out of the trees and round the adobe to the front yard, Cable came out of the barn. But in the same moment he stepped back inside again.

Two riders were coming along the bank of the river on the meadow side. Then, as they jumped their horses down the bank, starting across the river, Cable turned quickly to the sorrel. He drew the Spencer from the saddle, skirted the rectangle of light on the barn floor and edged close to the open doorway.

From this angle, looking past the corner of the house, he saw Luz Acaso first, Luz standing close to her dun horse now, staring out across the yard. Then beyond her, he saw the two riders come out of the willows. One was Vern Kidston. Cable recognized him right away. The other was one of the Dodd brothers, and Cable was almost sure it was the one named Austin.

But why didn't they sneak up?

No, they couldn't have seen him. He had stayed close to the trees coming back from running the horses and he had been in the yard, after that, only a moment. Watching them now, he was thinking: If they wanted to kill you they would have sneaked up.

Unless—he thought—there were more than just the two of them. Vern could be drawing him out. Wanting him to show his position, if he was here.

So wait a minute. Just watch them.

But there was Luz to think of.

His gaze returned to the girl. She was facing Vern, still standing by her horse; but now, as Cable watched, she dropped the reins and moved toward the two riders, walking unhurriedly and with barely a trace of movement beneath the white length of her skirt. Vern Kidston came off his saddle as she approached them.

Cable heard him ask, "Where is he?" the words faint and barely carrying to him. Luz spoke. There was no sound but he saw her shrug and gesture with her hands. Then Kidston spoke again, a sound reaching Cable but without meaning, and he saw Luz shake her head.

For several minutes they stood close to each other, Luz looking up at Kidston and now and again making small gestures with her hands, until, abruptly, Vern took her by the arm. Luz resisted, trying to pull away, but his grip held firmly. Vern walked her to the dun, helped her onto the saddle and the moment she was seated, slapped the horse sharply across the rump. He watched her until she passed into the aspen stand a dozen yards beyond the adobe, then motioned to Austin Dodd.

Austin caught up the reins of Vern's horse and came on. Cable watched him, wondering where the other Dodd brother was. Wynn. He had seen them only twice, but still he could not picture one without the other. Perhaps Wynn was close by. Perhaps that was part of these two standing out in the open.

Austin reached Vern and handed him the reins. Cable waited. Would Vern mount and ride out? If he did, it would be over. Over for this time, Cable thought. Then he would wait for the next time—then the next, and the time after that. Unless you do something now, Cable thought.

Tell him, and make it plain—

No, Cable knew that to make his stand clear and unmistakably plain, without the hint of a doubt, he would have to start shooting right now, right this second. And that was something he couldn't do.

He did not see this in his mind during the moments of waiting. He didn't argue it with himself; but the doubt, the conscience, the whatever it was that made him hesitate and be unsure of himself, was part of him and it held him from killing Vern Kidston now just as it had prevented him from pulling the trigger once before.

Briefly, he did think: You can be too honest with yourself and lose everything. He hesitated because this was a simple principle, a matter of almost black or white, and whatever shades of gray appeared, whatever doubts he might have, were still not strong enough to allow him to shoot a man in cold blood.

Though there was more to it than that. A simple principle, but not a simpler matter. Not something as brutally, honestly simple as war. He couldn't shoot Vern in cold blood. But if he *could* . . . If the urge to end this was stronger than anything else, would his shooting Vern end it? Would he be sure of getting Austin, too? Then Wynn and Dancey and Duane . . . and how many more were there?

It wasn't good to think. That was the trouble, thinking about it and seeing it as black and white and good and bad and war or not war. Wouldn't it be good if they could go back six days and start over and not have the Kidstons here or Janroe, not having anything that has happened happen, not even in a dream?

No, it was not merely a question of not being able to shoot Vern in cold blood. It never was just that. It was being afraid, too, of what would happen to his family. To him, and then to his family.

If they would fight, he thought. If they would hurry the hell up and fight, you could fight back and there would be nothing else but that to think about and there wouldn't even be time to think about that.

He saw Vern Kidston draw his revolver. He saw Austin Dodd dismounting, pulling a Sharps rifle from his saddle boot. Both men walked toward the adobe and within a few strides, from this angle, watching them from the barn and looking past the front corner of the house, they passed from Cable's view.

They'll wreck it for good this time, Cable thought.

If you let them.

He felt the tenseness inside of him, but he was not squeezing the Spencer and his legs felt all right. Stepping from the barn, he glanced toward the back of the adobe. The clearing between the pine slope and the house was empty. Then he was running across the yard, watching the front now, until he reached the windowless side wall of the house. He edged along to the front, cocked the Spencer and stepped around.

Vern and Austin Dodd were coming out of the front door, under the ramada now, Vern with his hands empty, his Colt holstered again, Austin Dodd holding the Sharps in one hand, the barrel angled down but his finger through the trigger guard. Both men saw Cable at the same time, and both were held motionless by the same moment of indecision.

Cable saw it. He stopped, ready to fire if either man moved a finger, waiting now, leaving the decision with them and almost hoping to see the barrel of the Sharps come up.

"Make up your mind," Cable said, even though he felt the moment was past. He moved toward them, along the log section of the house, until less than a dozen strides separated him from the two men.

"You came to wreck it a second time?"

"I came to talk," Vern said flatly. "That first."

"With your gun in your hand."

"So there wouldn't be an argument."

"Well, you've got one now."

Vern's gaze dropped to the carbine. "You better put that down."

"When you get off my land."

"If you want a fight," Vern said, with the same sullen tone, "one of us will kill you. If you want to come along peacefully, I give you my word we won't shoot."

"Come where?"

"To Fort Buchanan."

Cable shook his head. "I've got no reason to go there."

Vern stared at him, his full mustache accentuating the firm line of his mouth. "I'm not leaving before you do," he said. "Either shoot your gun off or let go of it."

Almost at once Cable had sensed the change in Vern Kidston. Four days ago he had stood covering Vern with a gun and Vern had calmly told him that he would outwait him. But now something had changed Vern. Cable could hear it in the flat, grim tone of the man's voice. He could see it on Vern's face: an inflexible determination to have his way now. There would be no reasoning with Vern, no putting it off. Cable was sure of that. Just as he knew he himself would not be budged from this place by anything less persuasive than a bullet.

Still, momentarily, he couldn't help wondering what had brought about the change in Vern, and he said, "So you've lost your patience."

"You visited Duane last night," Vern said. "We're returning the call."

"I never left this house last night."

"Like you don't know anything about it."

"Well, you tell me what I did. So I'll know."

"In case you didn't wait to make sure," Vern said, "I'll tell you this. Duane's dead. Either one of the bullets would have killed him."

Cable stared at Vern, almost letting the barrel of the Spencer drop and then holding it more firmly. He could not picture Duane dead and he wondered if this was a trick. But if Vern was making it up, what would it accomplish? No, Duane was dead. That was a fact. That was the reason Vern was here. And somebody had killed him.

Janroe.

Janroe, tired of waiting. Janroe, carrying the war, his own private version of the war, to Duane. It could be Janroe. It could very well be and probably was without any doubt Janroe.

But he couldn't tell Vern that. Because to convince Vern it was Janroe he'd have to explain about the man, about the guns, and that would involve Luz and Manuel. And then Vern would go to the store and Martha and the children were there now, and they'd seen enough . . . too much. Besides, this thing between him and Vern still had to be settled, no matter what Janroe had done.

Cable said, "I didn't kill your brother. If I had sneaked up to kill anybody, if I'd carried it that far, it would have been to put a sight on you."

"You're the only man who had reason to do it," Vern said.

"That might seem to be true," Cable answered. "But I didn't. Like you're the only one who had reason to wreck my house. Did you do it?"

"I never touched your place."

"So there you are," Cable said. "Maybe we're both lying. Then again, maybe neither of us is."

"You're not talking your way out of it," Vern said flatly.

"I don't have to." Cable raised the carbine slightly. "I'm holding the gun."

"And once you pull the trigger, Austin will put a hole through you."

"If he's alive," Cable said, centering his attention on Austin Dodd who was still holding the Sharps in one hand, the tip of the barrel almost touching the ground. The man seemed even more sure of himself than Kidston. He studied Cable calmly, with an intent, thoughtful expression half closing his eyes.

Like you don't have a gun in your hand, Cable thought, watching him. He's not worried by it because he knows what he's doing. So you go for Austin first if you go at all.

In his mind he practice-swung the Spencer on Austin, aiming to hit him just above his crossed gun belts. When a man is stomach-shot he relaxes and there is no reflex action jerking his trigger, no wild dead-man-firing. Then he pictured swinging the carbine lower and farther to the left. Austin might drop and roll away and it would be a wing shot, firing and letting the man dive into it. No, it wouldn't be like that, but that's the way it would seem. He thought then: That's enough of that. If you have to think when it's happening, you'll be too late.

The silence lengthened before Austin Dodd spoke.

"He talks, but he's scared to do anything."

Kidston said nothing.

Austin Dodd's eyes still held calmly, curiously on Cable. "I've got him thought out but for one thing. Where'd he buy the nerve to kill Joe Bob?"

"Ask him," Kidston said.

"He'll say he killed him fair." Carefully, Austin raised his left hand and pulled on the curled brim of his hat, loosening it on his head and replacing it squarely.

"Maybe," he said then, "we ought to just walk up and take the gun away from him."

Cable watched him. A moment before, as Austin adjusted his hat, he was sure the man's eyes had raised to look past him. And just before that Austin had started talking. Not a word from him until now.

To make sure you keep looking at him, Cable thought. He felt his stomach tighten as he pictured a man behind him, a man at the corner of the house or coming carefully from the direction of the barn with his gun drawn. Austin was staring at him again. Then—there it was—Vern Kidston's gaze flicked out past him. Vern looked at Cable then, quickly, saw his intent stare, and let his gaze wander aimlessly toward the willows.

Now you're sure, Cable thought, wanting to turn and fire and run and not stop running until he was alone and there was quiet all about him with the only sounds in the distance.

But he made himself stand and not move, his mind coldly eliminating the things that could not happen: like whoever it was being able to sneak up close to him without being heard; or suddenly shooting Vern and Austin Dodd standing directly in front of him, in the line of fire.

So, it would be timed. The moment they moved, the second they were out of the way, the man behind him would fire. It came to that in Cable's mind because there was no other way it could be.

And it would come soon.

Watch Austin and go the way he goes.

It would be coming now.

But don't think and listen to yourself.

You'll hear it. God, you'll hear it all right.

You'll even see it. You'll see Austin—

And Cable was moving—spinning to the outside, pushing himself out of the line of fire and throwing the carbine to his shoulder even before Austin Dodd and Kidston hit the ground. With the sound of the single shot still in the air, he was putting the carbine on Wynn Dodd, thirty feet away and in the open, standing, holding his Colt at arm's length.

Cable fired. *Too soon!* He saw Wynn swing the Colt on him as he levered the Spencer, brought it almost to his shoulder and fired again. Wynn was turned, thrown off balance by the impact of the bullet and his Colt was pointing at the willows when it went off. Still, he held it, trying to bring it in line again; but now Cable was running toward him, levering the trigger guard, half raising the carbine and firing again. Wynn's free hand went to his side and he stumbled, almost going down. From ten feet, with Wynn's Colt swinging on him and seeming almost in his face, Cable shot him again, being sure of this one, knowing Wynn would go down; and now levering, turning, snapping a shot at Austin Dodd and missing as the man came to one knee with the Sharps almost to his shoulder.

Austin and Vern had held their fire because of Wynn, but now both of them opened up. Cable's snap shot threw Austin off and he fired quickly, too wide. From the ramada, Kidston fired twice. Before he could squeeze the trigger again Cable was past the corner of the adobe, beyond their view, and within ten strides safely through the open doorway of the barn.

He brought the sorrel out of its stall, thonging the Spencer to the saddle horn, then mounted and drew the Walker.

Now time it, Cable thought.

He knew what Kidston and Austin would do, which was the obvious thing, the first thought to occur to them; and they would respond to it because they would have to act fast to keep up with him or ahead of him and not let him slip away.

Only one man could watch the barn from the corner of the house. The second man would have to expose himself, or else drop back to the willows, to the protection of the cutbank and move along it until he was opposite the barn, directly out from it and little more than a hundred feet away. If that happened he would be pinned down in the barn until he was picked off, burned out or eventually drawn out by a need as starkly simple as a cup of water. If he waited, time would be on their side to be used against him.

So he would move out and he would do it now while they were still realizing what had to be done, while they were still scrambling to seal off his escape. He knew this almost instinctively after two and a half years with Bedford Forrest. You weren't fooled by false security. You didn't wait, giving the other man time to think. You carried the fight, on your own terms and on your own ground.

Now it was a matter of timing. Move fast, but move at the right time.

The sorrel was lined up with the doorway now, though still well back in the barn. From here Cable could see the corner of the adobe. As he watched he saw a man's shoulder, then part of his head and the dull glint of a Colt barrel in the sunlight. Almost at the same time he heard the horse somewhere off beyond the adobe—the other man running for the cutbank.

Cable's eyes clung to the corner of the house.

Now move him back, he thought, raising the Walker and putting the front sight on the edge of the house. He fired once. The man— Cable was sure it was Kidston—drew back out of sight. At that moment Cable moved, abruptly spurring the sorrel. He was suddenly in the sunlight and reining hard to the right, the Walker still covering the corner; and as Kidston appeared, coming suddenly into the open, Cable fired. He had to twist his body then, his arm extended straight back over the sorrel's rump. He fired again, almost at the same time as Kidston did, but both of their shots were hurried. Then he was reining again, swerving the sorrel to the left, passing behind the adobe just as Kidston fired his second shot.

Even as he entered the horse trail up into the pines, Cable saw the way to throw the fight back at them, to swing on them again while they were off guard in the true hell-raising, hit-and-run style of Forrest; and he left the trail, coming back down through the trees. Then he was in the open again behind the adobe, but now cutting to the right and circling the side of the adobe away from the barn. A moment later he broke past the front of the house.

Twenty feet away Kidston was mounting, looking directly at Cable over the pommel of his saddle. He saw Vern trying to bring up his Colt. He saw Vern's face clearly beyond the barrel of his own revolver; he was pulling the trigger when Vern's horse threw its head into the line of fire. Cable reined the sorrel hard to the right then, seeing Vern's horse stumble and go down with Vern falling and rolling clear.

He caught a glimpse of Austin Dodd already mounted and coming up over the cutbank, but that was all. There was one shot left in the Walker and now Cable was spurring, running the sorrel through the light- and dark-streaked aspen stand, then cutting to the left, reaching the willows, brushing through them and feeling the thick, heavy branches behind him, covering him as he splashed across the river and climbed out onto the meadow.

Get distance on Austin, that was the thing to do now. Get time to reload, and at the same time look like you're running. Now he would lead Austin, let Austin think he was chasing him, and perhaps he would become careless.

Austin fired the Sharps as he came out of the willows to the edge of the river, but he hurried the shot and now Cable was almost two hundred yards ahead of him, holding the sorrel to a steady run.

Cable was calm now. Even though he was sure only in a general way what he would do. Somehow, he would stop Austin Dodd just as he had stopped Vern.

But was Vern stopped? For how long? He could be coming too. He would find Wynn's horse, which might or might not take time; but he would come.

So it wasn't over, or even halfway over. It was just starting. He would have to be careful and keep his eyes open and stop Austin— Austin first. Now it was a matter of leading him on until he found the place he wanted to fight him. He was applying what he had learned well with Bedford Forrest. How to kill and keep from being killed. Though not killing with an urge to kill, not killing Austin Dodd because he was Austin Dodd. Though you could probably even justify that, Cable thought.

He would start up the far side of the meadow and be in the trees while Austin was still in the open. Then Austin would slow up and that would give him time to reload. That would be the way to do it, he thought, lifting his gaze to the piñon trees and the open slope that rose above them.

Yet it was in the same momentary space of time, with the heavy, solid report, with the unmistakable smacking sound of the bullet, that Cable's plan dissolved. The sorrel went down, shot through a hind leg, and Cable was suddenly on the ground. He rolled over, looking back in time to see Austin Dodd mounting again.

The man had reloaded on the run, got down for one last-chance long-shot with the Sharps at two hundred stretching to three hundred yards. And you weren't watching!

Cable started for the sorrel—on the ground with its hind legs kicking in spasms. The Spencer was still thonged to the saddle. The cartridge tubes and loads for the Walker were in the saddle bags. But he knew at once that it was too late to get them. If he delayed, he'd be pinned down behind the sorrel. In Cable's mind it was not a matter of choice. Not with a slope of thick piñon less than forty yards away.

He ran for it, crouched, sprinting, not looking back but hearing the hoof beats gaining on him; then the high, whining report of a Colt.

Before Austin could fire again, Cable was through the fringe of yellow-blossomed mesquite and into the piñons. From here he watched Austin rein in at the sorrel and dismount. Cable was moving at once, higher up on the slope, a dozen yards or more, before he looked back at Austin again.

The gunman was squatting by the sorrel going through the one accessible saddle bag. But now he rose, holding the Spencer down-pointed in one hand, stepped back and shot the sorrel through the head. He threw the carbine aside, looking up at the piñon slope.

"Cable!" Austin shouted the name. He paused while his eyes scanned the dark foliage. "Cable, I'm coming for you!"

Cable watched him, a small figure forty or fifty yards below him and out in the open, now coming toward the trees.

He's sure of himself, Cable thought. Because he's been counting shots and he knows it as well as you do. Cable pulled the Walker and checked it to be sure.

One bullet remained in the revolver. Extra loads, powder and percussion caps were all out in the saddle bag.

■　■　■

Luz kept the dun mare at a steady run, her bare knees pressed tightly to the saddle, holding it and aching with the strain of jabbing her heels into the dun's flanks.

She realized she should have taken the horse trail. It was shorter. But Vern Kidston had sent her off abruptly, and in the moment her only thought had been to keep going, to run for help as fast as the dun would move. And now she was following the curving five-mile sweep of the meadow, already beyond the paths that led up to the horse trail from Cable's land.

They would find Cable in the barn . . . She had seen him go in as she approached. And if he showed himself, they would kill him. Even if he didn't, he was trapped. She pictured Vern and the other man firing in at him, not showing themselves and taking their time. But if they waited, having trapped him, she might have time also—time to bring help.

If her brother was home. She had thought of no one else, picturing him mounting and rushing back to Cable's aid. He would *have* to be home. God, make him be home, she thought, closing her eyes and thinking hard so God would hear her; he said he would come today, so all You have to do is make sure of it. Not a miracle. Just make him be home.

And if he's not? Then Mr. Janroe.

No! She rejected the thought, shaking her head violently. God is just. He couldn't offer something that's evil to do something that's good.

Yet in the good act, saving Cable, Vern Kidston could be wounded or killed. And there would be nothing good in that.

She closed her eyes as tightly as she could to see this clearly, but it remained confused, the good and the evil overlapping and not clearly defined or facing one another as it should be. Because the wrong ones are fighting, she thought.

But why couldn't they see this? Vern Kidston and Paul Cable should be together, she thought, because they are the same kind of man; though perhaps Paul is more gentle. He has a woman and has learned to be gentle.

But Vern could have a woman. And he could also learn to be gentle. She knew this, feeling it and knowing it from the first time she saw him; feeling it like a warm robe around her body the time he kissed her, which had been almost a year ago and just before Janroe came. Then feeling it again, standing close to him and seeing it in his eyes as they faced each other in front of Cable's house.

She had told him Cable was not at home and he said, then they would wait for him. I will wait with you, Luz said. But Vern shook his head saying, go on home to Janroe. She told him then, without having to stop to think of words, what she thought of Edward Janroe, what kind of a half-man half-animal, what kind of a *nagual* he was. And she could see that Vern believed her when she said she despised Janroe.

She had pleaded with him then to put his guns aside and talk to Cable, to end it between them honestly as two men should. She had thought of the war being over, saying: see, they ended after seeing how senseless it was that so many men should die. End your war, too, she had said.

But he had taken her arm and half dragged her to the dun mare and told her to go. Because now it was this business with Cable and not a time for gentleness. He did not say this, but Luz could feel it. Just as she knew now why he had stopped seeing her after Janroe's coming.

Because Vern Kidston was proud and would rather stay away and clench his fists than risk discovering her living with or in love with Edward Janroe. That meant only one thing. Vern Kidston loved her. He did before and he did now.

But don't think of it now, she thought. Don't think of anything. Just do what you have to do. She told herself that this was beyond her understanding. For how could there be room for love and hate in the same moment? How could good be opposed to good? And how can you be happier than you have been and more afraid than you have ever been, both at the same time?

Within a few minutes she was in sight of the store with the dark sweep of willows bunched close beyond. She kept her eyes on the adobe now and soon she was able to make out a figure on the platform. She prayed that it was Manuel.

But it was Janroe, standing rigidly and staring at her, waiting for her as she crossed the yard and reined in the dun.

"Where've you been?"

She saw the anger in his face and in the tense way he held his body. But there was no time to be frightened; she wanted to tell him, she wanted to say all of it at once and make sure he understood.

"I went to the Cable place," she began, out of breath and almost gasping the words.

"I told you I was going there!" Janroe's voice whipped at her savagely, then lowered to the hoarse tone of talking through clenched teeth. "I told you to stay home, that I was going later—but you went anyway! I told you he wasn't there last night and I would see him this morning—but you went anyway!"

"Listen to me!" Luz screamed it, feeling a heat come over her face. "Vern Kidston is there—"

Janroe stared at her and slowly the tightness eased from his face. "Alone?"

"One man with him. Perhaps more."

"What happened?"

"Not anything yet. But something has happened to Vern and he wants to kill Cable. I know it!"

Janroe's chest rose and fell with his breathing, but he said calmly, "He probably just wants to talk to Cable."

"No—he was armed. Vern, and the one called Austin with two guns and a rifle on his saddle. . . . Listen, is my brother here?"

"Not yet."

"He said he was coming today."

"Probably later on."

She was looking at him intently now, trying to see something in him that she could trust, that she could believe. But there was no time even for this and she said, "Come with me. Now, before they kill him."

"Luz, Vern just wants to talk with him." Janroe was completely at ease now. "Vern's a patient man. Why would he change?"

"Then you won't come," Luz said.

"There's no need to. Come in the house and stop worrying about it."

She shook her head. "Then I'm going back."

"Luz, I said come in the house. It's none of your business what's going on between them."

She saw the anger in his face again and she raised the reins. Janroe came off the platform, reaching for the bridle, but the dun was already side-stepping, wheeling abruptly, and Janroe was knocked flat. Luz broke away and was across the yard before Janroe could push himself to his feet.

She held herself low in the saddle and kept the dun running with her heels and with her voice, making the horse strain forward and stretch its legs over the grass that seemed to sweep endlessly toward the curve of the valley.

She would do something, she told herself, because she had to do something. There was no one else. She wouldn't think of it being over. She would arrive before they found Cable and plead with Vern, not leaving this time even if he tried to force her. He would listen. Then Paul would come out and they would talk, and after a while the thing between them would be gone.

But only moments later she knew she was too late. Luz slowed the mare, rising in the saddle and pulling the reins with all her strength to bring the dun finally to a halt. She sat listening.

Now, in the distance, she heard it again: the flat, faraway sound of gunfire, and she knew they had found him and were trying to kill him.

SEVEN

Soon there would be two of them.

Cable could see the rider now—it would have to be Vern on Wynn's horse—already on this side of the river and coming across the meadow.

Below, closer to him, was Austin Dodd.

Cable waited until Austin came through the yellow mesquite patches at the edge of the piñon pines. As the man reached the trees, Cable began to fall back. He moved carefully up the slope, glancing behind him, not wanting to stumble and lose time, and not wanting to lose sight of Austin. He caught glimpses of the man moving cautiously up through the trees.

The slope was not steep here and the piñon seemed almost uniformly spaced, resembling an abandoned, wild-growing orchard. It was not a place to stand with one shot in his revolver and fight a man who had two Colt guns and all the time in the world.

Cable moved back until he reached the end of the trees. And now he stopped to study the open slope behind him. It was spotted with patches of brittlebush and cliffrose, but nothing to use for cover; not the entire, gravelly, nearly one hundred feet of it that slanted steeply to the sky.

Perhaps he could make it; but not straight up. It was too steep. He would have to angle across the slope and Austin would have time to shoot at him. But it was worth trying and it would be better than staying here. He would have to forget about Austin—and about Vern, almost across the meadow now—and concentrate on reaching the crest, not letting anything stop him.

He was in the open then, running diagonally across the rise, his boots digging hard into the crusted, crumbling sand. Almost at once he felt the knotted pain in his thighs, but he kept going, not looking back and trying not to picture Austin Dodd closing in on him; or Vern, at the foot of the slope now and taking out his rifle.

Cable cut through a patch of brittlebush, getting a better foothold then and running hard, but he came suddenly onto a spine of smooth rock—it humped no more than two feet above the ground—and here he slipped to his hands and knees. He tried to get up and stumbled again, then rolled over the side of the smooth rock surface before lunging to his feet. He was climbing again, less than twenty feet from the top when Austin's voice reached him.

"Cable!"

He stopped, catching his breath and letting it out slowly before coming around. He knew he would never make the crest. He was sure of it then, seeing Austin already well out of the piñon, to his left below him and less than sixty feet away. Austin's Colts were holstered, but his hands hung close to them. He came on slowly, his face calm and his eyes not straying from Cable.

"Pull anytime now," Austin said. He advanced up the slope, not looking at the ground but feeling his way along with each careful step.

"You want to. But you got only one shot." He was reaching the brittlebush now. "Count the other man's shots. That's something I learned a long time ago. Then when I saw your extra loads still out there with the horse I said to myself, 'I wouldn't want to be that boy. He don't have one chance between hell and breakfast.' "

Cable said nothing. He stood facing Austin Dodd, watching him move into the small field of orange-colored brittlebush. There Austin stopped.

"So when you pull," Austin said, "you have to make it good the one time." He seemed almost to be smiling. "That could tighten a man's nerves some."

Austin was ready, standing on his own ground. And to beat him with one shot, Cable knew, he would have to be more than fast. He would have to be dead-center accurate.

But he wouldn't have time to aim, time to be sure.

Unless Austin hesitated. Or was thrown off guard.

Cable's gaze dropped from the brittlebush to the smooth spine of rock where he had slipped. If he could draw Austin to that point. If he could jiggle him, startle him. If he could throw Austin off balance only for a moment, time enough to draw and aim and make one shot count. If he could do all that—

And Vern was into the piñon now.

No—one thing at a time.

Slowly then, Cable began to back away.

Austin shook his head. "You wouldn't come near making it."

Cable was still edging back, covering six, eight, almost ten feet before Austin started toward him again. Cable stopped. He watched Austin come out of the brittlebush, watched him reach the spine of rock and grope with one foot before stepping onto the smooth, rounded surface.

As Austin's foot inched forward again, Cable went to the side, dropping to one knee and bringing up the Walker in one abrupt motion.

Austin was with him, his right-hand Colt out and swinging on Cable; but the movement shifted his weight. His boots slipped on the smooth rock and even as he fired and fired again he was falling back, his free hand outstretched and clawing for balance.

Beyond the barrel of the Walker, Austin seemed momentarily suspended, his back arched and his gun hand high in the air. Cable's front sight held on his chest and in that moment, when he was sure and there was no doubt about it, Cable squeezed the trigger.

He was sliding down the gravel as Austin fell back into the brittlebush, reaching him then, knowing he was dead and concentrating on prying the revolver from the man's fingers. Cable took both of Austin's revolvers, both Colt Army .44s. He waited a moment, but there was no sign of Vern. He rose half crouched, expecting to hear Vern's shot, expecting to feel it, then ran for the piñon pines.

He went down beneath a tree, feeling the sand and grass patches warm and the thick branches close above him, and now he listened.

Vern would be close. In the time, he could have come all the way up through the trees. Perhaps not; but at any rate Vern would have seen him running across the open. Probably he was just not in position for a shot. But now Vern knew where he was; that much was certain.

So move, Cable thought.

He pushed up to one knee and waited, listening, then was running again, keeping low and dodging through the brushlike trees. Almost immediately a rifle report whined through the grove. Cable dropped, clawing then, changing his direction and moving down the slope. The firing began again, this time with the sound of a revolver somewhere between fifty and a hundred feet away from him. Cable kept going and the .44 sound hammered after him, five times, until he dropped into a shallow gully.

Cable rolled to his stomach, holstered one of the Colt's, and at once began crawling up the narrow wash, up toward the open slope. He moved quickly, using his knees and forearms, until he was almost to the edge of the trees, roughly thirty feet above the spot where he had entered the gully. He stopped then to listen.

There was no sound. Beyond the brush and rock shadows close in front of him, the slope glared with sunlight. He turned, looking back the way he had come, then removed his hat and rolled on his side, resting the Colt on his thigh so that it pointed down the length of the gully.

Minutes passed in dead silence. Then there was a sound; but not close or in the pines. It was the sound of horse's hoofs, distant, still far out on the meadow.

More of them, Cable thought.

He would have to take Vern quickly, before they came. He would have to keep it even if he expected to come through this.

And if you knew where Vern was maybe you could.

But he didn't. Vern could be close. Vern could even know he was lying here, and if he ran for the slope, Vern could very possibly drop him. Or even if he moved or stood up.

And if times if equals if, and there's no getting out of this. No running. Only waiting and letting it happen. Even Forrest waited sometimes. He waited for them to make mistakes. But he would be waiting this time—God, yes, he would be waiting—whether they made mistakes or not.

The horse sound seemed nearer. He concentrated, listening, until he was sure that it was only one horse coming. One rider. One helper for Vern.

Cable pushed up with one hand, trying to see the meadow over the trees below him, but he could see only the far side of the meadow and the willows marking the river and the dark, quiet, cool-looking slope beyond. The rider would be close to this side by now.

Cable's gaze fell, and held.

Vern Kidston was facing him. Vern not thirty feet away, one leg in the gully, half sitting, half kneeling at the edge of it and partly hidden by the brush. Vern with his revolver extended and watching him.

Neither of them moved. They stared in silence with cocked revolvers pointed at each other. Cable sitting with one hand behind him, the other holding the Colt on his thigh, his face calm and showing clearly in the sunlight that filtered through the trees. Vern's expression, though partly shadowed and solemn with his mustache covering the corners of his mouth, was as relaxed as Cable's. The tension was somewhere between them, waiting for one or the other to move. And as the silence lengthened, it seemed that even a spoken word would pull a trigger.

It was in Vern's tone when finally he said, "Cable," and waited, as if expecting a reaction.

"I could have killed you," he said then. "I had my gun on you and you were looking away. . . . Why didn't I?"

Cable said nothing.

"I could have ended it right then. But I didn't. Do you know why?" He waited again. "I'm asking you."

Cable shook his head, though he saw Vern as he had seen him two days ago—a small figure against the front sight of his Spencer—and remembered how he had not been able to pull the trigger. He had thought about it enough and knew the reason why he had held back; but it was not a clear reason; only a feeling and it might be a different feeling with each man. What did Vern feel? At the same time, what difference did it make? Vern had not been able to pull the trigger when he had the chance, and knowing that was enough. But it would be different with him now, Cable thought, just as it's different with you. The feeling wouldn't apply or hold either of them back at this point.

Tell him anyway, Cable thought; and he said, "I had my sights on you once. The same thing happened. Though I'm not sure I'd let it happen again."

"When was that?"

"Two days ago. You were with Lorraine."

"Why didn't you shoot?"

"It takes some explaining," Cable said. "And I'm not sure it makes sense when you say it out loud."

Vern nodded faintly. "Maybe it's called leaving it up to the other man."

"I didn't start this," Cable said flatly. "I don't feel obliged to keep it going either."

"But you'll finish what you can," Vern said. "What about Austin—he's dead?"

Cable nodded.

"I didn't think you'd have a chance with him."

"Neither did he," Cable said. "That's why he's dead."

"So you killed all three of the Dodd brothers, and Royce—"

"What would you have done?"

"You mean because each time it was them or you?"

"Or my family," Cable said. "I'm asking what you would have done? Two choices. Run or stand?"

"All right." Vern paused. "But Duane. That's something else."

"I didn't shoot your brother."

"There's no one else would have reason to."

"Stay with one thing," Cable said. "I didn't shoot him."

"Even after he rawhided you?"

"If I'd wanted to get back at him for that, I'd have used fists. I never felt a beating was a killing thing."

"That could be true," Vern said. "But how do I know it is?"

"Whether you believe it or not," Cable answered, "your gun's no bigger than mine is." But he said then, "I told you before, I didn't leave the house last night."

"And if you didn't do it—" Vern began.

"Why couldn't it have been one of your own men?"

Vern shook his head. "Everybody was accounted for."

Then it was Janroe, Cable thought, without any doubt of it. He said to Vern, "I can ask you the same kind of question."

"You mean about your house? I never touched it."

"Then it was Duane."

"I know for a fact," Vern said, "it wasn't anyone from my place."

"But you put Royce and Joe Bob on me."

Again Vern shook his head. "They came on their own."

"What about Lorraine?"

"I knew about that," Vern admitted. "I should have stopped her."

"What was the point of it?"

"Lorraine said wedge something between you and your wife. Split you up and you wouldn't have a good reason to stay here."

"Does that make sense to you?"

"I said I should have stopped her."

"Vern, I've lived here ten years. We've been married for eight."

Kidston nodded then, solemnly. "Bill Dancey said you had more reason to fight than I did."

"What did you say?"

"I don't remember."

"Do you believe him?"

"I'll tell you this," Vern said. "I'd like to have known you at a different time."

Cable nodded. "Maybe we would have gotten on. Even worked out this land thing."

"Even that," Vern said.

"I would have been willing to let you put some of your horses on my graze," Cable said, "if it hadn't started the way it did."

"Well, it doesn't matter now," Vern said.

But it could matter, Cable thought. "We were going to wait each other out," Cable said. "But Royce and Joe Bob got into it. Then your brother. I wonder how this would have turned out if he were still alive."

Vern was watching Cable closely. "I wish I could understand you. Either you had nothing to do with killing Duane, or else you're some actor."

"Like trying to understand why you brought Wynn and Austin with you," Cable said. "You're big enough to make your own fight."

"When a man's killed," Vern said, "it's no longer a game or a personal contest. It was time to get you, with the best, surest way I had."

"When the man's your brother," Cable said. "When Royce and Joe Bob were killed you went right on waiting."

"I've been wrong," Vern said, "maybe right from the beginning. I let it get out of hand too. I admit that. But there's nothing I can do about the ways it's developed."

"Then in time you would have backed off," Cable said, "if nothing had happened to Duane."

"Well, with the war on I could look on you as an enemy. Kick you off your land and tell myself it was all right. But now that it's over, I'm not sure about anything, not even my horse business. Though I might probably get a contract from the stage-line people when they start up—"

Cable stopped him. "What did you say?" He was staring at Vern intently. "About the war?"

"It's over. You knew that, didn't you?"

"When was it over?"

"A few days ago."

"You knew it then?"

"We learned yesterday." Vern seemed to frown, studying Cable's expression. "Luz knew about it. She mentioned it when I talked to her a while ago."

"Yesterday," Cable said.

"She would have learned it yesterday." Vern nodded.

And if she knew it, Cable thought, so did Janroe. Yesterday. Before Duane was killed. Janroe would have known. He must have known. But still he killed Duane. Could that be?

You could think about it, Cable thought, and it wouldn't make sense, but still it could be. With anyone else there would be a doubt. But with Janroe there was little room for doubt. This was strange because he hardly knew the man.

But at the same time it wasn't strange, not when he pictured this man who had lost his arm in the war and who had killed over a hundred Union prisoners. Not when he heard him talking again, insisting over and over that Vern and Duane should be killed. Not when he remembered the feeling of trying to answer Janroe. No, it wasn't strange, not when he put everything together that he could remember about Janroe.

It could have been Janroe who tore up his house. It occurred to Cable that moment, but at once he was sure of it: Janroe trying to incite him, trying to make him angry enough to go after the Kidstons. Janroe wanting to see them—the enemy, or whatever they were to him—dead, but without drawing blame on himself.

Janroe could even be insane. Something could have happened to him in the war.

No, don't start that, Cable thought. Just take it at its face value. Janroe killed a man you are being accused of killing. He did it, whether he had reason or not; though the war wasn't the reason, because the war was over and you are almost as sure as you can be sure of something that he knew it was over. So just take that, Cable thought, and do something with it.

He sat up, raising the Colt, then turned the cylinder, letting the hammer down gently on the empty chamber. Vern did not move; though when Cable looked up again he knew Vern had been taken by surprise and was puzzled.

"We're wasting our time," Cable said. "There's a man we ought to see."

He began to tell Vern about Janroe.

Luz reached Cable's dead sorrel before she saw the two horses grazing along the mesquite at the foot of the slope. These would belong to Vern and the one called Austin. She slowed the dun to a walk now, her eyes raised and moving searchingly over the piñon-covered slope. The firing had come from up there, she was sure of it.

But there had been no shots for some time now. They could be hunting for him among the trees. Or it could already be over.

When she saw the two figures coming down through the trees, in view for brief moments as they passed through clearings, she was sure that it was over, that these two were Vern and Austin coming back to their horses. They left the piñon and were down beyond the mesquite for sometime. Finally they appeared again and it was not until now that she saw the second man was not Austin but Cable.

She watched them approach with the strange feeling that this could not be happening, that it was a dream. They had been firing at one another; but now they were walking together, both armed, not one bringing the other as a prisoner.

Questions ran through her mind and she wanted to ask all of them at once; but now they were close and it was Cable who spoke first.

"Luz, did Janroe leave the store last night?"

The question took her by surprise. Without a greeting, without an explanation of the two of them together, without wondering why she was here, Cable asked about Janroe. The question must be so important to him that he skipped all of those other things.

She said, hesitantly, "He went to see you last night. But he said you weren't home."

"Where is he now, at the store?"

"He was a little while ago." She remembered him jumping down from the platform, trying to stop her from leaving. "But he's acting strangely," she said. "I don't think I've ever seen him the way he was."

Vern was looking at Cable. "Your wife and kids are there?" When Cable nodded, glancing at Luz again, Vern said, "I think we'd better go see Mr. Janroe."

Janroe watched Luz until she was almost out of sight. He turned, pausing to brush the dust from his knees, and was aware of Martha in the doorway. He looked up at her; from her expression he knew she had heard Luz.

"Well?" Janroe said.

"I would like to borrow a horse," Martha said tensely.

"You can't do anything."

"Just let me have a horse," Martha said. "I don't need anything else from you, least of all advice."

"And you'll take your kids with you?"

"I'd like to leave them here."

Janroe shook his head. "I don't have time to watch your kids."

Martha came out on the platform. "You would stop me from going to my husband? At a time like this you would stop me from being with him?"

"You couldn't help him," Janroe said. "Neither could I. Luz is wasting her time whether she thinks she's doing something or not. I tried to stop her, tried to talk some sense into her, but she wouldn't listen. That's the trouble with you women. You get all het up and run off without thinking." He had moved to the platform and was now mounting the steps. "If Vern's there to talk to your husband, there's no sense in stopping him. If he's there for any other reason, none of us could stop him if we tried."

"You won't let me have a horse?"

"Sit down on your hands, you won't be so nervous."

"Mr. Janroe, I'm begging you—"

"No, you're not." He moved her into the store in front of him. "You want to do something, get out in the kitchen and do the dishes."

Martha didn't want to back down—he could see that—but there was little she could say as she turned abruptly and walked away, down the length of the store counter.

Janroe said after her, "Don't leave the house. You hear me? Don't even open the door less I say it's all right."

He waited until she was in the next room before he moved around behind the counter that extended along the front of the store. From under the counter he took a short-barreled shotgun with *Hatch & Hodges* carved into the stock—it dated from the time the store had been a stage-line station—checked to see that it was loaded, then laid it on the counter.

From a peg behind him he took his shoulder holster with the Colt fitting snugly in it, and looped it over his armless shoulder. He wound the extra-long leather thong, which held the Colt securely, around his chest and tied the end of it deftly with his one hand.

Just in case, he told himself; though you won't need them. You can be almost absolutely sure of that.

Everything will go all right. Luz would be back within an hour. She would ride in slowly this time, putting off telling Martha what had happened. Then behind her would come Vern and Austin, probably both of the Dodd brothers, with Cable face-down over his horse. Vern would tell it simply, in few words; and if Martha cried or screamed at him, he would say, "He killed my brother." Or, "He should have thought about his family before he killed Duane." Or words that said the same thing. Then they would dump his body. Or let it down easy now that it was over and the anger was drained out of them, and ride away.

Then what? Then he would listen to the woman cry, the woman and the kids. There was no way of avoiding that. Afterward, he might even offer his services to the new widow. . . .

Then what? Kill Vern? No, forget about that for now.

Then think about it when the time comes. There was no hurry. He could go back to St. Augustine. Or he could stay here. That would be something, to stay here and be a neighbor of Vern's. Talk to him about Duane every once in a while, and Cable, and all the trouble Cable caused. That would be something; but the staying here, the living here and letting the time pass, might not be worth it. He would have to weigh that against the once-in-a-while satisfaction of Vern talking to him and not knowing he had killed Duane.

No, there was no hurry. There would be time later on to think of what he would do. With two arms he would have stayed in the army; even though the war was over.

Janroe caught himself. Is it over?

All right, it's over. You've had no word, he thought. But if they want to say it's over, then it is. It was a good war, part of it was; but now, as of right now, you can say it's over. You can't fight people who won't fight back.

First Luz would come, then Vern. Everything had happened just about the way it was supposed to and there was no reason for it to change now.

Finding Luz gone this morning had affected his nerves. He knew she had gone to see Cable, and he had pictured her telling him that the war was over. Then asking him if he was at home last night. Then why, she would ask, would Janroe lie and say you weren't home? Then he had pictured Cable coming to the store.

But it had worked out all right. Vern was there before her. Vern seeking vengeance.

So now there was no chance of Cable finding out and eluding Vern or beating him or coming here. No, he would come here, all right, but not alive.

But this damn waiting . . .

Janroe paced the length of the space behind the counter, but it was too confining. He went out to the loading platform and for some time stood gazing out at the sunlit sweep of the valley; then at the willows and the slope beyond. He went inside again, through the store to the sitting room. From here he saw Martha still in the kitchen. Davis, the older boy, was with her, standing on a chair to put the breakfast dishes away.

He heard a noise from upstairs, then remembered that the other two children were up there. Martha had sent Clare up to make her bed and the younger one had gone with his sister. They'd probably forgotten all about the bed and were playing.

He was out on the platform again in time to see the rider come down the slope and drop from sight behind the willows. Waiting, Janroe was aware of the tight feeling in his stomach and the ache, the dull, muscle ache, in the arm that wasn't there. But the next moment the tension and the pain were gone. He could feel only relief now, watching Luz appear out of the willows and come toward him across the yard.

He saw her watching him as she came, all the way, until she had reached the platform.

"What happened?"

"It's over."

"He's dead?"

Luz glanced at the doorway behind them, then back to Janroe and nodded quickly.

"Where is he?"

"At home."

"I thought Vern would be coming."

Luz shrugged. "I don't know." She dismounted and came up on the platform. "I'd better go tell her."

Janroe stepped aside. "Go ahead." He said then, "You don't seem broken up any."

Luz said nothing.

"Didn't Vern say he was coming?"

Luz shook her head. "I don't remember." She moved past him into the store.

Janroe followed. "Wait a minute. Tell me what happened."

"After," Luz said. She hurried now to the next room.

Janroe still stood at the edge of the counter after she was gone. But why wasn't she crying? She could be nervous about telling Martha, but she would have cried, if not now sometime before, and she would show signs of it.

From this the suspicion began to build in his mind. Why wouldn't she tell what happened? She seemed to want to get away from him, to see Martha too quickly; not holding back, putting it off, reluctant to face Martha; but wanting to see her, to tell her . . . to tell her what?

He moved through the store in long, hurried strides, across the sitting room and saw them in the kitchen, Martha and Luz and the little boy: Martha looked at him, her eyes alive and her hand going to Luz suddenly to stop her. "What're you telling her?"

Luz turned, stepping back as he came in. "Nothing. I was just beginning—"

"What did she tell you?" He turned to Martha abruptly.

"This doesn't concern you, Mr. Janroe."

"Answer me!" His hand clamped on Martha's arm and he saw her wince, trying to pull away. "She said your husband was still alive, didn't she? She said not to worry that he was all right, that he was coming." Janroe shook her violently. "Answer me!"

He heard Luz moving. He wheeled, reaching for her, but she was already past him. "Luz—"

She ran through the store ahead of him, out to the loading platform and jumped. Janroe reached the doorway. He pulled the Colt, cocking it, and screamed her name again, a last warning. But beyond Luz he saw Cable step out of the willows with the Spencer in his hand. Then Vern, closer, running past the corner of the building. Janroe pushed back inside. He thought of Martha and ran into the sitting room in time to see her starting for the stairs. She reached the first step before she heard Janroe and turned to face him.

"You couldn't leave the two upstairs, could you?" Janroe said.

Now they were in the willows watching the front of the store. Vern had been down farther, in view of the rear door, but he had come back as Luz ran out of the store and Janroe shouted at her.

"That nails it down," Vern said. "He killed Duane. I wonder what he's thinking, seeing us together."

Cable, at the edge of the trees, said nothing.

Luz was staring vacantly at the adobe. "I shouldn't have run," she said. "I should be there with your wife and children."

"You did the best thing," Cable said.

"But I ran, leaving them alone with him."

"We shouldn't have let you do it," Cable said.

"No," Vern said. "It was the only way and it had to be tried. It was worth that much." The plan had been for Luz to tell Janroe that Cable was dead. Then to tell Martha, somehow without Janroe hearing, to take the children and slip out. That would leave Janroe alone in the adobe and in time they would take him. But now they would have to think of something else.

"Where was Martha?" Cable asked Luz.

"In the kitchen."

"The children with her?"

"Just Davis." She looked at him then. "Could Clare and Sandy be outside?"

"They'd be close. But I haven't seen them." He glanced at Vern. "In back?" When Vern shook his head, Cable said, "Then they're all inside."

"He wouldn't harm them," Luz said. "He would be too afraid to do that."

"Now he'll be thinking of a way out," Vern said.

"Unless he's already thought of it." Cable was still watching the adobe. "I think I'd better talk to him."

Vern looked at him. "Just walk out there?"

"I don't know of any other way," Cable said. He parted the willow branches and started across the yard. Almost at once Janroe's voice stopped him.

"Stay where you are!"

Luz's horse, by the loading platform, raised its head at the sound.

Cable's eyes moved from the screen door to the first window on the right. One of the wooden shutters was open. If Janroe was there he would be in the store, behind the counter that ran along the front wall. Cable started toward the adobe again.

"Stand or I'll kill you!"

That's where he was, by the window. Cable was sure of it now.

"Janroe, you're in enough trouble. Let my family come out."

There was no answer from the store.

"You hear me? Send them out and nobody will harm you." He

saw Janroe at the window then, part of his head and shoulder momentarily.

"How do I know that?" Janroe's voice again.

"You've got my word."

"I've got something better than your word."

"Janroe, if you harm my wife and children—"

"I'm through talking to you, Cable!"

"All right"—Cable's tone lowered, became more calm—"what do you want?"

"I'll tell you when I'm ready. Go back where you were. Try sneaking up and you'll hear a shotgun go off."

Cable stared at the window, not moving.

"Go on!"

"Janroe," Cable said finally, "if you harm my family you're a dead man." He turned then and moved back into the willows to stand with Luz and Vern.

Soon after, Luz's horse moved away from the platform, the reins dragging. It wandered aimlessly at first, nosing the ground; but finally the horse's head rose and it came toward them, drawn by the scent of water.

Taking the reins, Luz looked at Cable. "He could threaten us to bring it back. Why doesn't he?"

"He knows he can do it any time he wants," Cable answered.

They waited, watching the store and seldom speaking. The afternoon dragged by and there was no word from Janroe; not a sound reaching them from the adobe.

In the late afternoon, with the first red traces of sunset, a rider came down the slope from the horse trail south. It was Manuel, back from Hidalgo. Back for good, he said.

He looked at Vern, then at Cable inquiringly and Cable told it, beginning with Duane and bridging to the present time. They had been here nearly six hours now, waiting for Janroe to make his move. There was nothing they could do. There wasn't much doubt that Janroe would take a hostage when he decided to make his run. Probably one of the children. Probably, too, he was waiting for dark. But you couldn't count on anything—it was Luz who added this—because something was wrong with the man's mind. But Cable was sure Janroe would know they would hold back for fear of harming the child, and Janroe would lose them long before daylight.

The question then, what would he do with his hostage?

Cable said it bluntly, calmly, though his stomach was tight and he felt the unceasing urge through his body to move about and to do something with his hands. To do *something*.

It was Vern who brought up the question of the back door. "He can't watch front and back both. Unless he locked the door."

Manuel shook his head. "There's no lock on it. But what if he heard you?"

"That's something else," Vern said.

The evening came gradually with dusk filtering into the willow grove before seeping in long shadows out toward the adobe store. There were faint sounds of birds up in the ridge pines, but close about them the willows were silent. Later on, perhaps, there would be a breeze and the crickets would begin. But now there was a silence that seemed never to end. They waited.

Luz and Vern sat close to each other and occasionally Cable would hear the murmur of their voices. Janroe had split them apart and now he had brought them back together. Maybe they would get married. Maybe some good would come out of this. Later on— days or weeks, sometime later—he and Vern would talk this out that was between them. Cable remained apart from the others, sitting near the edge of the river and watching the dark water.

After a while he began to think of something Vern had said, about the back door. And Manuel had answered that there was no lock on the door. "But what if he heard you?" Manuel had asked.

But, Cable thought, what if he didn't hear you?

He pictured himself keeping to the trees until he had reached the barn, then creeping along its shadows, then across the yard and carefully, quietly, into the kitchen. It would already be dark inside the house. But if you bumped something—

No, he thought then, you know the place well enough. You could blind your eyes and walk through the house without touching or bumping anything.

Janroe wouldn't expect anyone and there would be no sound. Janroe would be by the window watching Martha and the children, but glancing outside often. He would creep to the doorway that led into the store, see Janroe and be very sure of killing him with the first shot.

An hour passed. It was dark in the willows now and the last red traces of sun were gone from the sky. Cable kneeled at the sandy edge of the river to drink, cupping the water in his hands.

In the other time, Martha would be getting the children ready for bed now. They would come in and kiss him goodnight before Martha sat with them on the bed, their eyes wide and watching her, while she told them a story.

There had been a story the children liked and asked for often, about the little girl and her brother who were lost in the forest. When night came, the little girl began to cry and her brother put his arm around her. They sat huddled together, shivering with cold and listening to the night sounds. And when it seemed they could bear no more, neither the cold nor the frightening sounds, the little girl's guardian angel appeared and led them through the forest to their home.

The children liked the story because it was easily imagined and because of the good feeling of being safely at home while they pictured themselves in the frightening dark.

Soon part of this story would come to life for one of his children. Janroe would take one of them as a hostage, because a child would be easier to handle than Martha. He would need only one horse and hold the child in front of him on the saddle, moving south toward the border and keeping to the wild terrain that offered good cover. But somewhere along the way, when he was sure he had lost the ones trailing him, when he no longer needed his hostage, Janroe would drop the child.

He would have no concern for the child's life. There was no reason even to hope that he might. It could be Sandy. Three years old and alone somewhere in the vast, trackless rock country to the south. If they didn't find him—and it would be almost as miraculous as the story if they did—the boy would survive perhaps two days.

So you have no choice, Cable thought. He would have to stop Janroe before he left the store.

Or while he was leaving it—

Cable pushed himself erect. Perhaps that was it. With the back door idea to make it work.

Perhaps as Janroe came out with the child in front of him. But it would be a long shot, too far, and even now there wasn't enough light. But say Vern worked his way around to the side of the adobe and waited there. That could be done.

Janroe would come out, would call for one of them to come unarmed with a horse, threatening to shoot the child if he wasn't obeyed. He would mount first and pull his hostage up in front of him. Or he would put the child up first. Either way, there would be a moment when Janroe would be seen apart from the child.

That was the time. You'll be there, Cable thought. Through the store as he walks out, right behind him, and fire from the doorway, from close range.

But if the child was in the way then it would be Vern's shot. Vern shooting from about fifty feet, in the dark.

There was no other way.

When he presented his plan to the others there were objections; but finally, after talking it out and seeing no alternatives, they agreed to it. After that each of them thought about what he would do.

Martha sat on an empty packing case with her arm around Davis next to her. It was dark in the store with the night showing in the doorway and in the window behind Janroe. The counter separated them. On it, pointed at Martha and the boy, was the shotgun. It was within easy reach of Janroe sitting on a high stool with the cold revolver in his hand.

Davis stirred, squirming on the wooden case, making it creak and causing Janroe to look at them. Martha's hand, with her arm around him, patted Davis gently. There was no sound from the other children now.

They were still locked in the upstairs bedroom and through the long afternoon Martha had listened to the faint sounds of their crying. Perhaps they were asleep now, even though they were frightened and had had nothing to eat since breakfast.

That seemed such a long time ago.

First Luz coming, riding in with the excitement on her face and talking to Janroe. Then returning, coming into the kitchen and telling her that it was over and that Cable was alive.

Then Janroe. She remembered the fear, the desperation in his eyes as he herded them upstairs, pushing them to make them hurry. He made Davis go into the bedroom where Clare and Sandy were playing; but as if something occurred to him, he brought Davis out and locked the door. He herded them downstairs again; closed the kitchen door and kicked at it angrily when he saw it had no lock. From the kitchen he moved them into the store, where they now sat.

When Cable came out of the trees and Janroe called to him to halt, Martha stood up. She caught only a glimpse of her husband in the yard before Janroe ordered her to sit down. Once Cable's voice rose threateningly and Martha tensed, seeing the strained look of desperation come over Janroe's face again.

But as the morning stretched into afternoon, Janroe seemed to gain confidence. Gradually his expression became calm and he sat quietly on the stool, his movements, as he looked from the yard to Martha, less nervous and abrupt.

Martha noticed it. She watched him closely, noting each change in his manner as he became more sure of himself. Occasionally, as he looked outside, her eyes would drop to the shotgun on the counter. It was five feet away, no more than that; but it was pointed at her. It would have to be picked up and turned on Janroe; while all he had to do was raise his revolver a few inches and pull the trigger.

Twice she asked him what had happened, why he was holding them; but both times he refused to talk about it.

Janroe came off the stool when Luz's horse wandered from the platform to the trees. He stood at the window, his attention turned from Martha longer than at any time before. But finally he sat down again.

"My horse left me," Janroe said, looking at Martha. "But all I have to do is call and they'll bring it back." He seemed to be reassuring himself.

Martha watched him. "Then you're leaving?"

"In time."

"Alone?"

"Now wouldn't that be something."

"I didn't think so."

"Your boy's going with me."

Martha hesitated. "Will you take me instead?"

Janroe shook his head. "Him. He's big enough to hold on, little enough to be managed."

Martha felt Davis close to her. She glanced down at his hand in her lap, then at Janroe again. "What will you do to him?"

"That's up to him. Tell him if he cries or tries to run, I'll hurt him something awful." Janroe's eyes moved from the boy to Martha. "He's no good to me dead; least not while I'm getting away from here."

"And after that?"

Janroe shrugged. "I suppose I'll let him go."

"Knowing he'd be lost, and possibly never found?"

"Honey, I've got to look out for myself."

"If you leave him or harm him in any way," Martha said quietly, "My husband will kill you."

"If he finds me he'll try."

"He gave you his word," Martha said. "If you release us, he'll let you go."

"But will Vern?"

"At least talk to him again," Martha urged. "Tell him where you'll leave our boy."

"That would be like giving myself up."

They spoke only occasionally after that. Now the room was silent but for Davis's restless movement. Martha watched Janroe, seeing his heavy-boned profile against the dull gray light behind him.

She thought of Clare and Sandy upstairs and of Davis, not looking at him, but feeling his small body pressed close to her side. If Janroe left with him she might never see her son again. Janroe would sacrifice Davis, admitting it with an offhand shrug, to save his own life. Could that happen? Would God let something like that happen?

No, she thought, don't blame God.

Cabe had an idea about that. People, he said, blamed God for bad luck because they had to blame somebody. Some things you can do something about, and with God's help you can do it even better. But others you can't do anything about, so you wait and try not to worry or feel sorry for yourself.

Which was this?

You can do something, Martha thought. Because you have to do something.

Her eyes went to the shotgun. A dull, thin line of light extended from the breech to the blunt end of the barrel. Two steps to the counter, Martha thought. Her right hand would go to the trigger, raising the gun, swinging it on Janroe at the same time. Three seconds to do that. Four at the most. But it would take him only one.

Janroe turned from the window. "All right. Tell him he's going with me."

"You won't talk to my husband again? To Vern?"

"Tell him!"

She saw Janroe turn to the window again and call out, "Cable— send Luz over here with the horse!" He waited. "You hear me? Just

Luz. If anybody else comes I'll kill your boy." His voice rose to a shout. "I mean it!"

Then it's now, Martha thought. She could feel her heart beating as she bent close to Davis and whispered to him. The boy started to speak, but she touched his mouth with the tips of her fingers, her own lips still close to his ear, telling him calmly, carefully, what he would have to do. The boy nodded and Martha kissed his cheek.

Janroe was looking at her again. "Is he ready?"

Martha nodded.

"As soon as she starts over with the horse, we go out to the platform."

Janroe's elbow rested on the window sill, his right shoulder against the side frame. The Colt in his hand was close to his body and pointed to just below the top of the counter.

When he moves it, Martha thought. The moment he turns.

Janroe looked out, but the Colt remained in the same position. Martha's gaze held on it. She heard him call out again, "Luz, bring the horse! You hear me? Luz—"

Janroe wheeled, seeing Martha already at the counter. She was less than four feet from him, raising the shotgun, turning it on him. He slashed out with the Colt, knocking the barrel aside as Martha's finger closed on one trigger. The blast was almost in his face and he struck the barrel again, lunging against the counter and turning Martha with the force of the blow.

"Janroe?"

Martha heard it—Cable's voice—and in the same moment saw Janroe's Colt swing toward the sound of it. Cable was in the doorway to the sitting room. He fired and Janroe stumbled against the wall. Cable fired again, but this shot smashed into the window frame. Janroe was already moving. He had been hit in the body, but he reached the doorway and lunged out to the platform.

Vern stepped away from the corner of the building. He fired three times, deliberately, taking his time, each shot finding Janroe, the last one toppling him from the edge of the platform.

Martha felt Cable move past her, past Davis, moving quickly but making almost no sound in his stockinged feet. She thought of the children upstairs.

"Davis, get Clare and Sandy."

She heard the boy run into the darkness of the next room before she turned and walked out to the platform to where Cable stood at the edge. Martha looked down, not seeing Janroe on the ground, but thinking of her children and her husband and wanting to be held.

The shotgun barrel slipped through her fingers until the stock touched the boards. She let it fall, feeling Cable's arm come around her.

THE
LAW AT
RANDADO

ONE

At times during the morning, he would think of the man named Kirby Frye. The man who had brought him here. There had been others, most of them soldiers, but he remembered by name only the one called Frye. He had known him before and it had been a strange shock to see him last night.

Most of the time, though, Dandy Jim stood at the window of the upstairs jail cell and watched the street below in the cold sunlight and tried not to think of anything.

He would see riders walking their horses, then flat-bed wagons—most often with a man and woman on the seat and children at the back end with their legs swinging over the tailgate—and now and then a man leading a pack mule. They moved both ways along the street that appeared narrower from above with the ramadas making a shadow line along the building fronts.

Saturday morning and the end of a trail drive brings all kinds to town. The wagon people, one-loop ranchers and their families who would be on their way home before dark. A few prospectors down out of the Huachucas who would drink whisky while their money lasted, then buy some to take if their credit was good. And the mounted men, most of them on horses wearing the Sun-D brand—a D within a design that resembled a crudely drawn flower though it was meant to be a sunburst—men back from a month of trail driving, back from pushing two thousand cows up the San Rafael valley to the railhead at Willcox, twenty days up and ten back and dust all the way, but strangely not showing the relief of having this now behind them. They rode silently, and men do not keep within themselves with a trail drive just over and still fresh in their minds.

Dandy Jim knew none of this, neither the day nor why the people were here. Earlier, he had watched the street intently. When he first opened his eyes, finding himself on the plank floor and not knowing where he was, he had gone to the window and looked out, blinking his eyes against the cold sunlight and against the throbbing in the back of his head that would suddenly stab through to above his eyes.

But the street and the store fronts told him only that this was no Sonoita or Tubac or Patagonia, because he had been to those places. Now he looked out of the window because there was nothing else to do, still not understanding what he saw or remembering how he came here.

Dandy Jim was Coyotero Apache; which was the reason he did not understand what he saw. The throbbing in his head was from tulapai; and only that much was he beginning to remember.

His Coyotero name was Tloh-ka, but few Americans knew him by that. He had been Dandy Jim since enlisting as a tracker with the 5th Cavalry. They said he was given the name because he was a favorite with the men of the "Dandy 5th" and they called him Jim, then Dandy Jim to associate him with the regiment, because to say Tloh-ka you had to hold your tongue a certain way and just to call an Apache wasn't worth all that trouble. Tloh-ka was handsome, by any standards; he was young, his shoulder-length hair looked clean even when it was not, and his appearance was generally better than most Apaches. That was another reason for his name.

He slept again for a short time, lying on his stomach on the bunk, a canvas-covered wooden frame and an army blanket, but better than the floor. He opened his eyes abruptly when he heard the footsteps, but did not move his face from the canvas.

Through the bars he saw two men in the hallway. One was fat and moved slowly because of it. He carried something covered over with a cloth. The other was a boy, he saw now, carrying the same thing and he stayed behind the large man, moving hesitantly as if afraid to be up here where the cells were.

As they came to his cell the Coyotero closed his eyes again. He heard the door being opened. There was whispering, then a voice said, "Go on, he's asleep." Dandy Jim opened his eyes. The boy was setting a dishtowel-covered tray in the middle of the floor. As the boy stood up he glanced at the Coyotero. Their faces were close and the boy looked suddenly straight into the open black eyes that did not blink.

"Harold!" The boy backed away.

"What's the matter?"

"He's awake!" The boy was in the hallway now.

"We let them do that," the fat one who was called Harold said, and locked the door again.

They went to the other cell and the boy took the tray while Harold unlocked the door. The boy went in quickly and put the tray on the floor, not looking at the two Mexicans who were lying on the bunks. The door slammed and they were moving down the hall again. Dandy Jim could hear the boy whispering, then going down the stairs Harold was telling him something.

The Coyotero sat up and ate the food: meat and bread. There was coffee, too, and after this he felt better. The throbbing in his head was a dull pain now and less often would it shoot through to his eyes. The food removed the sour, day-old taste of tulapai from his mouth and this he was more thankful for than the full feeling in his stomach. And now he was beginning to remember more of what had happened.

He heard the cell door close again, this in his mind. It was dark and he was lying on the floor and now he remembered the men leaving, one of them carrying a lamp. They walked heavily and the floor against his face shook with their walking. Then darkness, and silence, and when he opened his eyes again he was here. But before that—

Tulapai. No, before that.

It came to him suddenly and his mind was not ready for it. The shock of memory stiffened his body, then left him limp the next moment and he groaned, closing his eyes tight to squeeze the picture of it from his mind. He saw her face clearly. She was on the ground and he was astride her, holding her arms with his knees. Her eyes were open wide, but she did not scream, not until he drew the knife, and holding her head down by the hair, slashed off part of her nose.

It was the fault of the tulapai, the corn beer he had been drinking as he rode home; but it was also his rage. The shock of seeing her with Susto. Across the stream, through the willow branches, seeing the two of them lying close to each other. He was halfway across the stream when they saw him. Susto ran for the brush thicket and disappeared; but Dandy Jim's wife ran to their jacale, as if she knew she would be caught, but should at least run at a time like this. And that was where he found her and did what he had to do, what had been the customary act of a cheated Apache male longer than anyone could remember. A woman without a nose would not easily fall into adultery again.

And now he remembered more of the things that had happened the evening before: sitting with his friends drinking tulapai, drinking too much while they told him what he had done was the right thing. Then the sudden warning that soldiers were approaching the rancheria; but it was hard to think, even then with the tulapai, and they made noise fleeing on their ponies. Their minds would not calm long enough to think out their escape and do it properly. So they just ran, and all the time, for hours, the soldiers were never more than a mile behind. Just before dark the soldiers caught up and shot Dandy Jim's pony and that was the end. He remembered walking, stumbling, between their horses for a long time until they reached a place that was light and there was much noise.

And he remembered briefly, vaguely seeing a man he had once known, Kirby Frye. Then up the stairs . . . the plank floor of the cell, then daylight and the sour taste of tulapai.

He did not know what had happened to his companions. Perhaps they are still fleeing, he thought. With the darkness they could have escaped the soldiers. And that one whose name is Frye . . . he was there. I have not seen him for a long time. But he is not here now.

He looked at the two Mexicans in the cell across the hallway. One of them was eating, but the other man was still lying on the bunk with his arm over his eyes. For a moment the Coyotero wondered why they were there.

Downstairs, the boy was talking to Harold Mendez. His name was Wordie Stedman; he was eleven and he liked better than anything else to sit in the jail office with Harold Mendez or Kirby Frye and have them tell him things. Sometimes he got upstairs; like just a while ago when Harold let him carry one of the trays. The boy had an excuse to stay there now. He had to wait for the prisoners to finish eating before he could take the trays back to the Metropolitan Café.

He said to Harold, who was middle-aged and at this moment looked comfortable in the swivel chair with his feet propped on the desk edge, staring out the window, "I'm glad I got a chance to see them close-up. They really look mean, don't they?"

Harold Mendez said, "Everybody looks that way when they wake up."

"Those two Mexicans, I saw them the other day when Kirby brought them in. One with his hat gone, shot smack off his head." Wordie grinned. "Kirby must've been off a ways else he'd a hit him."

"Maybe he was aiming at the hat."

"Why would he do that?" the boy said. "When you catch two men stealing other people's cattle you might as well aim a little lower and save the county some hangin' expenses."

"How much does it cost to hang a man, Wordie?"

"What?"

"You've been overhearing your father." Harold Mendez, the jailer, lighted a cigar now and drew on it gently, holding it the way a man does who considers cigar smoking a luxury.

"The one in the other cell'd scare the wits out of anybody," Wordie Stedman said.

"Dandy Jim?"

"That 'Pache."

"He's considered a nice-looking boy."

Wordie nodded, indicating upstairs. "There wasn't anything nice about him a while ago. He stunk to high heaven."

"I'll see he gets a bath and rinses out his mouth," Harold Mendez said.

The boy was thinking, looking absently at the stairway, then he said, "I'll bet he murdered somebody and Kirby come up and caught him red-handed!"

"The only thing he was murdering was his stomach."

The boy looked at the jailer, frowning and twisting the corner of his mouth. "He was drinking tulapai," Harold Mendez explained. "Soldiers from Huachuca out looking for stills found him and some others with tulapai. They chased after the Indians, about six braves, to get them to tell where the stills are, but Dandy Jim's the only one they caught."

"What are they doing with him here?" the boy said.

"He was close by when they caught him, so they asked Kirby if they could keep him here while they chased after the others."

The boy said excitedly, "And Kirby went along to give them a hand!"

Harold Mendez nodded. "Of course."

"He'll find them," the boy said confidently.

"What if he doesn't?"

The boy looked at the big jailer. "What do you mean?"

Harold Mendez shrugged. "I mean what if he doesn't bring them back?"

Wordie looked at him, frowning again. " 'Course he'll bring them back."

"I've known him to come home empty-handed."

"Nobody's perfect," the boy said. But if that's true, the boy was thinking, then Kirby Frye's sure the closest thing to being it. He said now, "Should I get the trays?"

"We'll give them a few more minutes."

"I don't see how they can eat. In jail." The boy went to the window and looked out just for something to do. "There's sure a lot of people here today."

"It's Saturday," Harold Mendez said.

The boy turned to Mendez suddenly. "The Sundeen crew's back."

"So I heard."

The boy seemed disappointed that what he said wasn't news, but he tried again, saying, "I'll bet there's something you don't know."

"There might be," Harold Mendez said.

"They haven't been paid off yet."

Mendez turned his head to look at the boy. "No, I didn't know that."

Wordie Stedman grinned. "I heard my dad talking about it a while ago with Mr. Tindal. Says they moved that big herd all the way up to the railhead, come all the way back, and still haven't been given their trail wages."

"Your dad say why?"

"No, but Mr. Tindal said a man does that just once and then he finds himself without a crew. Even a man like Phil Sundeen. Mr. Tindal said Old Val Sundeen used to always pay off the hands when they reached the railhead, like it should be. He said Phil better take some lessons from his dad pretty soon if he wants to stay in the cattle business. Said if Phil minded his ways instead of drinking and carousing he wouldn't be losing stock and refusing to pay rightful trail wages."

"What did your dad say to that?"

"Mr. Tindal was doing most of the talking. My dad would just nod his head. I never seen my dad or Mr. Tindal look so worried."

"They might have good cause," Harold Mendez said. He drew

on his cigar thoughtfully and his hand idly fingered a name-plate shingle that was on the desk. Harold Mendez had carved the lettering on it himself, an inscription that read: KIRBY FRYE, and under it: DEPUTY SHERIFF—RANDADO. It had taken him almost a month to carve it.

TWO

Across the street, in De Spain's cardroom, R. D. Tindal was about to make a speech.

He had begun forming the words in his mind the night before as he lay in his bed staring at the darkness and because of it he did not fall asleep until long after midnight. In the morning, as soon as he opened his eyes, he began recalling the words, hearing his own voice as it would sound, going over and over again the opening sentence that had to sound natural. No, more than natural, casual; but words that would hold them right from the start, words he would speak dryly in a sort of don't-give-a-damn way, an off-the-cuff understatement, but loaded with meaning. Eating his breakfast he smiled thinking of the reaction. They wouldn't laugh when he said it, because he wouldn't; but they'd shake their heads thinking: By God, that R. D. Tindal's something! His wife watched him from the stove; his daughter, Milmary, watched him while she drank her coffee, and neither of them spoke. Opening the store, The R. D. Tindal Supply Company, and waiting on the first Saturday morning customers, he went over the other things he would say, even anticipating questions and forming the exact words for the answers. At ten o'clock he put on his hat and coat and told Milmary to hold down the fort till he got back. Milmary asked him where he was going and did it have anything to do with his being so quiet all morning?

Going out the door he said, significantly, "Milmary, the Citizens Committee." That was all.

And now he looked at the men at his table and the ones beyond at the other three tables and the men over against the wall, De Spain, one of them, standing with his back to the closed door and his hand behind him on the knob. He stood by the door, in case he was wanted out front. Saturday his saloon did good business even in the morning. And in the cardroom they could hear the sounds of the good business, the boots and the chairs scraping and the whisky-relaxed laughter.

R. D. Tindal wished they'd be quiet, these men laughing over nothing, only because it was Saturday. His eyes returned to the three men at his table—Earl Beaudry, landowner, probably his closest friend. George Stedman, manager of the Randado Branch of the Cattlemen's Bank, a good man to know. And Haig Hanasian, owner of the Metropolitan Café, a man you'd never know in seven hundred years, Tindal thought—and then he was ready to begin.

He cleared his throat. He had not intended to, because there was a chance someone might think he was nervous, but it just came out. He remembered though to sound casual and began by saying, "Gentlemen, it just occurred to me a minute ago, watching you boys file in, that there isn't one of us here who hasn't been shaving at least twenty years." He watched some of them finger their chins, as he had known they would. "Yet those people up to the county seat would have a special representative down here just for wiping our noses if we'd let them."

He paused to give them time to shake their heads and appreciate fully this dry, spur-of-the-moment humor.

Beaudry, Stedman and Haig Hanasian kept their eyes on Tindal, but did not shake their heads, not even faintly.

Across the room De Spain shook his head, but he was thinking: He isn't even a good actor.

Tindal leaned forward resting his elbows on the table and said, "Now I think we're all old enough to take care of ourselves, regardless of what opinion the people up to the county seat hold." He paused again, but not so long this time. "Which means we're old enough to take care of our own affairs right here in Randado without crying help from the county. Isn't that right, Earl?"

Earl Beaudry looked up. "Absolutely."

Tindal went on, "Earl's lived right here for a long time, even before there was a Randado, and his dad before that, one of the first men in the Territory. Now I'd say a man like Earl Beaudry should have a *few* words to say about how his town affairs are run. There are others of you who've been out here almost as long, got your roots planted firm now. There are some who've been here only a few years, like our friend George Stedman, but men who're damn well the backbone of the community." R. D. Tindal's mouth formed a faint grin. "What do you say, George? You think we're old enough to wipe our own noses?"

George Stedman grinned back. "I don't see why not."

De Spain blew his nose and every man in the room looked at him stuffing the handkerchief into his pocket again. He said to Tindal, "You'll have to excuse me. I've got to get back to work."

"Wait a minute now," Tindal said. "This is important."

"This is Saturday."

Tindal glanced around the room, leaning on his arms. "I'd say the question we're discussing is a shade weightier than whether or not some hands get drunk."

De Spain nodded resignedly. "All right, but get to the point."

Tindal gave him a stare, took time to suck at his teeth, then leaned back as slowly as he could. "Three days ago," he began, "our sheriff brought in single-handed two men caught in the act of rustling Sun-D stock." He grinned. "That wasn't too hard for Kirby, doing it alone. You know he's a Randado boy, done most of his growing up right here." Seriously again. "But we had something to say about signing on Kirby. Pima County give him to us as a deputy, but by God our committee passed on him! We looked over this Kirby Frye, along with others, and accepted him only after we were sure he qualified. He's young, but he's a hard-working boy and we know he can do the job. See what I mean? This committee took hold of the problem and we come up with the best deputy in the county!" Now get to the point, quick.

"Kirby Frye, Deputy Sheriff of Randado, brought in two men caught stealing cattle from a citizen of Randado . . . yet we have to wait until John Danaher's good and ready to send for the two outlaws before they're tried. We sit here waiting on the whim of a county sheriff eighty-five miles away from us." Now give 'em the big casino! "Gentlemen, here's the point. We sit here doing nothing while we're damn-right able to handle it ourselves!"

Earl Beaudry and George Stedman both nodded.

From the door De Spain said, "When was Phil Sundeen talking to you?"

Tindal looked at him, momentarily surprised, because this wasn't one of the questions he had anticipated, and feeling a sudden embarrassment he kept his eyes steadily on De Spain's dark face as if to prove that he was sincere and he said, "Do you think I'm trying to hide something? I'm not denying we talked to Phil

Sundeen. I was coming to that . . . if you'd give me time to tell it my own way. Maybe I'm not a polished enough speaker for you!" De Spain shook his head. "I'm sorry. Go ahead."

"I'm trying to do a job that could be a damn sight pleasanter. I don't see anybody volunteering to head this committee."

"You're doing a fine job," George Stedman said encouragingly. "Go ahead, tell them the rest."

"If this is an imposition on Mr. De Spain, maybe we should meet somewhere else," Tindal said.

De Spain said nothing.

George Stedman spoke up. "Go on with the rest."

R. D. Tindal cleared his throat and was embarrassed again and swore at De Spain in his mind. He said, almost angrily now, "Those two Mexicans over in the jail belong to Randado, that's what I'm getting at. And it's *our* duty to see justice done to them . . . nobody else's!" He brought his fist down on the table for emphasis.

Earl Beaudry half turned in his chair to look at the others. "You see, we—George and R.D. and me—were talking to Phil Sundeen last night. He come back last night, you know—"

Tindal interrupted, his face flushed, "Wasn't I telling it all right?"

Beaudry turned to him.. "Sure, R. D. Go ahead."

"If you want to take over, Earl—"

Beaudry waved his palm toward Tindal. "You tell it, R. D."

"As Earl said, we talked to Phil Sundeen last night here in town . . . in fact we were over to the Metropolitan when they brought in that drunk Apache. That right, Haig?" This was to show that they had met Phil Sundeen in a public place and there was nothing undercover about it.

Haig Hanasian nodded. He was dark with a heavy drooping mustache and his eyes appeared half closed because the lids were heavy.

"Haig saw us," Tindal said. "So did his wife. Well, we mentioned to Phil how Kirby Frye brought in the two Mexicans; which he hadn't heard about. Then he reminded us of something we'd known for a long time. He said his stock's always been rustled. With the border so close it's a temptation and his spread's hit harder than the ones up the valley. He said he'd complained to Mendez—that's when Harold was deputy—but nothing was ever done about it. Phil said he's always had the suspicion Harold

Mendez never did anything because the outlaws were always up from across the border and Harold being about ninety-nine percent Mex didn't give a particular damn so long as they were stealing from white men.

"Well, we got rid of Harold Mendez and got us a Randado boy, one we can trust. Harold Mendez isn't going to bother anybody being jailer." Tindal grinned. "With what it pays, Harold's the only one willing to do that kind of work." This was Tindal's view, not something Sundeen had told him.

"I told Phil how Kirby was deputy now. He didn't know that because he'd already started his drive the time we appointed Kirby. Then Phil made a pretty good point. He said, 'All right, let's say this new sheriff does grab a rustler. He's carted up to Tucson for trial. The man he stole from has to leave his work for at least a week, maybe longer, and go all the way up to the county seat to testify. Chances are, the rustler's only given a term in Yuma and in a year or so he's back driving stock over the border again.' That's what Phil said and by God I think it makes some sense."

Tindal leaned forward in his chair. He remembered well how he was to say this next part. He looked over the room slowly and then said, "Now what would there be to stop us—I mean us—from trying those two Mexicans?" The room was still silent and he added, quietly, "Right here and now."

Some of the men, looking at each other now, started to talk and one man's voice, above the others was saying, "Now wait a minute!" Earl Beaudry turned in his chair. "Well why not?" And a man at another table shrugged and said, "That's right. When you get down to it, why not?"

George Stedman said, "Like R.D. mentioned this is a crime committed against a citizen of Randado. Now common sense would tell us that the citizens of Randado, as a body, ought to be qualified to see that justice is administered."

The man in the back who had spoken now said, "We'd be nothing more than a lynch mob."

Earl Beaudry said, "We're going to try them first."

George Stedman brought his fist down on the table. "If we're a lynch mob then that's what the court up at the county seat is, that's what any court is if you look at it that way. Can't you see we're talking as the people, and there isn't any court on the face of the earth that's more than that!"

R. D. Tindal waved his hand in the air. "Gentlemen." He said louder, "Gentlemen, here's the point. Why should we let outlaws take advantage of us, just because the courthouse is eighty-five miles away? We establish law here, deal with those two Mexicans ourselves, and then, by God, others will think twice about stealing out of the San Rafael valley!"

De Spain said, "R.D.," and when Tindal looked at him, "I don't mean to sound disrespectful, but I've got a suspicion you're asking us to do another man's work."

"We all live here!" Tindal said angrily.

De Spain shrugged. "You can make it sound like whatever you like. But . . . on the chance of sounding blunt, I'd say you were kissing Sundeen's hind end."

Tindal colored, but he kept control of himself because everyone in the room was watching him and he said, "You've always had a notion you can say whatever enters your head. Now that might be a pretty funny thing you said, but just what does it mean?"

"I'd have to draw a picture," De Spain said, "to make it plainer."

Tindal was still controlled, but with an effort. "Maybe I'm just so dumb I have to have it spelled out."

"Well," De Spain said. "Whether he looks it or not, Sundeen's the biggest man in the San Rafael. He's got the most land, he hires the most men and, what should have been said first, he's got the most money. Now being friends with a man like that can make you feel pretty important, and have some advantages besides."

Earl Beaudry grinned, shaking his head. "You been drinking your bar whisky."

"Earl," De Spain said, "I understand you lease winter graze to the Sundeens and haven't worked a day in your life. What if Phil was to lease it somewhere else?"

De Spain looked at Tindal now. He wanted to accuse him of scheming to marry his daughter off to Phil, but that might be going too far, so he just said, "To some people feeling important's the best feeling in the world." He looked at Stedman to include him.

George Stedman was composed. He said, "Since you mention dealing with Sundeen, where would you be if he and his men stopped drinking whisky?"

"I happen to have the only saloon in town."

"Well, let's say someone borrowed enough money from my bank to open another."

"I've taken the bar apart before," De Spain answered, "and thrown it in a wagon."

"Gentlemen," R. D. Tindal said. "Let's stop talking nonsense." He looked at De Spain. "We're discussing a judicial system for our citizens, nothing else, regardless of how you want to twist our words."

De Spain shrugged. "It's your affair."

"Then you don't want to be on the committee?"

"I never was, really." De Spain added, "You picked a good day with Kirby Frye away."

"Kirby'd be with us a hundred percent."

"You know damn well that's not true."

Tindal ignored him and looked at the others. "I don't think the loss of one man's going to hurt us any. If anybody else objects, speak up now. If not, nominations are open for City Judge. Next, City Prosecutor." That was the way to do it, fast. Then there wouldn't be unnecessary arguing.

Haig Hanasian stood up. He said, "I won't be a part of this." De Spain opened the door, stepping aside, and Haig went out without saying another word.

Tindal waited. Three other men left hurriedly and Tindal put their names down in his memory. When the room was quiet again he said, "All right, nominations are now open for City Judge."

Dandy Jim saw more people as noontime approached. Most of the men seemed to be entering and leaving the building directly across the street and there were many of them standing in the ramada shade, more there than anywhere up or down the street; just standing, talking to each other with their hands in their pockets and sometimes spitting out into the sun of the street. There were two buildings here, both adobe, but only the different signs indicated that there were two—DE SPAIN'S, and a little farther down, METROPOLITAN CAFÉ. Dandy Jim could not read the signs, but he put it down in his mind that these must be important places.

He thought again of the one whose name was Frye, as he had been doing from time to time. The first time he saw him had been at San Carlos when they were both much younger. He remembered the lean boy, tall and with light-colored hair with his hat off, standing watching their games. Then joining their games finally, after weeks of watching. The foot races, pony races, wrestling, and seeing how far one could run with a mouthful of water, or seeing how far a boy could travel without water at all. And even from the first, this one named Frye did well, for a white man; and he did get better.

He remembered seeing him at Fort Huachuca during the past year. Every few months this Kirby Frye would come with two Apache boys and a string of half-green horses. Sometimes he and Frye would talk, because they remembered each other from the times they played games together and the few times in between when they would meet by chance.

Then, only a month ago, they had been together at Galluro after the raid by the renegade Chiricahuas, and Frye had gone off with the one who was called Sheriff. Dan-a-her was his name.

And now Kirby Frye was here, or at least he had been last night. I would like to talk to him again, Dandy Jim thought. He is an easy man to talk to.

The two Mexicans, who were in the cell across from Dandy Jim, spoke to each other very little. They were here because a man in La Noria—it had been in the cantina—told them how easy it was to steal cattle from this ranch that was so large its riders could never be watching all of it. Drive the cattle across the border, the man told them, down to the Hacienda of the Mother of God. The Mayordomo there will pay good money and ask no questions. Even eat some of the beef yourselves, the man told them.

The younger of the two Mexicans spoke only a few words during the morning and only touched the fork to his food, because he was trying to picture what would happen to them. The other man, who wore a mustache and now needed a shave badly, had slept well, had eaten all of his morning meal and now looked forward to the next. He thought most often of the present, sometimes the past, if it was a pleasant remembrance, never of the future.

The younger man asked, "What will they do to us?" He was frowning and talking to himself as much as he was to his companion.

The other man said, with finality, "Shoot us." He was tired of hearing this question asked.

The younger man looked up, with fear clearly on his face. "But won't we be given a trial?"

"How would I know that?"

"You've lived in this country before."

The older man was so tired of this conversation now that he did not bother to answer. But as he looked about for something to interest him he saw, across the hallway in the other cell, Dandy Jim. He said to the younger man, "Ask that barbarian there. He's lived here all of his life."

"Here comes Sundeen!" Wordie Stedman said, turning his head from the window.

Harold Mendez drew on his cigar. He was thinking: I'm glad I'm no longer deputy. In about an hour I would have to go over to De Spain's and ask Phil to stop firing his pistol . . . and probably get the barrel across my skull. Kirby hasn't had to do that yet. But the time will come.

"There're two men with him," Wordie said.

"One of them is Digo," Harold said, though his back was to the window.

The boy nodded, looking out of the window again. "I don't know who the other one is."

"It could be anyone."

"He don't look like a trail hand."

Harold Mendez swiveled in his chair. He saw the three men dismounting in front of De Spain's and Sundeen and the one they did not know handing the reins to Digo who led the horses away, probably taking them to the livery.

"He's new," the boy said. "I never saw him before."

Harold Mendez nodded, studying the man stepping up on the porch with Sundeen. No, he wasn't a trail hand, but he wasn't a doctor or a lawyer either. Harold Mendez thought: What is there about a man like that which singles him out? I would be willing to bet my pay for a year this one is hired for his gun. Still, even thinking this, he wasn't afraid; because he knew he would never be a bother to this man.

The boy said, "Who do you think he is?"

"Just a friend of Phil Sundeen's."

"He don't look like a trail hand though, does he?"

"No, he doesn't."

"Know what he looks like to me?"

"What?"

"A gambler."

"What do they look like?"

"Always wearin' a full suit and face pale from never being in the sun."

"You couldn't tell from here whether he was pale or not."

"Well, what else might he be?"

"He could be lots of things."

"Now here comes Digo back. Boy, he's big!" Wordie said. As if looking for an argument he added, "You know he's the best horse-breaker in the whole Territory."

Harold Mendez shrugged. "He's killed as many as he's broken."

"Boy, he's fast! I've seen him in that mesquite corral. One minute talking to the bronc real sweet, close up to the bronc's ear . . . the next minute clobberin' it across the nose with one of them big fists of his. Boy——" Wordie Stedman shook his head, grinning with admiration.

After a minute, the boy said, "Can I help you get the trays now?"

"I suppose it's time." Harold Mendez came out of the chair slowly, with an effort.

Then the boy said, "Here they come back out already!" Harold Mendez looked toward the window. "And there's my dad and Mr. Tindal and Mr. Beaudry——"

Mendez saw them stepping down out of the shadow of the ramada, crossing the street, coming directly for the jail and he said to Wordie Stedman, though he wasn't sure why, "Boy, you better scat out of here!"

Wordie Stedman opened the door. "Dad——"

"Wordie! What're you doing here?" George Stedman was in the lead with Tindal and Beaudry.

"Just talking to Harold."

"Kirby Frye's not here?"

Tindal scowled. "You know he rode out last night."

"I'm making sure," Stedman said. Then to the boy, "Go on home, Wordie."

The boy frowned. "I was supposed to help Harold get the dinner trays in a minute."

Tindal said, "You let Harold do his own work . . . what he's paid for."

"Go on home now, Wordie," George Stedman said. The boy started to back away, then was walking sideways as Stedman looked over his shoulder. Behind him were Phil Sundeen, Digo and the new man whom Phil had introduced as Clay Jordan.

"He wants to be a sheriff when he grows up," Stedman said

smiling. The three men behind him did not smile, but Phil Sundeen's eyes lifted and he said, "There's Mendez, the son of a bitch."

At one time Harold Mendez smiled often. He used to say, "Good morning, Mr. Stedman. Good morning, Mr. Tindal." Smiling. "Yes, sir, it certainly is a fine day." Get on the right side of the town's leading citizens and you're on your way. Now, standing in the doorway, he looked at them sullenly, his eyes on the men in front, but seeing Phil Sundeen and the new man, being conscious of the men behind them and the crowd that was gathering, and he said, "What do you want?"

"We want your two prisoners," R. D. Tindal announced.

"Which two?"

"The chilipickers," Earl Beaudry said.

"Which two are they?"

"The Mexicans."

"What for?"

Beaudry said, "To lynch 'em, for cry-sake!"

This wasn't the way to go about it and Tindal said, "By the power vested in my office as city prosecutor, I order you to hand over the two Mexican outlaws."

"City prosecutor?"

Tindal nodded his head once. "City prosecutor. George Stedman now presides over our municipal bench."

Harold Mendez frowned.

"Harold, we'll explain this just once. Not a half hour ago the Citizens Committee elected everything we need to try persons accused of crimes in Randado or against Randado citizens. George Stedman is judge. I'm prosecuting attorney. We called a jury to hear the case of those two Mexicans. Well, they heard it, Mr. Sundeen's testimony and all . . . and they rendered a prompt, just decision."

Harold Mendez shook his head. "I don't work for you. I take orders from Kirby Frye. He takes orders from Danaher, and Danaher said keep the prisoners here until he sends for them. Kirby will be back some time today. If you want to take this up with him, all right. It's none of my business."

George Stedman felt the crowd behind him and seeing just the one man in the doorway he felt foolish. "Harold, stop wasting time and bring those prisoners down. Representatives of this town, the most qualified people in the world to pass sentence on those two men, did just that. Now it's time to administer justice."

Harold Mendez shook his head. "I want it down on the record that I'm opposing this."

Someone in the crowd said, "It'll be down on your tombstone." There was scattered laughter.

Phil Sundeen pushed Tindal and the storekeeper lurched forward almost off balance. "Step up to him."

Digo grinned and pushed Beaudry and Stedman, a big hand behind each man.

"Go on,' Sundeen said. "Use your authority."

"Look, Harold," Tindal said. "We've explained it to you. We didn't have to, but we did so you'd understand what we're doing is legal. This is the same as a court order, Harold. Now if you had a court order given to you you'd hand those prisoners over fast."

Harold Mendez said, as if they were words he had memorized. "I take orders from Kirby Frye, who takes orders from John Danaher, who takes orders from the Pima County authorities. If you want to talk to Kirby, all right. It's none of my business."

Phil Sundeen looked over his shoulder and said, "What time is it?"

The man called Clay Jordan, who was now standing a few steps to the side with his thumbs hooked in the gun belt beneath his open coat, moved his left hand and drew his watch from a vest pocket.

"Ten minutes shy of twelve."

"It's getting on dinnertime," Sundeen said thoughtfully. He was squinting in the morning sunlight; a bright sun, but with little warmth now at the end of November. Looking at Harold Mendez again, he said, "Digo, you think you can get Harold out of that doorway by yourself?"

Digo did not bother to answer. He pushed between Beaudry and Stedman, going for the doorway, and as he neared it Harold Mendez, who had been standing with his feet apart watching him, stepped back into the office. Digo turned his head to glance at Sundeen, then followed Harold Mendez inside. The jailer stood in front of the desk stiffly.

"Sit down," Digo said.

"It's all right."

Digo shifted his body suddenly and swung his left fist hard into the jailer's face. Mendez went back against the desk and holding himself there groped for the arm of the chair. Blood was coming from his nose as he turned the chair and eased himself into it.

Digo went to the door and called out, "He says come in."

Sundeen came first, but he stepped back inside the door to let Tindal, Stedman and Beaudry pass him. Clay Jordan was next, but he did not come in. He said, "You don't need me." Only that. Sundeen watched him walk away, going wide around the people in the street, then up into the shade in front of De Spain's, then inside.

I shouldn't have let him do that, Sundeen thought. But now he was looking at the people and he saw in the crowd, and over across the street in front of De Spain's, many of his riders. He called out, "You Sun-D men, get over here!"

In the crowd a few of them started to come forward, but stopped when someone called out, "When do we get paid?"

"You don't do what I tell you, you never will!" Sundeen answered.

They came forward out of the crowd, almost a dozen men, and stood restlessly in front of Sundeen.

"Where are the others?"

One of the men shrugged. "I don't know."

Sundeen's gaze went to the people in the street again and his eyes singled out one man standing near the front, a lean man with his hatbrim low over his eyes and a matchstick in the corner of his mouth. Merl White, one of his riders.

"Merl, what's the matter with you?"

"Nothin'."

"Get over here."

"I don't work for you no more," Merl White said. He stood his ground and did not move.

"Since when?"

"Since you stopped paying wages."

Sundeen smiled. "You don't have enough patience."

"I lost it," Merl said. "I can name three or four more lost theirs."

"Who are they, Merl?"

"You'll find out."

Sundeen's mouth still bore part of the smile. "Tell you what, Merl. You and those other three or four meet me over to De Spain's when I'm through here and I'll pay you off."

Merl kept his eyes on Sundeen and he said, "We'll be there."

Tindal was next to Sundeen in the doorway. He called out, "Where're the rest of you committeemen?" A few men came toward him, then behind them more were pushing through the crowd. "Get in here!"

"That's the ticket," Sundeen said. He slapped Tindal on the shoulder and moved back into the office. "What happened to him?" He nodded toward Harold Mendez.

"He got a nosebleed," Digo answered.

"Where're the keys?"

"Right here." Digo held them up.

Sundeen looked at Tindal. "You think you can do the rest?"

Tindal hesitated, but he said, "Of course we can."

"Like hell." Sundeen shoved past him and started up the stairs, Digo behind him and the rest of them following.

The Sun-D riders and the committeemen who had come inside moved up the stairs now, hurrying in the noise of dozens of boots on the narrow stairway and suddenly there was an excitement that could be felt; it came with the noise and the hurrying and there was an anxiousness inside of each man now, the last ones not wanting to be last, going up the stairs two at a time to be a part of the excitement, not wanting to miss anything now that it was underway and everybody was in on it. Suddenly a man felt himself very much a man and the ones who had reached the upper floor first stood with their hands on their hips waiting for all the stragglers to come up, looking at the two Mexicans who were both standing, but well back from the bars, and then looking at the Apache in the other cell who stood by the window, but with his back to it.

A man who had never seen either of the Mexicans before spat on the floor and yelled, "Pull them bean-eaters the hell out!"

They crowded in front of the cell, looking through the bars at the two Mexicans who stood close together staring at the crowd with their mouths foolishly, wonderingly open; then the younger one wetting his lips, his eyes going over the crowd of men, wetting his lips again and now his hands were clenching and unclenching with nothing to hold on to. He could feel the hot tingling in his body and his heart beating against his chest, his legs quivering—he was aware of his toes moving against the straps of his sandals—but there was nowhere to run.

The older Mexican stood dumbfoundedly, not moving his body, and as his body began to tense he tried very hard to remain calm, talking to himself very slowly, telling himself not to become excited and act like a child, but this took a great effort and it was almost unbearable.

He heard his companion's voice—"Mother of God . . . Virgin Mother of God . . ."—and for some reason he did not want these men to hear this and he rasped at the younger man, "Shut up! Hold on to yourself!" A man was opening the door now, a big man who looked Mexican but who wore the hat of a gringo—like the one who had brought the food with the boy, but it was not that one.

"Pull it open, Digo!"

The sound of metal striking metal, clear, even with the voices, then Digo saying, "This goddamn key's no good."

Someone said, "That one was praying . . . you hear him?"

"He better."

"That's the way they are . . . pull their own sisters in the stable on Saturday night, then go to church on Sunday!"

"Give me it," Sundeen said. He took the key from Digo, turned it in the lock effortlessly and pushed the door open hard making it swing clanging against the bars. "Get 'em out!"

Digo went in, pushed in with men close behind him. He jabbed his elbows making room, then took hold of the younger Mexican who had backed away, but was now against the bunk and could go no farther, grabbing the Mexican's arm and bending it behind his back.

The younger Mexican screamed out, raising himself on his toes.

"Let him walk like a man!" the other Mexican said.

Digo pushed the man he held toward the cell door and as he did came around with his clenched fist swinging wide. The mustached Mexican started to duck, but not quickly enough and the blow caught him squarely on the side of the head sprawling him over the bunk and against the adobe wall. He sat up shaking his head as Earl Beaudry and another man each took an arm and dragged him out.

Digo was grinning. "He walks strange for a man."

"Come on," Sundeen said. "Get the other one."

As Digo took hold of him again the younger Mexican said, "We are to be tried now?"

"You've been tried."

"But when?"

"What do you care when?"

Close to Sundeen, Tindal said, "Tried and found guilty by legal court action. Now, by God, take your medicine like a man!"

"But it was only a few of those cows—"

"Listen, you took a chance and lost. Now face up to it!"

"They were returned . . . every one we took!"

" 'Cause you got caught."

"Come on!" Sundeen said suddenly, with anger. "Get him out of here." He stepped aside as Digo twisted the man's arm and pushed him, raising him to his toes, through the cell door, then down the crowded hallway, pushing the Mexican hard against the men who couldn't get out of the way quickly enough.

"Don't touch me with that greaser!"

"Then get out of the way!"

Sundeen said to Tindal, "Digo's a wheel of justice."

Tindal, looking at Sundeen's beard-stubbled, sun-darkened expressionless face, hesitated, not knowing whether to laugh or not, then just nodded.

Someone said, "What about this one?"

"That's an Indin."

"I got eyes."

"What'd he do?" a third man said.

"That's the one the soldiers brought in."

Another man said, "Fool around with army property and you get a bayonet in the ass."

"We'd be doing them a favor."

"Look at the eyes on the son of a bitch."

"Imagine meetin' him alone out on the flats. Just you and him, no horses, not another livin' soul around—"

"For cry-sake come on . . . they're taking them down already!"

Dandy Jim had not moved from the window. Without expression he watched them take the Mexicans. He heard the men talking about him, understanding only a few of their words, and a moment later the hallway was deserted, the last sounds going down the stairs.

Then suddenly voices again, a cheering from the people in the street as the men, dragging the two Mexicans, seemed to burst from the front door of the jail into the sunlight.

And now the excitement, the not wanting to miss anything, the not wanting to be left out, was in the street. It was there suddenly with the noise and the stark violence of what was taking place. People joining the crowd, running neck-straining behind the ones closer to the Mexicans, some running ahead to the livery knowing or sensing that it would take place there; and others, standing in the long line of ramada shade and in windows; a man with his family standing up in the flat bed of a wagon and their heads turning as the crowd pushed by them; those in doorways watching fascinated, wanting to see it and not wanting to see it. Some went inside. A woman shooing three children into the doorway and the little boy yelling something as she herded them.

De Spain was alone behind the bar. He had one customer, a man who drank beer slowly, sipping it, smoking and sipping beer, leaning on the bar. It was the man who had come in with Sundeen earlier. Clay Jordan. He paid no attention to what was going on outside; he did not even glance toward the windows at the noise. But when the noise was farther down the street he finished the beer and went out.

Haig Hanasian, watching from the door of his café, saw them come out of the jail. He turned away and went back to the kitchen where there was no cook now. No cook, no waitresses. And looking toward the front again, down the whitewashed adobe length of his café and through the open doorway he could see his wife, Edith. She was standing with one arm about a support post raising herself on tiptoes, straining to see over the crowd; and as he watched her, she moved out of view.

Now they were passing a sign that read R. D. TINDAL SUPPLY Co. Milmary Tindal was standing beneath the sign.

"Dad!"

"You go inside, Milmary."

"Dad—"

"I said go inside!"

Now they were beyond, almost to the livery stable that was set back from the corner with the fenced yard in front and in the middle of the fence, the main entrance gate—two upright timbers and a cross timber over the open gate.

"We don't have ropes," Sundeen said. "Digo, get ropes!"

"Mine?" Digo said. "That's bad luck."

"I don't care whose."

"We'll have them."

Earl Beaudry looked up at the cross timber, then back to Sundeen. "Here, Phil?"

"Why not?"

R. D. Tindal waved his arms. "All right, you men back! Move back and give us some elbow room."

Now the two Mexicans were lifted to their feet to stand under the cross timber. The younger one put his head back to look at the beam, then looked at the crowd again, at all of the faces close in front of him, and he began to cry. His companion told him, for the sake of God, to shut up and to hold on to himself.

"This is as good a place as any," Tindal said.

"How are you going to do it?" Sundeen said.

"What?"

"How do you go about hanging a man?"

"All you need is rope."

"Just tie it around their necks and yank 'em up in the air?"

"I don't know . . . I guess I never thought about it."

Digo came across the livery yard with a coiled rawhide riata in each hand. He handed one to Earl Beaudry and they began to uncoil the lines and bend a loop into one end of each.

The older Mexican said, "Your justice is not slow."

Close by, George Stedman said, "Nobody's talking to you."

"Listen," the older Mexican said. "You have us now . . . and you are going to kill us. But grant one last request."

"Go to hell."

"It isn't much. Just get a priest."

"There's no priest here."

"At La Noria," the Mexican said. "What difference does it make if you put this off a few hours?"

"If you think somebody's going to ride all the way down to La Noria to get a priest, you're crazy."

Earl Beaudry looked up. "On Saturday."

"Look," the older Mexican said. "We are going to die. Is that much to ask?"

"You should've thought of that before."

Beaudry added, "Before you stole that beef." He had tied the knot and now pulled on it, testing it.

"Whether we should have or not is past. But it remains we need a priest."

"That's tough luck," Stedman said.

The older Mexican said no more, but after a moment he leaned closer to his companion and said, "Pray. But pray to yourself."

"Who's going up?" Sundeen said, looking at the beam.

Digo grinned. "I'd break it."

"Need somebody light." Sundeen's eyes went to Tindal.

Tindal forced a smile. "My climbing days are over."

Beaudry said, "Hell, give me a boost."

Digo stooped and they helped Beaudry up onto his shoulders,

steadying him, holding his legs as Digo rose slowly. He threw the lines over the beam, looping them three times, then gave each a half hitch so that with weight on the hanging end the line would be pulling against itself; and when he came down the loops were hanging just longer than head high to a mounted man.

Now Digo went into the livery stable. He was gone for a few minutes and when he reappeared he was mounted and leading two horses with bridles, but without saddles.

"Mount 'em up," Sundeen said.

"Wait a minute."

Sundeen turned at the words behind him. Clay Jordan was coming toward him through the crowd. "You going to help out now?" Sundeen said.

"Nobody rides that horse." Jordan nodded to one of the mounts Digo had brought.

"It won't be but for a minute," Sundeen grinned.

"Nobody rides him."

"You superstitious?"

"Either you tell Digo to take him back, or I do."

Sundeen shrugged. "You tell him."

Digo looked at them, not understanding. "What's the difference?" But he saw the way Jordan was watching him and he said, "All right," and led Jordan's horse back to the stable. When he returned with another, Jordan was no longer in the circle beneath the cross beam.

"Let's get this over with," Stedman said.

Tindal said, "We got to tie their hands."

"What for?" Beaudry asked.

"You always do."

"It's better if you don't . . . they fight longer trying to hold their weight off the rope, then their arms give out."

Tindal frowned. "What's the matter with you?"

"This isn't a church meeting, R.D."

"You talk like a crazy man." Tindal turned from Beaudry and saw that Stedman was already tying their hands. He had cut enough length from the free ends of the riatas hanging from the beam.

Now the older Mexican said, "What about a cigarette first?"

Tying the man's hands behind his back, Stedman said, "Go to hell."

"Don't you have any customary last things?"

Digo rolled a brown paper cigarette, lit it, then placed it between the man's lips. "Here. Don't say I never gave you anything." The Mexican inhaled and with the cigarette in the corner of his mouth blew out smoke in a slow stream. "You've given me enough already."

Digo said in Spanish, "You feel you are much man, don't you?"

"Not for long," the man answered, also in Spanish.

"It's too bad this has to happen to you."

The Mexican shrugged.

"Does your companion wish a cigarette?"

"Ask him."

Digo smiled. "He looks already in another world."

Barely above a whisper the younger one was reciting, ". . . *Santificado sea el tu nombre, venga a nos el tu reino . . .*"

Digo grinned at him and said, "Remember to have perfect contrition."

The older Mexican said suddenly, "Do this quickly and stop talking!"

Now Digo shrugged. "As you say."

They lifted the Mexicans to the bare backs of the horses and now no one in the crowd spoke. In the silence, Digo mounted. He kneed his horse in a tight circle between the two Mexicans, reached up and adjusted the loop over the older Mexican's head and tightened the honda at the nape of his neck. The younger one tried to move his head away, but Digo's hand clamped over his jaw and held the head still until he dropped the noose over it and tightened the knot.

Now he moved out behind them and dismounted. Still there was silence and he took his time, with everyone watching him, walking up close behind the two horses. In front, an opening had been cleared to let the horses run.

Digo waited for a signal, but none came. So it was up to him. All right. He raised both hands in the air, said, "Go in peace—" and brought his hands down slapping the rumps of the horses.

They swung out, then back toward him on the ropes and turning, jumping aside, Digo could hear the horses breaking away down the street. The bodies jerked on the tight lines, but only for part of a minute. He heard Tindal say, "My God, look at their pants—'

Someone else said, "I don't feel very good."

And it was over—"

THREE

Kirby Frye rode in shortly before nine o'clock.

He tied his dun gelding in front of the jail and started for the front steps, but at the walk he thought: A few more minutes won't matter to Harold. He turned and crossed the street, walking slowly with the stiffness of all day in the saddle. He was hungry, he felt the taste for a glass of beer and he was anxious to see Milmary Tindal; all three were before him and he didn't know which to do first.

It felt good to walk and he was thinking how good the beer would taste. Sit down and stretch your legs, even before washing up, take the first glass and drink it better than half right down, though it burns your throat. Then sip what's left. Smoke a cigarette and drink the beer slow. Then have another one and sip that.

De Spain's windows, above the painted lower half, showed every lamp up to full brightness. Frye opened the door. But he closed it again and went on. Smoke and noise and he didn't feel that much like having to make conversation in a Saturday night crowd. The Metropolitan was still open, and a few doors down he saw light coming from Tindal's store. Well, he could always see Mil at home if she closed the store; but if the café closed—

He opened the door of the Metropolitan and almost bumped into the cook who was coming out.

"Too late, Ed?"

"Hello, Kirby. Too late for me."

"Can I get something?"

"Sure, Edith's still there."

"I'm starvin'."

"You get them drunk Indins?"

"All of a sudden they disappeared."

"Ain't that the way. Well . . . Edith'll fix you something. I got catchin' up to do."

"Thanks, Ed."

The café was empty. The counter was clean and most of the tables had been cleared, all but two that were near the front and still cluttered with supper dishes. With the emptiness was silence. Frye walked back toward the kitchen, hearing his steps and the metallic ching of his spurs which seemed louder because they were the only sounds in the room.

Nearing the open doorway to the kitchen a voice said softly, "Phil?"

Frye hesitated, then went into the kitchen, looking to the left. Edith Hanasian, Haig's wife, was sitting at the table against the wall with a cup of coffee in front of her.

"It's me."

"Oh." She looked at Frye with surprise.

"I wondered if I could get a bite."

"Of what, Kirby?"

"Whatever might be on the stove."

"You look tired."

"Been working all day."

"Would you like a drink?"

"That'd be fine."

"Sit down then."

Frye moved to the table. "Where's Mr. Hanasian?"

The woman shrugged. "I don't know."

"You want me to sit out front or here?"

Edith smiled. "If he didn't trust the deputy, who would he trust?"

"I just didn't know where you wanted me to sit."

"Here. Then I won't have so many steps."

Frye pulled out the chair opposite to Edith and sat down. "The coffee smells good."

"Would you rather have that?"

"I just said it smelled good."

The woman rose. She went to a cupboard and returned with an almost-full whisky bottle, picking up a glass from the serving table as she did. She placed the glass in front of him and poured whisky into it.

"Whoa—"

"You're a big boy now."

"I'm not that big." He drank some of the whisky and putting the glass down felt Edith move around next to him. She took his hat off and sailed it over to the serving table.

"I've had that on so long I forgot it was there."

"You look younger without it."

"Do I?"

She moved her fingers over his sand-colored hair. "Sometimes you look like a little boy," she said quietly.

"Do I look like a hungry one?"

She moved away, as if reluctantly. "What do you want?"

"I don't care."

"Enchiladas are still warm."

"Fine."

She went over to the stove, then looked back at him. "Or lamb stew?"

"All right. Stew."

"You're easy to please."

She placed a heaping plate of the stew in front of him, brought salt and bread, then sat down again.

"Tastes good."

"Does it?" She was leaning forward now with her elbows on the table, watching him eat. He glanced at her and the way she was leaning he could see the beginning of the hollow between her breasts. She was an attractive woman, not more than a year past thirty, but she smiled little. It showed in the way her mouth was set and in the eyes that seemed indifferent to whatever they looked at. Probably in another few years she would be fat. Now, there was only the hint of it, a pleasing softness that would become too soft.

"Where'd you say your husband was?"

"I said I didn't know."

"That's right." He ate the stew, pushing it onto the fork with a piece of bread, dabbing the bread in the gravy and eating that. When he was finished he wiped the plate clean this way.

"More?" Edith asked.

Frye looked at her still leaning close to the table. Then he began rolling a cigarette. "I wouldn't mind a cup of coffee . . . though I hate to ask you to move."

Edith smiled, still not moving. "Sometimes the little boy in you begins to disappear."

"Do you want me to get it?"

She rose then. "You're paying for it."

He watched her go to the stove and come back with the coffeepot.

"I thought eating in the kitchen like this I was a guest."

She poured them each a cup and sat down, but now she sat sideways in the chair, leaning against the wall, looking from the ceiling to the stove and at nothing in particular, not bothering to answer him.

"Business slow?"

Edith shrugged indifferently. "It's all right."

"You generally do better than this on Saturday, don't you?"

"Everybody's next door, celebrating."

"Celebrating what?"

"Their manhood."

"What?"

Edith looked at him. "Didn't you hear what happened?"

"I just got back."

"Go next door; you'll find out."

Frye shrugged. He wasn't going to beg her. He finished his coffee, stubbed out the cigarette on the plate and stood up. He was tall, but with a big-boned leanness, and he looked younger than twenty-four. "Maybe I will," he said. Then, "If I see Phil, you want me to tell him you're here?"

Edith hesitated, studying Frye's face. "Why would I want that?"

"You thought I was him when I came in."

"Don't jump to any conclusions."

"Wouldn't think of it. How much do I owe?"

"Thirty cents."

He felt inside his pants pockets. "I'll pay you tomorrow, all right?" He grinned. "I guess I didn't bring any money."

Edith shook her head. "Then the little boy comes back again."

Frye was smiling. "That's no way to talk to the deputy sheriff."

He went out the front door and stopped on the plank sidewalk to make another cigarette. The noise inside De Spain's would go on until late, dying out slowly, then the street would be quiet again. It had been quiet last night when he left. Friday night was usually quiet. He lighted the cigarette, looking across the street to the jail. Quiet as a church. He heard laughter from De Spain's.

Edith said they were celebrating—

She thought I was Phil Sundeen when I came in. That's it. Sundeen's back from his drive and his men are celebrating. Probably been at it since early this morning. Sitting in there all day drinking.

He shook his head faintly remembering this morning, miles away chasing like hell after nothing. His eyes went to the jail again. Harold would be asleep now, sitting up with his feet on the desk.

But Edith said something happened. Not just that they were celebrating, but that something happened—

Let it wait.

He flicked the cigarette into the street and moved away from the café.

Milmary Tindal was locking the front door of the store when he came up behind her. She heard the footsteps, then heard the footsteps stop and she turned coming around hesitantly, keeping her face composed, then her features relaxed suddenly and she smiled with relief.

"Kirby! You scared—"

Holding her shoulders he kissed her unexpectedly, his lips making a smacking sound against hers.

"Kirby!"

"Too loud?"

"Right out on the street—"

"You look good, Mil."

She brushed a wisp of hair back from her forehead. "I'm a mess."

"You going home?"

The girl nodded, looking up at him. "When did you get back?"

"Just a few minutes ago."

"Did you catch them?"

"This afternoon they made it over the border."

"Daddy was sure you'd get them." They started walking along the adobe fronts, hearing behind them faint sounds from De Spain's. Ahead were the shadowy forms of men sitting in front of the buildings, now and then a cigarette glow in the darkness, and passing them—"Good evening—"

"You get 'em, Kirby?"

"No, sir. They got away."

"That's too bad."

Nearer the end of the street the adobe fronts were deserted and now there was only the sound of their steps hollow on the plank sidewalk, and out behind the adobes and in the yard of the livery stable they could hear crickets.

"It's a nice night," he said.

The girl was walking with her head down watching her steps and did not answer. Standing straight she would come just past Frye's shoulder. Now she seemed smaller. Her figure was slight, almost boyish, but her face was delicately feminine: dark, almost black hair combed back from her face and small features softly pale in the darkness. They turned the corner and started up the low sweeping hill, seeing the lights farther up. They flickered in an uneven row through the trees indicating at least five or six houses.

"What's the matter?"

"Nothing," the girl said.

"You're not talking."

"Well, I'm tired. That's all."

"How's your father?"

She looked up at him suddenly. "He's fine."

"What're you so jumpy about?"

"Well, why're you asking me so many questions?"

"All day long I've been talking to a horse."

"I'm sorry."

"Has he said any more about you marrying Sundeen?"

"Of course not. I thought that was settled."

He said quietly, "I hope so."

Their footsteps were muffled and Frye's spurs chinged softly. Abruptly Milmary said, "I suppose you heard all about what happened today." In the darkness her voice seemed natural.

"You sound like Edith."

"You were with her?"

"All we talked about was supper."

"She didn't tell you?"

"Uh-uh."

"Well, there was a trial today."

"A trial?"

"Our town's first legal court action."

He was frowning. "The county judge was down here?"

Almost defensively she said, "We have our own judge and prosecuting attorney," and went on quickly now as if to tell it and get it over with. "The Citizens Committee met this morning and elected a city judge and a city prosecuting attorney."

"They don't have the—"

"Let me finish. Mr. Stedman was elected judge and my father, prosecutor. It was done legally, by vote of the Citizens Committee, and they represent all of the people here."

"You sound like your father."

"Will you please have the courtesy to let me finish?"

"Go on."

Her face was flushed now looking at Frye, who for a moment had smiled, but was now frowning again. "After the elections they decided to hold the first court session and they tried the two cattle thieves you've been holding. Phil Sundeen was made to testify even though everybody knew those two men were the ones. You said yourself you caught them driving off the cattle. So they were found guilty."

"Then what?"

Milmary hesitated. "Then they were taken out and legally hanged."

Frye was silent.

"The men felt, why should they wait for a court way up at Tucson to get good and ready before something's done. Our citizens are just as qualified . . . more so even, since it was one of our people whose stock was stolen."

"Your father explained all this?"

"Of course he explained it to me, I'm not a lawyer"

"Neither is he."

"He's got common sense!"

"Mil, you can't just set up a court any place you want. We're part of the county, protected by the county. Maybe we should have a judge and a prosecutor here, but to get them would take some doing up at Tucson, not just a self-made committee deciding in one morning."

"Kirby, those two men were guilty. You caught them yourself," she said pleadingly.

"But you can't set up the law *after* the wrong's done. You got to have the authority before. I even know that much."

"I suppose my father and Mr. Stedman aren't as intelligent as those people up at Tucson?"

"Now you're talking like a woman."

"What do you want me to talk like?"

Frye said quietly, "The point is, the law is already established to handle things like this. Everybody's agreed to it, so you can't just come along and set up your own law."

"Even if it's something we should have had a long time ago?"

She's using her father's words, Frye thought. And she wants to believe them. He said, "Where did they hang them?"

Milmary hesitated. "At the livery."

"Did you see it?"

"Part of it."

"A big crowd?"

"Of course."

"Was Harold Mendez there?"

"I didn't see him."

Frye said, "They were taken from the jail, marched down to the livery and hanged. Just like that?"

"I didn't see all of it."

"Did the part you see look fair?"

"I don't suppose a hanging would ever look *fair*. You're using the wrong word."

"What's a better word?"

"Kirby, use some sense! They were tried by competent men and found guilty. Now it's over."

They started to walk again, slowly, and did not speak for a few minutes. Nearing the house, Frye said, "Is your father home?"

"He said he wouldn't be home till late. Kirby, what can you do about it now?"

"I don't know."

"It's over now."

"Part of it is."

Milmary said, wearily, "If you don't understand, there's no use talking about it"

"Maybe your dad can explain it to me."

Milmary did not answer. She went up the porch steps and into the house.

Harold Mendez could feel that his nose was still swollen. Now he was touching it gently, as he had been doing all afternoon and evening, still not sure whether or not it was broken, when Frye opened the door.

"I saw you tie up a while ago," Harold said, "but by the time I got to the door you were across the street."

"I was hungry."

"Did you get them?"

"No."

"Well—"

"Everybody's more concerned with whether we got those tula-pai drinkers than with what happened right here."

"You heard then."

"Milmary told me. Where're the bodies?"

"We took them down. There were two men here from La Noria who helped me. No one else I asked would."

"Did you try to stop them?"

Harold shook his head slowly. "I couldn't see any point to it. Even if I'd tried, they still would have hung them." His fingers touched his nose.

"It looks like you told somebody no," Frye said.

"Digo was showing his authority. Do you think it's broken?"

Frye looked at Harold's nose closely, feeling the bridge of it with his finger. "I don't think so."

"They came in like a flood once it started. At first only a few were doing anything. Tindal, Beaudry, Stedman . . . and Sundeen. But once it started you would have thought everybody in town was in here."

"The place looks all right."

"They didn't break anything. I don't know why, but they didn't break anything."

Frye said suddenly, "What about Dandy Jim?"

"He's still upstairs. How long are you going to hold him?"

"I don't know. It was out of their way to come back here, so they went straight to Huachuca. They'll send for him when they get ready." He was referring to the Fort Huachuca Cavalry Patrol.

"Like Danaher sending for the two cattle thieves."

Frye moved to the window thoughtfully. "Do you know if Tindal's across the street?"

"I think so. What are you going to do?"

"Talk to him, or one of the others."

"Wait a while."

"I've got to sooner or later."

"Not tonight." Harold Mendez shook his head as he spoke. "They've been over there drinking and playing poker. They even had their dinner brought in so they wouldn't have to leave."

"They're really celebrating—"

"Listen, why don't you go to bed? Then tomorrow you can talk to them one at a time."

But you don't come home, find out something like this has happened and just go to bed, Frye was thinking. They must have been drunk to do it. No . . . Sundeen. This was probably Sundeen's idea and those men would go out on a long limb to look good in his eyes. "Harold, who was the leader?"

"They say Tindal at the meeting. But he'd make speeches in an outhouse if someone would go in with him to listen."

"Sundeen then."

Harold nodded. "Tindal might think he organized it, Stedman might think his weight influenced the others . . . but it was Sundeen behind it. Sundeen drinks too much and he talks loud, but I think he watches, and he understands these men."

"When did he get back?"

"Yesterday. He came to town last night just before you left. He was in the Metropolitan with the committee heads for a long time." Harold studied Frye for a moment standing by the window. "Listen, I don't mean to sound disrespectful, this Tindal might be your father-in-law someday . . . but you know how he talks: 'Sure, General So-and-so, I remember a humorous account he told at dinner one time . . .' Or the way he looks off in the distance sucking his teeth like he's calculating a weighty problem, and all the time he doesn't know a goddamn thing. I don't like to say that, but that's the way he is. You haven't been here long as a grownup, but you should know it yourself by now."

"You can't pick your father-in-law," Frye said.

"Like he's trying to pick his son-in-law," Harold said. "He'd give his right one to have her marry Sundeen."

"Well, that's something else. Was De Spain there?"

"I don't think so."

"Or Hanasian?"

"I don't think he was either."

"And they've been in there ever since—"

"They came out just the once."

"When?" Frye looked at him.

"I thought you'd heard."

"No."

"Did you hear about Merl White being there earlier?"

Frye shook his head.

"Merl and some others wouldn't join Phil. Merl said they'd quit because Phil hadn't paid their trail wages."

"Why not?"

"Why does Phil need a reason? Like riding his horse into De Spain's. He does what he feels like doing. Right out in front of everybody Phil told Merl to come over to De Spain's after and he'd settle up. Well, Merl went over. He and two others walked into De Spain's and a few minutes later they were carried out. The story is, Sundeen threw whisky in Merl's face, then Digo hit him. The other two stood there until Digo started at them. They each took one swing before they were on the floor. Then Digo pulled their boots off and carried them one at a time to the porch and threw them out in the street. I saw what happened after that. Sundeen came out and this new man with him—"

"Who's that?"

"Jordan. Clay Jordan."

Kirby shook his head, not knowing the name.

"They stood on the porch until Digo came with horses, then Sundeen and Digo made them run, shooting at their feet. Sundeen went back inside, but Digo and some other Sun-D riders went out after them and made them keep running until they were out of sight . . . without any shoes on."

"No one sided with Merl then?"

"Of course not."

"And nobody's gone out to find them?"

"About two hours after it happened I took a wagon and started out. I wasn't even beyond the last house when Digo rode next to me and said 'Where are you going?' "

Frye's eyes were on Harold, but he said nothing.

"I told him nowhere and turned the wagon around." Harold sat down and his fingers touched his nose, stroking it gently.

Frye was leaning against the window frame, watching him. After a moment he said, "It's all right, Harold."

"I'm not apologizing," the jailer said.

"You don't have to."

"What if I had tried to stop them? I mean before. I would be dead now. I couldn't see where it would be worth it."

"It's all right."

"You're goddamn right it is," Harold said.

"Why don't you go home now?" Frye said.

Harold looked up at him. "I'll go over with you if you want me to."

"No, you go on home."

"What are you going to do?"

"Just talk."

"Don't try to arrest them They'll laugh at you."

Frye was silent. Then he straightened and walked away from the window. "It's a hell of a thing, isn't it?"

Harold nodded. He watched Frye open the door, then he rose slowly and followed him.

FOUR

Clay Jordan saw them first, because he was facing the open doorway. Sundeen was on Jordan's left, then around the table, Stedman, Tindal and Beaudry; Sundeen dealing cards over the stacks of poker chips in front of him, the other three watching. They were in De Spain's cardroom.

Past Tindal's right shoulder, through the doorway, down the length of floor in front of the bar to the double doors, Jordan was looking straight ahead and he saw one of the doors push in. He recognized Harold Mendez, and from that knew who the younger one, the one who came first, must be. He said nothing to Sundeen, but watched them come down the length of bar, passing Digo standing midway at the bar, Digo realizing they were there and turning to look after them. As Frye neared the doorway, Jordan's gaze went unhurriedly from the stiff-brimmed hat and the shadowed eyes to the Colt on the right hip and the hands hanging loose, then back to the eyes as Frye stopped inside the doorway.

"Mr. Tindal—"

Tindal looked over his shoulder, then smiled turning in the chair. "Kirby! Come on in, boy!"

Frye moved closer to the table. "Mr. Stedman . . . Mr. Beaudry—" He only nodded to Phil Sundeen because it had been a long time since he had seen Phil and he wasn't sure what to call him. He glanced at Jordan, then looked at Tindal again.

"Could I speak to you a minute?"

Tindal frowned. "What about?"

"This afternoon—"

"Oooh, that." Tindal's narrow face grinned. "You heard about it, uh?"

"Yes, sir."

"Well . . . I'll explain it to you tomorrow, Kirby. We're right in the middle of a hand. Sit down there and order what you want. Put it on my bill."

"I thought this might be important enough to talk about now," Frye said. He heard Stedman say, "I call," and saw him push two chips toward the pot.

"Sure it's important," Tindal said, "but it'll keep till tomorrow." Stedman said, "What do you do, R.D.?"

Tindal glanced at his cards. "How much to stay?"

"Two dollars."

"I'm in." Tindal had less than ten chips in front of him. He took two off the top of the stack and dropped them on the pile of chips in the middle of the table.

"Mr. Tindal, I want to find out your side—"

Beaudry threw his cards down. "I fold."

Frye glanced at Beaudry, then to Tindal again whose back was toward him now. He moved to the side so he could see Tindal's face. "I'd like to know how you could do a thing like that."

Clay Jordan pushed two chips away from him. "Some people don't know enough to go home," he said mildly. He glanced at Sundeen. "You're called."

Tindal turned his head, but did not look up at Frye. "Kirby, I said tomorrow!"

"Mr. Tindal, I can't find out something like this has happened and just go to bed and forget about it."

Jordan looked at Frye momentarily. "Maybe you better try."

Sundeen's hand slammed down on the table spilling the chips in front of him. "Goddamn it, we're playing poker!"

"All right, Phil," Stedman said quickly. He glanced at Frye. "Just a minute, Kirby." Then to Sundeen, again, "What've you got, Phil?"

Sundeen showed his hand. "A pair of ladies over," he said sourly.

"That beats me," Stedman said. He threw in his hand watching the others and saw that they were beaten too. "All right," he said then, "let's just take a minute and explain to Kirby what we did. Now I think being deputy sheriff he's entitled to some explanation." No one spoke.

Stedman took his time now. He said, "Kirby, briefly . . . the committee met this morning. We used our own God-given authority to set up a judicial system for our city. R.D. was elected public prosecutor and I, I was honored to accept as municipal judge. Then, under the power vested in us, we tried the two outlaws you brought in. Twelve men found them guilty, Kirby. Twelve men, after R.D. presented the evidence against them. I then felt it my duty to prescribe the death sentence. For the main reason, to let it be known how we deal with outlawry and that way discourage any future crimes against Randado. Kirby, this was done with clear conscience and, as I said before, through a God-given authority."

"Mr. Stedman," Frye said, "you know better than that."

Stedman looked at him surprised, then his eyes half closed to a squint. "We're not going to argue with you, Kirby."

Suddenly it was clear and he should have known it before, but this brought it out into the open without any words wasted. They considered him of little importance. Of *no* importance! Standing by the table he had felt self-conscious with no one paying any attention to him, but now he was suddenly angry realizing why. These were older men who didn't have to listen to a boy who'd only been deputy a month and before that never in his life had an ounce worth of authority. He felt his face flush and he said, "I'm not going to argue either. Tucson gets the report first thing in the morning. You can argue with them." He turned to leave.

"Kirby!" Tindal was around in his chair. He waited, sucking his teeth, making sure Frye would stay. He saw Harold Mendez just inside the room and Digo lounging in the doorway. "Kirby . . . you're a good boy. You work hard and you keep yourself presentable . . . but"—Tindal looked him up and down carefully—"maybe you're not as smart as I thought you were."

Frye waited, with his respect for this man fading to nothing.

"We've been on this earth a little longer than you have," Tindal said, and nodded, indicating the men at the table. "And I think maybe we've collected a little more common sense and judgment. That's nothing *against* you, Kirby, it's just you're young and got a little bit to learn yet."

Frye said, "Yes-sir."

"Now, Kirby, I want to remind you of something. We passed on your appointment as deputy. We could have gotten someone else, but we talked it over and decided you had the makings of a good one. Technically, you work for Danaher up in Tucson, but not if we hadn't passed on you. We used out judgment, Kirby . . . and our authority. Remember this, boy, as long as you're deputy you work for the people."

Frye said "And all the people hung those two men?"

"A majority is all that's necessary," Stedman said.

"After you hung them," Frye asked quietly, "did you bury them?"

"Mendez took care of that," Beaudry said.

Frye looked at him. "Didn't your authority cover that?"

Tindal chuckled softly. "Kirby, now you're talking foolish."

Frye turned on him suddenly. "Doesn't killing two men mean anything to you?" He felt the anger hot on his face again.

Sundeen, sitting low in his chair, was fingering the chips in front of him. He said to no one in particular, "You picked yourself a beauty." He looked sideways at Jordan. "Why does he pack that gun if he's so against killin'?"

Jordan said, "Maybe it makes him feel important."

"Now if it was me," Sundeen said, "I wouldn't pick a deputy that whined like a woman."

Jordan was looking at Frye. "Maybe that's what this deputy is . . . only dressed up like a man."

Sundeen grinned. "Maybe we ought to take his pants off and find out."

Tindal chuckled. "Come on, Phil . . . don't be rough on him."

Frye held his eyes on Sundeen. Keep looking at him, just him, and don't let him think you're afraid. He's not an animal, he can't smell it, he has to use his eyes. Just Sundeen—he felt his anger mounting—and don't look at the other one, don't even think about him. He looks like he would fight with a gun, not with his fists, and you don't know anything about him. One thing at a time.

"Sundeen, if you want to try, stop by the jail tomorrow."

"Clay," Sundeen grinned, "did you hear what he said?"

Jordan was still looking at Frye. "Why would you wait till tomorrow?"

"That's what I was thinking," Sundeen said. He looked past Frye to Digo who still lounged in the doorway. "You hear what he said, Digo?"

Digo straightened. "I heard him."

"You think we should wait till tomorrow?"

"What for?"

Sundeen was grinning. "Can you do it alone?"

"Sure."

"All right. Get his pants off in two minutes and I'll buy you a drink."

"All the way off?"

"Just down."

Frye heard Digo behind him. Suddenly no more could be said because it was handed to Digo and Digo wasn't a talker, and with it there was hardly time to think about being afraid, only that you had to do something fast, without waiting.

He took a half step back turning, cocking his right fist, starting to swing at Digo who was almost on him, and Digo was seeing it, rolled head and shoulders out of the way. There it was. Frye shifted and jabbed his left fist hard into Digo's face. The face came up exposed for part of a second and Frye was ready. He swung hard with his right and Digo went back against the wall, his head striking the adobe next to the door frame. He started to go down, but he held himself against the wall and shook his head, clearing it and now wiping the blood from his mouth with the back of his hand.

Frye was on him again. He feinted, jabbed and swung, his fist landing solid against Digo's cheek, then the left, the right again, now to the stomach and a cross over to the face as Digo's guard dropped. Digo was covering, hunching his shoulders, but suddenly he swung.

His big fist came up from below grazing Frye's chin, making him go back, and there was Digo's moment. Frye was open and Digo bore in, missing with his left but catching Frye's jaw with his right. Frye counterpunched with the ringing in his head, hitting Digo's face, but now Digo did not go back. An animal grunt came from him and he waded into Frye taking the stinging jabs, then swinging hard and now finding Frye's face with most of his blows. His guard went up and Digo's fist slammed into his stomach. Then the wall was behind him hard against his head, jolting his back, Digo swinging and the soft smacking sound of his fist against Frye's mouth. He tried to cover himself and Digo hammered through his guard, a grunting jab to the stomach. Frye's forearm went up for the blow to the head that would follow but it didn't come and again his body slammed against the wall as Digo went after his stomach.

He swung right and left backing Digo off, but only for a moment. Digo came again, taking jabs to the face and body as he closed in. He swung once, grazing Frye's head but his follow through was hard against Frye's cheekbone sending him back off balance. He kept after him until Frye was against the wall again and then he swung with every pound of his body behind it. Frye started to go down, but Digo held him by the front of his shirt and hit him again and again and again and each time he did Frye's head slammed against the adobe wall.

"That's enough, Digo!" Tindal screamed.

Digo let him fall. He backed away breathing hard, wiping his mouth. "He needs only twenty more pounds," Digo grunted, "and it could have been the other way."

Sundeen said, "You didn't do it."

Digo looked at him. "More than two minutes?"

Sundeen nodded. "But take his pants off anyway."

It was well after midnight when the wagon rolled into the street and stopped in front of the Metropolitan Café. Light framed the painted windows of De Spain's, but now there were no sounds from inside and across the street the windows of the jail office were dark. The street was silent, though the crickets could be heard if you listened for them.

Haig Hanasian climbed off the wagon seat and for a moment disappeared into the deeper shadow at the door of his café. He unlocked the door and returned unhurriedly to the wagon and close to the sideboard he said, "All right, come this way."

A man rose to his hands and knees in the wagon bed. He hesitated, then dropped silently over the sideboard of the wagon and as he did, two figures rose slowly, cautiously and followed him over the side. Haig Hanasian held open the door and they passed by him into the darkness of the café.

They stopped as he closed the door. "Be very quiet," he said. "The tables are just to your left all the way to the back. The counter stools are along the right. Walk straight and you will not bump anything." He moved past them and they followed his steps to the kitchen. They heard him close the door. A match flared in the darkness and Haig lighted the lamp that was above the serving table.

The three men, who were in range clothes and watched Haig with full-open shifting eyes in dirt-streaked faces, were the men Sundeen had forced out of town. Merl White and the two Sun-D riders who had sided with him.

Haig said, "Sit down," glancing at them and then at the smaller table against the wall, then at their swollen bare feet, the shreds of wool socks and the traces of blood on the floor as they moved to the table. Haig pulled the chairs out for them. He began clearing the few soiled dishes from the table, but hesitated as he picked up the plate with the brown paper cigarette mashed in it. He put these dishes on the serving table, then went to the stove.

Merl White said, "What about your horses out front?"

"They are patient," Haig answered. He was a short heavy-set man and he spoke quietly, as if he were tired, and the heavy mustache over his mouth covered the movement of his lips.

"If you want to tend them," Merl White said, "I'll see to the fire."

"It's all right," Haig said, looking at Merl. But then his eyes went to the serving table, to the cigarette mashed out on the plate. He lighted the fire and moved the iron pot that was on the stove over the well. "It will be ready soon." He walked to the rear door that opened to the backyard. "I'll be gone only a few minutes," he said.

The three men were watching him. Merl said quickly, "Where're you going?"

Haig turned. "Don't you trust me?"

Merl swallowed. "I'm sorry . . . I guess we're edgy. We wondered what you planned."

"When I come back we will talk about it," Haig said.

"A man can't go far without boots."

Haig nodded. "We will talk about that, too."

He went outside, then up the back stairs to the second floor porch and through a door which opened to a hallway and just inside the door he lighted a table lamp. At the end of the hallway the living room was dark. Haig opened the door on the left, the door to his wife's bedroom, but he did not go in.

The room was dark, but the light from the hall fell across the bed and he could see her form under the comforter. She was lying on her side with her back toward him as he stood in the doorway and she did not move.

"Are you awake?"

"I am now," Edith said drowsily. Still she did not turn.

"I have to tell you something." She did not answer and he repeated, "Edith, I have to tell you something very important." He moved into the room and stood by the bed.

"What is it?"

"Those three men that were chased out of town—they're downstairs."

He expected his wife to look at him now, but she did not. "Did you wake me up to tell me that?"

"It concerns you," Haig said, "because they will be here until Monday night."

"Then what?"

"Then I'll take them to La Noria."

"The good Samaritan."

"I only ask that you stop entertaining Mr. Sundeen as long as they are here." Haig said this quietly, without emotion, as he had said all the things before.

She turned now, but only her shoulders and head on the pillow, her body twisted beneath the comforter and now the faint light showed her eyes and the outline of her features.

"I'll try," she said, beginning to smile.

"He was here this evening," Haig said.

"How would you know that?"

"He ate supper in the kitchen and you had coffee with him while he ate."

Now she recalled Kirby Frye, picturing him sitting across the table from her, but she said, "I didn't know watching someone eat was a sin."

"With you," Haig said, "it could be a very near occasion to it."

"You're absolutely sure Phil was here?"

"Who else?"

Edith rolled over lazily and with her back to him again said, "Imagine whatever you like."

FIVE

Danaher came Sunday morning. He had been to La Noria on county business and had planned to stay there over Sunday before returning to Tucson, but two men rode in late Saturday afternoon with the story of the hanging at Randado and that changed Danaher's plans.

He left for Randado before sunup and all the way there he thought of Kirby Frye and wondered if he had returned. The two men told that the regular deputy had not been there, only the jailer.

And if Frye had returned, what?

Danaher had confidence in his deputy, though he kept reminding himself of it, because picturing Frye he saw a young man who looked too easygoing, who maybe smiled too readily and who called almost anyone older than himself mister. No, those things didn't matter, Danaher reminded himself. His confidence was based on a feeling and he relied on it more than he did the external evidences. A man could look like a lot of things, but Danaher let his intuition tell him what was beneath the surface. A good deal of the time, Danaher felt alone in his job, this being sheriff of Pima County, and he liked to think that sometimes God gave him extra help—an above-natural power that allowed him to rely on his intuition in appraising people—a compensation for the loneliness of his job, and to make up for the minimum of help he could usually expect from others.

His intuition told him many things about Frye. That he was sensitive without being emotional, that he was respectful without being servile, and that he was a man who would follow what his conscience told him ninety-nine per cent of the time. That was the quality which sold Danaher, because he was sure he could make many of his own principles a part of that conscience, and in time he would have a real deputy. He showed Frye that he himself was a man to whom principle was everything and this way, whether Frye was aware of it or not, he won Frye's respect.

At the same time, Danaher was honest enough to admit to himself that maintaining Frye's respect would even make John Danaher a better man and he thought: That's how God tricks you into being good.

It hadn't taken long for him to like Frye, and that happened with few people he ever met. He respected him as a man, and with Danaher respect was something to be given out sparingly and only after substantial proof that it was deserved. Once he caught himself pretending that Kirby Frye was his son and he called himself a damn fool; but when he did it again he thought: Well, what's so unnatural about that? But the next time he saw Frye he spoke little and he bawled hell out of him for letting cigarette butts collect on the jail floor.

The first time he ever laid eyes on Frye was at Galluro Station the day after the Chiricahuas hit—

Danaher received the wire on a Saturday afternoon, from Fort Huachuca, relayed through the Benson operator. BRING POSSE GALLURO STATION HATCH AND HODGES LINE URGENT CHIRICAHUAS.

They reached Galluro Monday before noon, Danaher and eight men, only eight because raising a posse on Saturday wasn't the easiest thing in the world. They moved along at a steady but slower pace keeping their eyes open on the chance they might be riding into the running Chiricahuas and that was why it took them until Monday to get there.

The station had been partially burned, the stable and outbuildings, everything that wasn't adobe, and the teams had been run off. The dead were buried: the station agent and his wife and the Mexican hostler. But two people were missing: the hostler's wife and the little girl, and it was naturally assumed the Apaches had taken them. The agent's wife had been in her forties, that was why she had not been taken.

A Lieutenant J. R. Davis told them this.

He was there from Fort Huachuca with half of a company, about eighteen men counting his Coyotero scout, plus two civilians who stood with their thumbs in their belts waiting for something to happen. The other half of the company had gone out the day before while the sign was still fresh, Lieutenant Davis told them; but he had waited in order to tell Danaher their plan, which was no plan at all, but the only alternative Davis could think of.

So, the first half of the company was to stay on the sign as long as possible, following wherever it led. Davis would taken the remainder of the company and angle east by southeast for the Dragoons, which was the logical place the Apaches would try to reach no matter what direction they took from Galluro. By Wednesday, Davis said, he hoped to have made contact with the rest of the company by heliograph. And if luck was with them, the Apaches would be somewhere in between their sun-flash messages.

Danaher was told to take his men west, back toward the Santa Catalinas, the way they had come, and keep a sharp eye, because perhaps these Apaches weren't heading for the Dragoons at all, but trying to get away in a westerly direction. Danaher was angry, because he could see the lieutenant didn't believe this, but only said it because he had come all that way from Tucson with eight men and it was a shame not to have him doing something.

"How many were there?" Danaher asked.

"Not more than a dozen," Lieutenant Davis told him, and glanced at his scout. "That's what Dandy Jim reads."

"And you're pretty sure," Danaher said, "you can handle these twelve Chiricahuas by yourself."

"What do you mean?"

"Well, you're sending us off for home now you don't need us."

The lieutenant's face reddened, but it was anger and not embarrassment. "What do you mean don't need you? Couldn't they just as easily have gone toward the Catalinas?"

"You're not even considering it."

"My God, I can't go all four directions with eighteen men!"

Danaher felt sorry for him momentarily. The lieutenant had problems of his own to live with and to him they were bigger than anyone else's. There was no sense in aggravating him further. It wasn't the lieutenant's fault Danaher had been brought here; still, the Pima sheriff couldn't help one more small jab and he said, "Well, Lieutenant, how do you suppose I'm going to watch your western frontier with only eight men?"

The lieutenant's face was still flushed and he said angrily, "How many men would you like, Mr. Danaher?"

"Many as I can get."

"Will two be enough?"

"If that's all you can spare."

Davis motioned to the two civilians who were standing with Dandy Jim. "You men go with the sheriff here."

One of the men said, "You're orderin' the wrong boy. When I start ridin' it's back toward Huachuca."

Davis looked at the other man, scowling. "What about you?"

He was standing hip-shot with his thumbs in his belt and he nodded. "All right with me."

The first man said, "Kirby, what you want to go way over there for?"

"Well, Frank, our deal's closed, I thought I'd go on up to Prescott and visit with my folks."

Davis said, "Mr. Danaher, you get one man."

"That'll have to do then," Danaher said.

He glanced at the man who was coming with him, but did not take a second look because there wasn't anything out of the ordinary about him—though maybe he was lankier and lazier looking than the next man—and Danaher didn't bother to shake hands with him, but turned to his eight men and told them they would eat before starting back. Then, drinking his coffee, Danaher looked over at Davis' half-of-a-company preparing to leave and he saw his new man and Davis' Coyotero scout squatting, talking together, and Danaher's interest advanced one step.

But it was not until later that he spoke to him. They had been riding for more than an hour and it came when the two of them happened to be riding side by side.

"What did that Coyotero tell you?" Danaher's first words.

"To stay awake."

Danaher looked at him because the boy's voice was calm and he had not been startled by the sheriff's abrupt question. "What do they call you?" Danaher said now

"Frye."

"Frye what?"

"Kirby Frye."

"Where're you from?"

"Randado originally."

"Is that so? What else did that Coyotero say?"

"That maybe part of them went this way."

"What do you think?"

"I think he could be right."

Danaher half smiled. "Don't go out on a limb."

Frye glanced at him, saying nothing.

Danaher asked, "Did he tell the soldier that?"

"No."

"Why not?"

'It wouldn't make any difference with the few men he's got."

"Davis thought they'd run for the Dragoons," Danaher said.

"Well, he's probably right."

"So they could have gone either way and both Davis and the Coyotero are probably right."

"I'm saying," Frye said, "they could have gone *both* ways. Any Chiricahua could dodge soldier patrols and get back to the Dragoons, but he'd stop and give it some thought if he was driving those stage horses."

"So maybe the ones with the horses went this way," Danaher concluded.

"That's right."

"But if they were to drive them west, then make a long swing back to the Dragoons, that would take time."

"They've got more of it than anybody else," Frye said.

They camped without a fire on flat ground, but with foothills looming in the near distance. It was the boy, Kirby Frye, who suggested no fire. The men grumbled because as far as they were concerned they were going home, not stalking hostiles; but Danaher agreed with Frye and said bluntly, flatly , no fire, and that's all there was to it. They ate jerked beef and biscuits, then lay on their stomachs to smoke, holding the glow cupped close to the ground. One man, with a cigarette in his mouth, stood up and walked off a few feet to relieve himself. He turned, surprised, seeing Danaher next to him, but had no time to dodge as Danaher's fist swung against his jaw. Without a word Danaher stepped on the cigarette and returned to the circle of his possemen.

In the morning as soon as they reached high ground, they saw the dust. Far off beyond the sweep of the grade below them, hanging clear and almost motionless in the distance, seeming only a few hundred yards off in the dry air but at least four hours ahead of them, beyond arroyos and cut-banks that were only shadow lines in their vision. Horses raised dust like that and every man there knew it. And when they moved on, down the sweep of the grade, there was an excitement inside of them that wasn't there before. Danaher could feel it and he knew the others did, but they rode loose and kept it inside and tried to look as if this was something they did every other day of the week.

Well, Danaher thought, watching his men when they weren't watching him, that was a good sign. They're good men and maybe I shouldn't have hit that one last night. Now they know they're not just riding home and they'll act like grown men.

But later on Danaher's men let their excitement show. Since noon they had been deep among the hills, winding through the shadows of brush and rock formations, moving single file with two men a mile or so ahead, moving slowly but gaining steadily on the column of dust which they would see only occasionally now.

About two o'clock they heard rifle fire up ahead and soon after one of Danaher's advance riders was coming back. They could read good news all over his face.

Danaher side-stepped his big chestnut gelding to block the trail and the rider came up short, almost swinging out of the saddle. He had been yelling something as he rode in and now Danaher told him to shut up and take a breath and they'd find out what happened a lot quicker.

"Now what's it all about?"

"John, we *got* one!"

The man's name was Walt Booth and he was the same one who had showed his cigarette glow the night before and Danaher had hit. He was quick tempered and easily roused to fight, but Danaher could handle him and that's why he always let Booth join the posses.

Now Booth told them what had happened. How they had topped a rise and there right below them, but beyond a brush thicket, were eight or ten horses in a clearing like they'd been held up to rest. It hit them right away, Booth told. Stage teams from Galluro! And that meant only one thing—

"We started to rein around and I heard it. A snappin' sound in the brush. Now I had my piece across my lap and my finger on the trigger—had it there all morning—and I'm broadside to the thicket when I hear the noise and the next second this son-of-a-bitchin' 'Pache's standin' there gawkin' at me. He starts to run, but he's a split-haired second late and I let him catch it right between the wings." Booth was grinning. "Didn't even have to lift the piece, just squeezed one off and he flops over like a sack of fresh cow chips."

Danaher asked him how many Apaches, but Booth didn't know. When he fired the horses started to move, just like that, like a signal, and they didn't see even one, though they fired at the horses because you know how the bastards cling to the off side of a mount and make you think there're no riders while all the time they're ridin' the hell out.

He told that the other advance man was watching the place and they'd better shake their tails up there if they were going to have 'Pache for dinner.

Danaher let Booth go first, then told the others to follow and he swore if a man made a sound he'd break him in two. But their excitement was up again and they did make sounds in the loose shale and brushing through mesquite and all Danaher could do was swear to himself.

The other advance rider was not in sight, but they found the dead Apache right away. Booth said damned if he oughtn't to lift the greasy scalp . . . show his wife he was really out here . . . but Danaher told him to keep away. Frye came up to him then. He watched Frye kneel over the dead Apache and heard him say something about the Apache being only a boy. Not over fourteen.

Well, that was too bad. Danaher had live Apaches to think about. He directed his men to the clearing where the horses had been and when they got there the other advance man who had been with Booth was coming out of the brush on the other side. He was running and pointing behind him.

"John, they're runnin' like blue hell down a draw!"

"How many?"

"Not a mile ahead! John, we got 'em runnin' for the open!"

"How many!"

The man reached them and he stopped, breathing heavily. "I didn't see 'em . . . I heard 'em! This draw's full of scrub pine— must slant down two miles before she opens up. Way off over the trees you can see open country where the draw comes out. And all the time I could hear the red sons beatin' down through the trees!"

"But you didn't see them come out," Danaher said.

"Settin' there was time wasted. I came back to get you."

Danaher swung up over his saddle and went through the brush at a gallop. The others followed. They topped the knoll that formed the beginning of the draw, listening and hearing nothing, but seeing off in the distance, below and off beyond the slanting brown-green smooth-appearing tops of the scrub pines, the dust trail. Dust that was rising thinly to nothing and pinpoint dots inching into the wide open flat glare of the distance. Booth said, "We're going to have us a late supper, but damn' if it won't be worth it."

Danaher was ready and he turned in the saddle to make sure that his men were. This is what they had come for and by God they'd run the Apaches till they caught them. His men were ready, sitting their mounts eagerly. All of them except the boy, Kirby Frye.

He was standing in front of his horse, holding the reins close to the bit rings and gazing up at the wild brush and rocks that followed a looming jog back off to the left of them.

Danaher asked, "You coming?"

Frye's gaze swung to Danaher. "I don't know about chasing after that dust."

"What do you mean?"

"It doesn't seem right they'd be running for open country."

One of the men said, "John, we got to move!"

Danaher scowled. "Hold on!" And to Frye, "Make some sense."

"I never heard of an Apache getting himself caught out on flat land. They mostly camp high, even if it's a dry camp, and *always* if somebody's on their sign."

Danaher said, "But is we surprised them they didn't have a choice but to streak for the best opening."

Frye shook his head. "I never heard of a Chiricahua raiding party being even approached without their knowing about it."

"That 'Pache over yonder," Booth sneered, "sure'n hell opened a surprise package when he stuck his head out the bushes." Booth's eyes held on Frye. "Who says you know so goddamn much about 'Paches? That stuff last night about no fire—"

"The one you got was a boy," Frye interrupted. "He hadn't yet learned the finer points."

Booth glanced at the rider next to him. "He's a goddamn Indin lover. Chief No-Fire." He looked back to Frye. "Chief No-Fire-In-His-Pants. Let me ask you a question, Chief. Are you tellin' us this 'cause you're an Indin lover or 'cause you're too goddamn scared to go down that draw?"

Danaher almost interrupted, but he glanced at Frye and suddenly checked himself. The boy hadn't moved, hadn't flickered his eyes from Booth's face. Booth was almost broadside to him, the Remington rolling, block across his lap, and pointed just off from Frye, and the boy still held his reins short, but his right hand was at his side now, thumb almost touching the hickory butt of his Colt.

Frye said, "Mister, were you asking a question, or telling me a fact?" Booth had been leaning over the saddle horn, but now he straightened slowly and the barrel of the Remington edged a wavering inch toward Frye.

"Take it any way you want," Booth said.

"If it wasn't a question," Frye said, "then you better start doin' something with that Remington."

"Hold on!" Danaher broke in. He had been intrigued by the boy's calmness, by the way Frye stared back at a rifle barrel almost on him and dumped the play back into the other man's lap; but it had to end. And Danaher was the man to end it.

"Time's wasting." He glared at Frye. "Get it out, quick. Why don't you think it's them? Even though you can see their dust."

"We make dust just like they do," Frye said. "I'll judge they sent a man back to look us over sometime yesterday afternoon."

"Go on."

"They decided we were getting too close, so the thing to do was throw us off. It was either keeping their skins or the horses. Their skins got the vote and the horses were elected to side-track us. That's what you see down there, the Hatch and the Hodges Stage horses they took from Galluro."

Danaher said, "And you think the braves are up here in the rocks somewhere."

Frye nodded.

"That boy getting shot," Danaher said. "Was that part of the side-tracking?"

A few of his men laughed, Booth one of them.

"That's the way they learn," Frye said. "They either graduate or get dropped out of school suddenly."

"What else?" Danaher said.

"The rest is guess."

"Go ahead."

"There were three boys and one warrior, the instructor you might say. Probably this run on Galluro was the first raid they've taken part in. They were to just take care of the horses and get them back home somehow. Now there weren't enough for an ambush and we were too close to be outrun, so they had only one thing left to do. Throw us off and get the hell home."

"You admit that's a guess," Danaher said.

"Most of it. I wasn't there when they talked it over."

Danaher shook his head. "That dust over there is something we can see. Maybe they're only horses as you say, but it's something there and you don't have to guess to know it."

Frye nodded. "Yes sir. You coming back this way?"

Danaher looked at him. "You mean you're going to stay here?"

"They come back for their dead when they can."

"That's presupposing quite a bit."

Frye shrugged. "When you come back I'll ride on to Tucson with you."

Danaher hesitated. There were words he could use to cut a fresh know-it-all kid down to manageable size. Words almost in his mouth. But he hesitated. The way the boy said it wasn't cheeky or show-off; it was perhaps just the words themselves, if you took them alone. So he hesitated because he was unsure and later on he was glad that he did.

He took his men down the draw, down through the scrub pine to the plain and pointed them into the distance, ran them until mounts and men were salt- and sweat-caked, halted them for the sake of the horses not the men, moved them again, gaining on the dust cloud, now making out pinpoint dots again, drawing closer, closer, until finally—there it was.

He drew up his posse and sat heavily, silently watching the riderless Hatch and Hodges Line stage horses streak into the distance again.

And all the way back to the draw, in the approaching dusk, he was silent. He was not angry because he had made a mistake. He did not expect to be right all the time. This was even a justifiable miscalculation for that matter. A bird in the hand always and any way you looked at it being worth more than the two in the bush. Well, maybe not always. He was thinking of Kirby Frye and the matter-of-fact way he had read the situation. No, the one in the hand isn't always the best. Not if somebody tells you the bush is right under your nose and all you have to do is stick your hand in.

Reaching the top of the draw Danaher was thinking: But he better not say, "I told you so."

Moving into the clearing he expected to see Frye get up and watch them ride in. Wasn't that him lying over there? It was in his mind and at the same moment Booth, swinging down next to him, answered the question.

"That's the 'Pache I shot!"

The Apache boy had been left in the brush, but now, strangely, he was near the edge of the clearing. And still Frye was not in sight.

"John, there's a note on him."

"What?"

"Right on his chest, a rock weightin' it down!" Booth looked at it, even though he couldn't read, before handing it to Danaher.

It was a yellow sheet of paper that had been folded twice but was now open and the side he looked at was a receipt form with the information that thirty-three cavalry remounts had been delivered and—

Danaher turned the paper between his fingers. Frye's message was on the other side, written in pencil.

Don't move the dead one. 35 paces off his right shoulder in the brush is a wounded Cherry-cow. Gutshot. Don't give him water. Will see you by dark.

And the last line: *Horses run like hell without saddles, don't they?*

One thought struck Danaher at that moment. It had been building in him since meeting Frye, evolving slowly as Frye, step by step, advanced in Danaher's estimation; first, seeing him talking to the Coyotero tracker; then last night, he was the one who had suggested no fire; then the way he stood up to Booth's nervous Remington with ice water in his eyes and a voice like he was asking the time of day; and the fact that he had read this Apache scheme like words on a printed page.

He'd make one hell of a fine deputy, was Danaher's thought. And he realized now that perhaps he had been thinking it, or half wishing it, all the time.

The note clinched it in Danaher's mind. He carries a pencil! Maybe he can't spell Chiricahau, but by God "Cherry-cow" was close enough and all the rest of the words were right.

He was still thinking about this when Kirby Frye returned. He came out of the brush and was next to Danaher before the sheriff realized he was there.

"Where've you been?"

"After the other two."

So he was right, Danaher thought. Four altogether. "You get them?"

"One. The other disappeared."

In the almost dark Danaher studied him. "Probably the older brave."

"I never got close enough to tell."

"Why'd they come back?"

"To pick up the dead one. They thought we'd all gone."

"Well, three dead out of four isn't bad."

Frye looked at Danaher anxiously. "The one I hit in the belly's dead?"

"Booth finished him." Danaher asked then, "Why didn't you?"

"I didn't create him," Frye answered. "I don't see where I had a right to uncreate him."

"What about the other one? You killed him."

"Not when he was lying on the ground gutshot."

"What's the difference?"

Frye hesitated. "Mr. Danaher, don't you see a difference?"

He did, but he wasn't going to stand in a mesquite thicket all night discussing Apache-country ethics, so he said, "Maybe we'll talk about it over a beer sometime."

And he was thinking: No question of it now. He's my man.

After they reached Tucson he asked Frye if he'd mind stopping by the jail. Danaher relaxed a little and smiled to himself when Frye said yes sir, he'd be happy to. Might even buy the boy a drink, he decided, after they had something to eat.

And later, after tacos and a glass of beer, now sitting in the jail office, Danaher with his back to the roll-top, Frye appearing comfortable slouched in a Douglas chair, both smoking cigarettes—

"I'd like to ask you a few things," Danaher began.

"Go ahead."

"There's a reason."

Frye shrugged. "I figured there was."

"Well . . . you said you were from Randado."

"Originally."

"How long ago?"

Frye looked at the beamed ceiling, then at Danaher. "I was born there. My dad was a mining man then and felt he ought to work the Huachucas. So we lived in Randado while he prospected."

"And how long did you stay?"

"I left the first time when I was fourteen."

"For where?"

"With a trail herd."

"Old man Sundeen's?"

Frye nodded. "Yes sir. That was before Willcox became a pick-up point for the railroad. We drove them all the way to Ellsworth."

"I imagine you learned a few things on Douglas Street," Danaher said seriously.

Frye grinned. "A few things."

"And then what?"

"The next year we drove part of the herd to McDowell and the rest over to San Carlos and Old Val sold them all as government beef for the reservation."

"Go on."

"Well, I didn't go back with them that trip, but stayed on at San Carlos and worked for the agent a while."

"And that's where you learned about Apaches."

"I learned some."

"I guess you did."

"That same year my folks moved up to Prescott and my dad started a freight line with what he'd scratched out of the Huachucas."

"He sounds like the one prospector in a thousand," Danaher observed, "with some sense."

"All he wanted was enough to start a business with," Frye explained.

"That's what they all say."

"Well, my dad was always good for his word."

"You favor him?"

"I don't know . . . they always said I favored my mother. She was from right here in Tucson. One of the Kirby girls . . . her dad was a lawyer, W. F. Kirby?"

"I've only been here for a few years," Danaher said. "What did you do, work for your dad?"

"Yes sir. I drove one of his freight wagons."

"Did you help him keep books?"

"Some."

"Your mother saw that coming when she taught you to read and write."

Frye looked at him surprised. "How'd you know that?"

"You don't talk like you came out of the hills, but you haven't had time to go to school. Which did you get tired of first," he said then, "the freight wagon or the ledger?"

"You sure know a lot about me."

"You left, didn't you?"

"Yes sir. I went to work for a man supplying remounts to the cavalry."

"How long did you do that?"

"For him, a couple of years."

"Then you went in business for yourself."

He frowned, the frown changing to a grin as Frye shook his head. "I don't know why I'm doing any talking."

"Did you work alone?"

"I had two Coyotero boys."

"And they taught you a little more."

"A lot more."

"Where'd you sell?"

"Huachuca mostly. I'd just sold a string of bangtails there when Davis said he was going to Galluro and asked did we want to come along."

"Was that tracker of his one of your boys?"

"Dandy Jim? No, he works just for the Fifth Cavalry. My boys quit on the trip before that one, so I took on a partner."

"The one who was with you at Galluro."

"Yes sir. But he didn't like to work much. I was glad when he said no about going with you; that gave me a chance to break our partnership. It was just on a trial."

Danaher was silent. Finally he said, "Then you haven't been back to Randado in about ten years."

"That's right."

"You remember Old Val Sundeen."

"Yes sir."

"And his boy?"

"I remember him. He was about six years older than me then."

"Phil."

"That's right, Phil."

"Did you get along with him?"

"Well—"

"Not too good, uh?"

"Not too."

"Phil's running the spread now. Old Val's got something eating at his insides and he hardly gets out of bed."

Frye said, "That's too bad," frowning.

"You remember R. D. Tindal?"

"I remember Mr. Tindal. He had a girl, Milmary."

"He still does. You remember Beaudry?"

"The name's familiar."

"What about Harold Mendez?"

Frye shook his head. "I don't think so."

"Harold's deputy at Randado, but he's quitting."

"Oh."

"Do you want his job?"

"What does it pay?"

Danaher had expected him to hesitate. He stared at Frye slouched comfortably in the chair returning his gaze calmly. "Seventy-five a month," Danaher answered, "plus a dollar for each drunk and disorderly arrest. You get something else if you have to collect taxes. I suppose it's less than you might make trading horses, but it's steadier. Do you want the job?"

Frye straightened in the chair and said, "I think it'd be fine." Just like that.

You can't be sure, Danaher told himself now, dismounting in front of the Randado jail. Even with Godgiven intuition you can't always judge a man quickly. He told himself that because Frye was only twenty-four and because, more than anything else, he didn't want to be wrong about him.

SIX

"I'm sorry you have to be kept in this cell," Frye said to Dandy Jim, who stood close to him but seemed to be farther away because of the heavy iron bars that separated them. He hesitated. "Listen," he went on, speaking to the Coyotero in Spanish, "I could leave this door open if it would make a difference to you."

The Coyotero seemed to consider this. "Why would it make a difference," he said then, "knowing I must remain here?"

"I promised the soldier in charge that I would hold you until he returned," Frye explained.

Dandy Jim said nothing. He could not understand this and that was the reason he did not speak; and he was not sure if it would be proper to ask why the soldiers had the right to hold him or request of another that he be held. And at the same time, looking at Frye, he tried not to notice his swollen mouth, the bruises on both cheek bones and the left eye which was purple-blue and almost closed. He knew it would not be proper to ask about his disfigurement. Perhaps, though, he could ask about the other since he had known this man many years—

"Tell me," he said, suddenly having decided to ask it, "why is what I did to that woman a concern of the soldiers?"

"I don't understand," Frye answered.

"It was my woman, I found her with another, this Susto if you know him, and did what I had to do."

"When was that?"

"Just before the soldiers came."

Frye was silent. Then, "After you disfigured her you drank the tulapai?"

Dandy Jim nodded.

"With others, and perhaps you made noise?"

"Perhaps."

"To be overheard by someone who might tell the soldiers if it meant a reward?"

"That might be."

"Well, that's why they chased you . . . the tulapai, not because of what you did to your wife." Watching Dandy Jim, Frye could see that this explanation did not seem reasonable to him, so he said, "I'll tell you, without wasting words, that when the Apache drinks tulapai, the soldiers are afraid. That's their reason for taking it away from you."

Dandy Jim said, "When the soldiers drink aguardiente, who takes that from them?"

"No one."

"Is no one afraid of them?"

"Some are, but in a way that is different."

Dandy Jim could not reasonably carry this further, so he said, "Then that about my woman has nothing to do with why I am here."

"I'm almost certain it does not." Frye asked then, "Do you need tobacco?" And when the Coyotero shook his head, he said, "I'll come back again to talk to you."

And when he was gone Dandy Jim thought and continued to think that even this white man whom he had known so many years, even him he did not understand. Something made the white men different from Apache and he did not know what it was. Yes, even this one who could do many things which were Apache, even he was different when you closed your eyes and thought about him, remembering the small things he said which were not really small but kept small because they were things that could not be explained. Like this tulapai thing. He said that soldiers were afraid of the Apache who drank tulapai. That was keeping it simple and small.

And probably he does not approve of what I did to the woman, even though he says I am not being held for that. But it was not his wife, and he did not see her through the willows lying with another man. Susto.

He thought about the woman again, though he had ceased calling her his wife.

It was the tulapai he had been drinking on the way home that brought the rage. He would not have done it sober. Beat her, yes;

but not mutilate her. But even as he thought of it he was angry again. It was not his fault that he was gone most of the time as a tracker for the soldiers. Did she expect him to grow corn? He was a warrior and would fight either for the soldiers or against them and at this time it was not only more profitable, but wiser to fight for them. He was not asked to go against Coyoteros. Only Chiricahuas and sometimes Mimbreños, people he did not usually approve of under any circumstances. But he did it as much for her as for himself and that was what angered him. That while he was away, working to be able to buy cloth and beads as well as ammunition, she would lie with another man. Susto. Susto of all men. She had been a Lipan woman, taken on a raid, and perhaps he should never have trusted her.

No, he was sure Frye did not approve of his treatment of the woman, though this did not show on his face. There was their difference again.

When Frye first became known to him he seldom thought of this difference. That time at San Carlos. And the first day they spoke—

They were just beginning the foot race and the white boy came up to them and asked if he could take part. For weeks he had watched their games while they pretended that he was not watching, but this day he asked if he might join. And while laughing to themselves they told him, seriously, yes he could join them, but would he not like to make a wager? Say his horse? All of this was half in Spanish and half Apache and English and it took time.

Then, after he had put up his horse they told him that of course he knew this was not an ordinary foot race. Dandy Jim himself, Tloh-ka then, pointed, explaining that they would run following the bending course of that arroyo to the clump of mesquite part of the way up the hill ("You will know it by the way it claws at your face"), then back again, a distance of two and a half miles. And, of course, the contestants would be blindfolded, their hands tied behind them and would carry a knife, by the blade, between their teeth. Whoever did not return with a knife still in his mouth would forfeit his horse to the winner of the race. There was an old Coyotero man there to see that each boy abided by the rules which forbade attempting a short cut or trying to trip an opponent.

Twice that afternoon they ran the race and when it was over Kirby Frye still had his horse. He had not won any of the races, but

he still had his horse. Later, years later, Dandy Jim learned Frye
had been practicing this alone for weeks.

There were other games in those days at San Carlos: Apache
games, and in all of them Frye did well and in competing in the
games there was never the thought that this boy was different from
them, not after that first foot race. In time he even spoke some
words of their language.

Thinking of those days now, it occurred to Dandy Jim, that, yes,
they were different even then, because whatever it was that made
them different was inside and must have been present from the
moment of conception. It was just that they did not have the time
then to notice it.

But he is a good man, Dandy Jim thought, and I think it
would be a rare thing to track with him or go to war as his companion . . . to do something which would leave no time for thinking about this difference.

Danaher had been talking to Harold Mendez for almost a
quarter of an hour when Frye came down the stairs. Time enough
to learn how the hanging had taken place and to learn again that
Frye had not been present; though he refrained from asking
what Frye had done about it.

And now, seeing Frye's swollen face, it wasn't necessary to ask.
He felt relief sag inside of him and he exhaled slowly, inaudibly, all
of the tension that he had carried with him from La Noria. Frye
had done something, there was no question about that.

"Kirby, you look a bit worse for wear," Danaher said, sitting
down and pointing with his eyes for Frye to sit down also. "How
do you feel?"

"I don't know. I think all my front teeth are loose."

"Don't eat anything chewy for a while and they'll settle again.
Who did it?"

"Sundeen's jinete."

"Digo the horsebreaker," Danaher said as if reflecting, picturing
him. Then, "What are you going to do about it?"

"I don't know."

"What about Tindal and the others; what're you going to do
about them?"

Frye seemed suddenly worn out and he only shrugged his
shoulders.

Danaher was silent for a moment watching Frye. He told himself to take it easy or he'd lose a deputy. But no, the hell with that, if he wants to quit then let him get out now, out of the way. Baby him and you'll be holding his hand from now on, Danaher thought. So he said, "How long are you going to sit here?"

"I don't know."

"You don't know very much, do you?"

Frye looked up. "What would you do?"

"I'd slap 'em with warrants."

"I don't know if I could do it."

Danaher said, "You've got a gun."

"I walk up to Tindal, and tell him he's under arrest, and if he objects I draw on him."

"You've got it fairly straight," Danaher said, "but I'll write it out if you want."

"John—" Frye hesitated; it was the first time he had called Danaher by his first name. It just popped out and momentarily he looked at Danaher as if expecting him to object, but there was no reaction from him, nothing on Danaher's face to indicate an objection. And Frye thought briefly, flashingly: You make a big thing out of everything. You make a problem out of whether you should use a first name or a mister . . . which was half the reason it didn't go right at De Spain's last night. You were being too respectful, so they shoved it down your throat.

"John," he repeated the name purposely. "Maybe I'm sitting here because I'm afraid. I'll get that out in the open first. But there's something else. Last night Tindal told me that I worked for Randado, that is, the people of Randado. And if the people of Randado elect to have a law their way, one that benefits them as a whole, then I have to go along with the people I serve."

Danaher nodded. "That sounds like Tindal. But there's one thing wrong with the statement. You work for me."

"I know I do, but these are the people right here I actually serve."

Danaher leaned forward in his chair. "Let me tell you something, if you don't already know it," he said quietly. "I'm paid pretty well to keep order in a stretch of land as big as any one man's been asked to watch. I've got people above me, but they give me a free hand; those were my terms. I'm the law here, Kirby. I've got a conscience and God to account to, but I'm the law and when

I say something's wrong, it's wrong . . . until a higher authority proves otherwise." Danaher continued to look at Frye, holding him with his eyes.

"You said you might be scared. Well, I was boogered once, shaking in my boots making my first arrest of a wanted man. After that I took men with me because it was quicker and I no longer had to prove to myself, or to anybody else, I could do it. You proved yourself by standing up to them. Now get some men behind you and slap warrants on Tindal, Beaudry, Stedman, Sundeen and Digo—"

"What about Clay Jordan?" Frye said, because he thought of him suddenly as Danaher named the others and he wanted to see Danaher's reaction.

"Was he here?" Danaher's face showed nothing.

"They say he wasn't in on the hanging."

Danaher paused. "Then don't touch him."

"Do you know him?"

"I know him." Danaher rose saying this.

"He looks like a gun-tipper."

"Don't try to find out," Danaher said.

"I might have trouble getting men to back me," Frye said, "when I pass out the warrants."

"That's your problem. You get paid for figuring out things like that."

Frye's swollen lips formed a smile. "I'll try. But I can't promise anything."

That was all Danaher wanted to hear. He said, "Wire Tucson when you've served them. If I don't hear from you by Wednesday I'll come back."

Frye nodded, but said, "How do you know I won't quit?"

"Kirby," Danaher answered, "I just have to look at your busted face."

SEVEN

"There must be a better way to do this," Harold Mendez said. He was watching Frye, who was sitting at the desk filling in the names on the warrants. The warrants already bore Judge Ira M. Finnerty's illegible scrawl in the lower right corner, which to Frye always seemed proof enough of Danaher's influence—anyone who could get Judge Finnerty to sign blank warrants that would be used sometime in the future—

"Maybe Danaher's right," Frye answered the jailer. "He'd throw them in jail and not make any bones about it."

"But you're not Danaher," Mendez said.

"I just don't think they have to be thrown in jail." The warrants would be served, but instead of jailing them they would be ordered not to leave the vicinity between now and the next court date scheduled for December 18, three weeks away. And since their families and businesses were here Frye decided it wouldn't be necessary for them to post bond. But it will be hard living with them, he thought. Then Judge Finnerty will decide to hold the hearing at Tucson and that will make it all the worse, making them ride eighty-five miles for their comeuppance.

Sunday, the day before, he did not see any of them. He came to the jail in the morning to relieve Harold and to talk to Dandy Jim; but after Danaher left he went back to his room—a boardinghouse down the street—and stayed there through most of the afternoon and evening, not even visiting De Spain's after supper. Let them cool off. Sunday might have a soothing effect on them and it would be easier Monday when he served the warrants.

"Harold, maybe you could find out if Beaudry's about while I visit Tindal and Stedman."

"All right," Harold nodded. "What about Sundeen?"

"I'll go out there about suppertime."

"When his whole crew's in," Harold added.

"I have to serve Digo, too," Frye answered. He left the jail, slipping the warrants into his inside coat pocket, and walked along the shade of wooden awnings to the Randado branch of the Cattlemen's Bank. He glanced across the street to Tindal's store before going inside and he thought of Milmary as he approached the railed-off section of the bank's office.

"Louise, could I see Mr. Stedman?"

The blond girl at the front desk looked up. "He isn't in," she said stiffly.

"Where would he be?"

"I don't know."

"No idea?"

"Maybe he's at dinner."

"It's a little early for that."

"Mr. Stedman doesn't tell me everything he does."

"All right." Frye started to go. "You might tell him I was here."

"Don't worry," the girl said after him.

He crossed the street to Tindal's. Opening the door and closing it with the jingling of the bell, he saw Milmary behind the counter. She was facing the shelves, a writing board in her arm, and Frye knew that she had seen him. She would have turned hearing a customer.

"Mil—"

"Just leave your warrant on the counter and get out of here."

He hesitated. "How do you know I have a warrant?"

"Everybody in town saw Danaher yesterday. Why else would you be here?"

Now it was out in the open and that made it simpler, if nothing else. "I'm looking for your dad."

"I don't know where he is."

"Maybe he's having dinner with Mr. Stedman."

"Why don't you"—she turned suddenly, hesitating as she saw his bruised face, and though her tone was softer she finished—"look for him. Isn't that what they pay you for, looking for criminals?"

"I thought you might save me some steps," Frye said. "Maybe he's at home."

"Maybe he is," Milmary said.

"Or at De Spain's?"

"Or in Mexico! Why don't you just leave?"

"All right, Mil."

"Kirby—"

He was turning to go and now he looked back at her. "What?"

"Who did that to you?" She nodded gently, almost frowning.

"Digo," Frye answered. He hesitated, still looking at her, but slowly her eyes dropped from his. He turned then and left.

Harold Mendez was at the window when Frye opened the door. He nodded to a line of Sun-D horses hitched in front of De Spain's and said, "They came while you were at Tindal's. It looked funny because as you were coming out they were going into De Spain's."

"Is Phil there?"

"Phil and Digo and Jordan and three or four more." Harold's eyes went to the line of horses and he said, "That's right, seven of them."

"I didn't even hear them," Frye said.

"You were thinking of something else," Harold said. He saw Frye look at the rifle rack and then at the desk, then walk over to the desk, not sitting down but only touching it with his fingers, then come over to the window and Harold was thinking: I'm glad I'm not in his shoes; and said, "Did you serve the warrants?"

"Neither one of them were there."

"Something funny's going on," Harold said. "Wordie Stedman was passing and I asked him if he'd seen Mr. Beaudry, but he went right on without stopping."

"He might have had something to do."

"Didn't even look back."

"Well, I don't know—"

"Kirby, the word's out on this warrant business and nobody likes it. That's what it is."

Frye nodded slowly, looking across the street. "It didn't take long for them to find out, did it?"

"They saw Danaher and they know Danaher wouldn't fool around," Harold said. "You know they can make it hard for you to serve those warrants."

"I don't understand that, Harold. Everybody wasn't in on the hanging. Why should they stick up for the few that were?"

Harold shrugged. "Maybe it's just that nobody likes Danaher. Or at least they feel closer to Tindal and Stedman . . . and Beaudry, and it's a matter of principle with them. Like helping out a kin who's in trouble. Not necessarily because you like him, but because he's a him."

Frye said, "Do they feel that way about Sundeen?"

"They don't have to worry about Sundeen. Listen," Harold went on, "probably everybody isn't against you." He hesitated. "But that isn't much consolation because it seems like everybody, doesn't it?"

Frye nodded.

"I know how you feel," Harold said. "I'm glad I don't have to feel that way any more. It's something that comes with the job but isn't important until something like this happens. You know I used to go out of my way to be nice to people . . . always with a good word; then one day I just got sick to my stomach of smiling, and I quit." Harold's eyes went to the window and he said abruptly, "There's Digo on the porch."

"I saw him," Frye said. He nodded. "He's going in again."

"What does that tell you?" Harold said.

Frye was silent, watching the front of De Spain's, and he was thinking: How long will it take? The tails of the horses switched lazily in the sunlight of the street, but the shade of the porch was deserted and nothing moved there.

"What did you say, Harold?" But now he wasn't listening and he knew Harold would not answer. He saw both doors of De Spain's swing open and hold open as they came out: Phil Sundeen first, Digo moving next to him as he started across the street; the one called Jordan was directly behind Sundeen and spreading out behind him were the four other Sun-D riders.

"Harold, unlock the rifles."

"You can't stop all of them."

"Before you do, go up and open Dandy Jim's cell."

"I'll give you a rifle first."

"No . . . get up there quick!"

Frye moved to the door and opened it. In the sunlight, halfway across the street, Sundeen hesitated. As Frye stepped into the doorway Sundeen came on again until less than twenty feet separated them. Digo came even with Sundeen, but Jordan stayed back. He was almost directly behind Sundeen.

Frye watched them, holding himself calm, knowing what would come, but not being sure what to do. They've rehearsed this, he thought, so let them play it.

"I hear," Sundeen called, "you got warrants to serve."

Frye hesitated. "That's right."

"You got one for me?"

Frye nodded.

"One for Digo?"

"That's right."

"What about the Committee?"

"For three of them."

"But they're not about."

Frye nodded again.

"What about Jordan?"

"None for that name."

Sundeen grinned. "None for Mr. Jordan. Why don't you have one for him?"

"He wasn't part of the hanging."

Sundeen stood relaxed. "I don't think that's the reason."

"I don't care what you think," Frye told him.

Sundeen glanced at Digo. "Listen to the boy sheriff."

Digo grinned, looking up from the cigarette he was shaping. "He's something."

"I think you're afraid to put his name on a warrant," Sundeen said. "That's the reason."

"You think whatever you like," Frye answered. Behind him he could hear Harold Mendez coming down the stairs.

Sundeen took a full step to the side, half turning, saying, "I don't believe you met Mr. Jordan."

"Not formally," Frye said.

"Mr. Jordan takes care of my legal affairs." Sundeen nodded to Jordan who was standing directly in line with Frye now, his coat open and his thumbs hooked close to the buckle of his gunbelt.

Frye said, "Then he can advise you about the warrant you're getting."

"He says I'm not going to get one. Digo either."

Now it's coming, Frye thought, holding himself still in the doorway, making himself relax. He didn't know what to say, so he kept his jaw clenched and his eyes steady on Sundeen.

"Jordan says I won't get one 'cause you're not man enough to serve it. He says when a sheriff's got a yellow streak then he's got no authority to serve warrants."

"Do you want it right now?" Frye asked.

"You can try," Sundeen grinned.

"But you'd rather see me try for my gun."

"You might just as well. If your hand went inside your coat how's Jordan to know whether it's for a warrant or a gun. He'd have to protect himself."

"What's he got to do with this?"

"I told you, he's my lawyer. Digo's too." Saying this he glanced at the Mexican. "That's right?"

"Nothing but the best," Digo said, taking the cigarette from his mouth.

"So if you got something to take out of your pocket," Sundeen added, "it's for Mr. Jordan."

Frye's gaze shifted to Jordan, then returned to Sundeen. He hesitated before saying, "You won't try to stop me because that would be resisting arrest, but there's no warrant for him and if I put a hand in my pocket he'll draw and you'll all swear he shot in self-defense . . ."

"This boy's a thinker," Sundeen said to Digo.

"That's if he shoots first," Frye added, and immediately, in the silence that followed, he was sorry he had said it.

Sundeen was grinning again as he turned to Jordan. "You hear what he said?"

Jordan's gaze remained on Frye. "I heard him." This was the first time he had spoken; his voice was calm and his eyes watched Frye almost indifferently though they did not leave him for a moment.

"He thinks he's faster than you are," Sundeen said.

"Maybe he is."

"Only one way to find out."

Jordan nodded, still looking at Frye. "Let's see those warrants."

"They're not for you."

"I didn't ask who they were for."

"I'll serve them when I'm ready."

Jordan nodded slowly. "How's your mother?"

"What?"

"Did she ever get married?"

Frye held back, not answering.

"I hear she works in a can house."

You know what he's doing, Frye thought, and he said quietly, "You're wasting your time."

Sundeen glanced at Digo, his gaze taking in the people standing off beyond Digo, and as his head turned slowly he saw the men gathered on De Spain's porch and in front of the Metropolitan, and on this side of the street the people standing watching as far down as the bank, then his gaze returned to Digo.

"If a man said that to me I'd be inclined to stomp him."

"Unless it was true," Digo said.

"Even then," Sundeen said. "Just on principle."

Frye stepped down from the doorway. He was looking at Sundeen and moved toward him quickly. Then he was standing in front of him, and looking straight ahead, over Sundeen's shoulder, he saw that Jordan had not moved.

"What if I said it to you, Phil?"

"Find out."

"I'll say something else—" Frye's hand brushed into his open coat. "You're under arrest!"

Close to him Sundeen was moving, shifting his weight, and as Frye drew his Colt he swung his left hand against Sundeen's jaw, Sundeen fell away and he was looking straight at Jordan, seeing the gun suddenly in his hand, half seeing the people scattering on De Spain's porch as he brought up his own gun, and he was conscious of himself thinking: Go down! as the rifle report filled the street. He saw the dust flick at Jordan's feet and Jordan suddenly going to the side, firing at the jail, at the doorway and then at both windows.

Get him! It was in Frye's mind as he swung the Colt after Jordan, but Digo moved. He was out of Frye's vision but less than three steps away and in the moment Digo's pistol was out and had chopped down savagely across Frye's wrist.

Stepping to the side Digo looked at Jordan eagerly. Jordan was standing still now watching the jail. "Where is he?"

"He's quit," Jordan answered.

Digo seemed disappointed, saying then, "Let's make sure." He raised his pistol and fired at the front windows, shattering the fragments of glass that remained, and when the gun was empty he called out in Spanish, "Mendez, you son of a whore, show your abusive face!"

Harold appeared in the doorway hesitantly. Seeing him Frye breathed with relief. He heard Jordan say, "Leave him alone."

"We should teach him a lesson," Digo said.

Sundeen picked up Frye's pistol. "We're going to teach both of them a lesson . . . like we did Merl White and his hardhead friends." He grinned watching Frye holding his wrist, bending it gently and opening and closing the hand.

"Digo, help the man off with his boots."

Frye turned to face Digo, who moved toward him with his pistol still in his hand. "Don't try it," he warned the Mexican.

"I've got something to convince you," Digo said.

"Not without bullets—" Frye lunged toward him, but Digo was ready, side-stepping, swinging the long-barreled .44 at Frye's head, but missing as Frye feinted with his body and dodged the blow. He was crouching to go after Digo again when Sundeen's forearm closed over his throat and jerked him off balance. Digo stepped in quickly and swung his free hand into Frey's face, then waited as Sundeen threw him to the ground and straddled him, sitting on his chest.

Digo holstered his pistol. "He's something," he said, shaking his head; then pulled off both of Frye's boots and threw them toward the jail.

Harold Mendez sat down in the street and removed his boots without a word.

From the window directly above the Metropolitan Café sign, Merl White watched them get up as Digo and Phil Sundeen, mounted now, came into view reining their horses behind the two men.

"They better walk faster'n that," Merl said. The two men who had stayed with him were at the window. Haig Hanasian was in the room, but he was seated, not wanting to witness this again. Neither of the men at the window answered Merl. They watched solemnly: Digo yelling now, taking his quirt from the saddle horn and lashing it at Frye's back, forcing him to go into a run, then lashing at Harold Mendez and Harold, starting to run, hunching his shoulders ludicrously and looking back and up toward Digo as if to escape the quirt.

Merl White said, "Which one would you rather have?"

One of the men, Ford Goss, said, "I'd take Digo, with a Henry rifle."

The other man at the window did not answer. He was older than Ford by ten years and was almost completely bald. His name was Joe Tobin.

"I'd take Phil," Merl White said. "I think with an empty whisky bottle."

Ford nodded thoughtfully. "That'd be all right."

"I wouldn't cut him none, not on purpose, but I'd sure as hell bust it over his head."

Joe Tobin said now, "You notice the others aren't in it."

He was referring to the four Sun-D riders who had backed Phil Sundeen a few minutes before, but who were not in sight now.

"They're having a drink," Merl said.

"You can stand just so much," Tobin said. "I don't know how I ever worked a day for a man like Phil Sundeen."

"It was different with Old Val," Merl told him. "Old Val worked you, but he paid pronto at the end of a drive. Sometimes even a bonus."

"Phil won't have any men left now," Tobin said. "He's gone too far."

"I think he's drunk," Merl said, squinting after the two horses nearing the end of the street now.

"He was drunk Saturday," Ford said. "He can be drunk and not show it."

"Everybody was drunk Saturday," Merl said, "but they didn't all go crazy."

"Many of them did," Haig said now, quietly.

Merl White nodded slowly. "I almost forgot about that."

"Jordan's gone too," Joe Tobin told them. "Try and figure him out."

Ford nodded. "It's got to be something against him personally, or something he's paid to do else he won't have a part of it."

"Just to have around," Tobin said, "a man like that would come high."

"He can afford it," Merl said. "Phil could pay us and still afford a dozen men like that."

"But why does he want him?"

"For days like today."

"I'll bet he pays him a hunnert a month."

Merl shrugged. "I guess a gunman comes high . . . just for the good feeling he gives you being around."

Ford was watching the street, pressing his cheek to the glass pane. "They're about out of sight."

"Will you go out and get them tonight?" Merl asked Haig.

"I was going to take you to La Noria."

"We can wait. Fact is," Merl went on, "I wouldn't mind waiting just to have a talk with this Kirby Frye. I think we got something in common."

■ ■ ■

Milmary Tindal moved out to the edge of the walk as they started down the street. She would catch glimpses of Kirby, then Phil or Digo's mount would side-step and she would not see him. When Digo's quirt went up she flinched imagining the rawhide sting and now she could not stand still. She moved along the edge of the sidewalk stretching and leaning to the side to see Kirby. Less than an hour before she had told him to get out of the store. She continued to think of that and even the quirting would not jolt it from her mind. And she was thinking that if she had been kind to him this would not be happening now. There was not time to reason it carefully; it was in her mind in a turmoil watching them move down the street. There was nothing she could do. She could make promises about the future, but right now, even though her nails dug into the palms of her hands and her knuckles showed white, there was nothing she could do.

"Do you think he'll come back?" Edith repeated.

She was in front of the Metropolitan now. Edith Hanasian stood a few feet away on the sidewalk. Milmary looked at her. "What?"

"Do you think he'll come back," Edith repeated.

Milmary was looking down the street again, but now her glance went suddenly to Edith. She had not asked herself that question and uncertainly, fearfully, she heard herself answering, "I don't know."

Edith said, "If you don't know then you haven't been treating him right."

Milmary said nothing. Edith moved to the edge of the walk and stood close to her and looking down the street they saw the horses at the far end now.

"He'll come back," she heard Edith say, and she could feel Edith looking at her closely. "Maybe it won't be for you, but he'll come back."

EIGHT

Kneeling, Frye looked through the pine branches down the slope to the dim outline of the road, then glanced at Harold Mendez hearing him moving toward him.

"What is it?"

"A wagon," Frye said. They could hear the creaking and the labored sound of a pair of horses in harness and Frye was thinking: It couldn't be them, because they wouldn't come out in a wagon. And they wouldn't come out after dark when there are other things to do.

Now they could see the shape of the wagon below them, but there was not enough moon to make out the man on the seat. He moved the team slowly, letting him have their heads going up the grade that rose gradually between the pine slopes.

Frye felt the ground in front of him until his hand found a small enough stone. He waited until the wagon was even with them, then threw the stone. It struck the wagon bed, a sharp sound in the darkness, bouncing out and almost immediately the creaking and the harness rattle stopped.

There was silence. Then from the wagon, "This is Haig Hanasian—" the words carrying clearly in the stillness.

Harold murmured, "That's his voice."

"Up here!" Frye called. He rose and stood at the edge of the jackpines waiting for Haig to reach them.

"I didn't hope to find you so quickly."

Frye took his hand as he reached them. "You came out just to find us?"

Haig nodded.

"We're obliged to you."

"How are your feet?"

"About worn through."

"I brought your boots."

"You found them?"

"They were still in front of the jail."

Frye was smiling. "We're really obliged."

"Perhaps," Haig said, "the boots will not fit now." He pulled two pairs of socks from his pocket. "These will help some. But put them on quickly, it isn't good to delay long on this road. It leads to Sun-D."

"Haig," Frye said. "We appreciate this—"

"Quickly now—"

"You go on back, Haig."

"What?"

"Danaher," Frye explained, "is due to ride by Wednesday sometime. We figured to go back in with him."

"Well," Haig said, "I can't blame you for that, but it's a long time to have to sit here."

"We'd have to hide out anyway, even in town, till we got our bearings."

Haig's dark face was serious, even saying something in a light vein. "That is done every day. This man, White, and his companions have been there since Saturday night."

"Where?"

"In my rooms."

Frye shook his head. "Right across the street."

"I was going to take them to La Noria tonight—"

"We appreciate this, Haig." Frye had spoken to Haig only a few times before this, but suddenly he felt very close to him. But he felt sorry for him at the same time and he wasn't sure why.

"Merl White is anxious to meet you."

"I guess we have something in common."

"He said the same thing." Haig lifted a .25-caliber revolver from his coat pocket and handed it to Frye. "Take this. I'd better get the wagon moving." He started to go, but stopped. "You don't have any food."

Frye shook his head. "We figured we'd grub around and make out. There's a spring back a ways." He nodded toward the deep pines.

"Tomorrow you'll have food," Haig said. "And I'll bring something for your feet." He hesitated again. "You don't have blankets."

"Or clean sheets," Harold Mendez said.

"Wait a moment," Haig told them. He hurried down the slope and returned with a rolled tarpaulin over his shoulder. "This will help some."

"Haig," Frye said, "we owe you a lot."

"You don't owe me anything. God forgive me, but I would like to see something bad happen to this Sundeen." He started to go. "You say Danaher comes Wednesday?"

Frye nodded. "That's what he said."

"To make sure, I could go to Huachuca tonight and wire him."

"He'll come," Frye said.

"I want to be there when he does," Haig said, and after that he left.

As they strung up the canvas shelter they could hear his wagon far down the grade, the faint creaking fading to silence as they gathered wood for a fire. And when the fire was burning they sat close to it, listening to the silence, then becoming aware of the night sounds, the crickets and the soft hissing of the wind through the pines.

"I'm going to quit," Harold murmured, staring into the fire. "I don't have to take this."

Frye watched the fire and said nothing.

After a moment Harold asked, "What are you going to do?"

"I'm not sure," Frye answered. "Right now, sleep."

But he did not sleep, not for some time, thinking of Danaher coming and what would happen when they rode into Randado. He knew what he would do. He was sure, even though he told Harold he wasn't sure. There was no sense in arguing with Harold. If Harold wanted to quit that was his business.

You don't have to do it though. You don't *have* to do anything. But you will, huh? You'll go through with it and have it out with Phil Sundeen and Digo . . . and Jordan, if that's the way it has to be. And Tindal and the others. Don't leave them out. "You're under arrest . . . Mr. Tindal." What do you call a man when you arrest him?

You should have stuck to mustanging.

Danaher will back you, but probably he'll give you another chance to do it by yourself if you want. He'll say, "Kirby, this is your jurisdiction. If you see fit, handle it your own way, with your own deputies. I'll only make suggestions." The Danaher let's-see-what-kind-of-a-man-you-are test. And if you're smart you'll say, "John, you can take this job and—" But something won't let you say that and you'll see it through now. Are you mad enough to see it through? Danaher said he just had to look at your beat-up face. And after what they did this morning—You're damn right I'll see it through.

Something will happen soon now to end it . . . one way or another. And that's good because it should never have started. A silly damn thing that's grown . . . no, it wasn't silly, not hanging two men, but it was stupid . . . and now there's a chance more will be dead before it's over. Sundeen will fight. Maybe he doesn't want to; maybe he knows he's gone too far, but he's not the kind who'd admit it. Like Harold said, a man who rides his horse into a saloon doesn't have to have a reason. And he didn't hire a gunman out of humility. It's too bad there isn't a way he can back down and still hold on to his self-respect. No, you have to beat him, beat him once and for all.

Tindal and the others, that's something else. They might give themselves up. If they did, Judge Finnerty would probably go light. Maybe just a fine, because he's known them all his life. They know they did wrong, else they wouldn't have run this morning. So maybe there isn't any problem . . . except living with them after. "Mr. Tindal . . . sir . . . you're under arrest." "Mr. Tindal, I wonder if I might marry your daughter . . . while you're in jail."

Wouldn't that be just fine.

You better ask Mil first.

But most of the time, until he fell asleep, he thought of Phil Sundeen, his horsebreaker and his hired gunman.

Sundeen came to Randado again late Wednesday morning. He brought with him Digo and Jordan and they went directly to De Spain's. Many of his riders had left during the past two days, including the four who had been present when he ran off Frye and Mendez, and he believed that if they were still around he would find out at De Spain's.

Sundeen stood at the bar, but Jordan and Digo took a bottle and glasses to a table.

"He drinks too much," Jordan said.

Sitting down at the table, Digo shrugged. "He holds it . . . and it's his money."

"And the more he drinks, the less you have to work."

"Watching him is work in itself."

"It's starting to wear thin."

"You get used to it," Digo told him.

"How long have you been at it?"

"Almost since the day he was born." Digo smiled. "I taught him to ride . . . how to break a horse . . . how to drink. I taught him many things."

Jordan's gaze left Sundeen standing at the bar and returned to Digo. "And now there's nothing left to teach."

Digo nodded. "Now I watch. I told this one's father I would watch him, so that's what I do."

Jordan's eyes went to Sundeen again, who stood with his elbows on the bar and his back to them talking to De Spain behind the bar. "Was his father like that?"

"At times. But he worked harder than this one," Digo said. "I've been with him twenty years and I know. He saw that the work was done and then he drank. This one does what he feels like. He always has. Even when the father was strong and would try to break him with his fists, this one continued his own way . . . and now it's that father who's broken. When there was no strength left to use on him, the old man said, 'Digo, watch him—' He gave me my name, Digo. Once it was Diego, but the old man said it Digo and now everyone does. He said, 'Digo, watch him as I would.' " The horsebreaker closed his eyes as if to remember the words. "He said, 'Watch him and keep him alive as long as he's bad, for if he dies the way he is, his next meal will be in hell.' " Digo grinned. "That was something for the old man to say, uh?"

"What about his mother?"

"She never counted. And now she's dead anyway."

Phil Sundeen came over to the table. He pulled out a chair and put his foot on it and stood leaning on his leg, looking at no one in particular. "De Spain says they haven't been in since Monday morning. And this is—"

"Wednesday," Digo said. "That's four more men you don't have."

"They might turn up. If they don't, so what? I can sign four waddies any day of the week."

"Eleven more," Jordan reminded him. "Counting the three you chased off Saturday."

"All right, eleven. I'd let go almost that many over the winter anyway. I don't need riders to scatter hay and drop salt licks. That's farmer work."

"If you don't care," Jordan said, raising his eyes to look at Sundeen, "why did we ride all the way in to look for them?"

Sundeen looked down at Digo. "He's the serious type."

"I think so," Digo answered. This was when he liked Phil the best, when he kidded with a straight face.

"The serious ones are always worried about little things," Sundeen said. "Like where to pick hands."

"I've noticed that in life," Digo said. "Some even pray before they know they're going to die."

Phil nodded. "That's the serious type."

Jordan leaned back in his chair placing his hands gently on the edge of the table. He said to Phil, "Remember what that boy said when I tried to prod him into a fight? I insulted his mother and he told me I was wasting my time."

"He was scared to fight," Sundeen said.

"Maybe so, under those conditions. But he didn't rile up and get shot. He held on until he saw an opening . . . one that you made."

Sundeen said, "What's the point?"

"The point is you tend to underestimate people. You chased that boy out of town and you don't think you'll ever see him again. Just like you think you and Digo can go on joshin' back and forth and I'll sit here and listen as long as you keep it up."

Sundeen said, "Digo . . . that's what I mean by the serious type."

Jordan rose. "I'm going to eat."

Sundeen just nodded, then followed him with his eyes as he left De Spain's.

"Don't think what you're thinking," Digo said.

Sundeen grinned. "And what's that?"

"You'd try anything once."

"How do we know he's fast? Just because somebody else said so."

"Just look at him."

"You can't go by that."

"You didn't see him draw when Harold Mendez opened up."

"Fast?"

"Fast! Listen." Digo said earnestly, "there isn't anybody in this country can touch him. I'd bet my life on it."

Sundeen shrugged. "You know how things enter our head."

"Keep that one out," Digo said, and exhaled silently as Phil straightened up, pushing the chair under the table.

"I'm going to get something to eat."

"It sounds good," Digo said.

"You get back home. Somebody's got to work."

Digo shrugged. "All right. But don't run off any sheriffs without me."

Now it was almost noon and half of the tables in the Metropolitan were occupied. Sundeen glanced at the men sitting along the counter and then his eyes went down the row of tables. There he was. Jordan. Sundeen walked toward him, but beyond he saw Tindal and Stedman sitting together and he walked past Jordan who looked up at him but said nothing.

Stedman half rose, holding his napkin to his stomach. "Phil . . . how are you?"

Tindal made himself smile, offering, "Sit down, Phil."

Sundeen pulled out one of the chairs and stepped over it sitting down.

"That's just what I meant to do." He was grinning, looking from Tindal to Stedman and said, "Haven't seen you in a few days."

"We were away," Tindal explained evasively, "on business."

"That's what I'm told."

Stedman pushed his plate forward putting his elbow on the table. "Earl Beaudry's thinking about buying some property in La Noria. Wanted us to take a look at it."

"You missed a show the other morning," Sundeen said.

Tindal nodded and now his face was serious. "You shouldn't have done that, Phil."

"You heard about it?"

"It's all over everywhere."

"Yeah, I suppose it got to La Noria else you wouldn't be back."

Stedman held his eyes on Sundeen. "Do you think we left for any other reason than because Earl asked us to come with him?"

Sundeen shook his head, grinning. "George, you old bastard, you should have been on that stage."

"Phil, I swear, when we left we didn't know Danaher was in town."

"Everybody else did."

"We can't help that."

"Why didn't Earl come back?"

"He's still looking at the property."

"Look," Tindal said, lowering his voice then, "we got no reason to lie."

Edith Hanasian came to their table and handed Sundeen a menu. His had touched her arm as he took it and she drew back.

"What's the matter, Edith?"

She returned his stare, but not his smile. "What do you want?"
Phil winked at her. "The special."

"What else?"

"Edith"—his grin widened—"you're somethin'."

"I mean to drink."

"Coffee." He was still grinning, watching her walk back to the kitchen.

"Phil, what about Kirby?" Tindal was leaning close to the table. "Is he coming back?"

"He's got no reason to."

"He won't just sit down and forget this."

"He doesn't have any choice."

"Hell he hasn't," Tindal said anxiously. "He'll go to Danaher."

"That's a long barefooted walk to Tucson."

"Phil," Stedman said as seriously as he knew how. "You got to do something."

"Like what?"

"I don't know. Explain to Danaher you were drunk and didn't mean anything by it. You're a big enough man, the most he'll do is fine you a little bit."

Sundeen looked at Stedman for a long moment. "What do you mean *you*?"

"Well, it was you that ran Kirby out."

Sundeen's face relaxed. "Why, I was working by request of the Committee. After the trouble he caused Saturday night you said we needed a new deputy and would I ask this one to leave."

Tindal's mouth opened, but no sound came from him. Stedman's words were a hoarse whisper, saying, "We never told you that!"

Sundeen shrugged. "Danaher would believe it whether it was the truth or not after the stunt you pulled Saturday."

"We can explain that to him," Stedman said hastily, "but not running off a deputy!"

"Well, now you'll have to explain both." Sundeen leaned back as Edith placed his dinner in front of him. He said pleasantly, "Where's Haig?"

"He's around."

"That's too bad, isn't it?"

She turned away without answering.

"Phil!" Tindal's tone was impatient. "You've got to think of something!"

Sundeen watched Edith until she reached the kitchen.

"That's what I'm doing."

"Be serious for a minute!"

Sundeen raised his fork and pushed it into the fried potatoes. He picked up a slice of ham with his fingers and curled it, biting off a piece. "Let me tell you something," he said, chewing the ham. "Everything I did, you did. And everything you did, I did. That includes Earl Beaudry looking over property down in La Noria. Now shut up while I eat."

They remained silent, stirring their coffee, letting it get cold and finally pushing the cups away untouched. When he was finished Sundeen stood up, taking a toothpick from the table. "Come on. I'll buy you a drink."

Stedman said absently, "I'd just as soon not."

"George, I'm not askin' you."

They went next door to De Spain's and stood at the bar, Sundeen leaning with his back against it, enjoying Tindal and Stedman's discomfort and watching Jordan, who had left the café before they did, sitting alone at a table now reading a three-day-old Tucson newspaper.

"Look at my lawyer," Sundeen said, amused. "He's not worryin'... and he's the serious type."

Jordan looked up, but said nothing.

Stedman finished his drink, scowling at the taste of it. "I've got to get back." He hesitated, as if expecting Sundeen to object.

"I do too," Tindal said. Stedman moved away from the bar and Tindal followed him. "We'll see you later."

"All right." Sundeen nodded and watched them head for the door. Stedman put his hand on the knob, but stepped back clumsily against Tindal as the doors swung in abruptly.

Digo pushed past them. He was breathing heavily moving toward Sundeen and one word came from him as a gasp—

"Danaher!"

NINE

Frye swung down from behind Danaher and went to the jail as Danaher's posse tied up along both sides of the street. Twelve men. He recognized a few of them: three men who had been with Danaher at Galluro Station. Two others were deputies from Sonoita and Canelo. Danaher had picked them up on the way down from Tucson. All of them were heavily armed; grim-faced men who spoke little and watched Danaher for orders.

There had been fifteen originally. Three were now scouting the Sun-D buildings. To Danaher this was merely going through the motions. He knew Phil Sundeen, and he was moderately certain where to find him.

From the jail doorway Frye glanced back seeing Danaher going toward De Spain's. He's not fooling, Frye thought. And neither are the rest of them.

Dandy Jim was sitting on the floor with his back against the wall and he rose as Frye entered the office, seeing the look of surprise on Frye's face.

"I thought you'd be gone."

"If you thought that," Dandy Jim said, "why did you have that man bring food yesterday and today?"

"Well, I wasn't sure, so I mentioned it to him." He had told Haig about Dandy Jim when Haig came out to them Tuesday morning.

"He said that he saw you"—the Coyotero spoke in Spanish—"and that you would come back soon."

Frye asked, "You saw what took place the day before this?"

Dandy Jim nodded. "All of it."

"Have you seen those men today?"

"They left hurriedly before you came."

Frye's eyebrows raised. "Will you wait here?" When the Coyotero nodded he added, "Only a short time," and went out, crossing the street to De Spain's.

As he pushed through the doors, De Spain was saying, "Sundeen wanted to fight. He'd been drinking all morning and the idea of a posse on the way seemed to appeal to his sporting blood. I'd never seen a man so eager to fight . . . until Digo reminded him he didn't have enough men. Digo kept saying, 'Man, you lost eleven already—' "

Following De Spain's glance Frye saw Merl White. He was standing next to Danaher and behind him was Haig Hanasian.

"You see, besides Merl and Ford and Joe Tobin," De Spain went on, "some more left after the stunt Phil pulled with Kirby. Phil knew they had quit, but it looked as if it didn't really sink in until that moment. Still, he wasn't going to budge and he told Digo, 'Well, go on home and get who's left!' But Digo argued there was no way of telling if any of the other men were still about, and if he rode all the way to Sun-D, then came back without anybody, it would be too late to dodge Danaher's posse. Phil argued back, but you could see it sinking in that suddenly he was almost alone . . . that Phil Sundeen, who owned the biggest spread in San Rafael, had only Digo and a hired gunman left."

Danaher broke in, "Jordan's still with him?"

De Spain nodded. "He was when they left. You see Digo kept it up, looking like a crazy man the way he was pleading, and finally Phil said, 'All right, we'll ride out.' He looked at me then and said, 'But you tell 'em I'm coming back!' "

"I don't think he'll be that obliging," Danaher murmured. "What kind of a start did they have?"

"Not two hours," De Spain told. "But Tindal and Stedman should slow them down some."

Danaher's eyes showed surprise. "They're along?"

"They were here when Digo came in," De Spain said. "They tried to leave but Phil held them and said, by God, if he was running then they were too. They argued and pleaded until Phil pulled his gun and told them he wasn't going to hear any more." De Spain shook his head. "They were a couple of sorry sights riding off with him."

Danaher said, "But Earl Beaudry wasn't there?"

"I haven't seen him in four days."

"They didn't say where they were going?"

"No. They couldn't go toward Sun-D because you were coming

from that direction. Though it seems to me as they were going out Digo said something about circling around to Sun-D and seeing who's about, then meeting Sundeen later."

"I hope he does," Danaher said. "He'll find three men there I'm sure of. Three of mine."

Later on, while they were in the Metropolitan eating—Frye, Danaher, and the Sonoita and Canelo deputies sitting at a table together—a man came in from the street and went straight to Danaher.

"John"—he was excited and grinning, eager to see Danaher's reaction—"you sure must live right. Those three boys you mentioned watching Sun-D . . . they just brought in Digo!"

They walked across the street, pushing through the men crowding in front of the jail. Frye went in first, seeing Dandy Jim and then Digo, Digo sitting in a chair against the wall and a man standing close to him on both sides; but Danaher stopped in the doorway. He told the men outside to go over to De Spain's and take it easy.

Turning, he looked at Digo, then to the two men guarding him. "Go have a drink, boys."

They moved reluctantly and one of them said, "John, maybe you'll need a hand," glancing at Digo as he said it.

"I got two of my own," Danaher told him. "Close the door behind you." He waited until he heard it slam and then he removed his coat, not taking his eyes from Digo who sat low in the chair watching him. Danaher folded the coat deliberately and draped it over the chair by the desk.

Frye half sat on the edge of the desk with one foot on the chair. Dandy Jim stood near him. Frye moved slightly as Danaher lifted his revolver and placed it on the desk, then watched Danaher as he moved toward Digo again.

"Where'd they go, horsebreaker?"

The Mexican's chin was close to his chest, but his eyes were lifted watching Danaher and he did not answer.

Danaher stepped closer. "Where did they go?"

Digo did not move, looking up at Danaher sullenly.

"Once more. Where did they go?"

"Gimme a cigarette—"

He was saying it as Danaher hit him; his head snapped back and his eyes came full awake and he put his hand to his face.

"When I ask a question, you answer it."

"I don't know where they went."

"You were to meet them."

"No, we split up."

"You were to check for riders and then meet them."

Digo shrugged. "You know so much, why ask me?"

Danaher hit him again, his right fist landing solidly against Digo's cheek.

"The next time I'll knock you out of the chair."

Digo's hand covered the side of his face. "We did not have a place to meet."

"Maybe you've just forgotten it."

"Maybe that's it."

"Be careful, Digo."

"Listen . . . I don't know where they went!"

"You were to meet them tonight."

"There was no plan."

Danaher glanced at Frye, who had not moved from the desk and was smoking a cigarette now, and then to Dandy Jim. "We got a boy," Danaher said to Digo, "who could pick up their sign within an hour."

Digo shrugged. "All right."

"We're giving you a chance to square yourself."

"I didn't ask for favors."

"If you helped of your own accord, Judge Finnerty would go light on you."

"Go to hell."

Digo saw it coming and brought his shoulder around, but Danaher's right hand tightened in the air and the left hand swung viciously against the exposed side of Digo's face. The chair went over and Digo sprawled on the floor.

He came to his hands and knees slowly, his eyes raised to Danaher. And as he brought his legs under him, he lunged. Danaher was waiting. He shifted his weight and his right hand swung like a mallet against Digo's head. The Mexican staggered and Danaher hit him with the other fist. Digo gasped as Danaher found his stomach. He tried to cover, but Danaher's fists broke through his guard. A jab to the head straightened Digo and a right cross slammed him against the wall.

Danaher picked up the chair, then helped Digo into it.

"I was saying, it would be easier on you if you cooperated."

Digo's mouth was bleeding and he touched his jaw, moving it gently.

"We're trying to help you."

"You know where you can put that," Digo muttered.

Danaher's arms were folded; but suddenly they uncoiled and his right fist lashed back-handed across Digo's face.

"First we want proper respect. Then the right answers."

Digo held his sleeve to his mouth, wiping it gently. "I can tell you nothing."

"Maybe," Danaher stated, "they went north."

"I don't know."

"Over toward Tubac?"

"I don't know."

"Or South. To La Noria."

"He didn't tell me."

"First to La Noria, then over the border."

"You're wasting your time."

"I've got more of it to waste than you have."

Digo's eyes stayed on the sheriff, but he said nothing.

"You know why?"

Digo shook his head. "Why?"

"Because before Christmas you'll be dead."

Digo shrugged.

"You'll hang for taking part in that lynching . . . even though it wasn't your idea."

"Maybe it was."

"Why should you protect Phil Sundeen?"

"He pays me."

"His old man pays you."

"One or the other—"

"What will you do after we hang Phil?"

"You won't hang him."

"Why not?"

"He has influence."

"All right," Danaher said, "then we'll hang you and shoot him."

"What do you mean?"

"I'll give orders to shoot him on sight. Sound asleep, taking a bath or sittin' in the outhouse, shoot him . . . and then bring him in."

Digo was silent. "But," he said finally, "you have to find him first."

"Which brings us around again," Danaher said. "Maybe you were to meet him somewhere on Sun-D land."

"He didn't say."

"In a line shack."

"He didn't say."

"Let's try the Huachucas."

Digo nodded. "All right."

Danaher's face tightened. "Watch yourself."

"You don't scare me."

Danaher stood close to him, looking down and both fists were clenched. "Digo, before the night's over I'll break you."

"I can wait."

Danaher moved a half step and his fist slammed into Digo's chest. He tried to rise, Danaher letting him, but it was momentary. Digo was pushing up, both hands on the arms of the chair, and Danaher hit him again, in the stomach and then in the face, standing in close, keeping Digo pinned against the chair, now driving both fists, grunting as he hit the Mexican, not hurrying because Digo could no longer defend himself. And when he stepped back Digo sunk into the chair, his arms hanging over the sides, and did not move.

"I've had them that tough before," Danaher said, moving to the desk. "Not many hold out."

Frye said, "He won't tell you anything if he's dead."

"If he won't alive," Danaher said, "then what difference does it make?"

"Dandy Jim asked me what you were doing. I told him and he said, 'There are many better ways to do it.' "

"I was giving him a chance, not like the Apache does it," Danaher said. "He could fight back any time he wanted."

"If he could get out of the chair."

"Don't you approve, Kirby?"

"It's none of my business."

Danaher looked at him, trying to read more than was on Frye's face, then he picked up his coat. "I'm going across the street."

"Maybe I'll work on him while you're gone," Frye said.

Danaher studied him again. "You do that, Kirby." He went to the door, but looked back before opening it. "Let me know if he tells, huh?"

When the door closed, Frye went to Digo. He pulled him forward in the chair, then stooping, let Digo fall across his shoulders.

He stood up and this way carried the man up the stairs, into the cell that the two Mexicans had occupied and lowered him to the bunk. He stepped into the hall and poured water into a cup from a canvas bag that was hung there for the prisoners, then returned to Digo and raised his head gently to let the water trickle between the man's swollen lips.

Digo's eyes opened. His hand went to the cup and he emptied it drinking thirstily.

"More?"

"A little."

Frye returned with the cup filled and handed it to him. He made a cigarette while the man drank and lighted it and when Digo handed him the cup he offered the cigarette. Digo took it hesitantly, then inhaled and blew out the smoke slowly.

"When do you take your turn?" Digo asked.

"Do you think I should?"

"You have a good opportunity." Digo's eyes raised to Frye. "If it was the other way around, if I was in your shoes, I'd take a turn."

"Danaher's doing all right."

"He's doing too good."

"Just keeps it up, doesn't he?" Frye said.

"I think he must be crazy."

"That's the way he is when he makes up his mind to something," Frye said. "He stays with it. Good for his word."

"He doesn't scare me."

"Then you're in for some more."

"That's all right."

"John gets mad and he keeps most of it inside . . . for a while. Then he has to blow off steam, like poking his fist through a door. The less you talk, the madder he gets." Frye paused. "But this time he's lucky."

"What do you mean?"

"He can blow it off on Phil."

"If he finds him," Digo said.

"There's nothing to that," Frye said. "You saw that Coyotero boy. He's the best tracker ever read sign. It would just be a matter of time." Frye grinned. "With old Danaher getting madder and madder."

"You mean that about shooting him on sight—"

"You think he was kidding? Listen, that man's word is gospel."

"I thought he was just talking."

"Danaher doesn't just talk."

Digo shook his head. "If he's so sure of getting him why does he question me?"

"It could save him a day or two if you told."

"Giving Sundeen that much more time."

"It wouldn't matter," Frye said. "Phil doesn't have a chance. And all the time the steam's building up in Danaher."

Digo was silent. He said angrily then, "This is none of his business! Why is he here?"

"Just to help out."

"Why don't you do your own work?"

"If he wants to help out it's all right with me."

Digo looked at Frye intently and asked, "Would you shoot him on sight?"

"Well, I've got no reason to."

"You'd try to arrest him for trial?"

"Probably." He knew what Digo was thinking, that if Sundeen stood trial he would most likely get off with little more than a fine. Digo had used the word influence before and there was truth to that.

"This is your territory. Would Danaher let you handle it yourself?"

"If I asked him."

"Listen." Digo was breathing heavily and his face was alive with what he was about to say. "It would be senseless for him to die just because Danaher is a madman."

"Go on."

Digo said it quickly. "If you promise to handle this yourself I'll tell where he is."

"How do you know you can trust me?"

Digo shook his head violently. "Keep Danaher off of Phil . . . swear it to God or I won't tell you!"

Frye stooped close to Digo. He said quietly in Spanish, "Where is he, man?"

"Promise in the name of God—"

Frye nodded. "I promise."

But Digo hesitated. His swollen face was strained and he closed his eyes as if in pain. "Give me another cigarette," he said, relaxing. He took it from Frye and smoked it down as he convinced himself that this was the right thing. Keep Phil alive. Perhaps it would break some of him, but it would keep him alive. He rolled toward Frye and whispered close to his ear, even though they were alone in the cell.

Danaher closed the door behind him as Frye came down the stairs.

"Where is he?"

"Upstairs."

"Did you work on him?"

Frye nodded, and he could see that Danaher was keeping himself from smiling.

"Did he tell where Phil is?"

Frye nodded again. "La Noria. You guessed it once yourself, John."

Danaher stared. There was nothing he could say.

TEN

"They got no business coming here," Earl Beaudry said.

Behind him, sitting at the table, the woman watched him as he stood in the doorway looking past the deserted bandstand with its grayed wooden awning to the row of two-story adobes across the square. One of these was the La Noria Cantina and lettered on the weathered expanse of wall next to it was the one word, MOCTEZUMA. Now, in the evening dusk, with rain clouds approaching, the word was obscure, losing its meaning in the fading light, though its form stood out against the pale adobe.

The woman watched him and said nothing. This was her adobe, hers alone since the death of her husband three years before; though when Earl Beaudry came she assumed a different role: the submissive role she had known so well when her husband was alive. When this mood was on him it was better not to speak at all unless he asked a direct question.

"Why did they have to come?" Beaudry muttered.

Her eyes lifted, looking at the back of his head. No, that was not a question expecting an answer. He was talking to himself. It was bad when he was in this mood. Like Sunday night when he had beaten her for no reason at all. But he was good to her, too. He brought printed cloth . . . and flour and chocolate and— One learned to accept the good with the bad. Sometimes though, she was thinking now, it was better to speak out, then take the beating and it would be out of his system.

She was a handsome woman, firmly built, and the part of her blood that was Tarahumare showed strong in the clean dark features of her face.

"As long as they are not in this house," the woman said, "what difference does it make if they are here?"

Beaudry turned from the door, not answering her question, but came to the table and lifted the mescal bottle that was there and poured some of it into the glass he held. He had been drinking the mescal all day and it showed in his eyes and in the way he breathed with his mouth open, the corners of his mouth filmed with the colorless liquor. He returned to the doorway and looked across the square as he sipped the mescal, and now it began to rain.

"What difference does it make if they are here?" the woman said again.

"Just keep still."

"It would be less cold with the door closed," and as she said it she wondered if this might not be going too far. But he did not turn and now she knew that whatever it was that bothered him was a grave matter.

She was a simple woman and she said, "Are you thinking of your wife?"

This time he looked at her. "God, no!"

Then it was something else. Often, when he was silent and did nothing but drink mescal, she believed he was thinking of his wife, thinking that it was too bad she existed. Men did that, she knew. Even unattractive men such as this one. They felt that their wives were great weights and if they could be free of them they would be men again.

This one came here thinking himself irresistibly virile (until he slipped into his black mood), reliving a part of him that had been dead for a dozen years. Even being a simple woman she could see the kind of man that he was: at home, speaking words to his wife only when it was necessary and sentences only when they were arguing; but most of the time silent, thinking what a great beast she was, a dumb-eyed animal without feeling, a woman who no longer knew what it was to be a woman, and no longer cared. These were the men who never looked at themselves, yet wandered from home.

Even when he came here picturing himself something else, the Mexican woman knew this about him; but she did not mind it and she thought of it little, having learned to accept the good with the bad. She did feel obligated to respect him. A man from the village had told her Señor Beaudry owned . . . how many? . . . thousands of varas of land. And he did no work! Something was said how he allowed others to use the land and they paid him for it. But, the woman would think, it is too bad he isn't attractive.

Beaudry turned now and said, speaking to himself more than to the woman, "He's over there lappin' it up, not caring a damn what happens."

"Who is?" the woman asked.

"Phil Sundeen."

"He was not here Sunday?" She could not remember the names of the two men who had come, but she knew neither had been called Sundeen.

"That was Tindal and Stedman," he said, answering the question that was in her mind.

And it occurred to her as he said their names what it was that must be bothering him. The hanging of the two La Noria men. Sunday the three of them had talked about it over and over again and in the end there had been an argument because Beaudry would not go back with them.

Tindal and Stedman. Those were the ones. Both of them beyond the middle of life, like Beaudry, though they dressed better than he did and they used language that was less coarse. She remembered now they had seemed frightened when they left. As Earl was now.

"I thought there were four of them," the woman said, remembering how they looked entering the square earlier that evening, riding almost single file.

Beaudry looked at her intently. "You've got a lot of questions."

The woman shrugged. "It doesn't matter."

"The other one works for Sundeen. That makes four."

"They are all your friends, but you don't want them here?"

"Friends," Beaudry muttered, "bringin' the law on me."

She did not understand this fully, but it seemed reasonable to say, "Then why don't you ask them to leave?"

He poured another drink before turning from her and this time didn't bother to answer.

Why don't you ask them to leave? Across the square, now, light showed in the two windows of the cantina. Why don't you ask Phil Sundeen to quit drinkin' and join the monastery? That'd make about as much sense. A woman's brain is just big enough to take her from the stove to the bed. For anything else it's got to strain. Ask them to leave . . . just like that. "Phil, you and your friends move along. This is my home . . . my second home, but I got first rights to its use." "Why sure, Earl, we'll pack up and be out by the thirty-second of December." Beaudry swore under his breath. In the doorway he could feel a mist of rain against his face as the

breeze changed. All right. You can't talk nice to him. "Phil—"
Look him square in the eyes and stand close and don't hardly move
your mouth. "Phil, I'm not buyin' any more of that. You're not out
of here in ten minutes I'll come for you with a gun!"

His elbow touched the bulk of the Colt beneath his coat as he
looked across to the two lighted windows. The gun was the answer.
But why take a chance facing him head on? (He allowed it to be in
his mind, as if challenging Phil Sundeen was one way; although
there was not even a remote possibility he would bring himself to
do it.) The gun brought out the ultimate plan. The gun and the
lighted windows.

Now if he were to throw some shots inside, not trying to hit anybody—If he pulled it right they'd think *posse*. Sure, the first thing
they'd think of . . . a big *posse!* They'd run. By God they'd run to
China!

He turned to the woman abruptly. "Didn't I bring a rifle this
trip?"

You can smell a Mexican pueblo, Frye thought to himself. Even
with the rain. Not a soul in the square and the adobes without windows look deserted, but you can always smell the good smell of
the mesquite cook fires. If it wasn't raining there'd be people sitting by that bandstand. He was thinking then that La Noria was
like a lot of pueblos; crumbling sun-dried adobe out in the middle
of nowhere, but with people in it to make the cook-fire smells and
keep it alive.

Frye was standing at the edge of an aspen thicket looking
through the rain drizzle and across the open one hundred yards to
the wide break between the adobes that showed the square. The
bandstand, a dim outline of it, was on a straight line with his eyes
and he knew that the cantina was along the row of adobes on the
right. Merl White was next to him and Dandy Jim was one step
behind.

He'll be in the cantina, Frye thought, thinking of Sundeen. Bet
all you've got and borrow more to put on it, that's where he'll be.
If he's not, then he's changed his ways—and you'd better change
yours.

Turning his head, keeping his voice low, he said, "Merl, would
you say he'd be in the cantina?"

Merl nodded and water rolled off the curled brim of his hat. "I
wouldn't think about it twice," he said.

"Just go in?"

"We could wait for them to come out."

"Which could be a wet all night," Frye said.

"Let's just go in and get it over with."

"All right. You want to get the others?"

Merl said he would and moved back through the trees. Dandy Jim waited with Frye.

Now, waiting, listening to the rain, Frye thought: You shouldn't ask a question when you tell somebody what to do. He shrugged within himself. You don't have to kick Merl in the tail. No, it's not a question of the man. If you're in an order-giving position then give the damn order and don't be so damn hesitant. You don't say, "Do you want to get the others?" What if he'd said no? Watch Danaher and learn a few things. Learn how to tell men what to do.

He felt very much alone now, even though Dandy Jim was a step away from him, and he thought: I wonder if Danaher ever feels all by himself? Like the night after Galluro and John hit that man for smoking out in the open. I'll bet he felt all alone that night. It probably goes with the job. You better watch Danaher and learn how to give orders and meet the cold looks that come back half the time. But he'll be watching you tonight.

Frye had told Danaher his promise to Digo. He had promised to bring Sundeen back himself, without shooting. Danaher had agreed. This is what he had hired him for. If he didn't care to use his gun, that was all right. As long as he brought him in. Danaher mentioned that the shooting Sundeen on sight business was half scare anyway. Then Frye asked Danaher if he'd care to come along and Danaher said yes without hesitating.

Frye turned now, hearing the others coming up through the trees. He saw Danaher and he thought for one last time: Just tell them.

Merl White and the two other ex-Sun-D riders, Ford Goss and Joe Tobin, were following Danaher and behind them were a half dozen men Danaher had brought along to "fill out the posse."

Frye waited for all of them to come up close. "Merl and Dandy and I," he said then, "are going into the square. The rest of you will wait till we pass the first adobe, then John"—he nodded to Danaher—"you and two of your men will follow to back us up. You other four men will stay here with the horses, mounted in case anybody slips through us."

He looked at Ford Goss and Joe Tobin. "The cantina is on the

right. The . . . fourth adobe down, next to a wall. You'll recognize
it. Skirt around the back from here and watch the rear door."

Ford Goss said, "Do we shoot if they come out?" Almost as if
he were anxious to.

"If you see them," Frye said, "you'll know. Watch Clay Jordan."

One of Danaher's men said, "I don't want any part of him."

Frye looked at Merl, then to Dandy Jim. "Ready?"

They both nodded and moved out into the open as he did. Frye
and Merl carried Winchesters and Dandy Jim held a Springfield
carbine up diagonally in front of him. Merl's Winchester had a
large ring-type lever and he jiggled it silently as they walked
across the open one hundred yards to the square.

They were almost to the first houses. Not looking right or left,
Merl said, "Did you see something cross the square? The other
side of the bandstand."

"I'm not sure," Frye murmured. He glanced at Dandy Jim. *"Vió
algo cruzar por la plaza?"*

Dandy Jim nodded and they were sure.

Beyond the first house they stopped. They were now at the edge
of the square and from here the pueblo showed more life. Not
all of the doors were closed against the rain and here and there the
doorways were outlined by the cook fires inside.

Merl White was looking toward the mescal shop. "The one over
there with the ramada?"

Frye said, "That's right," and pointed out the adobe to Dandy
Jim. It was diagonally across the square on their right; the front of
it, doorway and windows, in the deep shadow of the tin-roofed
ramada.

And looking at the shadowed front of the cantina Frye saw the
muzzle flash as the shot was fired. The sound of it slammed across
the square and another shot followed. Three in rapid succession
then, and going down it was in Frye's mind that the first one had
been a rifle and the ones that followed from a .44 Colt. Merl and
Dandy Jim were both on the ground with him, all of them down instinctively at the sound of the gunfire. There was a lull. Then two
rifle shots, barely spaced, but there was not the lightning-quick on-
off flash in the darkness this time. Coming from the side of the
house, Frye thought. Suddenly there was firing from inside the
cantina. Another lull followed. And again gun flashes at the front
window. After that there was no more.

Rising to his feet Frye could hear the others approaching from behind, but he was still looking at the mescal shop. He saw the figure run from the darkness of the porch going directly across the square.

One! It flashed in his mind. That's all there was. He called out, "Halt!" raising his Winchester, thinking of Sundeen, and Jordan. Merl was next to him. Merl with his face against the stock and his eyes along the rifle barrel that edged steadily after the running figure.

"Halt!"

The figure broke his stride, turning, raising a rifle, and threw a shot at them. He was moving as he fired, hunched, running sideways, and his shot was high and wide. Merl hadn't lifted his head. He fired, aiming low, and the man went down, dropping his rifle, and his hands went to his thigh.

Frye was running toward him, but he stopped at the sound of gunfire coming unexpectedly from off beyond the adobes to the right. He turned, seeing Danaher running toward the mescal shop.

Then Danaher stopped and now he was looking back the way they had come, shouting something toward the openness and the dark expanse of the aspen stand beyond. As the sound of his voice echoed in the square, his riders broke from the trees, angling across the open space and were suddenly out of sight beyond the first adobe.

Merl White glanced at Frye. "Behind the cantina!"

"That's where the firing was from," Frye answered. His Winchester was trained on the wounded man who was sitting, holding his thigh and rocking back and forth as if to ease the pain; but Frye was watching Danaher. The sheriff had reached the front of the cantina. Now he disappeared into the shadows and the men who were with him followed.

Still watching, Frye moved to the wounded man. He glanced down, kicked the rifle away from him and as the man rolled back looking up, the face glistening wet and drawn with pain, he recognized Earl Beaudry.

"Don't hold the wound," Frye said. "Grab the inside of your leg and squeeze it tight." He saw Beaudry's hand groping at his knee and he said, "Up higher. It'll stop the bleeding."

Beaudry gasped, "God . . . somebody help me," then began to moan and rock back and forth again.

"Quit moving. You'll keep it bleeding."

"God, it hurts like fire!"

Frye bent closer to him. "Wait about half an hour."

"Get me a doctor—"

"You'll get one."

"Right now!" Beaudry would moan and close his eyes tightly, but open them when he spoke.

"You'll have to hold your own a while," Frye said.

"I could lose my leg!"

"Earl, what were you shooting about?"

Beaudry was silent, breathing heavily. Then he said, "I wanted to make them surrender."

Frye smiled, but to Beaudry he said, seriously, "That was good of you, Earl."

"There's Danaher again," Merl White said.

Looking up, Frye saw Danaher coming out from between the cantina and the next adobe. He had gone through, out the back door, and now had come around. Behind him were his two men, and following them were Goss and Tobin.

Approaching, Danaher called out, "Who is it?"

Frye waited until they were closer. "Beaudry."

"What was he shooting for?"

"Earl says he's on our side now."

"I guess he would," Danaher said. "Let's get him in out of the rain."

One of his men said, "He might catch cold."

Beaudry screamed as they picked him up. They started to carry him to the cantina, but he groaned, "Not there!" and pointed to the adobe across the square where the woman stood alone in the doorway. All about the square now doors were open and people were standing hesitantly watching.

The woman stepped aside to let them carry Beaudry in, then moved to the hearth and placed on more wood to build the fire, filling the kettle with water after that. Rising, she saw that they had lowered Beaudry onto the straw mattress.

Merl White asked, "What was going on back there?"

"Sundeen," Danaher answered.

"He got away then," Merl said, and seemed disappointed.

Ford Goss shook his head. "I don't want to see Jordan that close again."

"What happened?" Merl asked him.

"We were almost back of the place when the shooting started. We stopped there by a shed to see what was going to happen and a minute later the back door flies open and there's Jordan. Sundeen came next and then what must have been Tindal and Stedman. They were moving fast for the stable shed that connects to the back of the place. Then Jordan spots us and he lets go like he's six men shooting at once. His shots come zingin' through the corner of the shed keeping us back. Then they stop. I stuck my head out and like to got it blown off. Sundeen was in the saddle using his rifle while Jordan swung up. See, they must of had them already saddled. Then when we heard the horses Joe and me ran out, but all four of them were around the stable shed before we'd fired twice."

Frye said, "John, I saw your boys come out of the trees."

Danaher shook his head. "They won't get them. It's too dark out in the brush. Sundeen could hold up and let them ride right by."

"And with the rain," Frye added, "by morning all the tracks'll be gone."

Danaher took a cigar from his pocket, bit the tip off and lit it. "We've got time."

"They're probably in Mexico by now," Merl White said.

"Well," Danaher said, "that's all right too. If they stay hidden, the world's a better place to live in. If they come back, we take them." Danaher looked at Frye. "What do you want to do."

"Take Earl back."

Merl said, "Maybe some of us could stay hereabouts and look around."

Frye nodded. "If you want to that'd be fine."

"You never know," Merl said.

ELEVEN

They had stretched a tarp over the borrowed wagon that carried Earl Beaudry and most of the way back to Randado Frye sat with him in the close darkness of it. The rain stopped during the early morning and they rolled back the tarp; but it was daylight before they reached Randado. There were figures in doorways and people standing by ramada posts watching solemnly as they passed down the street; watching curiously as they stopped in front of the doctor's adobe and lifted out Beaudry, straw mattress and all.

They had all returned except Merl White, Goss, Tobin and Dandy Jim.

Danaher's men moved off across the street to the boardinghouse, but the sheriff and Frye waited to hear the doctor's report.

And after that, out in the street again—

"He's got nothing to worry about," Danaher said. "When the bullet doesn't go all the way through, then it's time to worry."

Frye's hand moved over his jaw, feeling the beard stubble there. "I better go tell Mrs. Beaudry."

"What about the other women?"

"I'll have to tell them too."

"Why don't you go over and talk to the Tindals? I'll go up and see Beaudry and Stedman's women."

"I could talk to them, John."

"Seeing the Tindals is enough," Danaher answered.

"Now?"

"Might as well. I'll see you back at the office."

Frye watched Danaher cross the street diagonally toward the last adobe building. The small residential hill was just beyond. Then he turned and crossed the street himself in the direction of Tindal's store.

Milmary opened the door for him. She had been standing by it, watching, waiting for him to come, going over in her mind the words she would use, but now he was here and she said nothing. Frye removed his hat feeling it sticking to his forehead and nodded solemnly. Milmary passed him and his eyes followed her to the counter. Her mother stood behind it.

"Mrs. Tindal. Your husband's all right."

Her mouth formed a smile, but the rest of her face did not smile, and her eyes were picturing something that was not in the room. He could see that she was trying to be calm, and pleasant. And it went through his mind: Why did she ever marry him? She was a plain woman, her hair parted in the middle and drawn back tightly into a bun, though there were thin wisps of hair not in place. He felt sorry for her because he could picture her combing her hair, trying to make it look attractive; but it was not attractive now, and probably it never had been. He felt sorry for her because she was plain, because no one would attach any importance to her, not even in little things, though perhaps Mil would. He could picture Tindal scarcely paying any attention to her when she spoke. But she would serve him and smile when he expected her to smile and praise him when he expected to be praised. And Frye felt sorry for her because he knew she needed to be held; but there was no one, not even Tindal if he were here.

"Mrs. Tindal, I'm awful sorry about this—"

He hesitated. She was looking at him, but not trying to answer. "I wanted to talk to you before, but I never got the chance."

Milmary asked, "Where is he?" Her voice seemed natural.

He looked at her, conscious of his beard and his hair stuck to his head from the hat being on so long and his damp clothes shapeless and dirty looking. Maybe he smelled. All that riding, then under that hot tarp with Beaudry. He could feel her eyes on him when he was not looking at her.

He told them everything then, beginning with their arrival at La Noria. He told it quietly and most of the time he looked at Mrs. Tindal.

"Sundeen forced your husband to go with him, Mrs. Tindal. We know that for a fact."

Milmary said, "Be sure you're not blamed for anything."

"De Spain will testify that Sundeen forced them to leave his place at gun point."

"That's noble of Mr. De Spain."

"Mil, why don't you talk like you've got some sense?"

She held his gaze silently for a moment. "Are you finished now?"

"I guess I am." He started to put on his hat.

"Kirby."

He looked at Mrs. Tindal. She had not spoken before and now the sound of her voice surprised him.

"Did you see him, Kirby?"

"No ma'am, I didn't."

"What will happen to him?"

"Nothing, Mrs. Tindal. This is kind of a game with Phil Sundeen. Soon he'll get tired of it and come home."

"He won't do anything to them?"

"No ma'am, I'm sure he won't."

Milmary said, "But when he comes back—"

Frye nodded once. "He'll stand trial."

"Will you take him to Yuma, too?"

He ignored Milmary's question. "Mrs. Tindal, you can figure your husband won't get more than a fine, if that. Judge Finnerty's a friend of Mr. Tindal's." Frye smiled. "You know he wouldn't send him to Yuma."

Milmary asked abruptly, "But what happened to Mr. Beaudry?"

"He was shot in the leg trying to run."

"How do you go about dodging that blame?"

"Mil, he fired on us first."

"Did you shoot him, Kirby?"

"No."

"That was decent of you, since he helped get you your job."

He looked at Mrs. Tindal instead of answering. "Can I do anything for you, ma'am?"

"Haven't you done enough?" Milmary asked.

He thought: You asked for it. But she could have thought of something better than that to say. He felt his temper rise, hearing her words again in his mind. He moved to the door putting on his hat, then touched the brim to them and stepped outside.

Maybe this is a good thing, he thought as he walked toward De Spain's. You get to know a person better when something like this comes up. After you're married, how'd you like to have that the rest of your life, everytime you have a disagreement? She'd give you that silent act. If you said something she had to answer, then she'd come back with that ice-water tone. I think I'd rather have a woman who throws plates. She'd get it out of her system and it would be over with. Well, enough's enough. If she wants me, she knows where to come.

He told these things to himself but he did not completely believe them. They made him feel better, that was all.

He nodded to a group of men standing in front of De Spain's, then started across the street toward the jail. His back was to them when he heard one of them say, "Some people think they're pretty goddamn big."

Frye stopped and half turned. One of the men was holding on to a support post staring at him defiantly. He was drunk and without the post would have fallen into the street. Behind him, four men stood close as if in conversation. They paid no attention to the drunk, though before, when Frye nodded, the five of them had been standing together.

He continued across the street and entered the jail office. Harold Mendez came away from the window as he closed the door.

"Harold." He nodded to the jailer. "I see you fixed the windows."

"Digo did," Harold said, "he broke them. I tied his feet and held a shotgun behind his back while he did it."

Frye took off his hat and slumped wearily into the chair in front of the desk. He leaned forward to unfasten his spurs, then going back, lifted his feet to the desk and crossed them.

"I saw you come in with Beaudry," Harold said. "One of Danaher's men left his gear here. When he came in for it, he told me the whole thing."

Frye was silent. Then he said, "How are they talking about it at De Spain's?"

"I haven't been over there."

"Did you see that just before I came in?"

Harold nodded. "What did he say?"

"Some people think they're pretty goddamn big."

"He was drunk," Harold said. "When he's not cleaning the livery he's drunk. You never know what he'll say."

"He didn't say it. The four behind him did. They poured the words in and he used them."

"You have to expect a certain amount of that."

"What are they saying, Harold?"

"Well . . . last night a few men came over from De Spain's and one of them asked if the rest of the people could consider themselves safe or should they run too. It was supposed to be cutting, but he sounded as if he was reading it. He said when the manager of the bank and the town's leading merchant have to leave town, then it's time to look more closely at the one who's chasing them, and reconsider. Something like that."

"Did you mention," Frye said, "Sundeen's Colt making them run?"

"They're going back before that," Harold said. "Many of them took part in the hanging even if they didn't tie the knots. They're not wanted, but they probably still feel obliged to share a little of the blame with Tindal and Stedman. The way to do that is oppose you."

"How do they feel about Sundeen?"

"He's the biggest man around here. They're awed by him, even if they don't like him, and they don't see how a young deputy who's only been here a month gets off chasing him out of town. People are scared to death of Phil Sundeen, but they still look up to him. Because he's got money if for no other reason. A man with money must be important."

"Which is how the whole thing started," Frye said.

"That's right."

Frye shook his head. "There must be some sensible people here."

"Plenty," Harold answered. "They're the ones that hardly even talk about it. They probably think we're all children."

Frye was silent, but after a moment he said, "Harold, I'm tired."

The jailer nodded. "I know what you mean."

When Danaher came in Frye was shaving in front of a mirror propped on the desk. He was sitting on the edge of the chair and turned to look at Danaher as he entered.

"How was yours?" Danaher asked.

"Well, I didn't get the red carpet."

"Maybe you should have done that first." Danaher nodded to the razor.

"I needed more than a clean face."

"Ten years from now you and Mil will think back on this and you might even smile."

"How did you do?"

"The ladies were obliged to greet me with cold stony eyes and expressions that would've cracked like china had you touched them."

"How'd you expect them to treat you?"

"Kirby, I never *expect* anything."

"Yes sir," Frye said, not knowing, or caring, how Danaher would take it.

"You need sleep," Danaher said.

He wanted to say it again, because he was suddenly near the end of his patience. Yes sir—something a kid would say in a tone all of its own, thinking he was smart. He realized this, and held on; and moving the razor down his jaw line slowly, he said, "John you want to get something to eat first?"

They went to the Metropolitan and throughout the meal they spoke little. Once, Danaher said, "You feel all alone now, don't you?" and this stayed on Frye's mind even after they left the café. Maybe Danaher could read his thoughts—like when he was hiring him for the job after the Galluro thing. At the boardinghouse they bathed and went to bed, but before falling asleep Frye thought: He was talking from experience. Danaher feels alone too. And that was some consolation. Enough to let him fall asleep almost right away.

In the evening they ate at the Metropolitan again. Haig Hanasian served them and at the end of the meal he leaned close to Frye and said, "If you go out again, I would look upon it as a privilege to be along."

"We're not sure we will."

"Just if you do."

They returned to the jail office to smoke and theorize now. They would wait for Sundeen's move, but they could be thinking while they waited. Harold brought a bottle and glasses and in the semi-darkness they sipped whisky and talked until late.

Probably Sundeen had taken them across the border. That was logical; that made more sense than anything else. Still, Sundeen was not a man who lived by his reason. Frye remembered Danaher's words earlier in the day, "I never *expect* anything." That was the way to consider Sundeen. Don't say, "He probably did this." You'll find out he did the opposite.

So they didn't take for granted that Sundeen crossed the border. And the more they thought about it, the stronger the possibility was that he had not.

"He could even swing back this way," Danaher said, "to see what happened to Digo. He could even have in mind raising a fighting force. He's bullheaded enough."

"What about Tindal and Stedman talking him into giving up?" Frye suggested.

"Not a chance."

"They could circle up to Tucson and turn themselves over to Judge Finnerty."

"I don't think so."

"Digo talked him into running when he was set against it."

Danaher nodded thoughtfully. "That's right."

"Maybe he's not the stone wall we give him credit for," Frye said.

"But you can't predict the bastard. That's the trouble."

They were in the office again the next morning, Danaher having decided to return to Tucson since there was nothing to do but wait, and he was getting ready to go when Ford Goss rode in. Ford looked drained, as if he'd been riding all night.

He swung off, seeing them standing in the doorway, and the first thing he said was, "Dandy caught their sign!"

TWELVE

They rode southeast from Randado, Ford Goss showing the way, his saddle on a fresh mount and Ford in it again after a rest that lasted only as long as it took to drink a cup of coffee and eat a plate of meat and beans. He was bone tired, but he stayed in the saddle and followed his own trail without any trouble, without even thinking about it, because this was not something new. He couldn't count the number of watches he'd stood over a night herd, then stayed in the saddle the whole next day until sundown. It was part of a riding job.

At their first rest, Ford related the details of finding Sundeen's trail. How they had ridden south from La Noria and swung east along the border for half a day without seeing a track of any kind. Merl said maybe they crossed during the rain; but maybe they didn't go over the border after all, and that was worth checking. So they started bearing north in a wide circle. West was open country, but northeast from La Noria were the Huachucas and that way made more sense. By midafternoon they had picked up four tracks bearing more to the east, Dandy Jim spotting the hoof marks no white man could have. They followed. At a waterhole farther on they found two cigarette stubs and there the tracks of four horses were unmistakable. Then luck hit them right in the face. "Good luck that only comes from living right," Ford said. An hour from the waterhole they came across two Tonto-Mojave women dressing down a buck. The women told Dandy Jim they had watched from a distance as a party of white men shot the buck and took its hindquarters. Now they were only taking what had been left. Dandy asked them what the men looked like. They described each man—and then there was no longer any doubt. That evening when they camped, they matched to see who was going to ride all night to Randado. Ford lost.

Danaher was along with his six men—Danaher riding easily for a big man, unconcernedly, a cigar clamped in the corner of his mouth.

Frye and Haig Hanasian rode side by side most of the time. Frye slouched in the saddle, his straight hatbrim low over his eyes. He could have been asleep, the loose way he followed the dun gelding's motion; but he was not asleep and he missed nothing.

Haig Hanasian rode in silence. He made no comment about the weather, nor about the trail becoming rougher as they climbed into the foothills of the Huachuca range. Haig's hat was narrow-brimmed and he wore a full suit and a cravat. Everything about him seemed out of place except the expression on his face. Frye noticed this. Haig's silence and his masked expression told nothing; yet by their presence they told everything. At least to Frye. He remembered Edith mistaking him for Sundeen the night he entered the café late, as if she had been expecting Phil. Probably something was going on between them, Frye thought. Haig found out. And now he wants to do something about it.

Before noon they reached the camp where Ford had left Merl. Riding at night it had taken Ford seven hours to reach Randado; returning during daylight they did it in almost half that time.

"Merl and Joe and Dandy stayed the night here," Ford explained.

"You must have been close to them," Frye said. It was a dry camp and there had been no fire.

"So close we had to stop when we did," Ford said, "for fear of riding on them in the dusk. Merl said him and the boys would go on at daylight, but that we'd be able to follow him easy."

They rested the horses, then moved on following Merl's sign, crossing a three-mile length of meadow where the wild grass was broken and bent forward in a narrow path down the middle. Through scattered pine stands they followed branches Merl had broken and left hanging. Over rocky ground there were stones set in a row pointing the way. They could have followed the horse tracks, but this saved time and time was the important element. They entered a draw that was narrow and overgrown with brush and they moved through it single file, feeling the gradual rise and when it opened they were high up on a bench that looked down on a valley and the tops of jackpines far below. Dandy Jim was there waiting for them.

He led them along the bench, then down a slope through dim, silent timber. At the bottom, watering their horses in a stream, Merl White and Joe Tobin were waiting.

Merl was squatting on his heels at the edge of the stream. He looked over his shoulder, then rose as Dandy Jim brought them in.

"Where you been?"

Danaher stepped out of the saddle. "The other side of the mountain pickin' our noses."

Frye's gaze moved over the small clearing. He saw traces of the fire that had been smothered out, and close to him, at the edge of the clearing, the grass was trampled and broken off where the horses had been picketed. He watched Dandy Jim cross to the stream removing his red cotton headband. He dipped it in and out of the water quickly, then spread it out and rubbed mud into it from the damp bank. He shook it, then spread it out again to let the sun dry the mud. They're close, Frye thought.

He heard Merl White saying, "We got us a problem. They split up here."

"What?" Danaher was lighting a cigar but he held it and the match went out in his hand.

Frye swung down and let his horse go to the stream. "Maybe they split up leaving here," Frye said, "but meet again further on."

Merl shook his head. "Three of them went due north up the stream, but one crossed over and followed it down the other way."

Danaher lit his cigar and blew on it slowly. "Now which one would that be?"

"You wouldn't think Tindal or Stedman," Frye said.

"Unless," Danaher said, "one of them got a chance to sneak off during the night."

Frye asked Merl, "Where'd he cross?"

"Right there where your horse's watering."

"They were grazed over on the other side," Frye said. "That means he'd have to have brought his horse right through camp to cross the stream there."

"I didn't finish," Merl said. "We figure whoever it was, left a few minutes before the others, and in daylight. Dandy crossed over and followed his sign a ways, down the stream about a hundred yards, then up into the trees. Dandy says up there in a clearing the man had stopped. You can see this camp from there. The man waited there a while, least long enough to smoke a cigarette, because the stub of it was there. And he must have been watching the others."

"The careful type," Danaher said.

Frye said, "And he smokes cigarettes. You ever see Tindal or Stedman with anything but a cigar?"

"No," Danaher answered, "I don't believe I have."

"Are you thinking," Frye asked, "what I'm thinking?"

"Probably so," Danaher said. "Sundeen wouldn't be likely to walk out on his old committee friends after going to so much trouble to bring them along. And he doesn't strike you as the kind who'd sit over there and smoke a cigarette once he'd made up his mind to move. That leaves one man. Jordan. If they had an argument and Jordan walked out, I think he'd be inclined to watch them till they were out of sight."

Frye looked at Merl. "How far did Dandy follow him?"

"About an hour."

Frye went over to Dandy Jim and the Coyotero, squatting down, looked up at him and grinned as if to say: I've been waiting for you.

Danaher watched them and it reminded him of Galluro to see the two squatting together drawing lines on the smoothed dirt. He drank a cup of cold coffee from Merl's canteen, then saw them stand up.

The Coyotero took the cloth that was spread open next to him, folded it into a triangle and tied it over his long hair, knotting it in back. He looked like a color picture Danaher had once seen of a pirate, only now the head band wasn't red; it was a dull brown color that wouldn't be seen through the trees or stand out against rock. Then Frye came toward him.

"John, Dandy and I figure we can take Jordan before he gets anywhere near the border."

"Is that so?"

"Assuming he'll follow the stream as long as it bears generally south, we can make a straight line and be waiting for him when he comes out of the valley."

"Dandy knows the country?"

"Like his hand."

"Just the two of you?"

"We'd go a lot faster."

Danaher shrugged. "You're in charge."

"You'll keep after the others?"

"Of course."

"We'll catch up with you later."

"Kirby, just keep one thing in mind. He gets paid for carrying a gun."

Dandy Jim leading, they splashed over the shallow stream, then followed Jordan's tracks along the bank and up to the clearing where he had waited. From there Jordan had gone down again, following the stream south. But now Frye and the Coyotero slanted up through the timber, their horses going slower, more carefully, as the slope became steeper, then making switchbacks through the trees as the pines near the rim grew more dense. At the top they looked back. They could see the stream and the camp they had left far below on the other side, but there was no movement and they knew Danaher had gone on.

Daylight was beginning to fade, but here was open country dipping and rolling in long gradual swells and they gave the horses their heads, letting them run hard in the cool breeze of evening. Then, in gray dimness, they rode down the long sweep of land that stretched curving downward to the mouth of the valley.

Now, looking back into the valley they could see gigantic rock formations tumbled through the wild brush of the valley floor. Following the stream, Jordan would move slowly. And the rocks would slow him even more, Frye thought. He was confident that Jordan had not left the valley before they arrived to seal its exit.

Frye asked, "Where does the stream end?"

The Coyotero pointed to the trees, now a solid black mass between the steep sides of the valley. "Beyond there the time it would take to ride one hour."

Then that's where he will camp, Frye thought. By water. Because he doesn't know when he will see it again. And he would camp early; rest the horse well; and make the border in one ride.

"It is too wide here to wait for him," Frye said.

Dandy Jim nodded, agreeing. They moved their horses into the mouth of the valley that began to narrow abruptly after only a few hundred yards and now they angled toward the near side and left their horses in the dense pines that grew along the slope. They moved farther in on foot, then climbed up into the rocks to wait.

"It will be all right to smoke," Dandy Jim said, which was his way of asking for a cigarette. Frye made them and they smoked in silence. Afterwards, they ate meat which they had brought and drank water from their canteens. They smoked another cigarette before going to sleep.

At first light, the Coyotero touched Frye on the shoulder. He came awake, sitting up, looking out over the rocks to the floor of the valley.

"This is a good place," the Coyotero said.

"Even better than it looked in the dark," Frye agreed. Across to the other slope was less than three hundred yards; then, to the right, another three hundred to the trees and tumbled rocks through which Jordan would come. The trees seemed less dense on this side of the valley, which meant Jordan would likely be bearing to the near side. That, Frye thought, would make it all the better.

They decided how they would do it, watching the trees as they talked.

After, Frye rolled four cigarettes and gave them to Dandy Jim with matches, then watched as the Coyotero scrambled down the rocks. First he would check the horses, then return to the pines directly below Frye ready to run out and disarm Jordan after Frye commanded him to halt. Dandy Jim had said, "Why not shoot him from here?" But Frye explained that it would be better to take him back as a prisoner.

And now he waited, leaning on his left side, looking through a groove in the rocks in front of him. His Winchester rested in this V and from time to time he would sight on the break in the trees through which he expected Jordan to come.

The rocks that jutted out from the opposite slope were clean and clear in the early morning sunlight, but the floor of the valley, almost all the way across, was still in shadow. He could hear the cries of birds back in the trees in the direction he watched, and the soft sound of the breeze in the pines. The rocks beneath him were cold and he thought, feeling the dampness of the rocks but meaning the entire cool early morning stillness of the valley: By the time the sun is high enough to warm it, this will be over.

Keep listening to the birds. They'll give you warning when he comes. If they are in the lower trees they'll fly up as he passes them.

He looked at the shadow below him and he thought: Like rolling up a black rug. You almost see it getting shorter. Eight o'clock? Something like that. He's not rushing into anything. He looks ahead, and this morning he's making sure his horse will take him to the border. It would've been good to have seen what happened between him and Sundeen. Maybe it was payday and Sundeen didn't have the money. Maybe it was as simple as that.

He could not hear Dandy Jim below him and he did not expect

to. This is his meat. He's Apache and could sit in an ambush for ten years if he thought it was worth waiting for.

He could not hear the horses either. Purposely they were both geldings. There would be nothing between them that would be worth nickering about.

He saw the birds rise from the trees. They were in a flock, now swooping and rising as one, and they flew out of sight up the valley. Frye rubbed out his cigarette.

Jordan stopped at the edge of the trees. He dismounted and adjusted his cinch, pulling it tighter. Then he mounted and rode warily out of the trees.

Frye's front sight covered Jordan's left side, the sight barely moving, barely lowering as Jordan came on. The Winchester was cocked.

Mr. Jordan, Frye thought looking down the barrel, you're about to make a decision. And you won't have time to change your mind once you make it. The front sight dropped an inch as Jordan drew nearer to the slope and Frye's finger was light against the tightness of the trigger. Just flick it, he thought, and you've solved everything. No, let's take him home.

Now Jordan was even with him and Frye knew that this was as close as he would come.

"JORDAN! THROW UP YOUR HANDS!"

The words echoed in the narrowness and Jordan made his decision. Frye saw the horse wheel suddenly toward the slope and rear up, rearing the same moment he fired.

Jordan was reining again, pulling the horse's head to face the trees, and the horse moved with a lunge that took it almost to a dead run the first few yards. Frye hurried the next shot and it was low and suddenly he had to go down as Jordan returned the fire, emptying his gun, at fifty yards, straight up through the V where Frye was crouched.

Five shots! Frye was up, seeing Jordan slapping the gun barrel across the horse's rump. He heard firing below him. Dandy Jim. Jordan was running now, not looking back, his right leg out of the stirrup, holding close to the horse's off side. Frye fired, aiming at the horse now, but the horse did not go down. And in a moment it was too late. Jordan had disappeared into the trees.

THIRTEEN

How could you miss! Frye thought. He was angry because he had hurried the shot. Missing Jordan the first time was not his fault: the horse had reared. But the second shot: Jordan was running, for seconds less than a hundred yards away, and he had let himself be hurried. Now, there was not time to stand thinking about what he should have done, though as he went down the slope, scrambling from rock to rock, making sure of his footing, then sliding down on the loose gravel, he could still see Jordan crouched low in the saddle laying his pistol barrel across the horse's rump.

And as Frye reached the base of the slope, it went through his mind: Maybe you did hit him, but not where it would knock him down.

Dandy Jim approached along the edge of the pines. He was on his gelding and leading Frye's.

"How could we have missed?"

The Coyotero shook his head. "But I think we took the horse."

Frye looked across the open three hundred yards to the dense-ness of the trees and the rocks beyond. "He could be waiting for us to come after him," he said, squinting toward the trees, dark and unmoving beyond the sunlight. "But probably he won't wait, be-cause he doesn't know how many we are." He looked at Dandy Jim, but the Coyotero's face was without expression and he did not speak. "If his horse was hit, it might have dropped just in the trees. Then he would have gone on afoot . . . or waited, thinking one place to stand was as good as another."

Now the Coyotero nodded.

Frye swung up. "We could talk about it a long time, but there's only one way to find out for sure." He was looking at Dandy Jim as he kicked his dun forward and he saw a smile touch the corner of the Coyotero's mouth.

Riding across the meadow Frye could feel his shoulders pulled up tensed and he told himself to relax, thinking: A shoulder's no good against a .45 slug, is it? Still, he could feel the tightness inside of him and just telling himself to relax wasn't enough.

They covered most of the distance at a trot, then slowed to a walk the last few dozen yards and entered the trees this way, their carbines ready. There was no sound and slowly Frye could feel the tightness within him easing. If he's close, he thought, he would have fired when we were in the open or just coming in.

The Coyotero pointed ahead and Frye could see clearly the path Jordan's horse had made breaking into the brush. His gaze lowered, coming back along the ground, and now he noticed the streaks of blood that were almost continuous leading from where they stood to the brush clumps.

"There's no doubt we got his horse," he said to Dandy Jim.

The Apache nodded, answering, "It won't last very long."

"We'd better go on foot."

"I think so," the Apache said. "Listen," he added then. "I think I should go first, and you should follow, leading the horses."

"Why should you go first?" Frye said.

"Because I always do."

"There's nothing that says you have to." He could see that the Coyotero wanted to do this to protect him. "I'm the one responsible for bringing him back," Frye said.

"I think we're wasting time now," Dandy Jim said. He turned abruptly and started for the brush leaving Frye with the horses. But as he passed between the first clumps he looked back and saw that Frye was following him, leading the horses, holding the reins in his left hand. He had replaced the Winchester in its saddle boot and now he had drawn the Colt and was carrying it in his right hand.

They moved steadily through the brush patch stopping when they came to the end of it. From here the signs of blood angled more to the left, gradually climbing a bare slope, a slide of loose shale that reached openly almost to the rim high above them. He could be waiting up there, Frye thought. But if he didn't wait before, why should he now?

Halfway up the slope the blood tracks veered abruptly and

slanted down again into the trees. His horse couldn't make it, Frye thought. They followed, the shale crunching, sliding beneath their feet as they went down, and in the trees again it was quiet.

Now Frye watched Dandy Jim who was almost twenty yards ahead of him. He would see the branches move as the Coyotero moved steadily along, but he would hear no sound. Farther along, he began to catch glimpses of the stream through the pine branches to the right. Then ahead he could see a part of the stream in full view, and as he looked at it he saw Dandy Jim stop.

The Coyotero went down on his stomach, remaining there for what must have been ten minutes before rising slowly and coming back, running crouched, toward him.

"His horse," Dandy Jim said, reading him.

"Where?"

"By the stream."

"And you didn't see the man?"

"No. The horse is at the edge of the stream, part of it in the water."

"Dead?"

"Not yet."

"Quickly then."

The Coyotero turned and crept back toward the stream. Frye followed, but left the horses where they were.

Jordan's horse was at the edge of the stream, its hind quarters in the water and its head up on the bank. As the swell of stomach moved, blood poured from a bullet wound in the horse's right flank. It colored the water, red as it came from the horse, brown fading to nothing as it poured into the water and was moved along by the small current.

The horse had been shot again just behind the right shoulder; and as Frye started to cross the stream, looking down at the horse as he stepped into the water, he saw where another bullet had entered the withers; probably his first shot and he wondered briefly why it had not killed the horse on the spot.

He saw Jordan's footprints before he stepped out of the water. They bore to the left following the stream.

He signaled to Dandy Jim, who ran back through the trees for their horses. Then, watching him as he brought them back, he saw the Coyotero go to one knee next to Jordan's horse, then saw him bring out his knife and cut the animal's throat in one slash. The Coyotero brought their horses across then.

"Listen," Frye said, "let's do it this way now. You go up the slope and work along the edge. I'll stay on his sign and from time to time watch for you to signal. He won't climb out of here now, not without a horse."

"But he could when night comes," Dandy Jim said.

"We've got to pin him down before that."

They arranged a signal: every ten minutes the Coyotero would imitate the call of a verdin. If he located Jordan he would imitate a crow. Then he would either return to Frye or lead him on to Jordan by the same signals.

Frye watched Dandy Jim ride out of sight into the pines before he went on, following Jordan's footprints: at first, the marks of high-heeled boots that were easily read in the sand; but farther on, as the sand gave way to rocky ground, the marks were less apparent. And often he went on without a sign to follow, choosing one path through the rocks rather than another because it seemed more direct, less likely to bring him back to a point he had already passed.

Twice he heard the verdin, perhaps a hundred yards ahead of him and up on the slope.

Then again. This time it seemed to be closer.

Frye entered the narrowness of a defile and stopped in the deep shadow of it to drink from his canteen. He took a bandanna from his pocket and wetting it, wiped his horse's muzzle, cleaning the nostrils. Then, as he started out again, he stopped and drew back into the shadows instinctively as the sound of gunfire came from somewhere off to the right up on the slope.

Two shots from a revolver and a heavier report that was still echoing through the rocks.

Springfield, Frye thought. Dandy's on him and it must have been unexpected with no time for the signal. He reached past the horse's shoulder and drew his Winchester and turning back, his eyes momentarily caught a movement in the lower pines. He raised the Winchester, waiting as the minutes passed.

There!

The figure darted from the trees running crouched low. The sound of the Springfield came from higher up on the slope and the split-second he heard it Frye fired.

Too late. He was behind rocks now.

Frye had waited because he had not been able to identify the figure, and by the time the Springfield told him who it was, it was too late.

But now you're sure, Frye thought, looking at the rocks where Jordan had disappeared. Now you know where he is . . . and all you have to do is go in and get him. Or wait him out.

He studied the terrain thoughtfully. He was slightly higher than Jordan's position and beyond those rocks there appeared to be an open meadow. Probably, Frye thought, that's why he turned into the pines. He didn't want to cross the open. Not now. To the east was the pine-thick slope, and Dandy Jim. Frye was to the south. Beyond the stream was the steep slope to the west. It could be climbed, but much of it was bare rock and it would take time . . . if Jordan ever reached it, which was improbable. Still, Jordan could move around to some degree in a fifty-yard radius of rock and brush.

All of this went through Frye's mind and he concluded: He has to be pinned to one spot before dark and not be able to leave it.

He was sure that the Coyotero realized this. Now it was a question of working together. But first, Frye thought, tell Dandy where you are.

He aimed quickly at the spot where Jordan had disappeared and fired. Now be ready, he thought.

The Springfield opened up. One . . . two . . . on the second shot Frye was moving, running veering to the left . . . three . . . diving behind a rock covering as a revolver shot whined over his head and ricocheted off the crest of the rock. Frye exhaled, close to the ground. Now they both know.

He crawled along behind the cover of the rocks, then raised his head slowly until he was looking at Jordan's position from another angle. But he could not see the gunman even from here.

A little more around, Frye thought. And a little closer. He brought the Winchester up and fired quickly.

The Springfield answered covering him. Frye was up running straight ahead, then to the left again. He found cover, went to his knees, but only momentarily. The Winchester came up with his head—

Jordan! A glimpse of him disappearing, dropping into a pocket among the rocks.

Frye fired, levered and fired again—four times, bracketing the pocket and nicking one off the top of the rocks where Jordan had gone down.

It had worked. Jordan was still behind cover, but now he could not move, not three feet without exposing himself; and even darkness would do him little good.

Now we'll see how good he is, Frye thought. We'll see how good his nerves are—and if he has any patience. I should have told Dandy how he is with a gun. No, he already knows it. He was inside the jail when Jordan let go at Harold Mendez. And he heard how Jordan came out of the La Noria mescal shop. So he won't underestimate him.

Frye was on his stomach, but with his elbows raising him enough to see over the rocks and down the barrel of the Winchester in front of him. Mesquite bunched thickly all around him and even with his eyes above the rocks he knew Jordan would not see him. Not unless he fired. And Frye had no intention of firing. Jordan was flanked. He was cut off from water and cut off from escape—unless pure luck sided with him.

For the second time this day Frye settled down to wait. He knew Dandy Jim would do the same. He was Apache and would not rush into something that could be solved with patience. Dandy Jim has it figured out better than you, Frye thought. He's done this more times than you have. Let the quietness work on Jordan. Let him realize he's alone and there's nothing he can do about it. Let him think until he's tired of thinking. Then he will do something. He might even give himself up. If he does, wrap fifty feet of rope around him and still don't trust him. But it won't be that way, will it?

Frye waited and the time passed slowly.

It was less than two hours later, though it seemed longer, when Jordan started to do something.

"Frye!"

Frye looked up at the unexpected sound of his name. He could not see Jordan, but he knew it was Jordan who had called. He watched, feeling the stock of the carbine against his cheek, and did not answer.

"Frye!"

He waited.

"Goddamn-it that's your name, isn't it!"

I didn't think you knew it, Frye said to himself.

Then—"Frye! Come on out and we'll talk it over!"

Silence.

"You hear me!"

For a few minutes it was quiet.

"Listen . . . I turned my ankle and can't get out of this goddamn hole!"

Let's see you try, Frye said to himself.

"Come on over and we'll talk this thing out!"

You're doing all right as it is, Frye thought.

Silence again, but suddenly Jordan called, "Frye, you son of a bitch, come on out!"

Frye smiled, thinking: He's getting warmer.

"What kind of a law man are you!"

Silence.

"You're such a brave goddamn law man walk on over here!"

Keep talking, Frye thought.

"Frye . . . I'll make you a bet!"

Silence.

"I'll bet all the money I got you're not man enough to stand up the same time I do!"

What about your ankle?

"You hear me!"

I hear you . . . but I'm not buying in.

"I'm counting three and then standing up!"

Frye looked down the Winchester.

"One!"

Silence.

"Two!"

There was a longer pause.

"Three!"

Frye saw the crown of a hat edge hesitantly above the rocks. He was ready to fire. But the hat tilted awkwardly and he knew it was being held by a stick. His finger relaxed on the trigger.

The hat disappeared.

"You yellow son of a bitch!"

Work yourself up—it went through Frye's mind—till you can't stand any more.

"I gave you credit before . . . but you're nothing but a goddamn woman!"

I hope Dandy Jim can understand some of this, Frye thought.

Now there was a long silence that lasted for the better part of an hour. Then Jordan called for the last time.

"Frye . . . you win! But you're not taking me!"

Silence. Then a single revolver shot.

Frye smiled, hearing the shot die away. Clay, you should have been on the stage.

Throughout the long afternoon there was no sound from the pocket. Frye's eyes stayed on it. He shifted positions as his body became cramped and he smoked cigarettes to help pass the time. As dusk settled, coming quickly between the steep slopes of the valley, he removed his boots, his hat and cartridge belt. Then he cupped his hands to his mouth and whistled the call of a verdin.

He waited until it was darker, then moved on hands and knees a dozen yards to the left and imitated the call again.

Dandy Jim would know that he was moving. And if he was moving it meant only one thing. Close in and get Jordan.

He waited a longer time now, until the moon—what there was of it—appeared above the eastern slope; then Frye began to crawl forward, his Colt in his right hand, watching the rocks ahead of him pale gray in the moonlight.

Thirty yards to go.

All right, let's feel him out. Frye picked up a stone that filled his hand and threw it forward but to the left of Jordan's position.

He heard it strike and instantly the revolver answered.

Frye smiled in the darkness, even though he could feel the tension inside of him. He's good in a saloon fight, he thought, but he's not worth a damn at this. All right. Now you know for sure.

He inched forward a dozen yards and stopped. His hand groped for a stone. Finding one he threw it backhanded toward Jordan.

The stone rattled over the rocks and this time he saw the flame spurt as the revolver went off.

He's not taking any chances.

Now, off beyond Jordan's position he heard the hoot of an owl that he knew was not from an owl. Dandy Jim was closing in. Frye crept forward.

He heard the owl again much closer and this time Jordan's revolver answered it. Frye moved quickly and he reached the rocks that rose in front of the pocket as Jordan's shot echoed to nothing.

Now Frye could hear him: a boot scraped in the loose gravel. He could picture Jordan on the other side of the rock moving around the pocket trying to pierce the darkness, trying to see where they were hiding. Frye pressed close and shifting his Colt to his left hand, edged in that direction along the smooth side of the rock.

If he has one gun there are two bullets left in it. No, he thought then, hurriedly, you can't count shots. He's had time to reload.

Wait for Dandy. The next time is the one. In his mind he hesitated and he told himself: Just do it. Do it and get it the hell over
with.

God . . . help me—

It came suddenly, just beyond the pocket, not an owl sound as
he had expected, but the shriek of a coyote, the howl cut off
abruptly at its peak as the revolver went off.

Frye moved around the smooth turn of the rock bringing up his
Colt.

"Jordan—"

In the moonlight he saw Jordan turning, saw his eyes wide open
for a split second before he felt the Colt jump in his hand. Close on
the explosion he fired again and five feet away from him Jordan
went down, his hands clutched to his face.

Frye called out softly into the darkness, "He's dead," and a moment later Dandy Jim was standing next to him. Frye took Jordan's
billfold for identification and gave the dead man's gun and holster
to Dandy Jim.

"He died poorly," the Coyotero said strapping it on.

They buried Jordan in the pocket and at first light climbed the
slope and ran their horses again the way they had come. It was still
the early part of the morning when they descended the slope to the
clearing where they had left Danaher. They would water their
horses here, then pick up Danaher's sign. But as they crossed the
stream they saw Ford Goss standing next to his horse waiting for
them.

"You got him?"

Frye nodded. "Last night."

"I'd like to've seen that."

"What about you boys?"

"I came back to find you. We got the others holed up."

"Where?"

"Up a ways. Danaher wanted to wait for you." Ford grinned.
"They're hiding up in an old mine works and don't know we
know it."

FOURTEEN

From the window of the assay shack, looking down the slope, Tindal could see most of the deserted mine works: the ore tailings, furrowed gravel piles that stretched down the slope in long humps, and just behind the first tailing he could see the top part of the mainshaft scaffolding. Where the ore tailing petered out into the canyon floor he could see the crushing mill and giant cyanide vats, five of them, cradled in a rickety wooden frame.

He remembered the time he had visited here, a guest of—he could not think of the man's first name—something Butler. Butler had lived in Randado and had owned a small interest in the mine. They had not climbed the slope to the assay shack, but had stayed over there across the canyon where the company buildings were: now dilapidated and two of the four were roofless and you could see the framework of studs that the roof planks and tar paper had been nailed to.

The houses were built at the base of the slope and the verandas were supported on stilts. Butler standing on the steps, a cigar in his mouth, explaining the operation—

". . . it's got to be dry-crushed to pass a twenty by sixteen mesh . . . loaded into them vats . . . two hundred and fifty tons of ore, mind you, and leached in cyanide . . . strength of the solution is . . . to the ton of water . . . damn good thing we got water . . . right now the average tenor's thirty dollars to the ton and mister, that's pay dirt!"

It was the first and last time Tindal had visited the mine—"The Big Beverly," they'd called it—for months later the tenor dropped to two dollars and fifty cents a ton and from then on it was not worth working.

The shack he was in right now—

He remembered looking up the slope, up past the cyanide vats and the crushing mill, to the left and even higher than the main shaft scaffolding, and seeing the shack perched on a ledge that was almost halfway up the escarpment. Just sandstone above it; long, towering pinnacles of sandstone.

And Butler saying—". . . why would anybody want to build a shack way up there? Man, that's where the assaying is done. See those two dark spots on either side of the shack . . . the original mine shafts . . . in the shack they got shelves on the walls and bags of concentrates are stored there to be tested . . . you don't want to go up there . . . nothing to see . . ."

And there's nothing to see looking down from there, Tindal thought now. My God, it's funny what you can remember from even a long time ago. About fifteen years . . . but last week is a long time ago, too. It's how you look at it.

Last week—

Earl Beaudry coming into the store and saying that he'd seen Phil Sundeen and that Phil wanted to talk to them. Why in hell had Earl and George been so eager to stick their nose in another man's business! Sundeen's run-off cows were his own worry. My God, a man can change!

He was thinking of Phil Sundeen then, comparing how he was before with what he was like now. The difference was in Tindal's mind.

He had looked up to Phil Sundeen as everyone did, because Phil was an important man. He had always laughed when Phil started to cut up. When Phil did something that was genuinely funny, Tindal's eyes would water as he laughed and he would feel closer to Phil then, laughing without having to pretend that he was laughing. Those were the times when Tindal would feel justified for all the excuses he continually made for Phil, and the defending him to Milmary, who said he was a rowdy and wouldn't have anything to do with him. "Mil, a man of his stature is entitled to be a little eccentric." "Eccentric! Riding his horse into people's living rooms! Thinking he can do anything he pleases just because he owns a few cows!" "A few thousand." "I don't care how many!" "He's young yet, that's all." "Well, it's about time he grew up!"

He had even made an excuse for Milmary: you can't tell a woman anything. But always in the back of his mind was the hope that someday Milmary would change her attitude and marry Phil.

Marrying into the biggest spread in Pima County! For some things it was worth being a little extra nice. Hell, it didn't require much more of an effort. But, my God, the times when you had to laugh and it wasn't funny—

Everything in life isn't a bed of roses. It's just good business to put up with a few minor displeasures in order to make a profit in the end. Once in a while he would view his association with Phil Sundeen this way. Most often though, he would simply justify their association by making excuses for Phil's character. Either way Tindal kept his conscience clean and his pride intact. Doubts did not count.

But now—

Suddenly inside of only a few days there was nothing to gain and everything to lose and he could no longer make excuses for Phil Sundeen. He saw Phil as he actually was, the way Milmary had described him: a rowdy who thinks he can do anything he pleases. He blamed Beaudry and Stedman for getting him into this, but far less than he blamed, and hated, Sundeen now. It would come into his mind: Why can't we just start all over. No, not start over, but go back to the way it was and I swear to God I won't have anything to do with him. The two Mexicans were caught stealing . . . hell, that part's all right. But everything that happened after, Sundeen did. I got no cause to be hiding out. I haven't done anything! And the son of a bitch just sits there like God smoking a cigarette!

He glanced from the window to Sundeen, who was lounging in the open doorway, his back against one side and a booted leg propped up on the other knee. George Stedman was sitting cross-legged against the opposite wall. Stedman's head was down and he was staring at his hands, looking closely at his fingernails clenched against the palm, then with the thumb of the other hand he would work at the dirt wedged beneath the nails.

"Phil."

Sundeen did not look up. He was studying his cigarette, watching the smoke curling from the tip of it.

"Phil," Tindal said again. "Why don't we just go back home and see what happens?" Trying to keep his voice mild it sounded shaky and nervous.

Sundeen's eyes remained on the cigarette, but he said, "I told you to quit that talk."

"We can't stay forever."

"Why not?"

"Phil, we got rights. We don't have to stay out here like hunted animals."

"We do if I say we do."

"You're not being reasonable!"

"Nothing says I have to."

Tindal calmed himself. Getting excited wasn't going to help. "What about your cattle?"

"What about them?"

"You'd let your ranch go just because of this?"

"They know how to graze without my help."

"They'll be scattered all over the territory!"

"Then I'll hire me some men to bring them back."

"When?"

"When I get ready."

"Phil, here's the thing. If we give ourselves up, then Finnerty will let us off for coming in on our own accord."

"Who says so?"

"It stands to reason."

Sundeen looked up now, faintly grinning. "R.D., you old son of a bitch, you telling me we're wrong?"

"I'm facing the facts!"

"Facts don't mean a thing."

"They do when you're faced with them!"

Sundeen's glance went down the slope. "I don't see 'em facing me." He looked at Stedman then. "George, you got any facts facing you?"

Stedman's head jerked up. "What?"

"Phil—"

Sundeen cut him off. "R.D., you're a sad-looking old son of a bitch, but if you don't shut up I'm going to put you out of your misery."

Sundeen stood up stretching, then walked outside and away from the doorway.

Now he's going to look at the horses, Tindal thought. They were kept saddled in one of the old mine shafts that was on the ledge with the assay shack.

He doesn't worry about a solitary thing. Just piddles around like he was at home looking for some trouble to get into. You can see he's restless, but he puts on the act he's having a good time . . . like a spoiled kid who'd got to have his own way and even when he's wrong won't admit it. Hell, that's what he is, a snot-nosed kid, who should have had his ass kicked a long time ago.

He glanced at Stedman, then leaned head and shoulders out of the window and looked both ways along the ledge. Sundeen was not in sight.

"George."

Stedman's head lifted and he looked at Tindal almost angrily. "What do you want?"

Tindal glanced at the doorway, then moved closer to Stedman. "George, there must be a way out of this."

"You knew the way in," Stedman said, "you ought to know the way out."

"Me!"

"Who the hell else!"

"Now wait a minute, George. It was you and Earl who got me to talk to Sundeen."

Stedman's eyes narrowed and he said angrily, "You got a short goddamn memory is all I can say."

"You think I'm enjoying this!"

"I don't know why not. Finally you're in something with Phil Sundeen."

"Keep your voice down."

"You don't want him to hear you talking behind his back."

"George, make sense."

"Always shining up to him—"

"Don't talk so loud!"

"Always ready to kiss his hind end any time he bends over."

Tindal shook his head wearily. What was the sense of talking to him.

"Listen." Stedman lowered his voice and the sound of it seemed edged with a threat. "I'm getting out of here. I'm not taking any more off of him; no more of this goddamn obeying orders like we were his hired hands. I'm waiting for the chance and soon as it shows, I'm getting out. You can stay married to the son of a bitch if you want, but I've got a stomach full of him. A man can stand just so much. You wouldn't know about that, would you?"

"What do you mean—"

"Just stay out of my way from now on!"

Tindal felt his temper rise and he was about to curse Stedman and tell him to . . . to do something! But he was too enraged to speak. He turned his back on Stedman and returned to the window.

Imagine him saying that to me. Of all the goddamn spineless, yellow—Tindal gritted his teeth. He'll be sorry. Manager of a bank—If any two-bit illegitimate idiot couldn't be manager of a branch bank! Well, we'll see. We'll get home and see how much business Mr. George S.O.B. Stedman gets after this.

He's so panicky he doesn't even know who to trust. Blames me! He's as bad as Phil. Every bit as crazy!

Like that business with Jordan.

We're not bad off enough, Phil has to get in an argument with Jordan and Jordan leaves. Jordan said it was pointless to come back this way and be hunted like animals—the only one who had anything to say that made sense!

But suddenly Tindal stopped. What was he thinking of? He was reasoning to the point that they *needed* Jordan here. But Jordan wasn't one of them. Jordan was a gunman, a wanted outlaw, yet he had been wishing Jordan were here; missing the secure feeling of having him with them.

My God . . . I think I'm going crazy!

He slumped against the wall and wiped his face with his bandanna. Just take it easy. You've gotten along for forty-five years using your head. Just calm down. Keep your eyes and ears open, you'll make out all right. He looked across the room at Stedman. George can go take a running jump to hell . . . and take Phil with him.

He had made himself become calm and now he sucked at his teeth, the first time he had done this in five days.

Sundeen appeared in the doorway, unexpectedly, and Tindal felt himself straighten against the wall. Sundeen hesitated, looking from Tindal to Stedman, then said, as if reluctantly, "They're coming."

"Where!" Stedman was scrambling to his feet as he said it.

"Just stay where you are!" Sundeen was inside the doorway now looking past the frame. He was silent, then said, "They're coming up the road, just entering the canyon."

Stedman moved toward the window and Sundeen snapped, "I said stay where you are!"

Against the wall next to the window. Tindal could see them now straggling in almost single file. The first ones were reaching the company buildings now.

He heard Sundeen go over to the shelf along this side wall where his blankets were and slip his rifle out from between them.

Then another sound—

He looked back to see Stedman reaching the door and going out, stumbling as he started down the slope, then regaining his feet and running, sliding in the loose sand, shouting something to the men below—

FIFTEEN

In the directly above them sunlight of noon they entered the widening in the canyon that was the site of the mine. Frye and Danaher rode side by side a dozen lengths behind Merl White. The others were strung out behind them. Farther back, where there had been rock slides, the canyon was narrow and they had thinned out single file to pass through and had not closed up again before reaching the mine.

The day before they had followed the tracks up the canyon and spent the night a mile below the mine site. But before dark Merl had gone on alone to study the deserted building through Danaher's glasses. Just before dark closed in he saw the figure up by the assay shack. That was it. They would wait until morning to go in. It was Danaher who added that they would also wait for Frye. It was Frye's party.

Frye saw Merl White dismount in front of one of the company buildings and tie his reins to one of the support posts beneath the veranda. They can't be too close, Frye thought. His eyes moved across the open area to the mine works, then lifted to the sandstone escarpment high above. He thought: Where would you hide?

"John, where are they?"

Danaher nodded, looking up the slope. "That shack way up there. They used to use it for assaying."

"I was wondering about us just walking in."

"We're out of range."

"Unless Phil's a dead-eye."

"Three hundred yards is long for anybody."

"Maybe they sneaked out during the night," Frye said.

"Merl was here with the sun this morning," Danaher answered. "He saw movement up by the shack."

Merl White had the glasses to his eyes, now standing at the edge of the veranda shade studying the assay shack. They were up there and they might as well realize they were trapped. Maybe they would give themselves up and nobody would be hurt. Maybe. The trouble was you could not count on Sundeen to use reason.

"Look!" Merl shouted it without taking the glasses from his eyes. "Coming out of the shack!"

They could not see him at first, not until he came off the ledge and started down, a dark speck against the sand-colored slope, then dust rising in a cloud behind him. They saw him roll and slide head first and for a moment he was hidden by the dust. Then, on his feet again, running, pumping his legs to keep up with his momentum.

A rifle shot cracked in the stillness and echoed thinly in the wide canyon. Then another and another and puffs of sand chased the running figure down the slope.

Three shots before the men below had their rifles out of saddle boots, before they were scattering but moving their horses toward the slope to return the fire—aiming at the shack to cover the man coming down.

Then he was past the cyanide vats, swerving to find cover behind the massive structure, and the firing stopped.

Frye's men walked their horses back toward the company building where Frye and Danaher stood with Merl White as the man came across the open area toward them—every few steps looking back over his shoulder, up toward the assay shack.

Then as he became aware of the silent, grim-faced men waiting for him, he seemed to hesitate, walking more slowly now and he began to brush the sand from his clothes. He was breathing heavily and his face, gray with dust, bore a pained expression.

"I'm giving myself up," Stedman gasped.

No one spoke.

His eyes, suddenly wide open, went over the line of men, hesitating on Haig Hanasian before they came to rest on Frye.

"Kirby, I've wanted to give myself up . . . I couldn't with that madman!" He looked at Danaher, then back to Frye, waiting for one of them to speak. "I pleaded with him . . . I said, 'Phil, let's go on home and face up to it.' I tried everything humanly possible, but he'd just grin or else start cursing and there was nothing I could do about it."

Frye stepped toward him. "That's all right, Mr. Stedman." He opened Stedman's coat almost gently and saw that he was not armed. "You come on in here," Frye said, taking his arm, "in the shade and sit down."

"Kirby," Stedman murmured, "the man's crazy."

Frye nodded leading him by the arm under the veranda. "How many are up there now, Mr. Stedman, just the two of them?"

"Phil and R.D."

"How's Mr. Tindal doing?"

Stedman hesitated, but he said, "He's all right."

"Did Phil harm either of you?"

"He like to drove us out of our mind." Stedman was perspiring and his fingers pulled at his collar loosening it.

"Did he harm you?"

"Not like you probably mean."

"Or Mr. Tindal?"

"No . . . but you never know what he'll do. He picked a fight with Jordan. But Jordan had a gun. He wouldn't take any of Phil's airs and he left." Stedman added almost grudgingly, "He was smart to get out while he could."

Frye nodded, "Yes sir," and asked, "How are Phil's supplies?"

"Water and food for two days. No, that was for three of us. They could make what they have go four or five days if they had to."

"You said Mr. Tindal's all right?"

Stedman nodded. "He's all right."

"How do they get along?"

Stedman was calmer now and he said, "They quit sleeping together," and grinned. But he saw Danaher's cold stare and looking back at Frye he explained, "They're not getting along. But R.D.'s too goddamn scared to do anything about it."

Danaher smiled. "Not the man of action you are, George."

"Well, I thought why should I sit up there and—"

"Shut up!" Contempt was in Danaher's eyes and in his voice when he said, "Prisoners speak when they're asked a question. No other time!"

Frye said, "Sit down for a while, Mr. Stedman," and turned following Danaher out into the sunlight. Frye made a cigarette and stood next to Danaher looking up at the assay shack.

"That's a long open stretch up that slope," Frye said after a minute.

Danaher nodded. "Going up the off side of those ore tails we'd be covered all the way up to the ledge. But you still have to go in the front door of the shack once you get there."

Frye was looking at the sandstone heights that towered above the shack. "Phil might be just the one to try climbing his way out."

"He might at that," Danaher said. "But it would have to be at night else we could run up close and knock him off."

"If he wanted to do it," Frye said, "Phil wouldn't let a little thing like nighttime stop him."

"Well, we better have somebody get around there," Danaher said. "It would probably take a while."

Frye called over Dandy Jim and told him what they had been talking about. The Coyotero looked up at the heights, picturing the country behind it and the roundabout trail it would take to reach it, and then he told that it would be near dark by the time a man arrived there.

Yes, he would be willing to go. Merl White agreed, and when he volunteered so did Goss and Tobin and in less than ten minutes the four of them were riding back down the canyon.

"That," Danaher said, "closes the back door."

"But there're two side doors," Frye said, meaning up and down the canyon. His eyes roamed over the deserted mine works. "And enough good places to hide right here in the house."

"Well, Kirby, that just takes it out of the commonplace."

He looked at Danaher. "I think you're enjoying this."

"Kirby, if I didn't like my job I'd get the hell out."

"I can't picture you in anything else."

"Which makes it all the easier." Danaher said then, "Aren't you having a good time?"

"I don't know if you'd call it that."

"Would you rather be back trading horses?"

Frye shook his head. "No."

"Then get to work and figure a way to pry that crazy bastard out of there."

"We might go up and talk to him," Frye said. "Maybe he's calmed down. Take a white flag to show we're friendly."

Danaher thought about it before nodding. "So we can say we tried." He took a handkerchief from his pocket and smoothed it out before tying it to the end of his Henry rifle.

Frye leaned his carbine against a support post and they started across the open area, Danaher motioning his men to follow. When they had crossed to the cyanide vats, the sheriff motioned again. They strung out in a line, their rifles ready, as Frye and Danaher started up the slope.

They kept their eyes on the shack, going up slowly in the shifting sand, climbing abreast but with a few yards separating them. The shack seemed deserted: the boards bleached gray by years of sun and wind and there was not a sign of life in the dark opening of the doorway or in the windows.

They were fifty yards up the slope—

"If he doesn't show in the next minute"—Danaher's breathing was labored—"we're gettin' the hell back."

Frye's eyes remained on the shack. "What would you give to know what he's thinking?"

The answer came from the shack. On top of Frye's question the rifle shot whined down kicking up sand almost directly between them. Danaher's men were ready; they began firing, keeping it up as Frye and Danaher dove in opposite directions and rolled. Danaher came up firing the Henry, then turned and ran. As they reached the bottom of the slope the firing stopped.

Walking back, Frye said, "Now we know what George felt like."

Danaher was untying the white cloth. "I burned my best handkerchief."

"That's what you get for carrying a live truce flag."

Danaher grumbled something, then looking back up the slope he said, "With a clean conscience, Kirby, we can say we tried. Now we sit back and wait for Mr. Sundeen."

"And judging by his short patience," Frye answered, "that shouldn't be too long a wait."

Haig Hanasian warmed up their meat and made coffee on the stove inside the company building. The stove was almost beyond use and there was no stack on it to take out the smoke, but it didn't matter because they ate their meal outside under the veranda, watching the assay shack. Through the afternoon they played poker with matchsticks for chips or just sat smoking and talking, waiting for something that they knew would come sooner or later. As darkness settled they moved across the open area and paired off taking up positions along the base of the slope, then settled down again to wait. By Danaher's timepiece it was a little after eight o'clock. Haig Hanasian was told to remain at the company building and watch Stedman. It was to keep him out of the way. They knew Stedman would not try to escape.

At ten, Danaher ground the stub of his cigar into the sand, handed his timepiece to Frye, and rolled up in his blankets to sleep. Frye would watch the first part of the night; Danaher would then be up until daylight. He had instructed his men to do it the same way.

Frye sat in the darkness listening to the wind high up the canyon. It would moan softly, then rise to a dull hissing sound and he would hear the sand being blown against the deserted buildings. It kept going through his mind: What would you do if you were Phil Sundeen?

He smoked cigarettes thinking about Tindal up there with him; and from Tindal his thoughts went to Milmary. What would Mil be doing right now? He would light a cigarette and as the match flared look to see what time it was.

Eleven o'clock passed. Then twelve.

It was shortly before one (the way he figured it later) when he heard the revolver shot from up on the slope, and the first thing he thought of was Jordan—

Twice in two days!

Danaher was up, shaking off his blankets. Wide awake. "What is it!"

Frye was standing now looking up the dark slope. The moon was behind the clouds and he could see nothing. "Up there, John!"

"That was a shot, wasn't it?"

"A handgun."

In the stillness they heard one of the men down from them lever a shell into his rifle.

"John . . . Jordan pulled one that could be just like this."

"What?"

They heard a voice calling from up on the slope and there was no time to explain.

Then the sound of the voice came to them clearly—

"He's dead!"

Still they could not see him, but now they knew it was Tindal standing out in front of the shack.

"He shot himself!" The voice echoed in the canyon.

Momentarily there was silence.

"John, it could be a trick."

Danaher cupped his hands to his mouth. "Tindal, you come down!" To Frye he said, "Let's get him out of the way first."

"I can't!"

"I said come down!"

"I can't!" It came as a hoarse scream.

"We better go up," Danaher said. He waved to the men over on his right to start up the slope.

"John—" Frye hesitated. "Something's wrong."

They heard Tindal scream again, "He's dead!"

Danaher called again, "I said come down!"

"I can't!"

Danaher was suddenly at the end of his patience. He said roughly, "Come on!" and started up the slope.

Frye looked to the left, toward two of the men. He ran a few steps toward them. "One of you stay down . . . keep your eyes open!" then turned going up the slope after Danaher. The other man followed him.

Halfway up Danaher called, "Tindal!"

No answer.

Danaher muttered, "Damn him—"

They could make out the ledge now as the clouds passed from in front of the moon and suddenly Tindal was screaming again—

"He's getting away!"

They heard the muffled sound of hoofs somewhere off to the left.

"He's getting away! Stop him!"

The horse whinnied, over beyond the hump of the ore tailing closest to them.

"Phil's getting away!"

Danaher bellowed, "Shut up goddamn-it!"

He wheeled then, almost sliding in the sand, and called down to his men below, "Get him!"

Now they were running down the slope as firing broke suddenly from below—three shots . . . a fourth. Then the firing and the echoes of it dissolved to nothing and in the stillness they could hear the hoofbeats of the horse dying away up canyon.

They knew without going any farther. Sundeen had gotten away.

SIXTEEN

Now there was nothing they could do until morning.

They waited for Tindal to come down and he described what had happened as they walked back to the company building.

Sundeen had fired the revolver shot, he told excitedly, then had made him yell out that he was dead. "He had to get you all part of the way up the slope before he could make a break. He led one of the horses out of the mine entrance, then held his gun on me while I yelled . . . that's why I couldn't move. He'd a cut me down!"

As they brought Tindal under the veranda they heard three shots spaced apart and sounding far off, coming from beyond the escarpment.

"That's the others," Frye said.

He walked out to the middle of the open area leading his horse. Then he fired three shots into the air at ten-second intervals. That would tell the Coyotero there was no hurry. Then he mounted and rode up canyon almost half a mile and fired three times again. That would be the direction they would take. He knew the Coyotero would understand. If there was no hurry then they would leave in the morning, traveling up canyon.

He returned to the men in front of the company building after unsaddling and picketing his horse—cigarette glows in the darkness and low murmurs of sound as they talked about what had happened. He saw Tindal sitting against the wall next to Stedman, neither of them talking, and Haig Hanasian standing over them. Danaher stood off by himself near the end of the veranda.

He thinks it's his fault, Frye thought. Well, let him be. Don't interrupt a man when he's giving himself hell.

With first light they were saddled and making their way up

canyon. The sandstone walls seemed to shrink and become narrower as they followed the road that was almost overgrown with brush and in less than an hour they were out of the canyon, descending a long sweeping meadow toward distant timber. Coming out of the rocks they saw riders far off to the right following an arroyo down out of the high country and by the time they reached the timber they were joined by Dandy Jim, Merl White, Goss and Tobin.

Merl White said, "What's the matter with you boys letting one get away?" then shut up as he saw the look on Danaher's face.

Frye explained to him what had taken place. Then—"He angled across the meadow and right into the timber, Merl. That's almost due west. If he keeps going he'll run right into Sun-D land."

Merl nodded. "If I was him I'd at least want to take a look around home."

"It makes sense," Frye said.

"Well, let's go then."

"We got something else for you, Merl."

"What?"

"Taking these two into Randado."

"Not me."

"You and Ford and Joe's been riding longer than the rest of us."

"We got more of a reason to, Kirby; outside of you. Get somebody else to do it."

There was no sense in arguing it. Frye asked two of Danaher's men and they said they would, gladly in fact. He told Haig that he could go in also, but Haig shook his head and stated that he would rather stay out.

Before separating, Frye moved his gelding next to one of the men who was going back.

"Don't put them in jail."

"Why not?"

"They won't be going anywhere."

Danaher's man shrugged. "It don't matter to me."

Now they rode on toward Sun-D, watching the four horses move off, more to the southwest, toward Randado.

When they came out of the timber Danaher pulled his horse closer to Frye's. For a while they rode along in silence, but Frye knew what was coming.

Finally—

"Kirby, that was my fault he got away."

"No, you can't take the blame for something like that."

"I got impatient."

"Well, you were anxious."

"I got to learn to hold on to myself more."

"You been doing all right for forty years."

Danaher seemed not to hear. "Like with Digo . . . I beat the hell out of him and nothing happens. You whisper something in his ear and he runs off at the mouth."

Frye felt embarrassed for Danaher and he wished that he would stop talking this way. It seemed out of character, not like the rough-voiced, coarse-featured Sheriff of Pima County. But that was Danaher. He was man enough to admit when he was wrong, even if it made him feel like a fool to do it.

"John, why don't we just forget about it?"

"I intend to," Danaher said. "I just wanted to make it clear that it was my fault he got away."

And that was the end of it. After that, Danaher was himself again.

Within two hours they had crossed the eastern boundary of Sun-D land and an hour and a half later they were in sight of the ranch house and its outbuildings.

They pulled up in a mesquite thicket a hundred yards behind the main building, then waited while Merl, Ford and Joe went on, keeping to the brush, until they were beyond the bunkhouse and corral. They saw Merl come out of the mesquite far down and as he did, they rode toward the ranch house, splitting as they reached it, circling around both sides of the house to meet in the yard. They saw Merl and his two riders come around the corner of the bunkhouse.

A dog barked and came running toward them from the barn. The dog stopped, cocking his head to look at them, then went over to Merl as he dismounted and sniffed his boots. Merl reached down to pat him, then came up drawing his carbine from the scabbard. He looked at Frye, who was dismounted now, and Frye nodded toward the bunkhouse.

They heard the screen door of the ranch house open and close. A Mexican woman came out to the edge of the veranda.

Merl called, "That's Digo's woman."

Frye walked toward her touching his hand to the brim of his hat and he said in Spanish, "We are looking for the younger Sundeen."

"He isn't here," the woman said.

"When did he leave?"

"Days ago."

"His father is here?"

"He is ill."

"We won't disturb him . . . only long enough for a few words."
The woman shrugged and moved aside, but as Frye stepped up
on the porch, Danaher and Haig Hanasian following him, she
asked suddenly, "Where is Digo?"

"He is in jail."

The woman seemed to relax. "For how long?"

"It's not for me to say."

"Will they hang him?"

"No."

The woman half turned from them touching her breast and closing her eyes as they went inside.

"Who is it?"

They looked toward the sofa that was placed at a right angle
from the stone fireplace. Phil Sundeen's father was lying there, a
quilt covering him and a pillow at one end holding up his head. His
face was still leathery brown, but the skin sagged from his cheek-
bones and his eyes, lusterless, were half closed. Frye would not
have recognized him. He remembered Old Val as a robust, swag-
gering man always with a cigar clamped between the hard lines of
his jaw, and with thick graying hair that always seemed to have a
line around it where his hat fitted. Frey remembered that clearly.

They walked toward him and he said again, "Who is it."

"Val, this is John Danaher."

His eyes opened all the way. "What do you want?"

"This is Kirby Frye. . . . He used to work for you about ten years
ago."

"I don't place the name." The old man's voice was hard, but
with little volume.

"Mr. Sundeen," Frye said. "I'm sorry you're laid up."

"If you want a job you'll have to see Phil. I don't hire no more."

"No sir. I didn't come for a job."

Danaher said, "Val, that's who we're looking for. Phil."

"You try De Spain's?"

"Not yet. We thought we'd try here first."

"He might give the boy a job, I don't know."

"Val, was he here this morning?"

"I remember now we lost some boys a few days ago, so maybe Phil'll be hiring again."

Danaher exhaled slowly. "You didn't see him this morning?"

"I don't know if it was this morning or yesterday."

"Val, just try to think a minute. He stopped in here this morning to talk to you."

The old man's head nodded. "I think he did."

"Did he tell you what happened?"

"He didn't say anything about hiring any more men."

Danaher exhaled again. "Did he say where he was going?"

"But if he was going to hire men, he'd a told where he'd be, so I could send 'em to him."

Frye glanced at Danaher, then kneeled on one knee next to the sofa.

"Mr. Sundeen, I certainly admired working for you that time. The first year we pushed 'em all the way up to Ellsworth. You remember that?"

"Two thousand head," the old man murmured.

"Then the next year we went to McDowell and San Carlos and you let Phil trail-boss the bunch to the reservation."

The old man's eyes rolled to look at Frye. "I don't remember you. You see Phil, though, tell him I said it's all right to hire you."

"Well, I sure wish I could find him."

"You got to know where to look."

"Where do you start?"

"When I wanted Phil I looked where there was women. That's where I'd start and that's where I'd end."

"Maybe that's the thing to do."

"Hell yes it is. Phil's got a nose for women. He can smell 'em." The old man's mouth formed a weak smile. "Like a hound dog in heat, only Phil's like it all year round. I used to say, 'Phil, for cry-sake get yourself a woman and bring her home and be done with it. You'll wear out your seat ridin' to town every night.' And he used to say, 'I'll wear out more'n that,' and just laugh."

Frye said, "He's something."

"You looking for Phil? Go ask the women. They'll tell you where he's at." Old Val chuckled.

"Would you look any place in particular?"

"You want a job pretty bad, don't you?"

"Well I'd sure like to find Phil."

"Once he said, 'Why in hell does a man get married with all the women there are in the world just beggin' for it?' And I said, 'Son, when they're beggin' you ain't wantin' and when you're wantin' they ain't beggin'. That's why you got to have yourself one handy.'"

Frye said, "Yes sir."

"Are you married, boy?"

"No sir, I'm not."

"Do you want to?"

"I think so."

"Well, it'll be a long way off. Phil don't pay more'n forty a month to top hands." The old man grinned. "And you sure don't want to take your wife in the bunkhouse."

"Mr. Sundeen, I better try and catch up with Phil."

"Phil don't poke along. You'll have to move."

"But you're sure he was here this morning."

"A man's a fool to say he's absolutely sure about anything."

"He might have been here then."

"He might have been."

Frye rose. "Maybe we'll talk again some time soon, Mr. Sundeen."

The old man rolled his eyes and Frye could see the yellowish cast to them as he looked up. "You better make it soon if you've got anything to say."

Frye nodded. "Yes sir." He turned and followed Danaher outside to the porch. Then he stopped, looking out to the yard seeing Merl and the others standing by the horses. He glanced back at the screen door, then at Danaher.

"John, what happened to Haig?"

Danaher looked toward the horses. Haig's was not there. "I don't know. He walked out while you were talking." He called over to Merl, "Where's Haig?"

"He rode off," Merl answered. "Didn't say a word, just rode off."

SEVENTEEN

Sundeen waited in the shadow of the adobe wall until the wagon started down the alley, moving away from the Metropolitan Café, then he crossed the alley to the stairway that slanted up to the back porch.

He had left his horse in the thicket that bordered Randado's small Mexican community and had crept from one adobe to the next, keeping close to the walls, occasionally hearing siesta hour snoring coming from within, until he reached the alley that was in back of the café. The wagon had been a small delay, already unloaded when he reached the last adobe wall.

Now he hesitated before going up the stairs. He moved to the wall next to the back window and looked into the kitchen. Noontime activity. The cook facing the stove, a waitress just pushing through the door to go out front. The door swung back and Edith Hanasian came in with it. She was looking in his direction, but did not see him and he thought: Call her now! But she turned toward the stove, saying something to the cook, and it occurred to him: No. Wait a while, till the rush is over. He was tired, dust-caked and wanted a drink. The best thing would be to go upstairs and wait for her. Have a drink and take a load off your feet, he decided.

He climbed the stairs and went inside, following the hallway to the living room at the front. He took off his hat and coat, dropping them on the floor, and sank down into a stuffed leather chair stretching his long legs out in front of him. But he had forgotten the drink.

Phil pulled himself up and went down the hall to Edith's bedroom. He went directly to her dresser and lifted the half-full bottle of whisky from the lower right-hand drawer, then returned to the easy chair.

For some time he sat in the chair, his head low on the bolster, and drank from the bottle. Then he placed it on the floor next to him and made a cigarette.

He felt pretty good now even though his legs were stiff and he had a kink in his back from all that riding. He felt good enough to grin as he thought: Damn room looks different in the daylight.

He thought of Edith then and wished she would hurry up and get finished with the dinner trade. Won't she be surprised! He laughed out loud.

I'll tell her I saw little Haig.

Edith, I think that little hairy-faced husband of yours is quit the restaurant business and taken to mining. Him and some others were looking over that Big Beverly claim in the Huachucas yesterday. Edith, why else you suppose he'd be snooping around over there? Phil laughed again and took another pull at the bottle.

About Haig Hanasian, Phil had no feeling one way or the other. He was indifferent to him, as he was about most things. If a man couldn't hold on to his wife, that was too bad. He shouldn't have married her to begin with. If Edith wanted to fool around that was Haig's own fault. Hell, he got her through a Prescott marriage broker. Edith had admitted that much herself.

He remembered when Haig had come here to open his café, bringing Edith with him. There had been a lot of talk about them then, but Phil had never been too interested in the talk; he had just watched Edith, waiting to catch her eye as she served him, and when their eyes would meet he would tell her things without even opening his mouth. He never forced his attention on her. He didn't have to. To Phil it seemed the most natural thing in the world that she should want him; if anything, he considered that he was doing her a favor.

What fun would she get out of Haig? What was he, a Greek? No . . . something that sounded like ammonia. Well, he looked like a goddamn Greek. Came over on a boat and opened a restaurant in New Orleans; then packed up and came out here. Probably his health. Or maybe they wanted to send him back where he came from, so he ran.

Haig had gone to Prescott first. He traveled through the whole southern part of the territory until deciding to locate in Randado. Then he returned to Prescott to find a wife.

Edith told Phil she had come from San Francisco to marry a soldier in Whipple Barracks, but he had died while she was on the way. Killed in action against the Apaches. She would lower her eyes telling it. To Phil, that was as good a story as any; but he always had the suspicion that the Prescott marriage broker had to raid a whorehouse to fill Haig's order. One way or another, it didn't matter to Phil.

As soon as he saw Haig at the mine he had thought about coming here. Habit, he thought grinning. That comes from duckin' up the stairs every time you see him ride out.

Then when he arrived at the ranch and did not find Digo, he was sure he would come here. Digo's wife did not know where he was; but Edith would know. Only now was the awareness that he was alone beginning to take hold of him. He had been alone from the start. Tindal and Stedman and Jordan had never been a consolation, only company; company he had to force to stay with him, and now he did not even have that.

As soon as he found Digo everything would be all right. Hell, it wasn't any fun playing this game by yourself. Digo would have some ideas. Probably he's out looking for me. But he'd have left word with Edith so we could meet in case I came back.

With Phil it was that simple. This was something to do; something to relieve the boredom of tending cows all year long. But with Digo along it would be a hell of a lot more fun.

Only occasionally during the last few days did he try to think what the outcome of this might be; and always he had gotten it out of his mind by thinking of an immediate concern. Hell, don't worry about tomorrow. It might not even come.

But just since this morning, since not finding Digo at the ranch, it had crept into his mind more often: How is this thing going to end? And what seemed more important: What if I don't find Digo?

But now he had whisky, and he was relaxed.

He had almost finished the bottle when Edith came in.

Surprise showed on her face momentarily, but it vanished as she glanced from Phil to the whisky bottle on the floor next to him.

"Why don't you help yourself to a drink, Phil?"

Sundeen grinned. "Edith, you're somethin'."

"When did you get in?"

"About an hour ago."

"Alone?"

"All by myself."

"What happened to your friends?"

"They got sick and went home."

"Somebody said Tindal and Stedman were brought in, but I didn't see them." She was silent, watching him grinning looking up at her. "What do you want, Phil?"

"I didn't come for a haircut." He winked at her.

"You could use one."

Sundeen laughed. "For a woman affectionate as you are you can sure act cold."

"What do you want, Phil?"

Sundeen's expression changed. "Edith, you sound funny."

"I'm not used to having wanted outlaws in my living room."

He straightened in the chair and his mouth came open in surprise as he stared at her. "Well god*damn* . . . ain't we somethin' all of a sudden!"

"Why don't you just get out?"

He came up out of the chair suddenly taking her by the shoulders. "What's the matter with you!"

"Let me go!"

"You think I came to see *you*!"

"Take your hands off of me!"

He shook her violently. "You think I came for you!"

"I don't care why you came!"

He threw her away from him and shook his head slowly, saying, "Son of a bitch," spacing the words. "When I learn to figure out women then I'll be the smartest man walking this earth!"

She asked hesitantly, "Why did you come?"

"To find Digo. God almighty, not to see you!"

Edith smiled faintly as if taking pleasure in saying, "He's across the street."

"Where across the street?"

Edith moved to the window and pointed out. "Right over there. They call it the jail."

"What!"

"Take the wax out of your ears—I said he's in jail!"

Sundeen went to the next window and pushed the curtain aside roughly.

"When'd they get him?"

"The same day you left."

"You're sure?" He kept staring at the front of the jail.

"I saw them take him inside," Edith said calmly. "I haven't seen him come out."

"Edith, if you're pullin' a joke—"

She smiled. "What will you do, Phil?"

Sundeen did not answer her. The side of his face was pressed against the glass pane and he was looking down the street. Edith studied him for a moment not understanding, then she moved closer to the window and looked in the same direction. She saw then, halfway down the block, Frye and Danaher riding side by side and a line of riders strung out behind them.

"Mr. Sundeen—"

Edith heard the voice behind her, recognizing it, seeing Haig even before she turned. Phil wheeled, drawing his gun, and stopped dead seeing Haig Hanasian standing in the door. He carried a rifle in the crook of his arm, but it was pointed to the floor.

"Your father said I might find you here," Haig said.

"What? He didn't even know I was home."

"You don't know your father."

"Haig, do you aim to use that rifle?"

"Why should I?"

"Then set it against the wall." Sundeen grinned. "I thought you had designs of using it on me."

"Not now," Haig said quietly.

Edith moved toward him hesitantly. "How long have you been here?"

"For a few minutes," Haig said. "I believe I came in when you were reminding Mr. Sundeen that you weren't used to having outlaws in the living room."

"Oh—"

"I agree, Edith."

She looked at him surprised, then dropped her eyes again.

Sundeen shook his head. "I feel sorry for you, brother."

"I think you're the one to feel sorry for," Haig said.

"Why?"

"You're all alone. Now you have to run all by yourself."

And as if this brought it back to mind, he said, angrily, "Where's Digo?"

"He's in jail."

"He can't be."

Haig shrugged. "Go see for yourself." He watched Sundeen go to the window, then turn from it abruptly and start to make a cigarette. His fingers seemed clumsy and rolling it he tore the paper, spilling the tobacco. He threw the shreds of it to the floor and walked over to the whisky bottle.

"That Frye——" he mumbled. He picked up the bottle and drank from it. "That goddamn Frye . . . he's the one——" He sank into the chair then and hunched over, leaning on his knees holding the bottle between them, and for a time he seemed deep in thought and did not speak.

He took another drink. Frye was the one. Frye started it. A kid who thinks he's something. Well maybe we ought to show this kid. Maybe we ought to throw it in his face and see what kind of a man he is——

What're you doing runnin' from a kid!

And suddenly it was no longer a game.

He stood up, looking at Haig. "You get ahold of this Frye. Tell him I'll be in De Spain's. Tell him in front of everybody I want to see him there . . . and if he says he won't come, tell him then he better ride out of Randado before the hour's up else I'll gun him the hell out!"

EIGHTEEN

As they entered the street, Danaher sidestepped his chestnut closer to Frye's dun. "Are your friends in jail?"

Frye glanced at him questioningly.

"Tindal and Stedman," Danaher said.

Frye shook his head. "No."

"I didn't think so."

"I didn't see any reason for it. I told your man to let them go home."

"You didn't see any reason for it once before."

Frye grinned. He was tired, but relaxed and for a while he had even stopped thinking of Sundeen. He was looking forward to a good meal and a bed with sheets. After that he would start worrying about Sundeen again. He'd send wires to every major town in the Territory. Never finding him would be just as good, perhaps better than bringing him back. Frye sat in the saddle loosely following the walking motion of the horse. It felt good for a change not to be sitting on the edge of his nerves.

"I think they've had enough punishment for right now," he said to Danaher, "without being locked up."

Danaher shrugged. "They're your prisoners." He said then, "That reminds me, what are you going to do with Dandy Jim?"

"I'll have to hand him over to the Army."

"What was he doing, just drinking tulapai?"

"That's all, though he caught his wife with somebody while he was drunk and fixed up her face."

"They don't care about things like that," Danaher said. "Somebody will give him a lecture on the evils of tulapai and that'll be the end of it."

Along both sides of the street now Frye saw people stopping and turning to watch them ride by. Some of them waved; a few called out a welcome and he heard Danaher say, "They're a little friendlier this time."

Frye nodded thinking of the morning they had brought in Earl Beaudry.

"Maybe letting Tindal and Stedman go was a good idea after all," Danaher said pleasantly. "Now all you have to do is nail Sundeen's ears to the door and you'll have their respect."

There were more men under the wooden awning at De Spain's. A hand went up here and there and Frye nodded to them. He was reining toward the jail when he saw Milmary Tindal standing in front of the store. She was watching him, her eyes remaining on him even as he returned her stare.

Go on in the jail, he thought. You don't owe her anything. Let her wait a little bit if she's got something to say. But he hesitated. What good would that do? He flicked his reins back again and turned away from Danaher, urging his gelding toward her now.

She looked up at him and for a moment neither of them spoke. Then he said, "Mil," and stepped out of the saddle.

"Are you back for good, Kirby?"

"I don't know. We didn't get Sundeen."

"Maybe he'll turn himself in now."

"Maybe."

She hesitated, not knowing what to say, and her eyes left his. "How's your father?"

She looked at him again. "Fine. He's resting. Kirby . . . we appreciate you not holding him in jail."

"That's all right."

"Mama says he must've lost ten pounds." She smiled and said this as if to make all of what had happened seem light and of little importance.

"He might've at that," Frye said.

She hesitated again and for a moment neither of them spoke.

"Mil . . . I thought I'd call on you this evening."

She smiled. "That would be fine, Kirby."

He could see relief in her eyes and she looked suddenly as if she might cry.

"Why don't we have supper together?" he said.

"All right—"

"Call for you at the store?"

"Fine, Kirby."

He smiled at her, then turned away leading his gelding across the street. They'd have a long talk tonight; and in the darkness it would be easier for both of them.

Harold Mendez opened the door for him, stepping aside as Frye entered. Danaher was seated, swiveled around with his back to the desk.

"Everything all right, Kirby?"

Frye nodded. "It'll take a few days to get back to normal."

Harold Mendez said, "Everybody's talking about you letting Tindal and Stedman go."

"They still have to face the judge," Frye said.

"But you *could* keep them locked up," Harold said. "That's what they're talking about." Harold's gaze went to the open door, then shifted quickly to Danaher. "I thought you said Haig had disappeared?"

"He did," Danaher said.

"He's coming across the street."

Frye turned to the window and Danaher came out of the chair. Suddenly Harold said, "My God . . . look!"

De Spain's doors were open and men were hurrying out, separating both ways along the adobe fronts, but most of them coming out to the street, then stopping to look back at De Spain's. They were forming groups, talking, still keeping their eyes on the open doors. A man came out of the Metropolitan and called something and from the crowd someone called back to him, "Sundeen—"

Now Haig Hanasian came into the jail office. His eyes sought out Frye.

"Did you hear?"

"You mean he's in De Spain's?"

Haig nodded. "I have a message from him. He wants you to meet him inside."

"You were talking to him?"

"For a few minutes. He came to find Digo."

"Where?"

"In my living room."

"Oh—"

"He was talking to my wife."

Frye said quickly, "He came to find Digo and when you told him he's in jail he asked for me?"

Haig nodded. "I think he finally realizes this is not a game . . .

and he holds you responsible for what has happened. I think he enjoyed it when he had others with him, but now he is alone."

"No, it's not a game," Danaher said mildly. He went to the gun rack and took down a Henry. "I'll round up the others."

Frye hesitated. "John, I better do this myself."

"You don't get extra pay doing it alone."

"He's calling me."

"All right, you'll show with a full house."

"Remember, you said before I'd have to nail his ears to the door to get everybody's respect."

"I was just talking. What you did to Clay Jordan is enough. After that spreads around you're good here for life."

"John, I'm going over to talk to him."

Danaher studied his deputy. He took a cigar from his breast pocket and bit the tip off. "Kirby, as far as I'm concerned you've got nothing to prove. Phil's crazy enough to start shooting." Danaher hesitated. "It wouldn't be worth it."

"He'd like to back me down," Frye said. "Just to look good one last time."

"Taking men with you isn't backing down," Danaher insisted.

"It would be to Phil," Frye said. "And it might be to all those people outside."

Harold Mendez said, "The hell with them."

"It's not that easy," Frye said.

Harold shrugged. "It's as easy as you want to make it."

Frye started for the door and Danaher said quickly, "Kirby, he doesn't use his head. You watch his gun now!"

"I will, John."

He was outside then, going down the three steps and the men in the street were turning to look at him, those in his way stepping aside as he started across. He saw Milmary in front of the Metropolitan and he looked away from her quickly, his eyes returning to the dark square of De Spain's open doorway.

His right hand hung at his side as he stepped up onto the porch and he felt his thumb brush the grip of the Colt. Take it slow, he thought. Don't try to read his mind.

He walked into the dimness of De Spain's.

Phil Sundeen stood three quarters of the way down the bar. He was facing the front, his left elbow on the edge of the bar and a three-ounce whiskey glass was in his hand held waist high. His eyes stayed with Frye.

Behind the bar, De Spain waited until Frye stopped, ten feet separating him from Sundeen now. Then De Spain moved toward him.

Sundeen's eyes shifted momentarily to De Spain. "Pour him a drink."

Frye watched Sundeen and said nothing. He could see that Phil had been drinking. And now he watched him gulp the shot of whisky he was holding.

Sundeen brought the glass down on the bar. "Go ahead . . . drink it."

"Why?"

"We're seeing what kind of a man you are."

"Then what?"

"I think," Sundeen said, slowly, "you're scared to raise the glass."

Frye hesitated. He half turned to the bar, lifted the shot glass with his left hand and drank it in one motion. His eyes flashed back to Sundeen and he saw him grinning now.

"You thought I was going to draw on you," Sundeen said.

"That can work both ways," Frye said.

"If you're man enough." Sundeen grinned. He glanced at De Spain and the bartender filled their glasses again. Sundeen raised his, looking at Frye coolly, then drank it down.

"Why didn't you try?" Sundeen said.

Frye said nothing.

"Maybe you're not fast enough."

Still Frye did not speak.

"Maybe you're just a kid with a big mouth."

"I'm not saying a word."

"A kid with a big mouth and nothing to back it up," Sundeen said evenly.

Frye hesitated.

"Take a drink!"

Frye half turned and drank the shot, using his left hand, taking his eyes from Sundeen only long enough to swallow the whisky. He watched Sundeen signal again and De Spain refilled their glasses.

"Kirby, you look nervous." Sundeen lounged against the bar with his hip cocked.

"I'm just waiting for you," Frye said.

Sundeen raised his whisky and drank it slowly, then turned to the bar to put the glass down, taking his eyes from Frye for a full five seconds before facing him again.

"There you had plenty of time," Sundeen said. He grinned again. "Plenty of time, but not plenty of guts."

Frye raised his glass unexpectedly and drained it. He saw the look of surprise on Sundeen's face, then saw De Spain fill the glasses again, this time without a signal from Sundeen.

"Now he's drinking for guts," Sundeen said. "A couple more of them and he'll be taking that goddamn warrant out." He drank off his shot quickly. "Kirby, did you bring that warrant with you?"

"Right in my pocket," Frye said. He saw De Spain fill Sundeen's glass again.

"Let's see you serve it."

"Right now?"

"It don't matter when. It's no goddamn good anyway."

"It's got Judge Finnerty's name on it."

Sundeen grinned. "What else you got?"

"A witness outside. Merl White."

"I can handle Merl any seven-day week."

"What if Merl was standing right here?"

"That'd be his second big mistake."

"Everybody's wrong but you," Frye said. He watched Sundeen take another drink. He did not touch his, but said quickly, "We let Tindal and Stedman go, but we're going to lock you up tight until Judge Finnerty's ready for you."

"You're not locking anybody up."

"You'll sit about three weeks waiting for the trial. Then Finnerty'll send you to Yuma for a few years." Frye glanced at De Spain and the bartender slid the bottle along the bar to Sundeen and filled his glass to the top. "Be the driest years you ever spent," Frye said.

Sundeen raised the glass and drank it off, slamming the glass down on the bar. "I'd like to see Finnerty with enough guts to send me to Yuma!"

"You'll see it."

"He's got guts like you have," Sundeen said. "In his mouth."

"Phil," Frye said mildly, "how long have you been bluffing people?"

Sundeen grinned. "You think I'm bluffing?"

"You can shoot quicker, ride faster . . . drink more than anybody else."

"You sound like you don't believe it."

"Well—"

Sundeen reached to the inside edge of the bar and picked up two of the shot glasses that were lined there and placed them next to the one he was using. He pulled the bottle from De Spain's hand and filled them himself. And when the whisky was poured he raised each shot glass in turn, drinking the three of them down without pausing. His eyes squeezed closed and he belched, then he relaxed and rubbed the back of his hand across his mouth.

He looked at Frye. "Now it's your turn."

"I never made any claim as a drinker." He saw Sundeen start to smile and he said to De Spain, "Go ahead," then watched Sundeen again as the bartender filled the glasses. Sundeen lounged against the bar staring back at him.

Frye took his eyes from Sundeen momentarily, picking up the first glass, making himself relax. He glanced at Sundeen, then tossed it down, breathed in as he picked up the second one and drank it, feeling saliva thick in his mouth as he raised the third glass, then gulped it and made himself place the glass on the bar again gently. He breathed slowly with his mouth open, then swallowed to keep the saliva down, feeling the whisky burning in his chest and in his stomach. Nausea that was there momentarily passed off.

Now he felt more sure of himself, but he knew that it was the whisky and not a feeling he could trust. He could take more, if they did it slowly; but not many more even then. If he had to drink three consecutively again he knew he would not get the last one down. And thinking this he was suddenly less sure of himself. God, help me. Help me to hold on to myself. He breathed slowly, making himself relax. He's had more than you have, but he wants to make a fool out of you and that's all he's thinking about. He watched Sundeen steadily and it stayed in his mind: He's drinking more than you are. De Spain was filling the glasses without waiting for a nod from Sundeen and this also stayed in his mind.

He watched Sundeen take another drink.

Sundeen set the glass down, blowing his breath out slowly, then nodded to Frye. "Your turn."

He lifted the glass, smelling the raw hot smell of the whisky as it reached his mouth and he started to drink.

"Frye!"

The glass came down and he choked on the whisky, coughing,

only half seeing Sundeen in his eye-watered vision. He dropped the glass, blinking his eyes, rubbing his left hand over them and now he saw Sundeen. He was laughing, still leaning against the bar. Frye stopped, picking up the glass.

Sundeen said, "You thought that was it, didn't you?"

For a moment Frye watched him in silence. Then he said, "You want the warrant now?"

Sundeen straightened slowly. "Let's see you serve it."

"Without Jordan to help you?"

"I don't need Jordan."

"You did once."

"He was just earning his wages."

"How much did you pay him?"

"Enough."

"Was he worth it?"

"Maybe."

"They say he was pretty good with a gun."

Sundeen grinned. "That's what they say."

Frye's hand dipped into his coat pocket. He brought out Jordan's billfold and threw it down the bar to Sundeen.

"But not good enough," Frye said mildly.

Sundeen glanced at it. "What's that?"

"Jordan's."

"You got him?"

"We buried him."

Sundeen hesitated. "Who?"

"Me."

"What, from behind?"

"Five feet smack in front of him."

"I don't believe it."

"You mean you don't want to believe it."

For the first time, Sundeen had nothing to say. He lifted the whisky glass, drank it and moved his hand slowly putting the glass down.

Frye glanced at De Spain. The bartender filled Sundeen's glass again and Sundeen lifted it and drank it down as soon as the neck of the bottle tilted away from it. Frye held his glass in his hand, but did not drink. "You might as well fill it again," Frye said. "Mr. Sundeen's got some thinking to do."

Sundeen glared at him. "You think you're scaring me?"

"I think you've slowed down some."

"You don't scare nobody."

"Take that whisky, Phil. You'll sound more convincing." He raised his own glass to his lips, seeing Phil tighten, then drank it down, taking his time, and placed the glass on the bar. Sundeen was still tensed.

"Phil, you almost did it that time."

Sundeen gulped his drink. Bringing his glass down he lurched from the bar a half step and had to reach with his right hand to catch the edge of it.

"You almost went for your gun, Phil."

"Listen, you son of a bitch—"

"What stopped you?"

Sundeen hesitated. "I'm waiting to see that warrant."

"You're waiting, but not to see the warrant."

"You do a lot of talking—"

"You're waiting because you don't know what to do."

"Try serving it and I'll show you what I'll do!"

"Jordan had his gun out."

Sundeen flared, "You're a goddamn liar!"

Frye waited momentarily. "Why'd he leave you?"

"That's my business!" Sundeen stared at him with hate in his eyes, then picked up the whisky, spilling some of it, and drank it down. "Your turn!"

Frye kept his eyes on Sundeen as he raised his glass, then took it quickly. Setting it down he saw Sundeen raise another.

Phil drank it, exhaling loudly as he brought the glass down. "Your turn!" he said thickly.

"Phil," Fry said quietly, "I think you're drunk."

"What!"

"You look drunk, that's all."

"I'll drink you into next week!"

Frye shrugged. "You look to me about ready to fall over."

Sundeen's face tightened as he stared at Frye, then seemed to relax though his hand still gripped the edge of the bar. "Now you're calling," Sundeen said, "but you're going to show what you've got, too." Still watching Frye, his hand reached across the bar knocking down some of the shot glasses lined there, but clutching two and bringing these back to the middle of the bar. He reached across and took one more. "I look drunk, huh?" He glanced at De Spain then. "Fill up!"

De Spain said, "Yes, sir," though his expression said nothing and he placed the six shot glasses in a line. He poured whisky into two of them, finishing what was left in the bottle. Then took a fresh bottle from the counter behind him and filled the other four, glancing at Frye as he put the bottle down.

"Well, I've got to see it to believe it," Frye said.

"You'll see it," Sundeen grinned. "Then I'll watch you do it."

He took the first two standing straight with his feet spread and planted firmly, then backed up a step from the bar, holding the edge with his left hand, as he drank the third one. Frye moved toward him, watching him spill part of the fourth shot, the whisky running over his chin as he gulped it. His hand slipped from the bar and he started to go back, but he lurched forward and caught it again. His mouth was open gulping in air as he raised the fifth whisky and as his head jerked back to take it he spilled most of it. He dropped the glass to the floor and reached for the sixth one, now holding his body tight against the bar. He drank it and brought his hand down, but the glass hit the inside edge of the bar and shattered on the floor. He held on to the bar now with both hands, swallowing, taking in breaths of air with his mouth open. He swayed and began to fall back, but he reached for the bar and fell against it heavily, his arms on the smooth wet surface, his head down breathing heavily and now saliva was coming from his mouth.

Frye stood two steps away from him.

"Phil, you want the warrant now?"

Sundeen lifted his head, squinting at him, blinking his eyes, "Wha—"

"Here's your warrant, Phil."

Sundeen pushed himself from the bar, holding it with one hand, turning, then stumbling again, falling against it with his back. He hesitated, studying Frye as if he could not focus his eyes. Suddenly then, his hand slapped against his holster, fumbling momentarily, his body swaying away from the bar as his hand came up with the Colt and waved it toward Frye.

Frye took one step. His left hand covered the cylinder of the Colt and he twisted, holding Phil's shirt front with his right hand. The Colt came free and he pushed Sundeen at the same time.

Sundeen fell heavily against the bar. He held on momentarily, but it seemed too great an effort and he let himself slide down to the floor. He rose to his hands and knees, shaking his head, then sank down again and did not move.

Frye exhaled slowly and looked at De Spain. "Send him the whisky bill. I'll see that he pays it."

He took the warrant from his pocket and tucked it inside Sundeen's shirt. Then he stooped, pulling Sundeen up over his shoulders and this way he carried him out the front door and across the street. He saw faces, wide open eyes, move from in front of him, but there was not a sound until he reached the steps of the jail. He heard it behind him then, sharp in the stillness, and he knew it was De Spain—

"Didn't even draw his gun!"

Danaher helped him upstairs with Sundeen. They put him in a cell and the last thing Frye remembered was Danaher saying, "Why don't you go in here . . . lie down for a while—"

Danaher went downstairs shaking his head. It was a strange world. He saw Tindal and Stedman turn around as he reached the last step. They must have just come and were talking to Harold Mendez, who was sitting at the desk.

Harold looked up. "They want to talk to Kirby."

"Kirby's taking a rest," Danaher said. "He's had a busy day."